CROSSING THE BORDER

The dragoons wore their bandannas over their noses to muffle the noxious odor. Buzzards dived squawking out of the sky, landing behind the next rise. Each soldier sought to strengthen himself for the horror that lay ahead.

Nathanial Barrington rocked back and forth in the saddle as he approached the crest of the hill. He'd seen massacres, mutilations, and rapes, but what he saw went beyond that: The wagons had been burned to the ground and cadavers were everywhere. Nathanial's practiced eyes could surmise where the Apaches had hidden, waiting for the miners. Getting closer, he could see tattered dresses of women—they'd died alongside the men, probably firing rifles. Yes, Apaches are beautiful pastoral nomads and root gatherers, he told himself, but they're also brutal murderers. Nathanial Barrington had crossed the border into Apache bloodlust. . . .

WAR EAGLES

Volume Two of
The Apache Wars Saga

by

Frank Burleson

A SIGNET BOOK

SIGNET
Published by the Penguin Group
Penguin Books USA Inc., 375 Hudson Street,
New York, New York 10014, U.S.A.
Penguin Books Ltd, 27 Wrights Lane,
London W8 5TZ, England
Penguin Books Australia Ltd, Ringwood,
Victoria, Australia
Penguin Books Canada Ltd, 10 Alcorn Avenue,
Toronto, Ontario, Canada M4V 3B2
Penguin Books (N.Z.) Ltd, 182–190 Wairau Road,
Auckland 10, New Zealand

Penguin Books Ltd, Registered Offices:
Harmondsworth, Middlesex, England

First published by Signet, an imprint of Dutton Signet,
a division of Penguin Books USA Inc.

First Printing, April, 1995
10 9 8 7 6 5 4 3 2 1

To Francesca

ONE

Eleven-year-old Perico peered at five antelope grazing in the chaparral ahead. He'd been stalking all morning, adroitly placing himself upwind of the tasty beasts. The small herd munched grama grass contentedly, oblivious to the brown-skinned boy withdrawing a hardwood arrow from his cougar skin quiver. Silently, Perico strung the arrow and drew back the catgut string. *Oh mighty mountain spirits, send my arrow true.*

The antelope ate their way across the sun-spangled valley as a barely perceptible shaft streaked toward them. The hardwood point penetrated the heart of the biggest buck, poked out the side of his ribs, and the animal's knees buckled as he stared blankly into the middle distance.

The other antelope galloped off, leaving their dead brother flat on the ground, a red ribbon extending from his mouth. Perico arose behind a cholla cactus, advanced toward the carcass, and held his bow and arrow ready to fire as he searched for movement or sign of danger.

Satisfied that all was safe, he dropped to one knee, poked the thigh muscles, and saw many meals spread before him. *How can I bring him back to camp?* he wondered. He hadn't worked out that minor detail.

He could carry one haunch on his shoulder, but the rest would be lost, he concluded regretfully. A lone buzzard squawked in the sky, impatiently awaiting his share. Perico wished he had a horse, but was not old enough to buy one. Perhaps, with this kill, my grandfather will give me a horse.

He stabbed his knife into the joint where the antelope's leg attached to his body, when a threatening sound drifted over the sage. In a second, Perico was on his belly, still as a lizard. The faint rumble of many riders was headed in his direction, but Perico needed proof of his kill, otherwise no one would believe him.

He cocked his ear at the oncoming sound as frantically he sliced antelope ligaments. The horses were shod, ridden by the *Pindah-lickoyee,* the White Eyes, or the *Nakai-yes* Mexicans, and they'd scalp him, but in a few seconds the leg would be loose.

Then he heard a more ominous sound, as something crashed into the thicket to his right. Down he went once more, then cautiously peeked around the tail of the dead antelope. A White Eyes scout was riding in his direction, and Perico lowered his head. The scout wore a brown beard, buckskin shirt, and wide-brimmed hat. He appeared looking directly at Perico, but the boy of the People was motionless and colored as the desert itself.

Perico felt contempt for the scout, for he hadn't seen an enemy in his midst. The scout's back disappeared, and Perico knew he should get moving, but maybe there was time to take the haunch, not to mention the loin. He raised himself up, sawed bleeding flesh anxiously, as the soldiers drifted closer. The leg was almost free when he noticed a fluttering red-and-white flag advancing against the pale blue sky.

Perico flopped down and wished he'd fled while

he'd had the chance. Dust billowed as the bluecoat soldiers rode toward him, loaded with equipment, weapons, and wagons pulled by mules. Then he spotted the flank guard headed straight for him. With a prayer to the mountain spirits, Perico tried not to cough as the cloud of dust drifted toward him. The flank guard was a soldier, not a scout, and Perico prayed he was half asleep.

The guard's horse rumbled onward, and the animal looked straight at Perico, but Perico didn't move a muscle. The rider's face was covered by an orange bandanna, except for his half-closed eyes. The guard passed five horse lengths from Perico, but the child of the People was well hidden. The Chihuahua desert looked the same wherever the guard looked.

Perico counted soldiers as they passed, because his grandfather would want to know. Why would warriors travel with such impediments? the boy of the People wondered. They need many comforts because they are weak, dull-witted creatures, easy to attack or elude. I have outsmarted you this day, bluecoat soldiers. When I am a warrior, you will not ride away so easily.

It was April 1851, and the dragoons advanced in a column of twos, their wagons bringing up the rear, guidon flag fluttering in the breeze. Some soldiers wore unmilitary sweaters or coats, for it was chilly in the higher elevations, but their commanding officer was attired in regulation blue tunic with polished brass buttons, and a wide-brimmed vaquero hat tipped forward at a rakish angle. He sat erectly in the saddle, shoulders squared, elbows close to his sides, as his horse carried him past scraggly trees and sharp-spined cactus.

Lieutenant Nathanial Barrington was twenty-eight,

tall, broad-shouldered, wearing a thick, dusty blond beard. A New Yorker, he loved the pungent fragrance of greasewood in the morning, unaware of an Apache boy lurking less than twenty yards away.

Nathanial rode with his hand near his new Colt Navy five-shot pistol, .36-caliber. He'd spotted Apache smoke signals several times since the journey began and had perceived odd shapes that looked like heads behind outcroppings of rock.

Attached to his saddle was a scabbard containing the U.S. dragoons' standard .54-caliber U.S. Percussion Rifle, based on the famed Mississippi rifle, employed by Colonel Jefferson Davis's Mississippi Rifles during the Mexican War. A West Point graduate and six-year Army veteran, Nathanial had received a bullet in the ribs at Palo Alto.

He turned in his saddle to examine his bedraggled men. The tension of the march made them cranky and sullen, and they were prepared to haul iron at a moment's notice. Most were fairly good soldiers, but Nathanial also carried troublemakers and slackers on his roster, plus German immigrants who didn't speak the same language as he.

He scanned rabbit and hackberry bushes, because Apaches could swarm a detachment before they knew what hit them. America was fighting undeclared war against the Apaches, but New Mexico was far from Washington, and most Americans cared little for their frontier Army.

The dragoons were on their way to the Santa Rita copper mines, at the southern end of the New Mexico Territory. The United States Boundary Commission was drawing a new border between Mexico and America, and Nathaniel's detachment had been ordered south to reinforce its escort. According to intelligence reports, approximately 1,200 to 1,400 Apache warriors resided in the area, whereas the Boundary Commission was defended by 150 officers and men of the Second Dragoons.

Nathaniel saw movement ahead and yanked his Mississippi rifle out of the scabbard. "It's Pennington, sir," said Sergeant Duffy, who looked like a cross between a leprechaun and a gorilla.

Nathanial permitted his rifle to drop back into its leather bed. Abner Pennington was his scout, a lean former Texas ranger thirty-five years old, sitting easily in his saddle as his horse trotted toward Nathanial. When close, he slowed and raised his right hand in the air. "The copper mines are straight ahead, sir. We should be there in time for supper."

Nathanial turned toward Sergeant Duffy. "We'll take a short break—tell the men to spruce up."

Sergeant Duffy shouted commands in his Irish brogue as Nathanial steered his horse toward a shady willow tree. He climbed down from the saddle, loosened the cinch beneath his horse's belly, and hobbled the animal amid clumps of blue grama grass. Then Nathanial sat beneath the tree and rolled a cigarette as he watched his men dust themselves off, adjust equipment on their horses, and blow deposits out the barrels of their guns.

Nathanial didn't relish his assignment and wished he were back in Santa Fe. It was his first separation from his wife since they'd married, and now he had a three-month-old son. He saw movement behind a barrel cactus, drew his Colt Navy, and called: "Sergeant Duffy—there's something over there!"

He pointed with the pistol, and soon Sergeant Duffy was organizing a detail to explore the disturbance. As the dragoons closed with the cactus, a black raven

swooped away. Everybody relaxed; at least it wasn't
the Apache nation.

Once Nathanial had fought an Apache warrior
hand-to-hand, and he'd never forget desperate moments when they'd clawed each other's eyes and tried
to ram boulders through each other's skulls. It had
been the most harrowing experience of his life, and
he'd survived only because a stampeding horse separated the combatants, whereupon the Apache fled.

Apaches constructed no cotton mills, munitions factories, or general stores. If a warrior wanted a new
caplock rifle, he had to steal it. A harsh land had
produced harsh people. Nathanial hoped he wouldn't
run into an Apache war party, on his way to the Santa
Rita copper mines.

Perico ran through the encampment, the haunch of
deer bouncing on his shoulder. Everyone noticed the
auspicious event, as he bent beneath his load. He
made his way toward the wickiup of Mangas Coloradas, chief of all Mimbreno clans and tribes. Six
feet, six inches tall, fifty-eight harvests old, the leader
sat in front of his wickiup and bit the shank of a
hardwood arrow, carefully straightening it with his
teeth, as Perico darted into his vision.

"Grandfather!" shouted the boy. "I have seen many
bluecoat soldiers." He pointed his small finger.
"There."

The warrior cheftain smiled. "We have been observing them for many suns, but what have you there,
Perico?"

The boy removed the haunch from his shoulder and
held it to his grandfather. "This is for you, sir. I have
killed the antelope, but could not bring more of him
with me."

"You could have used a horse, no?"

Perico closed his eyes in prayer. "Oh Grandfather, if you gave me a horse, I would be so happy."

Mangas Coloradas placed his hands upon the boy's head. "This is a great day for the People, for you have brought home the antelope. I will give a pony to the new hunter. From this day hence, you will be called Antelope Boy."

Hammering reverberated across the valley, as soldiers and workmen repaired abandoned buildings at the Santa Rita copper mines. Once they'd comprised a major copper producing region, but Apaches had either killed or chased all the miners away. Now it was being resurrected, for it had become headquarters for the U.S. Boundary Commission.

Nathanial led his detachment toward a triangular old presidio with parapets at the corners and the 2nd Dragoons flag in front. Mine shafts could be seen, and the valley was ringed with high, jagged peaks topped with snow.

Nathanial headed toward the command post headquarters, then climbed down from his saddle, and felt bowlegged as he threw his horse's reins over the hitching post. Drawing himself to his full six feet and two inches, he opened the door and saw a deeply tanned sergeant sitting behind the desk. "I'm Lieutenant Barrington, and I've just arrived with my detachment from Fort Marcy. Where do you want us?"

The sergeant arose behind his desk. "I'm Barnes, and we're glad to see you. In case you ain't noticed, there's Apaches sittin' up there on the ledges, watching us. They're fixin' to steal our horses, I'd say, so stay on your guard. You'll have to use your tents till we finish fixin' up the buildings. Pitch 'em anywhere you like."

A door opened behind Sergeant Barnes's desk, and a short wiry colonel with gray mustache and goatee appeared. He looked at Nathanial and said, "Who might you be?"

"Lieutenant Nathanial Barrington reporting, sir."

"I'm Colonel Craig—and it sure took you long enough to get here. Sergeant Barnes will take care of your men—I'd like to have a word with you in private."

Nathanial followed the colonel into his office, which had front and rear windows providing mountain views. Colonel Craig sat behind his desk. "See any Apaches on your way here?"

"No, but there were smoke signals."

"According to scouting reports, more Apaches have been coming to this area since we've arrived. We may be headed for a showdown, so prepare yourself accordingly. This isn't going to be a vacation."

"Looks like you're building permanent quarters, sir. How long will this detail last?"

Craig frowned. "Hard to say, but that's what happens when you put political hacks in charge. We're just an escort service for the Boundary Commission, but they don't know anything about Apaches."

"Is John Bartlett here?"

"Of course—he's in charge of the Boundary Commission. Why do you ask?"

"I know the gentleman. He used to own a bookshop in New York City, where I'm from."

"Bartlett may be a great scholar, but most of his equipment hasn't arrived, perhaps because his brother is in charge of his commissary. We've got to sit tight and wait while Apaches are looking down our throats.

And if Apaches weren't enough, Bartlett has hired the dregs of Texas for muleskinners, guards, assistants, and so forth, and they're always fighting amongst themselves." Colonel Craig looked both ways, then lowered his voice. "There's talk of gold in this area, and we've had three desertions already. If you want more information about local conditions, the most knowledgeable man is our interpreter, John Cremony, who speaks Mexican and used to be in the Army. Be careful what you say around him, because he's a newspaperman."

"I'd like to have a talk with Mr. Bartlett, sir. We're not exactly old friends, but my mother knew him fairly well. I ought to pay my respects."

"By all means, and perhaps you can convince him to wait for his equipment in a safer spot, such as Santa Fe. Welcome to the Apache nation, Lieutenant Barrington. It's going to be a hell of a summer, I'm afraid."

The great chief Mangas Coloradas sat cross-legged on a ridge high in the Santa Rita Mountains and peered down at bluecoat soldiers repairing the presidio. What are they doing here? he wondered. They aren't working the mines, but perhaps that will come later. A new detachment had arrived that day. Is their intention war against the People?

The Mimbreno chief didn't want White Eyes in the People's homeland, but hesitated to make war on his own. He knew well the massed firepower of the White Eyes, especially since many of his friends and relatives would be among the missing.

The copper mine shafts looked like gaping, anguished mouths to Mangas Coloradas, because the worst massacre in the People's history had occurred on the ground below. Only sixteen harvests in the past, a group of Mexican and American miners had invited the Mimbreno Apaches to a big feast at the Santa Rita copper mines, with all the whiskey a warrior could drink.

The People had come in great numbers, including Chief Juan José and a respected sub-chief known as Mangas Coloradas. They didn't guess that cannon were hidden behind foliage, and at the height of the feast, when the people were gorged with food and whiskey, the cannon boomed jagged metal at unsuspecting men, women, and children. Chief Juan José had been killed in the first volley, but wounded Mangas Coloradas had managed to crawl away.

Mangas Coloradas would never forget that horrific afternoon. The enemies collected one hundred fifty pesos for every male Apache scalp, one hundred for a woman, and fifty for a child. Mangas Coloradas hated, despised, and loathed the *Nakai-yes,* but tried to maintain an open mind regarding the *Pindah-lickoyee.*

Mangas Coloradas avoided contact with White Eyes, but occasionally a group of young warriors eager for glory and booty had taken them on. Most of the People considered themselves at peace with the White Eyes, although they weren't happy to see more arriving at the Santa Rita copper mines.

Three years ago, at the copper mines below, Mangas Coloradas had smoked with the White Eyes war father called General Kearny, who ordered him to stop raiding into Mexico. Mangas Coloradas tried to explain that the People had declared war against the Mexicans, but General Kearny refused to understand. Ever since, Mangas Coloradas knew the White Eyes had different hearts from the People, and there was something unbalanced about them, despite their wonderful weapons, fine horses, and splendid uniforms.

Mangas Coloradas gazed at soldiers like blue bugs rebuilding the settlement below. The People depended upon his decisions, but he found no ready solution to increasing numbers of White Eyes soldiers. He could wipe out the ones below, but more would surely come, with cannon that blew mountains apart.

I must make no hostile moves, he counseled himself, and I will keep my wild young warriors under tight control. Meanwhile, it would be wise to ask the Nednai, Bedonko, and Chiricahua People to confer with us, for these mountains are sacred to all the People. If the White Eyes attack us here, they will pay a heavy price.

John R. Bartlett, chief of the U.S. Boundary Commission, sat at the table in front of his ambulance and sketched the old triangular presidio on his notepad, taking special care with Moorish towers at each corner. A writer, lecturer, artist, bookseller, and former secretary of the New-York Historical Society, he was forty-six years old, married, and had two daughters back in New York City.

He hadn't been first choice to lead the Boundary Commission, a fact that rankled his sensitive pride. Andre Sevier, the eminent engineer, had been the original selection, but he'd died before assuming the position. Then John B. Wellsey, president of Bowdoin College, had been appointed, but removed due to his alleged squandering of public moneys. The third choice had been most illustrious thus far, John C. Fremont himself, the Great Pathfinder, who'd mapped much of California, the Rocky Mountains, and the Great Basin. But Fremont resigned after accepting the position, and around that time, Bartlett had been seeking government employment.

Despite Bartlett's academic credentials and honors, and his publication of a widely sold book of American colloquialisms, he'd never earned much income. But he'd been active in New York Whig politics, and a New York Whig, Millard Fillmore, had just become president of the United States. Bartlett had been fourth choice for leader of the Boundary Commission, his pay three thousand dollars per year, a tremendous amount by his usual meager standards.

Unfortunately, he knew nothing about surveying and mapmaking and had never met an Indian prior to his arrival in Texas. He'd led a cosmopolitan New York intellectual life far from bullwhackers, muleskinners, scouts, guides, and quarrelsome army officers. Bartlett wanted to discharge his duties conscientiously, but logistics and bad planning were delaying his expedition.

While waiting for special instruments to arrive, he passed his time sketching landscapes. Broad, ragged strokes represented the Santa Rita Mountains, when he became aware of a tall soldier walking toward him, a wide-brimmed hat on the back of his head. Oh-oh, thought Bartlett, it's the Army.

"Mister Bartlett—remember me?" asked the blond-bearded first lieutenant.

Bartlett examined him closely, but no connection came to mind. "Have we met?"

"My mother visited your bookstore at the Astor Hotel, and a few times I accompanied her. I'm Nathanial Barrington, son of Amalia Barrington."

Bartlett blinked his eyes as he recalled his well-appointed bookshop across the street from City Hall and Barnum's American Museum. Amalia Barrington had been one of his best customers. "I didn't recognize you behind that beard, Nathanial," said Bartlett jokingly as he arose from the table. In truth, he barely remembered Nathanial, although he'd never forget the mother. "Were you with the bunch that arrived today?"

"Yes—from Fort Marcy."

They shook hands as Bartlett recalled gossip regarding Amalia Barrington's scandalous son. The big officer standing before him was supposed to be a thoroughgoing scoundrel, rake, and drunkard, but it was good to see somebody from home. "Perhaps you can help me with Colonel Craig. I'm afraid his bellicose nature will set the Apaches against us."

"The colonel is concerned about your safety, sir." Nathanial glanced about, then said casually, "You wouldn't happen to have any spirits around?"

"The last thing we need here is liquor, and if the Apaches ever get their hands on some, I shudder to think of what might happen."

Nathanial thought it odd to view the former elegant Astor Hotel bookseller wearing work clothes in the middle of the Apache homeland. The big city on the Hudson linked them in a strange indefinable way. "The Army has had much experience with Apaches, sir, and the colonel knows what he's talking about."

"Have you ever met an Apache?" asked Bartlett, cocking an eye.

"I've been in a few fights with them."

"That's what I'm talking about. The military mind can't imagine peace. I've conducted considerable research on ethnology, and it's my belief that primitive people can be reasoned with."

Nathanial raised his eyes to the hues and hollows of the Santa Rita Mountains, where Apaches were watching. "Friends of mine have been killed by them, sir, and I've seen results of Apache depredations with my own eyes. One of their favorite tricks is to stake a man in the sun, wrap wet rawhide around his skull, and as the rawhide shrinks, it slowly crushes his skull. The Apaches outnumber us about ten to one in this area, and we can't be too careful."

Bartlett waved his finger in the air. "It is exactly that kind of thinking which provokes violence. Is there any way to invite them into our camp?"

Nathanial leaned toward him. "Mister Bartlett—you don't understand. You invite Apaches down here, they'll cut your throat when you're looking in the other direction."

"The military mind is always suspicious," sighed Bartlett. "How many times have soldiers dragged their nations into war? Napoleon is a good example of the dangers of military men making diplomatic decisions. I wonder if I could talk to their chief, Mangas Coloradas? Perhaps we can reach an agreement, and they can help us with our work here."

This man is a fool, mused Nathanial. But he's in charge, and he's an acquaintance of my mother's. "When do you expect your equipment to arrive?"

"Another month or two, I'd estimate."

"Sir, I don't think it's wise to sit idly in the middle of Apaches for two months."

"John Cremony made the identical remark at breakfast today?"

"Perhaps you should take his advice."

"In my opinion, it was journalists like Cremony that drove President Zachary Taylor to his grave."

"What's Cremony's experience with Apaches?" inquired Nathanial.

"He was riding point a few days ago and ran into a war party. He barely escaped with his life."

"How?"

"Why don't you ask the great genius himself? His tent is just over that hill."

The newspaperman's tent was pitched alongside a meandering stream, and Nathanial approached cautiously because it was six hundred yards from the presidio, hidden behind a hill, shaded by a cottonwood tree. This interpreter will probably get himself beheaded by Apaches one of these days, thought Nathanial.

The campsite was silent as Nathanial drew his Colt Navy and thumbed back the hammer. Why did he come all the way over here? wondered the first lieutenant of dragoons. Doesn't he realize that Apaches love creeping up on solitary individuals?

A head poked outside, a fleshy smile ensued, and a plumpish man appeared, not the victim of Apaches that Nathanial had expected. "What's the gun for, Lieutenant?"

"Don't you know there are Apaches out here?"

"I should hope so. I want to talk with them. You must be the new officer who just arrived. How many men did you bring with you?"

"Forty."

Cremony scowled. "The Army never sends enough to really do the job."

"All the more reason not to pitch your tent this far from the presidio. A war party might be sneaking up on us even as we speak."

"Apaches don't want trouble any more than we. I know what they want." He took out his bag of tobacco. "This. Want some?"

"You wouldn't have any whiskey lying around, do you?"

"The last thing you want is whiskey around Apaches. They go completely loco when they get likkered up." Cremony grinned like a shark against a background of sagebrush and ocotillo. "You have a curious mind, otherwise you wouldn't have come to talk with me, because everybody's afraid of the newspaperman, am I right?"

"They're afraid you'll write some dirty lie about them and ruin their careers. But I'm planning to resign my commission, so I don't give a damn what you say about me."

"I have no whiskey, but I can offer you a good cup of coffee."

They sat at the fire, and Cremony poured black coffee from a tin pot into a tin cup. "I take it you haven't had many friendly dealings with Apaches," he said, as he handed the cup to Nathanial.

"I've had a few encounters, but they weren't of a social nature."

"That's understandable," replied Cremony, "because an Apache is trained from earliest infancy to regard all others as his natural enemies. They'll kill you in a second if they calculate they can get away with it. And if you look calmly, you'll see one sitting about twenty yards to your right."

Nathanial blanched. "He's not pointing a bow and arrow at me I hope."

"He wants us to invite him over for a plug of tobacco."

"Let him find tobacco elsewhere. Is he alone?"

"As far as I can see."

"I think we should start walking slowly back to the presidio."

"Don't be afraid, Lieutenant. What if your men see you in this state?"

Cremony took a corncob pipe out of his shirt and stuffed the bowl with Virginia burly into which a few pinches of Turkish latakia had been mixed. He lit it, puffed mightily, and his head disappeared in a blue cloud. Then he arose and walked in the direction of the Apache.

Nathanial was tempted to yank his Colt, as Cremony beckoned with the pipe. "Have some tobacco," he said to the chaparral.

An Apache in his mid-thirties arose slowly. No weapons could be seen in his hands, but a knife was sheathed at his belt. "Baccy?" he asked.

"Come on," encouraged Cremony. "Have a puff."

The Apache advanced uncertainly, and Nathanial realized that the savage was taking a big chance for tobacco. He must be confident he can handle us, thought Nathanial.

The Apache's eyes darted suspiciously as he advanced, but his leathery face wore a smile. "Baccy." He accepted the pipe from Cremony and took a puff.

"It is yours," said Cremony. "A gift from me."

"The pipe?" asked the Apache.

"And this." Cremony held out the pouch.

The Apache appeared puzzled. "Why you give these things me?"

"We want to be friends, because we come in peace."

"If you come in peace, why soldiers too?" The Apache looked at Nathanial, who tried to grin pleasantly, his right hand hovering in proximity to his service revolver.

"In case of trouble."

"We no make trouble."

"What is your name?"

"I am Nana."

Nathanial stared at the half-naked savage, and noted that the insides of his upper arms were tattooed with crudely drawn circles, stars, and jagged lines.

"What you do here?" asked Nana as he puffed his new pipe.

"Measure the land."

Nana appeared confused. "For what purpose?"

"We make a boundary between us and the *Nakai-yes*."

"How long you stay?"

"A few moons."

"More soldier come?"

"Maybe. Where do you live?"

Nana pointed behind him. "The mountains."

"You must tell your chief we want peace."

"We too want peace," said Nana.

The Apache puffed his pipe, poised for danger. Nathanial had never studied an Apache at his leisure, and took note of the sunbaked skin, small nose, and slanted oriental eyes. Nana had risked his life for a few puffs of tobacco.

Then the Apache's eyes took on a sly look. "You have whiskey?"

"Whiskey bad for Indian," replied Cremony.

"If whiskey bad for Indian, why not also bad for white man?"

"It's bad for everybody."

The Apache held up the pouch of tobacco. "Many thanks for baccy." He arose, glanced about, and strode away quickly.

"Now there's a brave man," said Nathanial, watching him disappear into the chaparral.

"He didn't come just for the tobacco," replied

Cremony. "He came to look around. And it's just the beginning."

The Mexican captive boy sat sullenly in front of his owner's wickiup, watching other children play on the far side of the encampment. Twelve years old, Savero had been six when the Apaches visited his village early one morning. He still recalled the screams of his mother as she was massacred in the adjoining room. Older than most Mexicans when captured, he remembered a civilized life that the others had forgotten.

Apache captives were adopted into their respective families, but not Savero. He was used mostly as a slave by his owner, old Taza. Savero refused to accept the holy life-way, although he practiced it on the surface. He especially disliked Antelope Boy, who was considered so wonderful by the Apaches, and a favorite of his grandfather, the great chief Mangas Coloradas. I hope they all die, thought Savero.

Savero needed allies, but all he had was Taza's other captive child, the nine-year-old José, stolen when three years old. Unfortunately, José enjoyed being an Apache.

Sometimes Savero wanted to burst into tears. Never would he forget his mother's savage death, but had no idea how his father had died. He remembered the village priest strung up by his heels over a fire. Lost in tragic memories, Savero didn't notice Taza approaching, a stick in his hand. Taza was in his fifties, narrow of shoulder, pot-bellied, with thin legs. Before Savero could raise his arm, the stick came crashing down on his head.

"You lazy little devil!" shouted Taza, whacking the stick across the boy's hindquarters. "You haven't gathered the firewood yet! You useless little . . ."

Savero ran toward the wilderness, as nearby
Apaches laughed at his predicament. Soon he was out
of sight, crouching beneath a purple prickly pear cactus, trying to catch his breath. I will kill that old man
one day, he swore.

The fiery sun sank through molten red clouds, as
Nana returned to the encampment. In addition to
being a warrior of the People, he was also a *di-yin*
medicine man, not as dumb as he looked to the White
Eyes. He turned his horse loose in the grazing
meadow, then made his way to the wickiup of Mangas
Coloradas. The great chief's first wife roasted the
haunch of an antelope over hot coals as the medicine
man approached. "Where is Mangas Coloradas?"

She pointed toward the wickiup, then Nana said
loudly, "I have spoken with the White Eyes."

"Come in," said the deep voice of Mangas
Coloradas.

Nana entered the wickiup, a hut made of branches
and leaves with a smoke hole on top. The great chief
of the Mimbrenos lay on antelope and deer skins, rest-
ing his head on his hand. Nana held out his handful
of tobacco. "They gave me this. Perhaps we should
smoke it."

Mangas Coloradas found his clay pipe, then passed
it to Nana, who thumbed tobacco into the bowl. A
few hot coals burned in the firepit, and Nana caught
one between two twigs, then dropped the red-hot ball
onto the tobacco. He filled his lungs, then passed the
pipe to Mangas Coloradas.

"I visited the lone White Eyes," reported Nana. "A
soldier was there, we smoked together, and they said
they want peace with us."

Mangas Coloradas chuckled. "They want peace because there are so few of them. If they were numerous, they would attack us. The White Eyes do not fool me."

"The camp is strong, but it can be taken."

"If they truly want peace, we shall give it to them. Go back, talk more, and find out all you can.

The officers' mess consisted of one partially reconstructed room in the presidio, with a long table down the middle. Nathanial imagined ghosts of long-forgotten Mexican lancers lurking in the shadows as he sat for his first supper of the Santa Rita copper mines.

In the light of candles, his companions were the usual mixed lot of patriots, time-servers, and bumbling fools, and he wondered into what category they were placing him. Colonel Craig sat at the head of the table, while his executive officer, Captain Edward Stewart of Louisiana, was perched at the foot. Platters of roast beef and biscuits were placed before the officers by a crew of soldier waiters struggling not to spill a drop on anyone's uniform.

Nathanial looked hungrily at red meat steaming before his eyes, but had to wait for grace. He couldn't help thinking of his wife and son in Santa Fe, and felt odd in the presence of strange officers. His little dining room had radiated warmth and love, whereas the officers mess was cold, grim, official.

Before the prayer, Colonel Craig smiled and said: "Gentlemen, I would like to introduce the new member of our escort, if you haven't met him already. He's Lieutenant Nathanial Barrington, and he hails from New York City, but we won't hold that against him."

There were a few chuckles as everyone shook hands with Nathanial. Then Colonel Craig said grace, and Nathanial recalled Maria Dolores performing that function at home. One of the reasons he'd married her was she was a good religious woman, the kind you could rely on, or so he wanted to believe.

"Lieutenant Barrington knew Mister Bartlett in New York," added Colonel Craig. "Perhaps Lieutenant Barrington can talk some sense into him."

"We weren't exactly friends," admitted Nathanial, "but my mother was one of his customers."

Lieutenant Leonard Harper, a lanky Georgian, said: "I visited New York once, and I'll never forget Broadway at night. Within twenty blocks you could buy anything you wanted, and I mean anything."

Lieutenant Jack Whipple of Alabama scowled. "Bartlett is a symptom of what's wrong with America. Political connections are more important than experience and merit."

Colonel Craig turned to Nathanial. "You spoke with Bartlett today. What did he say about the Apaches?"

All eyes turned toward the new officer, and he knew they were weighing his every twitch. "He believes we should make friends with them."

"And make it easier for them to slit our throats?" replied Lieutenant Bob Medlowe, from Michigan. "Bartlett believes the lion should lie down with the lamb, but I'm no lamb."

"Neither am I," said Colonel Craig. "Well, Barrington—will you have another talk with him?"

Nathanial peered through the window of the adobe hut. One scientist read a book, another a manuscript, and the third a map, while Bartlett wrote on a pad, and a fifth man polished the lens of a sextant.

It was as though they were in a laboratory in New York, instead of the Apache homeland. Nathanial rapped on the door, and it was opened by one of the scientists, a slender man with eyeglasses perched on his nose, and hair growing out of his nostrils. "Yes?"

"I'd like to speak with Mister Bartlett."

"Come in, Nathanial!" said the high-pitched voice of Bartlett. "Let me introduce you to my colleagues."

Nathanial shook hands with the assembled surveyors, botanists, chemists, and students of rocks.

"Have a seat, Nathanial," said Bartlett. "Want some coffee?" A tin cup materialized in front of the West Pointer, and black, oleaginous liquid was poured inside. "Is this an official visit?"

"Just wondered how you were getting along," Nathanial replied. "The Army wants you to be happy here."

"I hope you're not going to deliver another of those boring military lectures on the evils of the Apaches."

"As a matter of fact," replied Nathanial, "we have reason to believe an attack might be imminent."

"It is *my* belief that the Apaches don't want trouble any more than we, but I suppose military minds are trained to think in terms of attacks and repulsions."

Nathanial sipped his coffee, far superior to the watered tar in the officers' mess. "I've never heard of peace-loving Apaches, but maybe you're right."

"Until the instruments arrive," replied Bartlett, "I was thinking perhaps we should take a little jaunt down Mexico way."

Nathanial blanched. "Sir, the worst Apaches are down Mexico way. You'll ride into a nest of hornets, except hornets generally don't kill you."

"There you go spreading panic and fear." Bartlett sighed. "Perhaps we can buy fruit and vegetables. Our diet is terribly boring."

"It's worse than boring," added Dr. Charles Webb, the Boundary Commission's resident physician. "I've got a mild case of scurvy, and so have most of the men. It wouldn't be a bad idea to buy ascorbutics, John. If the scurvy continues, the men won't be worth much when the instruments arrive. Hell, they're not much even in the best of circumstances.'

The scientists chortled amongst themselves, as Nathanial studied them carefully. They seemed a different breed from soldiers who lived with Sister Death at their elbows. Nathanial felt like an ignorant bumpkin before them, but that didn't prevent him from suggesting: "Why not go north to Albuquerque?"

"It would be beneficial to study the territory in which we shall work," explained Bartlett, "and that's to the south. I'm told there's good range for horses, so I could save on feed. Perhaps I can set up supply lines with local farmers."

"I wonder if Apaches get scurvy," said Dr. Webb. "Do you know what they eat, Lieutenant Barrington?"

"Anything with meat on his bones, and they have a strange cultural quirk of massacring strangers, but perhaps it's a lie, and the savages are really agrarian poets and philosophers."

"I don't mean to be disputatious," replied Bartlett, "but I think the Army *does* misunderstand, and I suspect much of the turmoil with Indians is provoked by soldiers themselves."

Nathanial smiled, because he was a fiercely disciplined man. "We'll have an opportunity to test your theory if we go south, sir."

The horses were gathered behind a newly constructed wood fence, and a three-quarter moon cast a silver sheen over their great sloping backs. Nathanial leaned his elbow on the fence as he searched for his horse, Duke II.

Duke II was a sleek chestnut roan with a black mane and huge, luminous eyes. He'd been named after the horse Nathanial had ridden in the Mexican War. Standing among other mounts, Duke II peered suspiciously at Nathanial, who'd acquired him from a trader in Santa Fe.

Nathanial slipped through the slats and approached his horse, while the other animals gazed solemnly at him. As he drew closer, one of them neighed and shook his head. Nathanial touched his hand to his horse's long nose. "How're they treating you, boy? I wish I had an apple, but there aren't any in this part of the world."

Duke II didn't shy away, for he and Nathanial had gone on many scouts together. Duke II had even met Nathanial's little son, not to mention his woman, so considered himself a member of the family.

Nathanial felt at peace with the horses, as faraway mountains were outlined against swirling constellations. The mighty equines continued examining him, and he wondered what they were thinking, or whether they could think at all.

Nathanial loved the vast expanses of the Southwest, but it seemed unnatural to go to bed without kissing his son, and as for his wife, mere words could not describe the many ways he missed her. Despite periodic disagreements, and the crockery she sometimes threw at him, not to mention pots and pans, he still considered her the most delicious creature in the universe.

I need a drink, he thought. He wondered how to obtain one, when he heard men's voices nearby. Holding himself still, he recognized the blue uniforms and orange bandannas of the U.S. Dragoons. What the hell's going on? he wondered, as he drew his revolver.

The two soldiers drew closer, and moonlight flashed on the saddles they carried. They approached the edge of the corral. "Don't take all night to make up yer mind," said one of them.

"I already know which one I want," replied the other.

Nathanial watched the soldiers slip bridles over the heads of their selections. They were preparing to desert the U.S. Army. Nathanial stepped out of the darkness. "Going somewhere?"

One deserter had the face of a weasel, and the other a duck. "I knowed this was a mistake," wheezed the latter.

"The next step," said Nathanial, "is the provost marshal's office. Get moving."

The weasel hurled his saddle at Nathanial, who triggered his Colt. The bullet hit the saddle, then the big leather apparatus landed on top of him. He pushed it out of the way, his arm entangled in a stirrup, as something clubbed him over the head. He staggered beneath the blow, the horses disappeared, and when he opened his eyes, he was lying on his back, and the deserters aimed their rifles at his chest.

A voice came to them from the presidio. "What the hell's going on over there?"

"Deserters!" shouted Nathanial.

The weasel said, "Maybe they'll catch us, but yer a-gonna die, you fancypants son-of-a-bitch."

The weasel aimed his rifle at Nathanial, who lashed out his left foot. His toe caught the barrel, the rifle fired, and lead blasted the ground near Nathanial's hip. Then Nathanial dived onto the rifle, trying to yank it out of the weasel's hands, while the duck poised his rifle for a slam into Nathanial's left ear.

A rifle shot shattered the fragile silence of the night. "Hold it right thar!" said a voice at the edge of the corral. "Next time I'll shoot to kill."

A corporal aimed the shotgun into the corral, and Nathanial snatched the rifle from the weasel, turned the barrel around, and aimed it at the deserter's head.

"Sir," cautioned the corporal, "don't do anything you might regret later."

Nathanial looked at the distended pupils of the deserter. "You're under arrest, and I hope they put you before a firing squad. Corporal, form a detail and march them to the stockade."

Several soldiers with weapons drawn marched the prisoners toward the presidio. I need a drink, Nathanial told himself. But there was no drink at the Santa Rita copper mines, as far as he knew. Yet surely a soldier from Kentucky or Tennessee had a still, because the dragoons were exceedingly clever when it came to whiskey. If they applied the same intelligence to their duties, Nathanial reflected, America would have the finest Army in the world.

It was night at the Apache encampment, and Taza snored in his corner of the wickiup, his great belly heaving with every respiration, his mouth hanging open. Savero was tempted to drop something vile inside Taza's throat, like a dead grasshopper. He stole me from my parents, Savero thought, and probably killed my mother.

Savero lay on smelly animal skins next to little José, Taza's other captive boy. In the darkness Savero slithered closer and gently shook the younger boy's shoulder. José opened his eyes and tensed, as Savero placed his hand over José's mouth. "Ssshhh. I want to talk with you."

José angrily pushed Savero's wrist away. "Leave me alone!"

"Please, I want to . . ."

José turned his back to Savero, leaving the older boy biting his lower lip. José is more Apache than Mexican, he realized with sinking heart. My most likely ally is someone like me, who remembers his Mexican mother.

Savero knew every captive in the camp, and most had been captured young, like José, but he knew that Francisco, captive of Delgadito, had been taken when old enough to remember his mother. I will talk with him, decided Savero. Perhaps he too is searching for a friend to help him escape these accursed people.

After locking the deserters in jail, Corporal Hannigan walked back to the command post to write his report. He was acting Sergeant of the Guard, responsible for the security of the tiny encampment. Jittery, he reached for his Colt Dragoon when a footstep sounded beside him.

"Relax, Corporal," said a friendly voice, as Lieutenant Barrington sauntered toward him. "The deserters give you any trouble?"

"No, sir. Hope they didn't hurt you too bad."

"As a matter of fact, I think the tussle opened my old war wound. It hurts like hell and about the only thing that helps is whiskey. There wouldn't happen to be any around, would there?"

Corporal Hannigan shook his head vehemently. "No sir—the colonel doesn't permit whiskey in camp."

Nathanial winked. "I'm sure there's a fellow in one of those tents, making a batch. I'd be grateful if you'd get me some, because it's the only way to beat the pain."

Corporal Hannigan looked from side to side, making sure no one was eavesdropping. "I'll see what I can do, sir."

Chief Mangas Coloradas sat cross-legged at the mouth of a cave high in the mountains and gazed at isolated flickering lights in the soldier camp below. In generations to come, he calculated, the White Eyes will swarm over the People's homeland, building towns and snuffing out the holy life-way.

What will become of the Yusn the Life-giver and the mountain spirits when there are no People to worship them? wondered Mangas Coloradas. How many generations will it take for the White Eyes to destroy us? In the darkness below he imagined bluecoat soldiers slaughtering women and children indiscriminately. The great chief shuddered with fear, not for himself, but for those he loved.

Is this the beginning of their military conquest? he wondered. Are they starting with few numbers because they don't care to provoke us yet? I could kill them all, but that might make matters worse.

His heart ached with the gravity of responsibilities. They called him the great chief Mangas Coloradas because of his many accomplishments, but his strength was leaving him, his vision blurred, and when it came to young maidens, they barely interested him.

Unlike some warriors and sub-chiefs, Mangas Coloradas respected the power of the White Eyes. Once, burdened with a herd of stolen cattle, he'd been attacked by bluecoat soldiers, and in the confusion, he'd fought one hand-to-hand, a big strong White Eyes war chief with sunny hair. Until that moment, Mangas Coloradas had considered the White Eyes weaklings, but would never take them lightly again.

I am at the age when I should have wisdom, Mangas Coloradas told himself. What should I do?

Nathanial's tent was pitched twenty yards from his detachment, within sight of the presidio. His orderly had set up his cot, desk, and chair, with his map in the top drawer. Nathanial took out the map and traced with his finger the route he'd taken from Santa Fe. The Mexicans called it *La Journada del Muertos*, the Deadman's March, because of Apaches. Maria Dolores and little Zachary Taylor Barrington were two hundred and fifty miles away, and Nathanial especially missed them in the evening. It was a pleasure to feast his eyes upon his shapely wife, while his son was a continual delight.

The night was cool; he threw his cape over his shoulders. He dreaded sleeping alone, with disturbing dreams instead of his voluptuous wife. Bootsteps approached, and he whipped out his service revolver. "Who's there?"

"Corporal Hannigan, sir. Got somethin' fer you."

The corporal entered the tent, didn't bother to salute, and reached into his back pocket, from which he withdrew a pint bottle. "I was able to find this, sir. You got somethin' I can pour it in?"

Nathanial located his silver flash, a gift from his club when he left New York City. Corporal Hannigan poured crystal clear liquid from one container to the other. "That ought to take care of your aches and pains, sir."

"What do I owe you?"

"Consider it a gift from the men, sir."

Nathanial knew he was breaking a regulation, but

needed something to settle him down. "Tell them I appreciate it, but nobody gets any special favors."

"Oh no, sir. It's not like that." The corporal tossed a casual salute, then retreated through the tent flap, leaving Lieutenant Nathanial Barrington alone with his medicine.

Without a moment's reflection, hesitation, or doubt, he raised the flask and took a swallow. The volatile liquid rolled over his tongue and dripped down his throat, producing a forest fire. Not bad, he thought, as his belly filled with heat. After another gulp, he sat on his cot, removed his boots, lay down, and covered himself with a scratchy wool blanket.

The cot was uncomfortable, his tent flaps lay open, and he could see the moon perched like a bowl of molten silver above saw-toothed mountains. Again he wished he were in Santa Fe with his buxom wife.

Why the hell am I here? he asked himself, as he took another swig. When I was young, I had a young man's ambitions. Now I'm a husband and father, and the world has changed. West Point is the finest engineering academy in America, and it's time I became part of American industry, instead of just another drunken soldier.

The makeshift stockade was a ten-foot-square room in the presidio, with a window too small for a man to crawl through. Not far away, at the edge of the encampment, a guard marched back and forth, with his rifle slung over his shoulder. Another guard sat in the front office, to monitor the prisoners though a small barred square in the door. The two deserters sat on the floor, discussing their aborted escape in muted tones.

"If that goddamned officer ain't been thar, we

would've got away," said Ronnie Dowd, the weasel-faced deserter.

"Wonder what the hell he was doin' in the corral," replied the duck, Gus Ethridge. "Do you think they'll give us the firing squad?"

Dowd was wanted in Pennsylvania for robbery and murder, while Ethridge had been a highwayman in Maryland. They'd joined the Army to escape the hot breath of the law, met at the Jefferson Barracks, recognized their mutual interests, and became partners in crime.

"If'n we say we're sorry," whispered Dowd, "they'll probably return us to duty. After all, we never kilt nobody, and the colonel needs all the men he can get."

"But I nearly broke my rifle over that officer's head."

"We thought he was an Apache, remember?"

Ethridge grinned. "Sure."

"We're good soldiers, but we was jest missin' our mommas back in Saint Looie."

"Ain't that the truth?" replied Ethridge. "We're weren't desertin' so's we could go to the gold fields, right?"

"O'course."

In Washington D.C., the White House was shrouded in darkness. One might think its occupants were sleeping, but the new president, Millard Fillmore, was wide awake, sitting at his desk in the Oval Office, afraid to light his lamp, because tomorrow the *Washington Globe* would report he'd been unable to sleep. The eyes of the world constantly were on the president, and sometimes he felt like an exhibit in a cage.

Millard Fillmore had never run for president, but

won the vice presidency under President Zachary Taylor. When that fine old soldier died in the second year of his first term, the former Anti-Masonic party activist from Buffalo, New York, had been vaulted into the White House.

Millard Fillmore was the son of a farmer, and a former farmer himself. Intelligent, ambitious, he'd perceived early on that a man could rise through the practice of law, so he'd studied part-time for ten years before admittance to the bar.

Millard Fillmore knew the meaning of a full day's work followed by half a night at the books, squinting at small print in the light of one candle, trying to absorb the principles of jurisprudence. Tall, silverhaired, considered handsome by the ladies, he'd always maintained his behavior above reproach, and no scandal had ever touched his name.

Slowly, painstakingly, he'd built a successful law practice in booming Buffalo, key port along the newly constructed Erie Canal. Then he'd entered politics and soon found himself in the state legislature. The Anti-Masonic party merged with the Whigs, he ran for Congress, won, and studied great orators like Henry Clay, James C. Calhoun, and Daniel Webster for one full term before introducing legislation of his own. His hard work and sober realism brought him to the attention of his peers, who voted him Speaker of the House, the post he'd held before receiving the Whig nomination for vice president.

Sitting at his darkened desk, with the full weight of the nation upon his shoulders, he asked himself why he'd ever got into politics. In America of 1851, the great burning issue was the newly enacted Fugitive Slave Law, part of the controversial Compromise of 1850. The Fugitive Slave Law had been drafted to placate the South, but abolitionist politicians in the North ignored it, and thus the Compromise of 1850 was causing more difficulties that it had solved.

President Fillmore couldn't simply abolish slavery, because the South would secede from the Union. Neither could he order abolitionists to tone down their criticism of the "special institution," because they considered it a sin before God. He didn't want to be the president who presided over the breakup of America, but the Congress was becoming increasingly contentious, with legislators carrying concealed weapons while giving speeches, and the atmosphere crackling with hatred.

Millard Fillmore had argued cases before the Supreme Court and knew even the most intractable legal mess contained solutions. If I could solve the slavery issue, I'd be remembered in the same breath as George Washington and Thomas Jefferson, thought Millard Fillmore. But no matter how hard he wracked his brain, the cancer of the slavery issue grew larger every day.

Two

Three-month-old Zachary Taylor Barrington rode in a special Navaho harness on his mother's back as she walked the sidewalks of Santa Fe. He gazed at brightly colored lights ricocheting off store windows, and the barber's pole was an instrument of wonder to his ever curious eyes.

Suddenly, he was indoors, dust filled his nostrils, and he coughed. His mother said to a hunchback midget with a broom, "Don't forget to polish the cuspidors."

Next, little Zachary found himself in a small room with a desk, chair, and crib. His mother removed him from the harness, laid him in the crib, placed a Mexican doll beside him, and kissed his cheek. He reached for her breast, but she sat behind the desk and proceeded to become extremely serious.

It was the same routine every day, and Zachary was getting tired of it. And if that weren't enough, she wouldn't give him his favorite toy, the one his father had made for him, and where was that gentleman? He'd disappeared, and Zachary felt a sad sense of loss. He began to cry, pushing the doll away.

Anger flashed momentarily in his mother's eyes, but she calmed herself instantly. "I know what you want, you little rascal," she said with a smile. Muttering beneath her breath, Maria Dolores withdrew from the drawer the miniature painted wooden replica of a Colt Dragoon that his father had carved. "Here."

Zachary reached for the toy, and his sniffling stopped as his finger pressed against the trigger. He didn't appreciate the toy's significance, but it reminded him of the old man. Zachary made soft burbling sounds, as he recalled his father's stubbled cheek and interesting smell. *Have I done something wrong?*

Maria Dolores frowned as she watched her son fondle the toy gun. The boy had been cantankerous since his father left, and she wasn't holding up so well herself. *Of all the men passing through Santa Fe, why'd I marry a soldier?* she asked herself.

A child needs his father, and I need my husband, she told herself. Nathanial had considered quitting the Army, but then was transferred to the Santa Rita copper mines. She feared he'd become reaccustomed to barracks life, with the usual drinking, gambling, and whoring, and soon he'd forget his family in Santa Fe. Maria Dolores's youthful delusions were long gone, and now she viewed her husband somewhat objectively.

She'd never seen him roaring drunk, but his speech frequently was thick, his eyes drooped, and he developed that sweet and not altogether unpleasant whiskey smell. On the plus side of the ledger, he was fairly intelligent, but had no talent for business. Once she'd tried to interest him in real estate, but he'd yawned in her face.

He was an overgrown schoolboy, and like many sons of wealthy families, never worried about money. Whenever he needed some, his mother or uncles sent it. They'd bought the very house in which Maria Dolores resided.

Maria Dolores appreciated her husband's endearing qualities, such as his sense of fun, a much-needed antidote to her own melancholy nature. It was laughable and touching to see him with Zachary, for the child had his father wrapped around his little finger.

Third, and in many ways most important, Nathanial loved her. She had no doubts about that. A woman knows when a man is dissatisfied, but Nathanial never appeared indifferent to her presence, especially when they were alone. She carried certain frustrations and dark compulsions that he soothed, and he was just the kind of man she'd always wanted.

He belongs with me, she told herself, as she counted the take from last night's whiskey sales. What kind of marriage is this, with the father of my son so far away?

The children of the People played the hoop and pole game on a plateau not far from the encampment. The object was to roll the hoop, and then try to catch your pole in it. Hoop and pole was the most popular game among the People, and adults waged fortunes on how deeply the pole penetrated the hoop before it fell.

Little Savero despised the game, which appeared pointless to his Mexican Catholic mind. It is a pastime for murderers, he told himself. He'd prefer being an altar boy, or helping his poor murdered father in the store.

The Apaches didn't even have outhouses, so they did it on the ground like animals. They were always moving the campsite, after befouling one area after the other, while raiding parties frequently left on murder expeditions. Their drum-pounding ceremonies raised the hair on the back of Savero's neck, and sometimes he thought they were devils.

He noticed Francisco, captive of Delgadito, lose a game. With an angry gesture the boy stalked into the wilderness. Savero promptly followed him, stepping on a twig that cracked loudly, as he tried to determine the direction in which Francisco had gone. Savero shuffled across sharp grass, found himself at the edge of a dry wash, leapt across, and darted around a pokeweed bush.

Have I lost him? He asked himself. And where is the camp? He paused to orient himself, when something knocked his legs out from beneath him. He was thrown onto his back, and when he opened his eyes, a knife pointed at his nose.

"Why are you following me?" asked Francisco.

It was shameful for Savero to be bested by a younger boy, but the knife was a powerful argument. "I wanted to talk with you."

"Talk."

"Not like this."

"You are lucky I did not kill you." Francisco spat derisively. "You are just a weakling *Nakai-yes*."

"So are you," replied Savero evenly.

Francisco pressed the point of his blade into Savero's throat. "I am not a *Nakai-yes*," he said. "I am of the People now."

"But you were born a Mexican, and their blood still runs in your veins."

"My spirit is of the People, but you do not appreciate the holy life-way. You should go back to the *Nakai-yes*."

"Taza will never let me, and I cannot do it alone. I'd hoped you'd come with me."

"I like it here."

Savero looked into his eyes. "Do you remember your mother?"

"No."

"I remember the People killing mine, and heard her beg for mercy. I wish I were like you, but I was too old when the People took me."

Francisco sighed, sheathed his knife, and raised himself off the bigger boy. "You do not appreciate what you have, Savero. Look at the sky, mountains, the birds, flowers. The People have honor, whereas the *Nakai-yes* are rats beneath our feet."

"Where is the honor in killing mothers?" asked Savero.

"The People are my mother now, and I understand why everyone hates you. Stay away from me, because next time you follow me, I will beat you up. You are not of the People."

That is true, thought Savero, as a tear rolled down his cheek. Francisco returned to the encampment, as Savero sank to his knees, clasping his hands together. "One day I shall escape from the Apaches," he swore. "Otherwise . . ." He pulled out his knife and poised it in both fists above his heart. "All I have to do is push," he whispered, so he grit his teeth and pressed the point against his skin. It hurt, but he lacked the will to proceed. A lost, motherless boy, all he could do was sob uncontrollably.

The court-martial was convened at eight in the morning, one week after the deserters were apprehended. The two miscreants, bathed, shaven, and wearing clean uniforms, were marched under the gun to Colonel Lewis Craig's office, site of the proceedings.

The colonel was judge, jury, prosecuting attorney, and defense attorney, while Nathanial and Corporal Hannigan were witnesses. Army law was based on the

Articles of War, a vastly different document from the Constitution.

Sergeant Barnes read: "The defendants are charged with desertion, assault of an officer, and theft of military property, to wit two horses, their uniforms, and weapons!"

"How do you plead?" asked Colonel Craig.

"Guilty," the prisoners said in unison.

Colonel Craig was surprised, because usually deserters tried to lie their way out, but usually ended with a more severe sentence. Colonel Craig could turn them loose or place them before a firing squad, depending upon his personal opinions, prejudices, education, etc. "Lieutenant Barrington, would you care to make a statement to the court."

Nathanial stood at attention, hands down his sides. "Deserting is one issue, while attacking an officer with intent to commit murder is quite another. These are dangerous men, and I think they should receive the maximum sentence before they do more harm, sir."

Everyone knew what "maximum sentence" meant, and the prisoners glanced at each other in dismay. "But sir," protested Private Dowd, before he knew what he was saying. "I ... I ... made a mistake, and I 'pologize. Everybody should have the right to one mistake, don't they?"

Nathanial replied icily: "I would hardly classify attempting to murder an officer a 'mistake'. I'd call it what it was: *Attempted murder*."

"But," replied Ethridge, "we din't mean to kill you."

"If you didn't mean to kill me, what did you think would happen when you hit me in the head with your rifle butt?"

"We jest wanted to knock you out fer a spell, that's all. Hell, I don't even know you."

"Sir," said Nathanial to Colonel Craig, "We're talking about premeditated assault on an officer. Again, I argue for the maximum sentence. In my opinion, these men can never be good soldiers."

Dowd clasped his hands together. "I knowed I was doin' wrong, and I guess I'm too damn greedy fer gold, but my momma is sick in Pittsburgh, and I wanted to help her out."

"Horseshit," replied Nathanial. "Sir, if you've got qualms about drawing up a firing squad, hell—I'll shoot both of them myself."

Colonel Craig had never heard an officer make such a statement in a court-martial. He realized there was something odd about his new detachment commander. "Guards, remove the prisoners to their cells."

The guards marched the prisoners out of the office, then the colonel dismissed Sergeant Barnes and Corporal Hannigan. Nathanial was left sitting on a rough-hewn wooden chair in front of the uneven desk. "I apologize if I seemed vindictive, sir, but those two nearly killed me."

Colonel Craig folded his hands on his desk. "I agree—they should be shot at dawn—but if I executed every criminal in this escort, we'd have twenty to fifty percent fewer men. They apologized—a good sign. There's nothing like contrition, says the Bible. I'm sorry you were hurt, but we're surrounded by Apaches, and I need every man I can get. If you have nothing further to add, and I doubt you do, I'd suggest you return to your detachment."

At the request of Mangas Coloradas, warriors and chiefs from across the People's homeland gathered in the Santa Rita Mountains. Every afternoon, they sat in a large circle and debated the fate of the White Eyes.

The younger warriors, such as Juh of the Nednai and Geronimo of the Bedonko, wanted to wipe out the White Eyes in one bold stroke. Cooler heads, such as young Cochise of the Chiricahuas, suggested that the White Eyes be ordered to leave, and if they refused, *then* they should be annihilated. A third faction, led by Mangas Coloradas, urged no rash moves.

Juh was dark-skinned, of medium height, and his muscles glistened in the sun. "What is the point of waiting?" he asked, stammering slightly. "Do they wait to destroy our camps and kill our women?"

"We have not yet experienced open conflict with the White Eyes," explained Mangas Coloradas. "Why start?"

"The White Eyes are no different from the Mexicans, and should be treated the same way!"

Lucero, a popular Mimbreno sub-chief, agreed. "Whenever we are conciliatory, we pay with blood. There can be no peace with enemies."

"One night," replied Mangas Coloradas, "many harvests ago, I lay on my belly in the hills near Matamoros. It was the beginning of the great war between the *Nakai-yes* and the *Pindah-lickoyee*, and I realized there were more enemies before me than all the People in the world. I have since learned there are many White Eyes in eastern lands, breeding like dogs. If we destroy those soldiers down there"—he pointed toward the Santa Rita copper mines, and the gathering followed his finger to the tiny dots that were buildings and soldiers in the valley below—"these mountains will be full of White Eyes soldiers. We shall not be able to come here anymore."

Juh smiled sarcastically. "It is true there are many

White Eyes, but they are as cowardly as Mexicans. Show them their own blood, and they will never visit this land again."

"What if they come in greater numbers, and kill us all?"

Juh spat at the ground. "What do they know of mountains? They drop seeds into the ground and watch them grow. I am not afraid of their warriors."

Grumbles of assent reached Mangas Coloradas's ears, and he knew he was being challenged. "Once I fought a bluecoat soldier, and he nearly killed me. Do not underestimate these people."

Juh shrugged. "Mangas Coloradas is no longer a young man. Perhaps he should not go on raids in the future."

The convocation was silent, for the great chief Mangas Coloradas had been insulted by the impudent Juh. But Mangas Coloradas appeared more amused than angered. "You think I am too old to fight, young Juh?"

Juh glanced about nervously. "When warriors become old, they lose strength. Does anyone doubt this?"

"But I am not old," replied Mangas Coloradas. "Would you care to wrestle me?"

"I would not fight a great chief such as you."

"Afraid of losing?"

"I would be afraid of *winning*."

It was another insult, but Mangas Coloradas only laughed. "You should never be afraid of winning. Come, let us wrestle as brothers."

Juh arose from his sitting position, worked his shoulders, and measured himself against Mangas Coloradas. He is bigger than I, but I am younger. I should be able to defeat him.

Mangas Coloradas strolled casually to flat ground near the campfire, and removed his blue cavalry shirt. Juh took off his deerskin v-necked blouse and inhaled deeply. It would be no dishonor to be defeated by a famous chief, but if Juh won, perhaps one day he would become a great chief too.

There was no judge or referee, and the loser would be first to touch the ground with any part of his body other than his feet. Mangas Coloradas and Juh faced off, as the tribe coalesced around them. Then the combatants wrapped their arms around each other's waists, the traditional method for beginning a match. Juh's head reached the middle of Mangas Coloradas's chest.

The chief was an unusually tall Apache with an immense head covered by a full mane of black hair streaked with gray and reaching his waist. "Are you ready?" he asked Juh.

Juh planted his feet firmly on the ground, and gripped Mangas Coloradas more tightly. "Yes, sir."

"Let us begin."

Juh heaved, and the wily chief used the younger warrior's strength against him. Juh was yanked off his feet, and felt himself falling to the side, but at the last moment performed a flip and landed on his feet a short distance away. I am going to lose this match, he realized, as he set his jaw.

They closed once more, pawed at each other's arms, trying to catch each other. Mangas Coloradas feinted toward Juh's thighs, and as Juh bent lower to protect himself, the chief grabbed him suddenly in a headlock, twisted, and Juh found himself, falling toward the ground. Again Juh tried to flip around, but this time landed on his hindquarters.

Everyone laughed, as the blushing Juh bowed be-

fore the great chief Mangas Coloradas. But the chief
didn't strut proudly, puffing out his chest. Instead, he
turned to the others and said: "Tonight we shall ask
the mountain spirits to banish the White Eyes from
this land."

John R. Bartlett, chief of the U.S. Boundary Commission, sat in his covered wagon and wrote in his
journal:

> I spoke with Colonel Craig today, and he argued
> strenuously against our trip to the south. I re-
> minded him who was in charge, and told him I
> intend to leave in two days.
>   It is my opinion that reports of Apache deviltry
> are greatly distorted. The military is always look-
> ing for excuses to increase their budget, and the
> best way to accomplish that is make it appear a
> threat is looming in the persons of poor hunters
> who dwell in this land.

Bartlett read what he'd written so far, and realized
his political appointment would terminate if it became
known how much he distrusted the military. "Keep it
sweet and light, John," he told himself with a grin, as
he tore the page out of his journal. "We wouldn't
want the wrong eyes to see this, would we?"

"Mister Bartlett?" asked a voice outside his wagon.
"May I speak with you?" Nathanial poked his head
through canvas flaps. "I thought you were with
someone."

"I was speaking with myself," replied Bartlett as he
dropped the shreds of paper into his trash bucket.
"I'm the most interesting conversationalist I know."

Dirty canvas covered the wagon, and Bartlett was

surrounded by boxes of documents, surveying equipment, food, and a variety of weapons close at hand, for John Bartlett, despite humanitarian impulses, wasn't taking any chances in the Apache homeland.

"I wonder if I could ask you a favor, sir."

Here it comes, thought Bartlett.

Nathanial unbuttoned his shirt and displayed scars on his chest. "I have these old wounds," he said confidentially, "and sometimes the pain can be quite severe. I was wondering if you'd do me a favor and ask Dr. Webb to give me some laudanum."

Bartlett felt relieved, because he'd thought Nathanial wanted to borrow money. "I'll write a note for you."

He scratched his pen on a sheet of paper, then handed the request to Nathanial, who tossed a salute, then backed out of the wagon. "Thank you, sir."

Nathanial turned around and was staggered by the orange afternoon sky shimmering against white-topped mountains. The air was clear, brisk, pungent with the fragrance of greasewood. In New York, all he ever saw were the buildings across the street, whereas the frontier provided spectacular vistas that continually filled him with wonder and delight. I don't have to be in the Army to enjoy this, he reminded himself. The view is just as good in Santa Fe.

He arrived at the wagon of Dr. Webb, who invited him to enter. The good doctor sat amid books and medical instruments, looking through a magnifying glass at a dissected red-and-black striped salamander lying pinned to the board before him. "Remarkable how similar the human body is to the common lizard," he declared. "What can I do for you?"

Nathanial handed him the note. "I need some laudanum."

The doctor lay down his scalpel and magnifying glass, then pulled a large metal flask out of a crate. "What should I put it in?"

"This." Nathanial held out his flask.

The doctor poured. "Isn't it strange for New Yorkers such as we to be together here? It may interest you to know that I was rather friendly with your Uncle Caleb when we were students at Columbia College. If you need more laudanum, you don't need a note from Mister Bartlett. Would you like me to look at your wound?"

"Some other time perhaps. Thank you, sir."

Nathanial returned to his tent, poured a few drops of laudanum into a tin cup half filled with water, and drank it down. He tossed the flask into his desk, then left in pursuit of his duties.

His men sat in front of their tents, cleaning weapons or preparing equipment for the march to the south. They stopped talking as he approached, then resumed conversations after he passed. It was his impression that some feared him, other's were in awe of him, and a few would like to put a bullet through his brain.

On his way to the stable the laudanum kicked in. He felt woozy, the ground undulated beneath his feet, and mountains in the distance sported pink and gold stripes. He realized he'd taken one drop too many and feared he'd faint in full view of the soldiers.

He changed direction abruptly, headed back to his tent, and struggled to keep his spine straight. Nathanial's father was a colonel in the War Department, and if he ever heard that Nathanial passed out from excessive laudanum intake while on duty, there'd be hell to pay. Head spinning, black shrouds falling around him, he arrived at his tent, closed the flaps, and dived onto the cot, where he promptly sank into a deep stupor.

Every day at sundown, Maria Dolores attended the Vespers Mass at her neighborhood church. She removed Zachary from his harness, dipped her finger in holy water, and made the sign of the cross on his forehead. Then she blessed herself, slipped into a pew, lay Zachary beside her, and dropped to her knees.

She clasped her hands together and prayed for Zachary, Nathanial, and her strange old father, whom she suspected of going insane. He spent his time alone in a house she had bought him, reading books and practicing his strange religion.

Maria Dolores lived with a secret she'd uncovered only recently. She'd been baptized and raised a Catholic and believed in the principles of Holy Mother church, but she'd discovered by accident that her father was a Marrano, the Spanish word for pig.

The Marranos were Jews who pretended to be Catholic, but practiced their ancient oriental religion in secret. She was the only one who knew her father's secret and hadn't even told her husband. Her father feared he'd be burned at the stake for being Jewish, but she felt no reason to give up the Catholic habits and customs of a lifetime. She gazed at her robust son and pinched his cheek playfully. What would your father say if he knew you're one-half Jewish? she asked silently.

The procession of priests and altar boys entered the cathedral as the holy sacrifice of the Mass began. Incense was lit, and a cloud of smoke billowed over the congregation. Little Zachary sniffed the exotic smell, delighted by flickering lights, while the choir sang the Kyrie Eleison. The boy feel sweet inside, and sensed that his mother was relaxed. He raised his voice and tried to sing with the choir.

Maria Dolores smiled at the efforts of her son. She didn't believe in asking St. Anthony to find her lost scarf, but didn't hesitate to request St. Jude to send her husband home. Bowing her head, she wondered if Nathanial missed his family, or was overjoyed to be away from them. Loneliness probed cruel fingers into her mind. *If Nathanial doesn't return soon, what will I do?*

The deserters shuffled into Colonel Craig's office, as guards stood on either side of the desk, armed with rifles. Dowd and Ethridge were dirty, ragged, unshaven, and gaunt from reduced rations. "Prisoners—atten-hut!" hollered Sergeant Major Barnes.

The deserters snapped to attention clumsily, hampered by shackles and chains. Colonel Craig cleared his throat and said: "I have reached a verdict in your case. Your unprovoked attack on Lieutenant Barrington is worth the firing squad, but I have decided to be lenient, and give you another chance. You will forfeit all pay and allowances for one year and be confined to quarters for the same period. If you commit further violations, you can reasonably expect a firing squad. Any questions?"

The two deserters looked at each other, then Dowd turned to the Colonel, put on a sincere expression, and said, "I'd like to thank you, sir, fer yer kindness."

"Me too, sir," added Ethridge, gloating inwardly. "We'll be good soldiers from now on."

"Take them away," ordered Colonel Craig.

The prisoners marched out of the office, and Nathanial was fuming. "Sir," he protested, "they're getting off scot free. If you don't enforce regulations, the men will lose respect for them."

"Don't you believe in redemption, Lieutenant Barrington?"

"Not for men like that. I'd call them varmints, but that's an insult to common household rats. You haven't heard the last of them—mark my words. I hope I'm not the one they kill next."

The bloated red sun sank toward purple and gold mountains in the distance, as especially selected warriors and *di-yin* medicine men walked in single file to a secluded brush shelter located a substantial distance from the People's encampment. It was considered hazardous for the People to see masked dancers donning their costumes.

The candidates entered, formed a circle, and bowed their heads in gratitude. It was an honor to be selected for masked dancer, but a serious responsibility as well, and evil influences could be caused if mistakes were made.

One of the masked dancers was thirty-two-year-old Geronimo, warrior and *di-yin* medicine man from the Bedonko People. Much tragedy had touched his young life, for his mother, wife, and three children had been killed by Mexican soldiers near the town of Janos. Since then, Geronimo had dedicated himself to the destruction of the *Nakai-yes*.

Then Nana entered the shelter, accompanied by assistants. They proceeded to dress the dancers according to the parts they'd play. Geronimo would be the black dancer, who represented evil.

The bodies of the dancers were painted with holy designs, then the ceremonial blouse and skirt were put on. Their faces were covered with masks, and tall rigid headdresses adorned their heads. It was unhealthy for one dancer to touch another dressed by a different assistant. If they rubbed their makeup absentmindedly, it could cause a rainstorm. If the dancer placed the mask over his head without proper prayers, he could become insane.

Assistants applied paint with sticks whose ends had been pounded and softened. Nana beat a pottery drum decorated with holy symbols, as he sang prayers requesting endurance for the dancers. When fully attired, faces hidden by swathes of cloth, the dancers prayed for power in the upcoming ceremony. Then, as darkness came to the land, they descended in a long file, headed toward the bonfire in the encampment below.

Shackles and chains were removed from the deserters, and they received clean uniforms. "Behave yerselves," said Sergeant Barnes, with one eye narrowed. "Next time we'll shoot you where you stand—got it?"

"Yes, Sergeant," replied Dowd and Ethridge.

"Get out of here."

Shoulders bent by remorse, the two ex-deserters walked out of the provost marshal's office. They headed for the nearest alley, stood in the shadows, looked at each other, and burst into laughter, hugging their bellies, jumping up and down like oversize imps.

"Goddamned fools," whispered Dowd as he struggled to catch his breath.

Ethridge mimicked Colonel Craig. "I expect you to be good soldiers from now on."

They giggled till tears came to their eyes. "And did you see the look on Lieutenant Barrington's face?" inquired Dowd.

"First time I ever seen a purple officer," replied

Ethridge. "Them stupid sons-of-a-bitches'll never keep us in the Army, and if that big ugly Lieutenant Barrington ever gets in my way again, I'll shoot him between the fuckin' eyes."

The masked dancers formed celestial circles as masked drummers pounded sticks against stretched antelope skins. The hypnotic rolling rhythm plus substantial quantities of *tizwin* transported the People into a trance, with every warrior, woman, maiden, child, and dog participating, locked together into the same insistent beat.

And through it all leapt the black dancer, symbol of evil. Geronimo appeared truly menacing as he brandished his ceremonial ax, and it wasn't difficult to get into the mood, for he was expressing rage at the murders of his wife and children. Growling like a bear, he split open the skulls of babies, and hacked the breasts of nursing mothers, as the *Nakai-yes* had done to the People. All the frustration and hatred of his soul was focused upon those fiends, and the People shrank away from him, as white dancers sought to impede his movements.

Firelight flickered upon his eyes gleaming brightly through slits in his black mask. I am the foul one, he told himself. But the People are greater than I. A white dancer performed a ceremonial gesture with his lance, and Geronimo pretended to stagger beneath the blow.

Drums hammered his ears, as he twitched and arched in pretended death throes. Even in agony he had to maintain the beat, as the white dancers hopped victoriously over his prostrate body. A wet knot of wood exploded in the firepit, hurling sparks into the air. Then Geronimo leapt to his feet, because evil always returns, according to the wisdom of the People.

> We stand on our holy place
> our strength comes from the mountain spirits
> Go away—all enemies
> or face the wrath of the People

After supper and a few drops of laudanum, Nathanial took a solitary stroll around the encampment, to make certain guards were properly alert. Once, not that long ago, his detachment had been attacked at night, and the experience was engraved indelibly into his mind. The trick was to spot the Apaches before they came too close.

"Halt—who goes there!" called a voice in the darkness.

"Lieutenant Barrington."

"Advance, sir, to be recognized."

Nathanial strolled closer to the soldier, a member of Colonel Craig's escort. "What's your name?"

"Toohey, sir."

"Where are you from, Private Toohey?"

"County Limerick, sir."

"Keep your eyes open, and maybe you'll visit your relatives someday."

Nathanial continued his rounds, as laudanum coursed through his veins. He saw multicolored camels galloping across the sky, which was tinged with silver, while the Milky Way sparkled like diamonds. Nathanial felt as if tendrils in his legs were growing into the ground, like roots of a tree, and he realized that trees led peaceful lives, because they didn't have to worry about Apaches. For the first time Nathanial considered the possibility of becoming a tree, his leafy arms extended constantly to the sky.

"Halt—who goes there!"

"Lieutenant Barrington."

"Advance, sir, to be recognized."

Nathanial sucked in his gut and squared his shoulders, as if marching on the plain at West Point. "Good evening, Private—I'm afraid I forgot your name."

"Private Travis, sir." The mustachioed soldier winked. "Have a bit too much to drink tonight, sir?"

"Where are you from, Travis?"

"North Carolina, sir."

"Why'd you join the Army?"

"Two bad crops in a row, lost the farm, had to do somethin', and here I am. Sir, I think you'd better lie down. You don't look so good."

Nathanial continued his rounds as he reflected upon what Private Travis had said. I'm in the Army because I chose to be here, but that man's alternative was death from starvation. Nathanial felt grateful that he was a rich man's son, yet had landed in the same boat as Travis.

It's a beautiful land, but a man doesn't have to be a soldier to enjoy it, he told himself. There's no reason on God's earth why I should have to worry about Apaches for the rest of my life. He saw a light coming from John Cremony's tent. The reporter sat cross-legged on the ground, writing in the illumination of his campfire.

"Hope I'm not disturbing you, Mister Cremony."

"Not at all, Barrington." Cremony continued to write feverishly, and in Nathanial's opiated eyes, sparks flew off the nib of his pen.

"What're you working on?"

"Maybe it'll be a book someday. Hear the drums?"

"What drums?"

Cremony raised his finger in the air, and said softly: "Close your eyes and listen."

Nathanial heard the breeze rustling sagebrush and cottonwood, but then became aware of steady distant pulsations. "If you hadn't pointed it out, I'd never have heard it," he admitted.

"You must learn to listen. Lieutenant Barrington. If you want to fight Apaches, train your ears as they train theirs."

"Think it's a war dance?"

"If the Apaches want rifles and ammunition, they can steal them more easily from the Mexicans. They attack only when certain of victory and are much more sly than you realize, Lieutenant Barrington. The more you learn about the savages, the more fascinating they become. They're cold-blooded murderers, but believe in a supreme being, just as we. Their women can be quite beautiful, if you like the wild type. They also have interesting legends, such as—do you know where the Milky Way came from, according to Apaches? Once long ago in the sky there was a burro carrying a load of flour, but a mouse nibbled a hole in one of the sacks. After several miles, the poor burro became covered with flour, and when it got into his nose, he began to sneeze. His pitching motion threw the flour off him, and it became what we call the Milky Way."

"How'd the burro get into the sky?"

"Don't be rational with Apaches, Lieutenant Barrington. The difference between the primitive mind and ours is we know it's just a story, but the Apaches believe it."

As Nathanial and John Cremony discussed

Apaches, a lone stagecoach meandered over the back roads of Illinois, about fifty miles south of Springfield.

Where once the Sac and Fox Indians roamed, farms and towns had grown. And wherever people settled, lawyers were required to draw up deeds, wills, writs, and so forth. No hamlet could support a full-time judiciary, so the government sent judges to hear cases in one town after the other. It was called "riding the circuit," and the judges naturally were accompanied by lawyers who'd defend hapless widows, orphans, the innocent and guilty.

On that balmy June night, the solitary stagecoach carried Judge David Davis on his circuit tour, and he was accompanied by four distinguished members of the bar. In court these latter gentlemen fought as if they despised each other, but they were also comrades of the road, regaling one another with tales, discussing fine points of jurisprudence, and otherwise amusing themselves.

One of the most popular lawyers on the 8th circuit rode in the stagecoach that lazy night. His name was Abraham Lincoln, six-feet-four, a former back-woodsmen, rail splitter, and boatman on the Ohio and Mississippi rivers. Forty-two years old, he knew all the latest jokes, was an expert mimic, and courtrooms became packed when Honest Abe Lincoln arrived in town.

Once Abe Lincoln had held lofty ambitions and even had been elected to the Congress of the United States. He'd served one term in Washington, and loved to tell about shenanigans in high places. But Abe Lincoln had opposed the popular Mexican War, and his constituents promptly voted him out of office. He'd also served as a state legislator, but politics were a luxury he no longer could afford. He needed to support his growing family back in Springfield.

His fellow passengers laughed at one of his slightly ribald Washington jokes so hard that tears came to their eyes. Then, after recovering his voice, Judge Davis said, "But Abe, they can't *all* be crooks and liars. When you were in Washington, who was the greatest statesman you ever saw?"

Abe Lincoln gazed out the window, the light silhouetting his rugged but clean-shaven visage. "Henry Clay," he declared.

"But didn't he drink like a fish and fool around with women?"

"Maybe, but Henry Clay saved this country twice, with the Missouri Compromise and last year's Compromise Bill. In his prime he was the greatest orator in America, and probably the most intelligent. They don't call him 'The Star of the West' for nothing, boys. Too bad he's getting old, because this country could use another Henry Clay."

"I don't know about that," replied H.C. Whitney, another Springfield lawyer. "It looks like the so-called great compromise of 1850 isn't worth a hill of beans."

"I don't follow politics much these days," replied Abe Lincoln.

It fell silent in the carriage, because they knew Abe's congressional defeat had been a painful blow. Abe Lincoln was a Whig, while Democrats controlled the state legislature. So now he was riding the circuit again, trying to forget wounds inflicted by the nation upon itself.

Abe Lincoln had studied Henry Clay's speeches and agreed that America possessed a great historic destiny. But the people themselves were not great, evidently, for they feuded among themselves constantly. Every month sectional hostility stoked hotter, and the most recent outburst had been northern mayors who'd refused to return escaped slaves, thus violating the new Fugitive Slave Law, part of the Compromise of 1850.

Prior to becoming a lawyer, Honest Abe had stood in the hot sun and chopped wood till sweat poured off him, while folks laughed because his ragged pants were too short. His stepfather had virtually thrown him out when he was seventeen, and he'd worked any job he could find to keep from starving.

Abe Lincoln was no rich man's son, but unlike some who rise from humble beginnings, he never forgot the miss-meal cramps. As a young boatman, his travels and adventures had taken him to New Orleans. He'd visited the slave market, looked into the eyes of Negroes, and decided they possessed the same feelings as white people. This forced him to conclude their subservience was unjust.

But Abe Lincoln also realized, with his logical lawyer's mind, that Southerners would never give up their "special institution," because their economy, philosophy, and entire society depended upon it. So both sides constantly harangued each other, describing the opposition in the most inflammatory language, as the debate descended deeper into the gutter.

Sometimes Abe Lincoln could feel the tensions and contradictions of America in his long limbs. But what does it concern me? he asked himself, as he tried to doze in the dappled moonlight. Nobody cares about my opinions, and they even voted me out of office. I'm finished with politics, and they can make a monkey of somebody else for a change.

THREE

The U.S. Boundary Commission departed the Santa Rita copper mines on a warm June morning. The order of march was Colonel Craig in front, followed by about half his soldiers, then the wagons belonging to the Boundary Commission, and at the rear, Nathanial's detachment. Faces covered by orange bandannas, they looked like a gang of highwaymen as they headed for Mexico.

Nathanial felt as if a silver thread linking him to his family was stretching to the breaking point. He wore his Colt in a special holster hanging from his belt, with his Mississippi Rifle close at hand. Dust billowed about him as he followed the column of twos past clumps of sagebrush, cholla, ocotillo, maguey, and prickly pear cactus.

He was sweaty and uncomfortable, coughing beneath his bandanna, and blinking at dust lodging in his eyes. All my life I've wanted to be a soldier, he reminded himself. Why?

High on the mountain, the lookouts of the People gazed with disbelief at bluecoat soldiers departing the copper mines. A runner was dispatched to the encampment to notify the great chief Mangas Coloradas. The runner was a warrior named Azul, and he found the chief preparing to leave on a hunting expedition. "The White Eyes have gone away!" shouted Azul.

Mangas Coloradas dropped the bag of dried mescal in his hand. He'd suspected the mountain spirits of deserting the People, or perhaps they'd never existed in the first place, but now the power of the People had driven the White Eyes away! The joyous word spread across the campsite, because the People believed their supplications had been accepted by the mountain spirits.

Eminent warriors and their women dropped to their knees and bowed their heads, while others sang victory songs. Children danced delightedly, dogs yipped at their heels, and couples embraced. Mangas Coloradas raised his arms in recognition of their purity. "Tonight—a victory dance!" he declared. "Let the women begin making *tizwin*!"

Maria Dolores often took meals at the saloon, now that Nathanial was gone. She selected an out-of-the-way table, lay Zachary beside her, and a waitress would bring a steak, beans, tortillas, and a bowl of soup.

As she dined, she casually observed men drinking, gambling, and pursuing prostitutes avidly. The women weren't employed by Maria Dolores, but were independent agents. She left them to their sordid careers, provided they caused no trouble. Maria Dolores maintained a clean establishment with two big, mean-looking, armed peacekeepers on duty at any given time, especially the dead of night.

Her other interests included additional saloons, a hotel, a rooming house, and five houses that she rented to families. Maria Dolores had learned that she needed to keep investing if she wanted her wealth to increase. She recalled being poor and worked hard so it wouldn't happen again.

Santa Fe was a rapidly growing town, and all forward-looking business people believed a railroad would come in good time. Maria Dolores saw herself on the way to success, yet felt no sense of joy or accomplishment.

Her sultry brown eyes fell on a prominent Santa Fe businessman fondling a lady of the night young enough to be his daughter. In another direction a young vaquero bussed the wrinkled cheek of a prostitute old enough to be his mother. Men played cards, read newspapers, held boisterous conversations, laughed, sang, and threw dice across gaming tables, snapping their fingers.

Maria Dolores accepted human nature as it was. Since her husband was a man much like the ones before her, she couldn't help wondering if he was lounging in a cantina down Mexico way, with a stray prostitute on his lap.

Maria Dolores considered her husband attractive to other women, and wished he were less so. True, some might consider him brooding, taciturn, or selfish, while others might say he was clumsy and childish. Nathanial wasn't a perfect man by any means, but she'd fallen in love with him for reasons not fully clear to her.

Nathanial appeared aimless in his ambitions, impractical by nature, the kind of man who preferred the outdoor life, a habitué of saloons, a professional soldier who read history and philosophy, and yet was truly wonderful in the little ways that a man endears himself to a woman.

She also knew he was morally weak where his pleasures were concerned. He could never turn down a glass of whiskey, and sometimes she feared her easy-going husband would meet another woman some lonely night, and he'd think, Maria Dolores will never find out, so why not?

An icy dagger pierced her heart as she contemplated the possible unfaithfulness of her husband. A mere glance around the saloon was enough to prove that men couldn't be trusted. I wonder if he's cheating on me? she asked herself, as Zachary dozed at her side. Who is this Nathanial Barrington that I married, and why am I always thinking about him?

The U.S. Boundary Commission crossed the border into Mexico, then plunged through the Sonoran desert. The days grew hotter as the dragoons sat on sweat-stained saddles, traveling across a vast, glittering plains dotted with sagebrush and cacti.

Flankers watched for Apaches, while scouts probed ahead for possible difficulties. Farther back in the formation, John R. Bartlett sat beside the driver on the front seat of his wagon, sketching on his pad, and reflecting upon the strange circumstances that had brought him into the wilds of Mexico.

Never had he dreamed such vistas could exist. How can anyone survive in such a barren place? he wondered. Yet he estimated that one day far in the future, cities would be built on the barren wastes over which he rode. Bartlett glanced up from his sketchpad, surprised to see a settlement in the distance. It didn't appear on his map, but that didn't surprise him. No reliable maps existed of the region.

The column of soldiers, surveyors, scientists, and political appointees drew closer to the village, and Bartlett found himself anticipating a bath, hot meal, clean clothes, and possibly a real feather bed. He wondered what his scholarly New York friends would think if they could see him sweaty and stinking in sunny Mexico.

"Oh-oh," said his driver, an Army private named Caldwell. "There ain't nobody thar."

Bartlett's heart sank as he realized that the buildings appeared deserted. "Perhaps an outbreak of disease," he ventured.

Caldwell spat a large quantity of tobacco juice to the side. "It was Apaches."

The carriage rolled closer, and Bartlett realized that many buildings had been burned to the ground, with others in various states of damage. The column rode down the main street and came to a halt. Bartlett jumped down from his wagon and joined Colonel Craig on his inspection of the ruined town. "When did it happen?" asked Bartlett.

"A few months ago, evidently."

"Why didn't they rebuild?"

"Who's *they*? The Apaches probably killed 'em all."

"Why does everybody blame the Apaches for every disaster that happens?"

"They're generally responsible. Sergeant Barnes—tell the men to take a rest."

The orders finally reached Nathanial at the rear of the detachment. Perspiring profusely, he slid to the ground, regretting all the whiskey and laudanum he'd drunk, not to mention his indolence during the past year at Fort Marcy.

I've got to toughen up, he told himself, as he surveyed the deserted settlement. He lowered his hat brim over his eyes, to keep the sun from blinding him, as he scanned the terrain. For all he knew, Apaches were examining him at that very moment.

And they were.

*   *   *

That night the U.S. Boundary Commission stopped for supper alongside a stream in the Cedar Mountains. At the officers' table, Southerners sat at one end, Northerners at the other, and Colonel Craig, a Virginian, ensconced himself at the head, among the Southern contingent.

Nathanial took his place in between, for he viewed himself as a mediator, although he'd never mediated anything in his life. Supper consisted of the usual roast meat, biscuits, beans, and coffee, same as dinner and breakfast, with no vegetables or fruits, and certainly no decent pie such as could be purchased at any decent New York restaurant.

The officers were tired by the march, frustrated by lack of advancement in the peacetime Army, and tense due to the possibility of Apache attack. When Lieutenant Farley of South Carolina asked Lieutenant Medlowe of Michigan to pass the sugar, the latter pushed the tin bowl down the table roughly.

Lieutenant Farley looked as though he wanted to stuff the sugar bowl down Lieutenant Medlowe's throat, but instead said, in a barely audible tone, "Goddamned Yankee son-of-a-bitch."

Nobody responded, although Colonel Craig's ears turned red. Then Medlowe murmured beneath his breath: "Slave-owning scum."

Before anyone could intervene, Lieutenant Farley dived over the table, reaching for Medlowe's throat, but Medlowe tagged him coming in with a hard right jab, opening a cut over Farley's eye.

Farley's forward motion landed him atop Medlowe, who fell off his stool, and soon Medlowe experienced a furious Southerner pounding his face. Nathanial and the other officers piled on, as Colonel Craig shouted: "That'll be enough!"

There's nothing like an angry colonel to bring lieutenants to their senses. Reluctantly, Farley climbed off Medlowe, who raised himself from the ground, his face bearing mute testimony to the ferocity of the attack. "Just like a *Southern gentleman* to jump you when you're not looking," he muttered.

Farley raised his chin in the air. "I would be happy to meet you on the field of your choice, sir."

Colonel Craig said calmly: "There will be no more fighting in this command. We're American Army officers, and we must elevate ourselves above petty sectional difference. Otherwise, I shall place a complaint in the records of the offending party, and he can pretty much forget about promotions for the rest of his military career."

Jocita, first wife of Juh, peered through fluted spines of yucca cactus at horses penned in the rope corral before her. She was a warrior woman of the People, muscular as any man, and nothing moved except her eyes. The horses didn't know she was there, and neither did the bluecoat guards, one at each end of the corral. Jocita admired the fine lines of the horses, which would fetch good prices from the commancheros. In the next corral were mules, and her mouth watered at the thought of roasting one of them, for mules were the favorite food of the People.

Twenty-five years old, she was dressed like a warrior, except for her short blouse of plain unadorned deerskin. She returned her gaze to the first corral, readied the rope, and drew her energies together.

The head of a guard nodded, while the other blinked and yawned. Jocita crept forward slowly as

the horses watched her fearfully. Whispering their language, she slipped into the corral. I have not come to
hurt you, she silently told them. She'd already selected
her thick-flanked mount, which she considered best of
the lot, and slipped the bridle over his head. "You will
be happy with the People," she whispered soothingly.

As if mesmerized, the horse followed dutifully. She
raised the rope boundary of the corral and led the
animal onto the open land.

FOUR

In the morning Private Rittenhouse approached the command post tent fearfully. "Lieutenant Barrington, sir?"

Nathanial raised his eyes from a map. "Yes?"

"Your horse is missink, sir."

Nathanial was flabbergasted. "But ... where has he gone?"

"If I knew that, he would not be missink, sir."

Rittenhouse was one of the German recruits, and Nathanial followed him to the corral, where Sergeant Duffy had gathered a group of men. "What happened to my horse, Sergeant?"

Perplexed, Duffy shook his head. "Damned if I know, sir."

"Did you question the guards?"

"Nobody seen nothin', sir."

"My horse didn't just fly away, Sergeant. He must be somewhere."

Private O'Neil, an escapee from the potato famine in Ireland, shrugged. "Maybe the Apaches got him."

The Nednai People had moved their camp to Rainbow Gorge deep in the Sierra Madre Mountains. Above the wickiups a fountain of water burst from a rock wall, providing a continual rainbow, with clear water flowing nearby. Nestled within a natural baffle of mountains, the holy place had never been seen by Mexicans.

Jocita returned at midday, seated upon her war pony, and parading her latest acquisition through the camp. She held her head high, wind rustling her jet black hair, as she enjoyed the oohs and aahs of family and friends. "Where did you find him?" asked one of the warriors.

"The bluecoat soldiers gave him to me," replied Jocita with a laugh.

She led the hapless Duke II to the pasture, where she hobbled him with her war pony. Then she returned to the wickiup in which she lived alone. Sitting in the dimness, she closed her eyes. I have a wonderful new horse, she told herself, and I am a respected warrior woman, but what do I really have?

She looked around her empty wickiup, which had been given her by Juh, her husband. He also provided her with meat, for he respected his first wife, despite her inability to produce children. Juh now spent his nights with his more fruitful wives, while Jocita slept alone.

She felt ashamed of her thoughts, because the People believed preoccupation with breeding was a sign of mental instability. The only thing to do was keep busy, and she had a tender slice of deer to cook that night, another gift from Juh.

She wandered into the surrounding foothills, to collect wood for her fire. As she reached higher elevations, she could see the encampment stretched beneath her, ringed by mountains, hidden from the outside world. She carried the firewood to her pit, built a fire, and prepared the meat for cooking.

Her husband approached, kneeled, and touched his

lips to her cheek. "What a beautiful horse you have found," he said with his usual stammer, son of a war chief killed on a raid against the Mexicans.

"If you find him so beautiful, you may have him, my good husband."

"But my dear wife, how could I accept such a valuable gift?"

"Graciously," she replied.

He bowed his head. "I do not deserve you, dear Jocita. You are a finer warrior than I, and certainly more beautiful. If only . . ." His voice trailed off. "But I shall always love you and never would have taken another wife if—"

"Let us not speak of it, my husband."

After he departed, she watched the meat spatter and crackle over hot coals. You left because I am a barren woman, she reasoned. And all the horses in the world will never win you back.

The long blue column continued south, passing abandoned towns, ranches, monasteries, and stage-coach stops. One overcast afternoon, Colonel Craig saw his two scouts riding hard toward him. It looked like trouble, so he raised his arm in the air. Sergeant Barnes passed the order along, as the column ground slowly to a stop.

The Pawnee scout saluted the colonel. "Funny business ahead, sir. Fronteras looks deserted."

"Any burned buildings?"

"It looks perfect, but no one's there."

Colonel Craig didn't know what to make of it. He recalled the story of the *Mary Celeste*, a ship found abandoned in the Atlantic Ocean, with warm meals on the tables. Where had the crew gone? A terrible foreboding came over him. "Sergeant Barnes—tell Lieutenant Barrington that I want to see him."

Sergeant Barnes rode toward the rear of the column, as Colonel Craig gazed at the deserted town through his brass spyglass. Not a soul in sight. Have Apaches massacred the citizens, then run away at the approach of the U.S. Army?

Sweating Lieutenant Barrington rode closer and threw a snappy salute. "You wanted to see me, sir."

"Take your men and find out what's going on in that town."

For all Nathanial knew, Apaches were hidden in Fronteras, waiting to ambush dragoons. He passed the order to Sergeant Duffy, then moved his detachment out of the line. They advanced alongside the other soldiers, and when Nathanial came abreast of Colonel Craig, he tossed another salute.

Nathanial prodded his new horse, a russet stallion named Duke III, onward as his men followed. Everyone wondered what would be waiting in Fronteras as they checked their weapons one last time. The town looked frozen in time.

Nathanial spurred Duke III, taking his position at the front of the detachment, and hoping Apache sharpshooters weren't aiming at him. A shiver of fear touched him, so he squared his shoulders, held his Colt Navy firmly in his right hand, and rode the last two hundred yards to his possible grave.

Anxiety increased among the soldiers with every passing hoofbeat. Nathanial raised his spyglass and scanned for rifles or bows with arrows behind windows, when suddenly he saw movement on the street! Duke III neighed, raising his front hooves in the air, and Nathanial was surprised to see armed civilians and

Mexican soldiers spilling outdoors, led by a mustachioed officer wearing a smile.

Nathanial pulled his horse to a halt in front of the Mexican officer, who declared: "I am General Carrasco. Who might you be?"

"Lieutenant Nathanial Barrington, U.S. Dragoons, sir. What happened?"

General Carrasco appeared embarrassed. "We thought you were Apaches. Have you seen any?"

"Not yet."

"It is a miracle they have not attacked you, but welcome to Fronteras."

That evening, officers and civilian leaders of the Boundary Commission sat to dinner as guests of General Carrasco and his top commanders. The walls of the officers' mess were decorated with crossed swords and lances, as candlelight gleamed on the long rough-hewn table.

"It is the old story," the magnificently uniformed general explained affably, gesticulating with a goblet of red wine. "Our territory is enormous, but our government weak. Every day I receive accounts of Apache rampages, with women and children carried into captivity, horses stolen, property destroyed, and entire provinces laid waste. To raise more soldiers, I have imposed a special tax on the rich, and impressed men into my Army. This has made me unpopular with all parties, and it wouldn't be surprising if I were assassinated one of these days."

The general spoke matter-of-factly, resigned to his fate. Meanwhile, the newspaperman John Cremony scratched wildly in his pad, and Colonel Craig looked pointedly at John R. Bartlett, who maintained the usual skeptical expression in the presence of the military mind.

"But General Carrasco," protested Bartlett, "can you be sure Apaches are doing the harm? Couldn't it be roving outlaw bands?"

General Carrasco turned down the corners of his mouth. "Roving outlaw bands we manage like that." He snapped his fingers. "But the Apache is quite another matter, because he possesses the ability to disappear and appear at will. My dear sir, I myself have been in towns under attack by Apaches and have seen them with my own eyes. In battle, they fight with a ferocity almost awesome to behold, but"—he coughed embarrassedly—"I'm sure your military gentlemen could tell their own unhappy stories about Apaches. How strange," he mused. "Only three years ago we were at war, and now we are allies fighting a common enemy, the Apache. Where are you headed next?"

"Arispe," said Colonel Craig.

"I hope you will not consider me presumptuous, but you should not travel this country with so few men. The Apaches are very bold and numerous here. They conceal themselves so cleverly, you may not see them until it is too late."

After supper the Mexican officers escorted the Americans on a walking tour of Fronteras. They saw mud hovels, sad-faced citizens, and children with rickety legs, while the stench of death and haplessness filled the air.

"This is a fertile land," the general explained, "but the people are afraid to farm, except small plots within sight of the presidio. Once I was interrogating an Apache prisoner, and he said they could kill us all easily, but they needed us to raise horses and cattle for them, and to supply them with weapons and ammunition. They have contempt for us, because we have been so ineffective here."

Jocita lay on animal skins, staring through the smoke hole in the top of her wickiup. Blazing constellations swirled above her, and she wished she could fly to them, disappearing from her agonized body.

She felt ill, her breath came in gasps, and she itched all over. Unable to sleep, she tried to imagine worlds beyond the stars, but her body insistently called to her. Ordinarily, she'd consult with a *di-yin*, but not about her present affliction.

She knew its source, though she hated to admit it. She needed to be loved by a man, but was a proud warrior woman, and wouldn't give a hint of her needs. Sometimes the intensity frightened her, and she feared she would do something ignoble, such as ask her husband to hold her in his arms.

Sometimes she regretted banishing Juh from her wickiup, after he'd selected another wife. But you either loved, or you didn't. Jocita despised the unmarried *bi-zahn* women who'd sleep with any warrior who'd give them a present, but her special wrath was reserved for married women unfaithful to their husbands. The People enjoyed favors from the mountain spirits according to the holiness of their lives, and she did not want licentious behavior endangering family members and friends.

In the past, she'd noticed warriors studying her in that certain way. A few had dropped suggestive hints she'd refused to acknowledge, for a wife must be judicious in all her habits, even if she weren't receiving the benefits of matrimony.

Despite her strong body and other attributes of a woman, motherhood had been denied her by the mountain spirits. Jocita had prayed for a child, but no longer. Instead, she fought the enemies of the People. But at night, alone in her wickiup, she possessed a hungry body that no food could satisfy.

After the walk through Fronteras, the scientists and soldiers of the Boundary Commission returned to their tents. Nathanial had been designated Officer of the Day while Colonel Craig and the others slept. So he prowled the perimeter of their camp, making certain guards were awake.

The Mexican government should evacuate this area, he determined, but pride won't let them, so they maintain weak presidios. Meanwhile, the Apaches harvest the peasants' cattle, sheep, and horses, and practice the old institution of slavery, just like Southerners.

Distant mountains were deep purple, while the moon cast a sheen on remote peaks. The night was breathtaking, yet a thousand Apaches could be hiding in the next ravine, ready to swoop down on Fronteras.

The longer Nathanial remained in the West, the more he hated Apaches. This land would be paradise without them, and who do they think they are, killing and plundering at will?

Nathanial's father and uncles had fought in the War of 1812, while his grandfather had served under General George Washington, and his father was presently a colonel in the War Department in Washington. Nathanial had been raised on military conversations, he'd read the theories of Jomini and von Clausewitz, and had studied the Napoleonic Wars. In addition, he'd read Thomas Paine, Ben Franklin, Thomas Jefferson, John Locke, and David Hume. But nothing had prepared him for life among the Apaches.

Ahead, seated on the ground, was a guard, his head

sunken between his knees. At first Nathanial thought the dragoon had fallen asleep, but then wondered if the Apaches had killed him. He drew his service pistol, then dug the barrel into the soldier's arm. "Are you all right?"

The soldier raised his head. "Huh?"

Nathanial's features hardened. "You're under arrest for sleeping on duty. On your feet!"

"But—"

Nathanial kicked him in the buttocks. "I said on your feet!"

The soldier was small, bearded, with sorrowful eyes, an elf or gnome in uniform, and not a member of Nathanial's detachment. "What's your name?"

The rapidly awakening soldier scrambled to attention. "Private Persinger reporting, sir!"

"You little ..." Nathanial's voice trailed off, because it wasn't a matter of being physically small. "You have endangered the life of every man in the camp!"

Persinger trembled before Nathanial's displeasure, and the West Pointer recalled that enlisted men had set up camp while officers imbibed fine wine in the presidio. Persinger had fallen asleep not out of malicious selfishness, but he couldn't keep his eyes open.

"I'm sorry, sir," the hapless soldier blubbered. "I din't mean it."

"Run to the mess tent and get some coffee. Then hurry back here. I'll watch your post."

Persinger stared at him in disbelief. "Thank you, sir. I'll never forget this, sir."

"You'll forget it as soon as I'm out of sight, you son-of-a-bitch," the battle-hardened officer growled cynically.

Nathanial didn't want to get the reputation as easy

with the men, because they'd walk right over him. He could barely see outlines of chaparral at the edge of camp, never mind Apache warriors. On one dark night, an officer-friend had been shot through the throat by an Apache arrow. In the Mexican War, the battle of Palo Alto had lasted a few hours, but the Apache menace was constant danger. Nathanial felt imprisoned by Apaches, muffled by War Department policy, and frustrated over separation from his family. His mood grew uglier with every passing moment.

Private Persinger returned, his eyes wide open and staring due to two cups of black Army coffee. "Sir, I want to thank you," he stuttered. "You could've had me shot."

"Stay awake," replied Nathanial sternly, "because next time you may not be so lucky."

FIVE

Maria Dolores carried little Zachary through the streets of Santa Fe, on the way to see her reclusive father. She hadn't visited him for several weeks, and sometimes feared he had gone insane.

She arrived at the home she had purchased for him, where the maid peeled onions in the kitchen. "Is my father in the office?"

"Sí, senora."

Maria Dolores carried Zachary down the corridor and knocked on her father's door. Frantic shuffling came from the other side, where she imagined him feverishly hiding his forbidden books. Something slammed, an object scraped the floor, and then she heard his approach.

The door opened, and he peered out suspiciously. "Oh, it's you, my dear." He placed his hands on her shoulders and kissed her cheek. "Is anything wrong?"

She sat on a chair and perched Zachary on her lap. The little boy examined his grandfather curiously, as Maria Dolores glanced about the room. It was dusty, disorderly, books piled on every surface except narrow paths from door, desk, and bed. One wrong move, a tower of books would tip over. "I was wondering how you were, Father, and if you don't mind me saying so, you look terrible."

He shook his head vehemently. "There is nothing wrong with me—I assure you."

"Your skin looks like the underbelly of a fish. You ought to take a walk once in a while."

"I've done enough walking in my life." The old bookworm's eyes fell upon his grandson, and he smiled. "I'm pleased to see that Zachary looks well."

"He is strong like his father, but unfortunately, his father is far away."

Her father raised his finger in the air. "There were plenty of decent men courting you, but you insisted on marrying an American Army officer, of all things." He cocked his head to the side, and looked more like a dotty old man every time she saw him.

"I wish I could tell my husband the truth about our background. I feel I am hiding something from him."

Her father appeared scandalized. "If you do, next thing you know—you'll be divorced. He might even take your child away. I don't think you appreciate the deep-rooted hatred people have for ... strangers."

Maria Dolores opened her mouth to respond, but her jaw hung agape as she recalled Catholic friends casually accusing Jews of the sacrificial murder of Catholic children. "I will respect your wishes of course, my dear father."

In a remote region of Sonora, a palatial hacienda slept beneath twinkling stars. Surrounded by an adobe wall ten feet high, guarded by armed vaqueros, the hacienda was owned by a wealthy and powerful Mexican named Don Carlos de Azcarraga. The People permitted him to raise cattle and horses, so they could acquire some when the mood struck them. No written or oral agreement existed between the People and the great caudillo, but both understood the arrangement full well.

But the arrangement was about to change, for two warriors of the People were eyeing the hacienda approximately fifty paces from the main gate. They were Juh of the Nednais, and his cousin, Geronimo the Bedonko, hidden beneath chaparral.

Naked except for breechclouts, knee-high moccasin boots, knives, and pistols, their faces were smeared with dirt, and leaves had been stuck into bandannas wrapped around their heads. They heard the rumble of a wagon in the distance and smiled merrily. Since childhood, both had been inordinately fond of mischief, and they'd do anything on a dare.

The wagon rolled closer, and the warriors tensed beside the road. They could kill the driver and guard without difficulty, but that wasn't their game. The wagon rolled by, casting bulky moon shadows, as the warriors eased themselves beneath it.

Crouching, holding their pistols ready to fire, they followed the wagon toward the main gate. The great portals opened, and the two warriors hunched through the darkness. When the guards closed the gate firmly, two foxes were in the chicken coop.

The warriors dived behind a stack of hay and peered at the courtyard. They knew where the kitchen was, for they'd observed the hacienda for long periods. No one was near, and they emerged from the hay, skirted the darkness, invisible except for their bright, sparkling eyes.

A guard stood at the door to the kitchen, but the window was open around the corner. The warriors crawled through, landed behind the stove, stopped, listened, smelled, and then commenced searching for the door that led to the cellar.

They'd never been in the kitchen before, and if the Mexicans found them, their heads would be cut off. But they were brave warriors, confident of winning glory. They slipped along the wall, opened the door, and found a pantry full of food. Chewing biscuits, they continued searching, soon finding another door on the far side of the kitchen.

Opening it cautiously, they saw a flight of stairs descending to the cellar. The delicious fragrance of fermented beverages rose to their nostrils, and they smiled in anticipation of a great debauch. Tiny windows permitted narrow slants of moonlight to enter the cellar, enough to illuminate barrels of brandy.

The warriors were delirious with joy, as they opened spigots and let liquid pour into bags made from horse bladders. In the dimness they couldn't help spilling some onto fingers, so naturally they licked them clean. Then, when their bags were filled, it would be a shame to leave so much firewater behind. They couldn't resist taking a few small swallows before departing.

The stalwart warriors weren't accustomed to fine brandy, and their minds soon became addled. They sat on the floor, to collect their thoughts, and decided to lubricate their dry throats more. Demons danced in corners as the warriors sucked the spigots of their respective barrels. Incredible visions flooded their minds, they stumbled in the darkness, and Juh burst into laughter, as he reflected upon the absurdity of their situation. "We must leave this place," he slurred to Geronimo.

"But where is the door?" replied his cousin.

Geronimo loved firewater, for it permitted him to forget the wanton murder of his wife and children. He felt free, happy, and full of possibilities, as he narrowed his eyes and groped for the stairs. He thought he saw them, but stumbled into a barrel of brandy, knocked it over, and fell into a shelf of crockery, producing a fearful sound. Juh tried to help him up, but slipped on the wet floor, and his face struck another spigot, opening a cut on his right cheek.

The warriors struggled to rise, laughing uproariously at their predicament. That's how the guards found them, helpless and foundering in squalor, staring balefully at lanterns and rifles surrounding them.

Diego Carbajal sat in his stuffy office, door firmly locked. A spare man of fifty-nine, with gold-rimmed eyeglasses perched atop his nose, he resembled a question mark as he bent over his ancient, tattered leatherbound copy of the *Zohar,* the sacred Book of Radiance written by thirteenth- and fourteenth-century Spanish kabalists.

The multitudes dwell in confusion
failing to perceive the truth of Torah
while Torah lovingly summons them every day
but woe, they do not acknowledge her.

Wherever you look in the world, there is strife, pain, vanity, and death, analyzed Diego. The Holy One, blessed be He, calls to us continually, but we have closed our hearts to Him.

Sometimes Diego believed he was being called by His Holy Name, and he wanted to run into the streets, preaching righteousness to anyone who'd listen, but then he remembered the prophet Jeremiah, who'd spent substantial sojourns in jails, or the prophet Jonah, who'd been eaten by a whale, not to mention the prophet Ezekiel, who'd been exiled by Nebuchadnezzar. Do not be a fool, he counseled himself. You are not going to convert this sinful Santa Fe to righteousness.

He heard footsteps in the corridor outside his office and jumped three feet in the air, as if he expected the Spanish Inquisition to appear at any moment. Immediately, his beloved Book of Radiance found itself in the bottom drawer. There was a knock on the door. "Who is it?"

"Miguelito."

Don Diego opened the door and looked downward at the mishapen creature before him, janitor at the Silver Palace Saloon. Alarmed, the kabalist scholar asked: "Has anything happened to my daughter?"

"Be calm, Señor Carbajal." Miguelito climbed onto a chair and sat with his legs hanging over the edge. "Nothing has happened to Maria Dolores, but she is not herself since her husband has gone away. She is alone with the business, the baby, and sometimes a woman needs her father."

A black cloak of guilt dropped onto Diego as his spine curved further beneath the load. "I will go to her at once," said Diego. "And I will not tell her you have visited me."

Geronimo opened his eyes and groaned. He was bound hand and foot, lying in a pool of his own vomit at the bottom of a wagon. His head felt as though someone had buried a hatchet in his brain, and his limbs were numb due to constricted blood circulation.

He rolled over and saw Juh passed out cold. Then he remembered the drunken orgy, falling barrels of firewater, sliding around in the darkness, and the final shameful capture. Geronimo wondered why they had not killed him, but was certain his end was near.

Geronimo wasn't afraid of death, and neither did

torture worry him, but he cursed himself for stupidity. "It is the firewater that does this to me," he muttered.

"One of them's tryin' to say something," declared a guard, riding alongside the wagon.

"Keep an eye on him," replied a new voice. "If he tries anything funny, don't hesitate to shoot. We can't take chances with them."

Diego Carbajal was astonished at the expansion of the Silver Palace Saloon since he'd seen it last. Evidently Maria Dolores had acquired adjacent buildings while he'd been studying sacred books. Diego felt weak in the knees, for he hadn't been outdoors for two months.

He entered the saloon, stepped out of the backlight, and realized that the former hole in the wall had become a spacious, dimly lit chamber with gambling tables, polished brass cuspidors, a spotless floor, gleaming wooden bar, and plenty of customers.

He couldn't help admiring the intelligence and skill of his daughter, for he had lost huge sums in a variety of businesses over the years, always managing to be in the wrong place at the wrong time. He'd actually opposed her when she'd suggested opening an American-style saloon, but she'd been right, a lesson in humility for him.

He made his way through the crowd, and no one paid any attention to the gangly old fellow with a gray beard, wearing a dark suit, white shirt, and black string tie, with a big sombrero perched atop his head. He wondered if he had become invisible and caught vague spectral images of angels sitting in the rafters, gazing down at him.

He found his daughter in her office, astonished to see him. Even little Zachary in his crib was surprised to see the patriarch of the family. Diego sat on one of the chairs and wondered what to say to his daughter.

"What are you doing here, Father?" she asked. "Are you all right?"

"I thought I'd pay you a visit," he said lamely. "I've been too involved with my books, but you appeared troubled when you stopped by. Is anything wrong?"

"I am fine," she said uneasily.

"Perhaps you have too many responsibilities."

"I do not have any more responsibilities than before, but I am not sleeping well."

Diego suddenly understood what was bothering his daughter, and found it embarrassing. "You cannot say you have not been warned," he said testily.

Her voice dropped a few octaves. "It does no good to dredge up the past."

"If you had listened to your father, you would not have married a soldier."

"But I love him," she replied.

"Then you must tell him to come home."

"I have mailed letters, but not heard a word. For all I know, my husband might be dead."

The wagon stopped in front of a building with barred windows, and Geronimo raised his head. Men on horseback surrounded him and Juh, aiming rifles at their captives, but the warriors didn't cringe, cower, or beg for mercy.

"Look at them defying us," said one of the vaqueros. "I am tempted to put a bullet into them, to teach them a lesson."

"Do not be so foolish," said one of vaqueros, "unless you want to be looking over your shoulder for the rest of your life."

A crowd gathered, staring with fear and horror at the Apaches. The door to a building opened, and a sergeant appeared with the chief of vaqueros. "Why have you brought them here?" asked the sergeant. "You should have killed them while you had the chance."

"We thought it best to turn them over to you, Sergeant Rodriguez."

"When the Apaches find out their two friends are here, they'll destroy this town."

"Then turn them loose. Anyway, they are your headache now, sir."

The Apaches were pushed off the wagon, and they fell to the ground like sacks of flour. With a laugh, the vaquero captain vaulted onto his horse, and wheeled him around in street. "Vamanos muchachos!"

The vaqueros yipped and yelled as they galloped out of town, taking their clattering wagon with them. They made so much noise, they wakened Juh from his stupor, and he tried to work himself to his knees, but the ropes bound him too tightly.

Sergeant Rodriguez was tempted to free the Apaches, but a court-martial would doubtlessly ensue. "Lock them up," he ordered his corporal. "I want two guards on their cell twenty-four hours a day."

Diego was amazed by the splendor of his daughter's saloon. After talking with her, he decided to stay for a drink. It amused him that the bartender didn't know him, so he paid for his mug of beer like any other customer, and carried it to a table against the far wall.

On the stage a man in a suit and string tie strummed

a guitar, barely making himself heard above the crescendo of conversation, laughter, arguments, the clatter of the chuck-a-luck wheel, and the spatter of
broiling meat at the chop counter in the rear.

It all seemed exciting and fabulous to a man who'd
been sequestered in his room for most of the past
three years. He recalled when he'd owned his own
ranch, and visited cantinas with his vaqueros. But then
the Apaches stole his cattle and killed most of his
vaqueros, forcing him out of business.

I should spend more time with other people, he
thought, as he quaffed the beer. I can recite abstract
tractates of Torah, but I'm not having any fun. He
appraised the prostitutes, but it wasn't difficult to fight
temptation at the age of fifty-nine. Romance is for the
young, he told himself, whereas a gentleman such as
I should be more dignified. What an interesting and
stimulating place is this saloon. I believe I shall take
my meals here in the future.

Two bearded and dusty Americans sat at the table
beside him, and a waitress brought them whiskey.
Diego couldn't help eavesdropping on their conversation and discovered they'd just arrived from Durango.
Diego was about to ask how things were in Mexico,
when the mood of their conversation changed.

"I'm so tired, I could sleep for ten years," said one
of the bullwhackers, who wore a torn red-and-black
checkered shirt.

"Know what you mean," replied his friend, with a
nose like a spoon. "I work all the damn time, but it's
the Jews that get the money. Now why is that?"

"Because they cheat better than everybody else."

"An hombre was telling me the other day that Mexico is bankrupt because of the Jews. They suck people

dry, and they own all the politicians. Nothing we can do about it."

Diego was on the way to the door, hands shaking, lips white. Just when I thought I was like everybody else, there it is again, he said to himself. He headed home, glancing back to make certain the two bull-whackers weren't following. Thank God nobody knows who I am, he thought, and that daughter of mine had better keep her big mouth shut.

Jocita sat alone at her fire, carving a slice of ante-lope on a spit. Children gathered nearby, for she always prepared extra for hungry little bellies. She tossed a chunk over her shoulder, and the children jumped into the air. It was Little Antelope who caught it, outdistancing taller boys. Jocita laughed as she reached for the haunch of meat. Suddenly, a commotion erupted at the far end of the encampment.

She reached for her bow and arrow, as two sweaty riders galloped toward the wickiups. Ill tidings were reported first to the chief, but it appeared that the warriors were headed directly toward her!

She drew herself to full height as her muscles striated in the flickering light of the fire. The warriors pulled to a stop before her, their horses frothing and wheezing after their long ride, sending up a cloud of dust. A dagger of fear struck her woman's heart, but Jocita changed her expression not one bit. "What has happened?"

"Juh and Geronimo have been captured by the Mexicans and jailed in Arispe!"

It was all Jocita could do to maintain calm, because she knew how the *Nakai-yes* treated the People. She'd never led a raid before, but her man might be beheaded if he was still alive. "I shall free Juh and Geronimo!" she told them. "Who is with me?"

Colonel Craig rode over the crest of a hill, and saw the city of Arispe sprawled beneath him in the night. No lamps were visible, although it wasn't late in the evening.

"They think we're Apaches as in Fronteras, sir," explained John Cremony. "We'd better announce ourselves before they start firing."

"Excellent idea." The colonel turned toward Lieutenant Barrington. "Since your voice is louder than mine, why don't you give it a try?"

Lieutenant Barrington cupped his hands around his mouth and shouted: "We're American soldiers—don't shoot!"

Men with rifles appeared at the edge of town. "Our prayers are answered!" yelled one of them, dropping to his knees and crossing himself.

A Mexican sergeanto strode toward them and threw a salute. "We are happy to see you, sir. Two Apache braves are in jail, and we expect an attack any moment."

"We'll set up camp on this plain," replied Colonel Craig. "If the Apaches are foolish enough to attack your town, we'll give them all the lead they can handle."

The prairie dog town was silent and motionless in the light of the moon. It looked like any other expanse of open range, but beneath the surface, tiny furred creatures slept peacefully in their lairs.

Then, barely perceptibly, a trembling came to those ornate tunnels, and soon a clod of earth fell on one of the creatures. He awoke and was about to sound the alarm, when three sections of the tunnel network caved in.

All the prairie dogs scattered, as thunder and violence came upon them. Frantically, they ran toward the surface, poked their heads out holes, and were horrified to see a huge number of monsters heading in their direction!

With fearful bleats the prairie dogs ran for their lives, but some weren't fast enough and got smashed by swift, sharp hooves. The horses of the People demolished the town as they galloped onward, and the warriors riding them were nearly naked, their bodies painted black, and sprinkled with holy pollen. They carried their best weapons and bent low over their horses' manes as they sped beneath a sea of stars.

Leading the way, as lithe and strong as any of the men, was Jocita, her long black hair trailing behind her. The men were bare-chested, but she wore her brown deerskin blouse a few shades darker than her skin, decorated with inked symbols of the sun and moon. Around her head was wrapped a red bandanna, and she wore her *Izze-kloth* Killer of Enemies Bandolier across her breast.

She prayed that Juh was still alive, as she urged her horse to greater effort. Juh was the only man she'd ever known, and the other half of her very own being was in jeopardy.

Ahead, far in the distance, faint twinkling lights came to her sharp eyes. She raised her arm in the air, then pointed straight ahead, as the warrior queen led her rampaging warriors onward through the endless Sonoran night.

After supper the officers and boundary officials decided to ride into town and look at the Apache prisoners. They stopped at the office of Sergeant Rodriguez, who escorted them to the stockade.

"How big is this city?" asked Colonel Craig as they sauntered down the main street.

"Twelve hundred souls," replied Lieutenant Rodriguez, "but you will notice no citizens on the street. Last year an Apache war party attacked a pack train within sight of this town. The muleskinners managed to get away, but the townspeople watched the plunder from their windows, and it left a deep impression."

They came to a squat adobe building, the sergeanto led them past a steel gate, and they came a cell. The guards held torches, illuminating one tall Apache and another of medium height.

"What did they do?" asked John R. Bartlett.

"They broke into a hacienda and stole some brandy."

"That's all?"

"By the time they were captured, they could barely stand."

I know the feeling, thought Nathanial, as he noticed their deep chests, muscled legs, powerful-looking arms, and the expression of defiance in their eyes.

Colonel Craig chuckled. "They look as if they want to scalp the whole lot of us. What are you going to do with them?"

"I am waiting for orders."

Nathanial saw unremitting hostility beaming from the eyes of the Apaches. They appeared more or less like other men, yet a fundamental difference radiated forth, as if they were related to wolves and wildcats.

"We expect their friends to attack tonight," said the sergeanto, "Should be interesting, no?"

"We're not authorized to guard your prisoners," replied Colonel Craig, "but if Apaches attack Arispe, we shall stand beside our Mexican neighbors."

The weasel-faced dragoon named Dowd waited until the others were asleep, then pulled on his boots, grabbed rifle, pistol, and ammunition, and headed for the latrine. The campsite was silent, all lights out, with guards posted.

He passed a strawberry cactus, and thousands of hairlike needles stuck his thigh. Cursing, trying to brush them off, he only caught them in his hand, producing a dull ache. He continued to the big, smelly hole dug into the ground, and Ethridge was already there, pretending to button his pants.

The conspirators were on their way to the gold fields of California or a firing squad. Without a word, they walked into the chaparral, glancing behind them to make sure they'd hadn't been seen.

They made their way through cactus claws and ended behind a general store. Dowd wrapped a rock in his shirt, gently forced a window, then reached around and unlatched the door. He and Ethridge sneaked inside, then stole beans, coffee, flour, and other staples, which they stored into gunnysacks.

Above them, the proprietor and his wife hugged fearfully in bed, because they thought Apaches were in the store. A pot fell to the floor, and the proprietor twitched in terror, while his wife strangled down a scream.

The deserters slung the gunnysacks over their shoulders, then made their way to the townspeople's stable. As expected, the Mexicans were afraid to guard their horses, preferring to give a few to Apaches rather than risk their skins. The deserters selected two mounts, saddled them, then decided upon a packhorse.

They rode out the back door where a cloud obscured the moon. Their eyes searched for Apaches, as they steered toward the gold fields of California.

John Cremony sat in his tent, writing in his journal:

The Mexicans on the northern frontier are the very lowest and poorest of their countrymen. Living in hovels and sustaining themselves in some manner never yet determined, almost wholly without arms or ammunition, and brought up from earliest infancy to entertain the most abject dread and horror of the Apache, they are forever after unable to divest themselves of the belief than an Apache warrior is not a man, but some terrible ogre against whom it is useless to contend, and who is only to be avoided by flight or appeased by unconditional submission.

Cremony heard footsteps outside, reached for his Colt Dragoon, and Lieutenant Barrington appeared, hat on the back of his head, a smile on his face. "Saw your light and wondered what you were doing up this time of night."

Cremony puffed his pipe as he measured Barrington. "I was writing in my journal. What are *you* doing wandering around?"

"Making sure the guards are awake."

"Don't worry—the Apaches aren't after us. They want to free their friends, and I imagine they will before long. You don't expect those eight frightened Mexican soldiers to put up a fight, do you?"

"What about us?"

"We didn't capture the prisoners, and I don't think

there's anything to worry about. You might as well go to bed."

Nathanial shuffled toward his headquarters, chagrined that Cremony hadn't felt like talking with him. Then he noticed another tent, this one belonging to dragoons of Colonel Craig's unit, with a candle burning inside. On his tiptoes, he sneaked closer, then poked his head through the flap. Five soldiers sat cross-legged on the ground, playing poker for payday stakes with a deck of dog-eared cards.

"Put the cards away and go to sleep," Nathanial told them. "This is the Army, not a casino."

He could have arrested them, but gambling didn't appear a terrible offense to an officer who needed whiskey to steady his nerves. Every Mexican town, no matter how poor, boasted at least one cantina, and no one would question the movements of an officer. But he didn't want to run into Apaches.

He sat on his cot and removed his boots, then stretched out and closed his eyes, his hand gripping the plain walnut handle of his Colt service pistol.

Juh and Geronimo sat on the floor of the jail, gazing at each other in the cold light of sobriety. "How foolish we have been," muttered Geronimo.

Juh looked out the back window. "I wonder if they will kill us."

"I cannot understand why they have not done so already."

They were accustomed to running free, but had been caged like wild animals. Juh looked at the confinement of his cell and struggled to control rising panic. "We deserve to die for our foolhardiness. It was my fault, because I should have known better."

"But I had such visions," replied Geronimo. "Red

and blue lights flickered before my eyes. I thought I understood everything."

On the other side of the bars sat two guards, and each appeared fearful as they stared at their Apache prisoners. Outside the guardhouse, two additional guards stood on either side of the door. They scanned rooftops, windows, and jumped at every creak in the buildings around them, as wood contracted in the cool night air. The other four soldiers were in the barracks, dressed, but lying in bed, their rifles nearby, hoping Apaches wouldn't kill them.

Civilians cowered inside their jacales, waiting for the Apaches to arrive. Some cursed the vaqueros who'd brought Apaches into Arispe, as if they didn't have enough problems. Even the cantinas were closed and boarded. In the tiny church the solitary priest kneeled before the Blessed Sacrament, rattling his rosary beads, and praying that God would spare the town from massacre.

The guard changed at two in the morning, and Private Sanchez took his post in front of the stockade. It was the moment he'd been fearing, and he'd hoped the attack would come on somebody else's watch.

Sanchez was a skinny peasant who'd joined the Army to receive regular meals, not fight the dreaded Apache. He was afraid to look for them, because he might actually see one. He held his rifle in both hands, ready to raise the butt to his shoulder and fire.

He glanced around, but nothing moved in his vicinity. His partner, Private Lopez, fidgeted on the other side of the door. "I don't like this," said Lopez. "We're in the open."

"Don't worry—we'll see the Apaches before they get too close."

Suddenly an arm clamped his chest, and something sharp appeared at his throat. "Do not move," said a woman's voice in his ear.

His eyes widened as Apaches materialized around him, and one held a knife to the throat of Lopez. Then Sanchez felt a soft breast pressing his shoulder blade. He felt aroused and terrified at the same time. "Please do not kill us," he begged. "We do not care if you take your friends away."

The People advanced toward the door, a warrior pulled it open, and the disarmed guards were pushed into the orderly room. "Do not move," said Jocita, aiming a pistol at the nose of one of the guards inside.

Juh stood behind the bars, a smile on his face. "I am so happy to see you, my dear wife."

"Open the door," she ordered a guard.

He dutifully inserted the key into the lock, the door swung open, and the prisoners caught the breath of freedom. Weapons were pressed into their hands, then the People turned toward the former guards, who were pale and trembling against the wall.

"Let them live," said Juh. "They were not cruel to us."

Jocita advanced toward the guards, the corners of her mouth turned down. "You be quiet," she said in broken Spanish. "If you call others, we kill you."

"Don't worry about us," replied Private Sanchez nervously. "Anything you say."

The People filed outside and took defensive positions, scanning the shadows for enemies. Like two lithe deer, Juh and Geronimo sped toward the horses, followed by the other warriors, and the Mexicans dared not stop them. The warriors mounted up, put their heels to their horses' withers, and in seconds were swallowed by the hungry black night.

*   *   *

The People returned to camp in the hour before dawn. Everyone exhausted, they made their way to their wickiups. As Jocita arranged her animal skins, Juh joined her.

She could barely see him in the darkness. "Yes, my husband?" she asked.

"You have saved my life, and I wanted to thank you."

"I did not do it alone," she reminded him. "You should thank all of us together."

"But you were leader of the raid." He leaned forward and pressed his lips against her cheek. "I love you more than ever."

"Go home to one of your other wives," she replied wearily. "I want to sleep."

"But you are the one I love most."

"Do not lie, my husband. If you loved me, you would never have left me."

"But I wanted children—I'm sorry."

"I wanted them too, but I would never have left you."

"You think no one is good enough for you, but I did not come here to fight."

"You came out of obligation, but you do not owe me anything. I would like to sleep."

She listened to him crawl out of her wickiup, her lips set in a grim line. When he was gone, she stifled a sob, then her warrior woman's strength deserted her, and she collapsed onto the antelope skins, crying herself to sleep.

The U.S. Boundary Commission departed Arispe without being attacked by Apaches and headed north for the long march back toward the Santa Rita copper mines. Four days later, in Guadalupe canyon, their scouts reported a large Mexican cavalry unit dead ahead.

Colonel Craig didn't think the Boundary Commission could be mistaken for Apaches, so he continued through the pass, glancing about the cliffs and gorges for possible danger. Apaches were continually on his mind; he was becoming obsessed with them, as he'd been obsessed with Mexicans during the last war.

He spotted Mexican cavalry straight ahead, with their guidons and dusty uniforms, not much different from the U.S. Army. If they'd met three years ago, it would have meant a cavalry charge. The colonel smiled in rueful memory of those great glory days.

He estimated about two hundred fifty lancers, and knew lancers were the crème de la crème of the Mexican army, its officers drawn from the first families of the nation. Colonel Craig held up his hand, signaling for the Boundary Commission to halt.

The Mexican officer passed the same order to his men, and both groups came together in the pass, as dust billowed about them. The Mexican officer was a lieutenant, and Colonel Craig urged his horse toward him. The Mexican saluted the higher rank respectfully, as John Cremony angled closer to interpret.

After pleasantries were exchanged, Colonel Craig asked: "What's the Apache situation ahead?"

The Mexican lieutenant's white shirt was damp with sweat, his eyes bloodshot. "We have had no trouble, but ten Americans were attacked by Apaches near Janos. One was killed, three wounded, and the rest managed to escape. When last seen, the Apaches were headed this way."

Colonel Craig guessed the Apaches had been Mimbrenos from the Santa Rita Mountains. More compliments were exchanged, the two men saluted each other, the units veered right, and each passed each other in the Guadalupe Canyon.

Colonel Craig was deep in thought for the remainder of the ride to the copper mines. Are the Mimbrenos on the warpath? he wondered. If they attacked an American pack train near Janos, what'll stop them from killing American surveyors in the Santa Rita Mountains?

Approximately nine hundred miles to the east, near the banks of the great mother Mississippi, Senator Jefferson Davis of Mississippi sat among distinguished guests attending a ball at a mansion in Jackson, the state capital. It was a warm summer night, and his companions were planters, politicians, Army and Navy officers, businessmen, and bankers, the top strata of Mississippi society. In heated tones they discussed the dangerous political situation into which the nation was sinking.

Jefferson Davis was forty-three years old, born in a log cabin, son of a county clerk. He wanted a vacation from politics, so he gazed at the dance floor not far away, where young blades in fine-tailored suits or military uniforms danced a Virginia reel with ladies wearing hoop skirts and crinoline pantaloons. Musicians perspired as they sawed their violins atop the elevated stage, while on the other side of the room, mature married ladies such as Senator Davis's second wife, the former Varina Howell of Natchez, gathered to discuss women's matters such as fashion, upcoming marriages, and how to manage recalcitrant household slaves.

Jefferson Davis sat in silence, puffing a long, thin cigar, as his companions debated the great issues of the day. He'd heard the arguments a million times, and in fact had advanced many personally on the floor of the U.S. Senate.

Often appearing cold and imperious, Jefferson Davis once had been a lighthearted Southern cavalier. Then his first wife, a daughter of former President Zachary Taylor, had died of malarial fever three months after their marriage. Jefferson Davis never fully recovered from her loss, and for seven years lived in deep seclusion on the family plantation at Brierfield. But then, in 1845, he'd met his present wife, eighteen years his junior, who'd melted the sorrow surrounding his heart. Shortly thereafter, he'd resumed his public career.

Unlike most politicians, Jefferson Davis wasn't a lawyer. Instead, he'd been educated at West Point, fought the Winnebago Indians on the Wisconsin frontier, and led the First Mississippi Rifles in the most tumultuous battles of the Mexican War.

Jefferson Davis was famous not only in Mississippi, but also in the country at large. A fiery orator and staunch defender of Southern rights, he was a national hero for having held the vital Saltillo Road during the Battle of Buena Vista.

Jefferson Davis had been named after Thomas Jefferson, and considered himself a Jeffersonian Democrat. But he feared the federal government was intruding increasingly into people's personal lives, producing a tyranny as onerous as the one his grandfather had fought in the Revolutionary War. Senator Jefferson Davis had opposed the Compromise of 1850 because he foresaw the Fugitive Slave Law creating more problems than it solved. Meanwhile, new territories were clamoring to come into the Union as states, while the proposed route of the transcontinental railroad was coming to debate in the Congress. Northern and Southern senators insulted each other daily in the hallowed halls of Congress, and following the death of Senator John C. Calhoun of South Carolina, Jefferson Davis had become floor leader for the Southern cause.

Jefferson Davis gazed longingly at dancers twirling beneath rows of crystal chandeliers. He remembered when he'd been romantic and lighthearted, but then he'd spent nearly seven years campaigning in Wisconsin and Michigan, caught pneumonia, and now suffered painful facial neuralgia, plus a strange disease that clouded his left eye.

A hand dropped onto his sleeve. "Jeff, may I have a word with you in private?"

It was Senator Robert Barnwell Rhett of South Carolina, guest of honor at the ball, and one of the most notorious "fire-eaters" in the South. Senator Rhett had been nominated to fill Calhoun's unfinished term, while his brother, Edmund Rhett, was editor of the influential Charleston *Mercury*, the main organ of secession in the South.

Senator Rhett, fifty-one years old, was heavyset, with gray chin whiskers but no mustache. He led Jefferson Davis up the stairs to a small library on the second floor. Senator Rhett sat opposite Jefferson Davis, floor-to-ceiling shelves of tomes surrounding them. "I hope you won't be offended by what I have to say," said Senator Rhett.

"Speak your mind," said Jefferson Davis. "It must be pretty bad, to judge from the expression on your face."

"Jeff," declared Senator Rhett, "you and I have known each other for a long time, and I know what you think of me—that I'm extreme in my views, and perhaps I am. But I love the South as much as any man, and I see great difficulty arising here in Mississippi. We cannot let Henry Foote become governor."

Henry Foote was the most popular stump speaker in Mississippi, a turncoat Whig secessionist who'd switched parties and become a Democrat unionist. It would be no exaggeration to say that Jefferson Davis heartily despised Henry Foote, who was running unopposed for the state house, following the recent resignation of Governor John Quitman.

"What would you like me to do?" asked Jefferson Davis.

Senator Rhett stroked his gray chin whiskers. "I think *you* should run for governor of Mississippi."

Jefferson Davis was aghast. "But I've only just finished the first six months of my new term in the Senate!"

"In a government that is increasingly irrelevant to the needs of the South," replied Rhett. "We both know it doesn't matter who's in Washington, because Washington is rigged against the South, but a good man is vital here in Mississippi. Neither of us can predict the future, but if secession comes, and I believe it will, Southern governors will be the most influential men in the new government."

Jefferson Davis couldn't dispute the logic, but he'd never dream of resigning his Senate seat. "I'm flattered that you've thought of me in this regard, but if the South expects to defend itself, we'll need more than good governors. The South has got to start building factories *now* to smelt steel, manufacture weapons, sew uniforms, build wagons, and furnish other critical supplies, because once secession comes, the damned abolitionists won't sell anything to us. Why, even the books we read are printed in the North, and the

schoolmasters   who   teach   our   children   are
Northerners!''

Senator Rhett smiled, patting his emotional friend
on the shoulder. "You understand the stakes, Jeff, and
the people trust you. The party believes you're the
best man to lead Mississippi through the ordeal that
lies ahead.''

SIX

The Boundary Commission returned to the copper mines, unaware of the consternation they provoked. The People thought their prayers had forced the blue-coat soldiers away, but now they'd returned, apparently to stay.

Mangas Coloradas felt as if the mountain spirits had played on a joke on the People, but then rebuked himself for thinking ill of those who'd taught the People to live. The great chief consulted leading medicine men and women, but they provided only vague salutations. "Perhaps we should have another dance," one of them suggested.

So a dance was scheduled, and on the appointed night, masked dancers descended from the mountains, waving their scepters in the air. Drums were pounded, huge quantities of *tizwin* consumed, and all the warriors, maidens, children, old people, and dogs danced their hearts out nearly until dawn.

When they awakened the White Eyes still were camped at the copper mines. And the White Eyes remained during the days to come. Finally, Mangas Coloradas was forced to send messengers to all the far-flung clans of the People. The White Eyes had returned to the sacred Santa Rita Mountains, and a decision must be reached about how to expel them.

*   *   *

A supply train arrived from Fort Marcy, bringing Nathanial packages from his wife and mother. He carried them to his tent and didn't know which to open first. Finally, he decided that his wife would deliver the most important information, so he drew his knife and slit open the wrapping.

She'd sent him cookies baked by herself and crumbled to bits by their journey at the bottom of a wagon. Her letter sounded unhappy. When are you coming home? she asked. We need you. Included were incomprehensible scratchings on paper by his son, plus a lock of the little boy's hair. Nathanial brought it to his nostrils, but it smelled like seven days of the *Journado del Muertos*.

He felt guilty about his abandoned family and hoped the Boundary Commission finished its work soon. Why can't Maria Dolores accept her situation as I accept mine? he wondered. I'm surrounded by the Apache nation, but I'm making the best of it. The problem with women is they're so damned emotional.

His gaze turned to the packet from his mother, and he wondered what glad or ill tidings it contained. He opened it gingerly, finding a letter, a stack of press clippings, and two just-published books: *Representative Men* by Ralph Waldo Emerson, and *Moby-Dick* by Herman Melville.

Nathanial couldn't rely on his mother to tell the truth about family matters, because she needed to live in a comfortable, orderly world. According to her written testimony, her health was fine, her husband happily engaged in his work, her younger son, Jeffrey, doing wonderfully in school, and her adopted son, Tobey, also a superior student. But the truth was probably opposite, Nathanial suspected, because he never knew what was true or false in his mother's communications.

He loved his mother not out of obligation or a warped sense of duty, but because he knew that she loved him, and every lie she committed was for his sake. She didn't want him to worry, but only caused him to worry more.

He sat on his cot and proceeded to peruse newspaper clippings, all from the *New York Daily Times*. The one on top described a riot in Boston, where a fugitive slave named Shadrach was captured by slave catchers. Shadrach called for help, a crowd formed, police were called, and the white citizens of Boston stormed the prison, freeing Shadrach, and spirited him away. The incident had received widespread publicity, enraging the South, while abolitionists everywhere praised the brave deed.

Another clipping told of a San Francisco fire that destroyed an incredible 2,500 buildings. A third reported a speed record set by an American sailing ship, the *Stag Hound,* thirteen days from Boston Light to the Equator.

He also read about John E. Heath, a Mississippi engineer who'd invented a mechanical agricultural binder. New York City estimated over 18,400 people living in 8,100 cellars. In France, it was rumored that Prince Louis Napoleon Bonaparte, president of the Republic, was planning to make himself emperor, thus following the footsteps of his illustrious or depraved uncle, depending upon one's point of view.

Nathanial felt as if life were passing him by, as he re-read the letter from his wife. He pictured her at her desk and recalled the curves of her rich, full body, the feel of her sumptuous breasts, the warmth of her arms, the touch of her tongue against his. A wave of frustrated desire passed over him, and he feared he'd go berserk if he didn't receive feminine companionship soon.

When in doubt, check the guards, he told himself. He put on his hat and wandered around the perimeter of the encampments, challenging the sentries. Toward the end of his rounds, he thought he'd pay a visit to John Cremony. As he drew closer to the interpreter's tent, Nathanial realized that Cremony was conferring with Apaches next to his fire. Nathanial recognized Nana, the middle-aged warrior whom he'd met before. Wouldn't it be something if I ran into those two Apaches I saw in Arispe, Nathanial mused.

There were five Apaches, but Cremony appeared unafraid. "Hello Nathanial," he said. "Let me introduce you to my friends."

Nathanial noticed the eyes of the Apaches darting to his rifle, pistol, boots, and hat, as if he were a walking general store. What would I do if they all attacked at once? he wondered.

The Apaches were named Ponce, Coleto Amarillo, Delgadito, and Lucero. "You have baccy?" asked the latter.

Nathanial handed him the pouch of tobacco sent him by his mother. "Help yourself."

Each Apache took a big pinch, and when Nathanial received the pouch back, it was nearly empty. The tobacco had been purchased in a shop on Broadway and would be smoked by naked savages in New Mexico. Nathanial became aware of the Apaches looking at him fixedly and realized he was as odd to them as he was to them.

"I was explaining," Cremony told Nathanial, "that if they want to know how long we'll stay in the vicinity, they should talk with Mister Bartlett."

"I don't think he knows himself," replied Nathanial. "He has much work to do."

The Apaches looked at each other in dismay. "In the mines?" asked Nana.

"No, they're measuring a new line between America and Mexico."

Now the Apaches were more confused than ever, and Nathanial realized that a tremendous gulf lay between their minds and his own. "Don't Apaches have boundaries between their lands?"

"We have always lived in this place," replied Nana. "Yusn has given it to us."

"Who?"

Cremony answered for his guests. "Yusn is their God. He is also called the Life-giver."

Ponce said, "Our chief would like to speak with your chief. Is all right?"

"Do you mean Mangas Coloradas?"

The Apaches nodded.

Cremony appeared suitably impressed. "I am certain that Mister Bartlett would be honored to meet the famous chief of the Mimbrenos. Let him come here tomorrow at noon."

Delgadito sidled closer and narrowed one eye. "Maybe you bring whiskey, yes?"

"We don't have whiskey," Cremony replied firmly. "Mister Bartlett thinks it is bad medicine. Don't you believe me?"

"I never heard of White Eyes without whiskey," replied Delgadito adamantly.

Colonel Craig sat in his office, drafting a request for reinforcements. *The Apache have committed countless recent atrocities against Mexico, and are on the warpath in this area.* He was describing the attack near Janos, when someone knocked on his door. "Come in."

John Cremony and Lieutenant Barrington entered his office in high excitement. "We've been speaking with Nana again, sir," said Cremony, "and he said Mangas Coloradas wants to meet with Mister Bartlett."

"About what?" asked Craig, a note of skepticism in his voice.

"He didn't say."

"You can't trust an Apache, Mister Cremony. No, I don't think so."

Nathanial cleared his throat. "Shouldn't you ask Mister Bartlett, sir?"

Colonel Craig's eyes became hooded. "You have a lot to learn about Indians, Lieutenant. Don't be so trusting."

The door opened, and Mister Bartlett appeared hat in hand. "Did I hear somebody mention my name?"

Silence came over the office, then Colonel Craig replied in the voice of a frog. "It appears that Mangas Coloradas wants to speak with you, and Lieutenant Barrington was reminding us that we could not guarantee your safety, sir."

"Do you think they'd try to kill me?" asked Bartlett. "But you'd be protecting me, wouldn't you? Yes, by all means I'll talk with Mangas Coloradas. He must be an interesting man, if he's leader of the Apaches."

"He's the best thief and murderer they've got," replied Colonel Craig.

At noon, Bartlett, Craig, Cremony, Nathanial, and six other officers gathered in front of Cremony's tent. All were heavily armed, tense, and primed for meeting Apaches.

Cremony briefed them for the upcoming meeting. "An Apache is taught from birth to view all other people as enemies," he explained. "And he learns soon thereafter that the best way to defeat enemies is to outsmart them. Thus the cleverest Apache is widely respected, and women are especially attracted to him, since he can provide food and their other needs."

Nathanial's eyes scanned the chaparral surrounding Cremony's tent. For all he knew, the tent would be cut off and everyone massacred before the soldiers in the presidio could respond. But what would the Apaches gain? he wondered.

Nana appeared in the foliage ahead, waving his empty right hand, a pistol in his belt and knife at his side. "Here they come," said Cremony.

"And they're armed to the teeth," replied Colonel Craig.

"So are we," replied Bartlett as he rose to his feet. He waved to Nana and hollered, "Hello, my Apache friends!"

Is he simply a well-intentioned fool? wondered Nathanial. The kind that gets people killed out of the goodness of his heart? More Apaches emerged from the wilderness, hesitant about proceeding. "They appear as afraid of us as we are of them," observed Nathanial.

"Nobody asked your opinion, Lieutenant Barrington," replied Colonel Craig.

Exasperated, John Bartlett turned to Colonel Craig. "Belligerence only produces more of the same. I must ask you to be conciliatory, Colonel Craig. Those Apaches have taken a great risk to come here."

"So have we," muttered the dour-faced colonel.

The Apaches turned toward a greasewood bush, and from behind it emerged an unusually tall Apache with waist-length black hair streaked with gray. Nathanial sucked wind because he recognized him instantly. My God—that's the Indian who almost killed me!

"It's Mangas Coloradas himself," said Cremony softly. "The Apaches consider him the greatest chief who ever lived."

The big Apache peered into every shadow, to make sure no cannons aimed at him. Never again would he trust enemies at the Santa Rita copper mines. He walked with great dignity, stomach sucked in, head erect, and on either side of him were his foremost sub-chiefs: Ponce, Delgadito, Colleto Amarillo, and Cuchillo Negro, in addition to other leading warriors. The great chief tried to feel the emanations of the bluecoat soldiers, but they appeared apprehensive as he. It was almost funny. Then his sharp eyes fell on a tall, strongly built soldier with sunny hair, and he nearly lost his smooth gait. It was the bluecoat soldier he'd fought in the Manzana Mountains! But Mangas Coloradas knew how to hide true feelings. As he approached the front of the tent, one of the White Eyes stepped forward and said something in his language.

Standing nearby, a pious expression on his face, John Cremony provided translation. "My name is Bartlett, and I am happy to meet you."

Happy to meet me? wondered Mangas Coloradas. What does that mean? He towered over Bartlett as he gripped his hand. "We come in peace to speak with the White Father."

"Sit, and let us be friends."

The crate was opened, and gifts of canned food, clothing, and trinkets were distributed by the soldiers.

"No whiskey?" asked Mangas Coloradas.

"I do not believe in whiskey," replied Bartlett.

Mangas Coloradas felt two eyes burning into the

side of his face. He turned toward the bluecoat soldier with sunny hair. Meanwhile, Bartlett proceeded to introduce the Americans, but the names made no sense to Mangas Coloradas. Then the chief introduced his warriors to the Americans.

A mound of tobacco on a square of canvas was placed between Mangas Coloradas and Bartlett. Everyone filled his pipe or rolled a cigarette, but each observed the hands of potential enemies. After they puffed together awhile, Mangas Coloradas opened the dialogue. "We have observed since you have first come here. What do you want?"

Bartlett replied: "We and the Mexicans are measuring the land for the new border that will separate our nations. We should be gone before the first snow." The Boundary Commissioner smiled cordially, secure in the belief that all men were reasonable. "It is not our intention to take anything from you."

It was silent for a few moments, as Mangas Coloradas pondered that statement. Then he spoke again. "If you do not intend to stay, why have you rebuilt the houses?"

"To be comfortable while we are here. Why do you not believe me? I am telling the truth."

The great chief Mangas Coloradas looked him in the eye. "If you are telling the truth, there will be no trouble here."

Bartlett realized that a silent but important verbal agreement had been reached. In the gush of goodwill, he told the chief: "You are welcome to visit our camp any time."

Mangas Coloradas reflected again, then replied: "I extend the same courtesy to you. And we shall move our camp closer to you, so you can see how we live. There is much hatred between the Apache and Mexicans, but we respect the Americans. Once, not long ago, I met the great White Father Kearny when he passed through this land. There was peace between us, and so it shall always be."

With great solemnity they strolled back to the chaparral, followed by warriors bearing gifts. Mangas Coloradas was so tall, his head so large, and his hair so long, he appeared a prehistoric creature, rather than a modern man.

After he was gone, Colonel Craig turned to Bartlett. "I didn't want to interrupt while you were holding so-called negotiations with that savage son-of-a-bitch, but you're really not going to let them wander through our camp, are you?"

"I meant what I said," replied Bartlett.

"You're going to get us killed—do you know that?"

"I'm not saying throw down your arms, Colonel Craig, but we must at least attempt to make peace with these people, and we can't have peace unless we trust each other. I'm taking a small step in that direction, and I must ask you to make it with me."

Colonel Craig looked at him as though he were insane. "This is what happens when they let civilians run military expeditions."

"Permit me to remind you that this is *not* a military expedition. It is a scientific expedition. We're not here to wage war against the Apaches."

"But it's all right for them to wage war against us. I wouldn't be surprised if Mangas Coloradas had attacked that wagon train near Janos."

"I am here by order of the president," declared John R. Bartlett, "and if we don't make peace with these people, they'll never let us do our work. I order you to behave in a friendly manner with them, or I'll notify President Fillmore of your obstruction."

*   *   *

In a soft yet deliberate voice, the great chief Mangas Coloradas explained negotiations. "They have invited us to visit their camp," he said. "And we shall try to be friends with them. It is what I have always desired."

Juh of the Nednais shook his head sadly. "I do not believe in desiring anything. We have used war successfully against Mexicans and must not hesitate with White Eyes. Only war can halt incursions."

"But," Mangas Coloradas reminded him, "do not forget the White Eyes are not Mexicans. They defeated the Mexicans in their big war."

"The White Eyes have been in the homeland too long!" declared Cuchillo Negro, one of the most famous of all sub-chiefs.

"They have guns that shoot five times without reloading," replied Mangas Coloradas. "Yes, we can wipe them out, but many of us will die and women will weep in their wickiups. They say they are leaving before the first snow, and that is not long. We must be patient, my brothers and sisters. You are all very courageous, but why fight for no good purpose?"

That night, the former concubine Blossom shivered in the arms of the great chief Mangas Coloradas. Captured three years ago, at the age of twenty one, she was his latest and favorite wife. They lay on the skins in her wickiup; it was the middle of the night, and fires blazed brightly in her eyes. "I am afraid," she whispered into his ear. "I do not want to live near the White Eyes."

He caressed her tenderly. "It is only for a short time."

"Something terrible is going to happen—I feel it in my bones."

He pinched her buttocks playfully. "You're being silly."

"I am afraid someone will recognize me."

He kissed the nipple of his naked wife, born a *Nakai-yes*. "No one will recognize you, and I will never let anyone take you away."

SEVEN

The Apaches moved their encampment within two miles of the Santa Rita copper mines, and both civilizations gazed at each other across the measureless gulf that separated them. Then warriors began drifting into the American camp, where cautious but friendly relations ensued. In days to come, Apache women and children were seen about the presidio, while Bartlett, Cremony, and the officers visited the Apache camp. All was smiles and gifts, and it appeared paradise had descended upon the Santa Rita copper mines.

As Bartlett strolled among the wickiups one sunny afternoon, he reminded himself that his judgments had been correct, and the Apaches were decent people after all, just like Americans. You have to know how to treat them, he mulled. Kindness and understanding are the keys to peace.

Mangas Coloradas was delighted by the suit of new clothes given him by Bartlett. What an intelligent people they must be, to know how to make such things, he decided.

Raising his eyes from burnished brass buttons, he saw Sunny Hair riding toward him. Mangas Coloradas drew himself to his full height, as the bluecoat war chief stopped twenty paces away, climbed down from the saddle, and walked toward the renowned chief of the Mimbrenos.

Sunny Hair took off his hat and smiled. "We have met before." Then he opened his saddlebags and took out a bag of tobacco. "For you."

Without hesitation, the chief drew his knife from its sheathe, and for a moment Nathanial thought Mangas Coloradas would finish the job he'd begun previously, but instead the chief turned the handle toward Nathanial. "For you."

Nathanial bowed as he accepted it.

Mangas Coloradas looked into Nathanial's eyes. "I have never forgotten you, Sunny Hair."

"I haven't forgotten you either, great Chief."

They scrutinized each other as though they were freaks, and neither knew what to say. "We will speak at another time," said Mangas Coloradas.

Dismissed, Nathanial performed an about-face, walked toward his horse, placed his foot into the stirrups, vaulted into the saddle, and wheeled the animal toward the copper mines.

The Apache town was the strangest place he'd ever seen. It wasn't just the strange beetlelike wickiups or half-naked children, the mangy dogs and old people with leathery skin, but something bizarre was in the air, alien to everything he believed. He recalled the expression in the chief's eyes, and wondered how he could communicate on the most basic level with such a creature.

Savero stood at the side of the wickiup, watching American officers rambling through the encampment. He wondered whether they'd rescue him if he threw himself at their feet and blurted his story. But what if they refused to take me back, because they didn't want to anger the Apaches? Trembling with indecision, he feared beatings from Taza. What do Americans care about dirty Mexican children?

"What are you doing here, you little scamp?" said a voice behind him. The hated Taza stood there, hands on his hips, eyes narrowed with anger.

"I was taking a walk," lied Savero.

"If you try to escape, I will cut your dirty little *Nakai-yes* throat. Now get moving to your wickiup, and wait until I call you."

Taza booted Savero in the rear, lifting him six inches off the ground. The boy lost his balance, but managed to right himself at the last moment. He ran back to the wickiup, afraid Taza would murder him for sheer pleasure.

Fifty miles to the south, in the Mexican province of Sonora, Jocita lay motionless beneath dirt and twigs on the side of a trail. Her head covered with a clod of dirt and grama grass, she breathed through a reed. This was the most dangerous time, because the People could receive fire at close range.

She heard the *conducta* draw closer, but only Juh, leader of the raid, was permitted to observe them, though he too was well-hidden, unmovable as a stone, part of thick, tangled desert vines. The wagon wheels creaked, the jangle of harnesses could be heard, and not even the mules appeared aware that the people were on a raid.

And then came the distant call of an eagle, but it was only Juh giving the signal. Jocita burst out of the ground, drew back the arrow, and let fly. The Mexican soldier in front of her received an arrow in the middle of his chest. He slumped, as Jocita swiftly strung a new projectile. She fired at another soldier, caught him

in the stomach, restrung again, but it appeared that
the soldiers had been incapacitated by the People,
while *Nakai-yes* women shrieked hysterically in the
carriage.

Jocita advanced with knife in hand, to help dispatch
wounded Mexican soldiers. The warriors swarmed
over the bodies, slashing and mutilating, while the carriage driver lay sprawled on his seat, one arrow
through his ribs, another sticking out his thigh.

Four warriors gathered horses and mules, while the
rest advanced cautiously toward the carriage. Jocita
aimed her bow at the window, when suddenly a Mexican woman appeared, aiming a double-barreled shotgun. It fired, and the warrior named Pinotay was
struck by hundreds of tiny pellets, as Jocita let fly her
arrow. It caught the White Eyes woman in the face,
throwing her backward into the carriage.

The warriors rushed the carriage, with Jocita leading
the way. She flung open the door, saw the dead
woman on the floor, while another pasty-faced female
creature quivered in the corner, trying to speak, eyes
glazed with madness. Without hesitation, Jocita
plunged her knife into the breast of the *Nakai-yes*
woman.

The Apaches loaded plunder onto a wagon, then
herded the animals together. Singing victory songs, they
rode away from the horseless carriage, around which lay
the stripped Mexicans like big white worms. You kill the
People, so we kill you back, thought the warrior woman,
as the Nednai band headed for the Mimbres Mountains.
Stay out of my land, *Nakai-yes* pigs.

A few nights later, Nathanial wandered through the
Apache encampment, the fragrance of roasted meat
lingering in the air. He found Mangas Coloradas gath-

ered with sub-chiefs and warriors around a fire, and waited at a respectful distance until the chief excused himself.

The tall large-headed chief noticed Nathanial, muttered something to his warriors, then strode toward the bluecoat war chief. "You wish to speak with me, Sunny Hair?"

"I have whiskey," replied Nathanial, tapping the flask in his back pocket. "Shall I give it to you here?"

Mangas Coloradas glanced at his warriors and subchiefs. "Let us walk together."

Nathanial followed him toward the edge of the encampment, and then they were on the open range, where nocturnal animals prowled for food, a three-quarter moon floating overhead. Nathanial had no idea what to say, and neither did the chief. They came to a gully surrounded by mesquite trees, sat opposite each other, and Nathanial pulled the flask from his pocket. "For you," he said, handing it to the chief.

The silver flask, purchased at A. T. Stewart's on Broadway and Chambers Street, and manufactured in Connecticut, came to rest in the hands of the Apache chief, who stared at it for a few moments. Then he unscrewed the cap, raised the flask to his lips, and threw back his head. Nathanial watched the chief's Adam's apple bob three times, then Mangas Coloradas came upright again and handed the flask back to Nathanial. "Drink."

They passed the bottle back and forth in silence as they sat in the darkness, alcohol sloshing through the corridors of their minds. Nathanial tried to think of pertinent or witty remarks, but everything seemed silly in the presence of Mangas Coloradas. I wonder what he'd think if he ever saw Broadway at curtain time, mused the native New Yorker.

The chief's features sagged, his great eyes were half closed, and the corners of his mouth turned down. "We can never be friends, White Eyes," he intoned.

Nathanial wanted to say *why not,* but knew it was so. Although both had two arms, legs, eyes, and everything else in roughly the same proportions, they were vastly different. "I don't suppose we can," he admitted.

"There will be much killing, and no one can stop it," Mangas Coloradas said thickly, then he leaned closer and grinned. "Perhaps one day we shall finish our fight."

"I hope not," replied Nathanial.

For the first time both laughed together. They took alternate swigs from the battle as the atmosphere relaxed. "Why have you come to this land, Sunny Hair?" asked Mangas Coloradas.

"I am a soldier," replied Nathanial. "My chief has sent me."

"The White Eyes have plenty of land. Why you need ours?"

"Many White Eyes have no land at all, and they want to raise cattle and horses."

"The price may be higher than they want pay."

"The People must learn to change."

"We have no reason to change." He pointed his finger at Nathanial's chest. "You are a land thief."

"I enforce my nation's laws. If you obey them, you will have no trouble from us."

"The only laws we obey are the laws of the Lifegiver. Why should we surrender our land to you?"

"How can we tolerate murder and theft?"

"We are at war with the Mexicans, and it is none of your business."

"Unless we overcome our differences, there will be bloodshed."

"You are the one who said it," replied Mangas Coloradas.

A chill crept up Nathanial's spine. The chief and lieutenant arose and looked into each other's eyes. They saw massacres, skirmishes, and ambushes, for they shared no common ground. In silence they walked side by side back to the Apache encampment, where Mangas Coloradas joined his friends around the fire, and Nathanial climbed onto his horse. The blue-coat soldier rode off, and all the People watched him go.

"What did he say?" asked Cuchillo Negro.

"Nothing," replied Mangas Coloradas.

Nathanial left his horse in the corral, then returned to his tent, removed his second bottle of whiskey from its position of repose in a spare boot, and sat in his rickety chair. He took a sip as he looked at the moon shining brightly above the mountains.

He felt as though he'd just returned from another planet. The Apaches were nomadic warriors, like Genghis Khan and his Golden Horde, only they were smaller in number, doomed to extinction, and Nathanial had seen it all in the great chief's eyes.

Mangas Coloradas is no fool, despite his lack of formal education, figured Nathanial. He knows what's coming, but he'll never back down. His manners are probably better than mine, and tonight we drank whiskey together, but someday he may kill me, or I may kill him. How odd.

Surrounded by thick chaparral, the Nednai raiders camped in a remote valley where the *Nakai-yes* and the *Pindah-lickoyee* never came. Their stolen livestock were hobbled in grama grass, as the warriors roasted slices of mule over a fire.

The valley was locked in a labyrinth of mountains, invisible to the outer world. The warriors felt safe, although they maintained two lookouts at all times. The wagon was full of plunder, but Pinotay's widow would scream and wail when she learned that her husband had been killed.

Jocita gnawed rare mule meat as she sat near the trunk of a cottonwood tree. Now at last her hunger was being satiated, for they'd fasted since the raid began. The nourishing food revived her, and she felt victorious over the *Nakai-yes*. She sat proudly, chin in the air, but eyes downcast like a good Apache wife.

It didn't escape her notice that she and the other warriors were sitting half-naked around the fire, and she was a lonely woman beneath her stern countenance. It had been four harvests since Juh had slept with her, and she felt certain nameless desires.

She'd seen cats and dogs in heat, but unfortunately wasn't a cat or dog. A woman of the People had to conquer inner drives, otherwise she would lose respect, not just for herself but also her family. She was first wife of Juh, and her behavior should be impeccable in the eyes of the Life-giver.

But she couldn't help wondering what it would be like to lie on her back and let them remove her breechclout. They would take turns, and even after they were all exhausted, it wouldn't be enough for her great need. She was entitled to Juh, but wanted him completely or not at all. An honorable warrior woman of the People, she refused to compromise her principles.

*   *   *

In another cranny of that vast wilderness, four miners cooked venison over an open fire, its flames throwing shadows on their wagon, as their horses grazed amid clumps of grama grass.

They'd selected a campsite near a stream, after riding through the Apache homeland all day, fingers on triggers at all times. They'd first visited the territory in '49, on their way to the gold fields of California, but hadn't prospered up Sacramento way because the best areas had been staked by the time they'd arrived. Then they heard rumors of gold in New Mexico, and were on their way back. This time they hoped to get in on the ground floor of a new mining region.

They glanced about suspiciously, hands near their guns, as they wolfed bacon and beans. Bearded, dirty, desperate, they'd followed dreams of vast wealth into a barren, hostile land.

"What's 'at?" asked Jed Riley, reaching for his rifle.

Bobby Finch twitched his little pug nose. "Horses."

"Put out the fire!" said Mike Stoddard, who wore a Mexican serape.

They kicked dirt into the pit, when someone called out "Halloooo there."

The miners looked at one another fearfully. "Who's there?"

"The Army!"

The miners breathed a sigh of relief. "We're over hyar."

Horses clopped closer as the miners stood with rifles in their hands, peering at two soldiers riding toward them out of the night. "Howdy," said one of them, who looked like a weasel, touching his forefinger to the brim of his campaign hat. "We're on a scout, and wondered if we could jine you."

"Hell yes," said Stoddard. "We're always glad to see the U.S. Dragoons."

The two soldiers climbed down from their saddles and looked around warily. "Whatcha doin' out hyar?" asked the second one, who looked like a duck.

"We're on our way to the Pinos Altos Mountains."

"Ain't nothin, thar 'cept Apaches."

"Mebbe so. Can we offer you some bacon and beans?"

Extra plates were produced, and the soldiers helped themselves. "If I was a miner," said the weasel, "I'd get my ass to California."

"California's played out," replied Stoddard. "That's whar we're comin' from." He winked. "When you git out'n the Army, you might want to stay right whar you are. Thar's old Injun legends about canyons full of gold nuggets in this territory."

The soldiers looked at each other. "I din't know that."

"I guess it won't be secret fer long if'n I keeps shootin' my mouth off, eh?" The miner laughed nervously. "What's it like in the Army?"

"Like anythin' else, I guess," said the weasel as he tossed a significant glance at his partner. "What's that over thar?" he asked, chinning behind the miners.

The three hapless gold diggers turned around. "Whar?"

The soldiers yanked their Army guns and opened fire at point-blank range. Roars of gunfire shattered the night, smoke rose into the air, and two miners fell, shot in their backs. The third turned around abruptly, eyes widened with desperation, as two bullets rammed his chest. He was dead before he hit the ground.

EIGHT

Word traveled throughout the territory about the Boundary Commission at the Santa Rita copper mines, and it wasn't long before traders with heavily laden wagons were headed in that direction. Soon a settlement grew alongside the presidio, and the soldiers could spend their pay on something other than poker games.

Colonel Craig frowned as he looked through his office window at Apaches buying whiskey from traders. He wanted to send the entrepreneurs away, but they were citizens, voters, and free to conduct business wherever they chose. Politicians would throw him out of the Army if he interfered with citizens in the pursuit of wealth.

But Indians often went berserk under the influence of alcoholic beverages, and even the most dignified chiefs became blithering fools. The line between savagery and civilization was fragile in the Indian mind, according to Colonel Craig.

He'd say the same about approximately one-quarter of his soldiers, and the colonel knew a volatile mixture was brewing in the Santa Rita Mountains. One of these days I'll have a crisis on my hands, he speculated. It'll start real small, and then it'll get real big.

* * *

The stolen mules, horses, and wagon filled with booty were nearing the Santa Rita Mountains, when Juh noticed one of his scouts riding toward him at great haste. "Bluecoat soldiers ahead!" the scout shouted. "About forty, and they might've seen us!"

Everyone looked to Juh for his decision. If he ran, he'd lose the booty, but if he stayed, the White Eyes might make trouble. He wanted to ask his wife's point of view, but not in front of the warriors. "We have bought these things in Mexico," he asserted, "and we are at peace with the White Eyes. But . . ."—he looked at each of them significantly—"if the bluecoat soldiers try to stop us, be prepared to fight."

Nathanial rode at the head of the column, the 1st Dragoon guidon on one side, and his bugler on the other. Behind him came about twenty more soldiers, then the wagons of the Boundary Commission, and finally his last twenty men. They were headed to the site of the Commission's next measurements, when Nathanial noticed his scout, Pennington, riding toward him. It looked like danger, so he held up his hand. "Detachment—halt!"

The clank and jangle of equipment could be heard as the detachment stopped in the middle of the trail. Nathanial pulled the cork on his canteen, took a swig of tepid metallic flavored water, and noticed John Bartlett striding toward him. "What're we waiting for, Lieutenant?"

"Don't know yet," replied Nathanial.

The West Pointer took off his hat and wiped his forehead with the back of his arm. Pennington galloped closer, then pulled back his reins. His horse danced excitedly, as he called out: "Apaches ahead, sir. About ten with horses, mules, and a wagon. Looks like they're comin' back from a raid."

Article Eleven of the Treaty of Guadalupe Hidalgo between Mexico and the U.S. ordained that the American Army must stop Apache raiding into Mexico, but the safety of the Boundary commission was Nathanial's prime concern. "Sergeant Duffy?"

"Sir!" The sergeant prodded his horse, who advanced to Nathanial's side.

"Tell the men to get ready for action, but they are not to fire unless I give the command."

Sergeant Duffy shouted back the orders, and all the men readied their weapons. Nathanial debated whether to form them into a skirmish line, but that would leave the Boundary Commission more vulnerable.

"Perhaps," said Bartlett, "you'd better let me handle negotiations with the Indians, Nathanial."

"The responsibility for your safety is mine, and I'm afraid I'll have to ask you to return to your wagon, sir."

"I hope you don't offend them."

"They're returning with stolen property, so the offense is theirs. Keep your head down, sir."

"But—"

"Mister Bartlett, if you don't return to your wagon *at once*, I'll be forced to place you under arrest."

Nathanial pulled his brass spyglass out of his saddlebags. Scanning ahead, he picked out Apaches coming into sight through the summer haze. They looked peaceful, but where did they get that wagon? Nathanial had heard Mangas Coloradas himself say that Apaches reserved the right to raid into Mexico, although it violated American laws. And I am the law out here, Nathanial told himself.

"The men are ready, sir," said Sergeant Duffy.

"Move them out," replied the detachment commander.

Juh had grown up believing violent death was normal, and hated fear most of all. "Let me do the talking," he told his warriors. "But if they reach for weapons . . ."

None of the warriors wanted to abandon plunder, otherwise poor Pinotay would have died in vain. Besides, why run from inferior beings? They drew closer to the bluecoat soldiers, and the officer raised his hand. "What have you got there?"

Juh felt rage, for how dare anyone ask a warrior of the People what he was doing in his own ancestral homeland? "Things we have bought in Mexico," he replied pleasantly.

The officer rode closer, and Juh realized how easy it was to kill him. The officer looked into the wagon at guns, ammunition, clothes, an axe, and some harnesses. "Are you sure you didn't steal them?" inquired the officer.

Juh refused to dignify the question with a reply, while Nathanial had no tangible proof. He looked at Juh closely, and he appeared familiar. "I believe we've met at a certain jailhouse in Arispe," he said.

"It is possible."

"What is your name?"

"I am called Juh."

Nathanial studied him carefully, embedding the face in his mind. Then he examined the other warriors. He was startled by an Apache woman in a buckskin shirt, her exposed legs and arms as bare and sinewy as the men's. Nathanial examined her pistol, knife, rifle, and bow and arrow. He didn't know what to make of her.

"You are blocking the road," said Juh.

Nathanial was mesmerized by the strangest being he'd ever seen. If Phineas T. Barnum could get his hands on her, reflected Nathanial, he'd have a bigger attraction than Jenny Lind. "If I receive word that these goods were stolen in Mexico, I'm coming after you," he replied. "I am Lieutenant Nathanial Barrington, First Dragoons. You'd better watch out for me, Injun."

Juh smiled thinly, but Nathanial's mission was not to start a war with the Apaches. "We will make way for you," said the West Pointer. "And I look forward to our next meeting."

"So do I, White Eyes, but *we* will move out of *your* way, since you have many wagons, and we only have one. We want to live in peace with the White Eyes." Juh threw his version of an Army salute, and his warriors burst into laughter.

Nathaniel's ears grew warm. "I will never forget you, Juh."

"Nor I—you." Juh wheeled his horse, and the animal turned off the road. Warriors guided the wagon to the side, and Nathanial motioned for the Commission to continue its journey. Then he looked once more at the warrior maiden bouncing up and down in her saddle, her back perfectly straight, and Nathanial found himself wishing he were her horse.

Sergeant Duffy, Scout Pennington, and the detachment drew closer, followed by the Boundary Commission. Pennington frowned at the Indians and their wagon at the side of the road. "They're Nednais, worst Apaches of 'em all."

The Nednais had combative light in their eyes, provoking Nathanial's fighting instincts. Taking his place at the head of the column, he adjusted his hat, then

turned casually to the side, for a last look at the warrior woman tall in her saddle, surrounded by half-
naked men, her face expressionless as the White Eyes
passed. That's the most interesting person I've ever
seen, he told himself. "Pennington?"

"Sir!" The scout rode alongside Nathanial, rolling a
cigarette as he rocked in the saddle.

"Who the hell was that woman supposed to be?"

"A woman warrior, and they'll kill you as quick as
any man."

"I didn't know the Apaches had women warriors."

"Every once in a while you'll run into one."

"Take the point, Mister Pennington."

Pennington rode forward, a man who practiced
every known vice, yet appeared in superb health. Nathanial turned backward, but the Apaches were obscured by clouds of dust. He speculated on the
possibilities of wrestling a wild warrior woman, but
then remembered he had a wife and son in Santa Fe.
I've been on escort duty so long, I'm going loco, he
told himself. If I don't see my family pretty damn
soon, there's no telling what I might do.

"It is not difficult to fool the White Eyes," Juh explained as he and his warriors headed toward the
Santa Rita Mountains. "They always back down—that
is their nature, even though they outnumbered us.
They knew we were on a raid, but have no courage."

The warriors listened silently, and among them rode
Jocita deep in thought. She knew that Juh was bolster-
ing morale, but she'd studied the bluecoat officer's
eyes, and seen a man under strict self-control, like a
warrior of the People.

Jocita was impressed by the officer, perhaps because
he was about the same height as the great Mangas

Coloradas, with big shoulders, a narrow waist, and long legs, but his most arresting features were his golden beard and sky blue eyes. I have been without a man so long, even the White Eyes are starting to attract me, she said to herself, smiling ruefully.

Nathanial sat hatless in the shade of a mesquite tree, sipping from his canteen. His men guarded surveyors shooting azimuths at mountain peaks, while botanists studied exotic new plants, naturalists searched for exotic wildlife, and Bartlett sketched the scenery for his friends in New York.

The West Point officer had studied the tactics of the Napoleonic wars, but they provided no guide for defending the Boundary Commission. An attack on a stray scientist could come at any time. He remembered the cruel eyes of Juh and realized the Army faced a wily and implacable enemy in the Nednai Apaches.

The government will never send enough soldiers, he analyzed, and the Apaches will never surrender, but what does it have to do with me? A man can always find a peaceful corner of the world, and that's what I'm going to do when I get out of the Army.

He scanned massive peaks and crags, while a rock formation in the distance looked like a man standing on his head, and distant perspectives enlarged the boundaries of his imagination. I love this land, he thought, but what in the hell are we going to do about the Apaches?

Not far away, on a high slope sheltered by pinyon trees, Delgadito lay on his stomach and peered at the activity below. The White Eyes aimed shiny reeds at each other, waved arms, wrote in books, and scurried about like squirrels, as others dug up plants and sniffed roots. It was the strangest spectacle of Delgadito's life, and he didn't know what to make of it.

What are they doing? Delgadito asked himself, as he scratched his head. And why?

Juh and his warriors arrived at the encampment of Mangas Coloradas in the early hours of the morning, when no White Eyes were about. The warriors hobbled their mules and horses, carried their booty to their wickiups, and scheduled no Property Dance, for they didn't want the White Eyes to know what they'd done.

Juh wanted the latest news from Mangas Coloradas, but the wickiup of the great chief was dark. Nearly all the People were asleep, but a light burned in the wickiup of Lucero. Juh poked his head inside and saw Lucero amid a group of other warriors, passing a bottle of whiskey around.

"Come in, Juh," said Lucero drunkenly, handing the bottle to the newcomer.

Juh accepted it. "I have mules, horses, guns, and cloth for the women," he said proudly. "A bluecoat officer tried to stop us, but I told him to go to hell." Juh laughed, threw back his head, and swallowed the firewater down. Its power struck him at once, his head skyrocketed through the tent, and for a few heartbeats, he saw himself vaulting across the sky.

"Is everyone well?" asked Lucero.

The rocket sputtered and fell to earth. "I have lost Pinotay."

There was murmuring and grumbling among relatives of Pinotay, and Juh felt guilty. "He led the last charge and died like a hero of the People," said the sub-chief. "In his memory I shall give my share to his family."

In Santa Fe it was two o'clock in the morning. Diego Carbajal sat at his candlelit desk, studying the legend of the *Lamed Vav*. One of the oldest folk beliefs of the kabalists, it claimed that thirty-six righteous men upheld the world, and the strangest part was sometimes they didn't even know who they were!

Diego had been fasting for a week, praying, studying, and entering deep states of meditation. Sometimes he heard cherubs singing above him, and once had dreamed of the prophet Ezekiel seated in his *merkabah* chariot, leading the faithful into heaven.

Diego's eyes were half-closed as he reached for another glass of water. Hunger had left him long ago, replaced by lightness in his stomach and mind. His hands shook before his bleary eyes as he turned the next page.

What a responsibility it must be, to uphold the world, he conjectured. One measly mistake could bring suffering to millions, and that is why a righteous man must be flawless in his behavior, for the fate of humanity rests upon him.

Then, out of nowhere, a simple thought nearly knocked him off his chair. What if *I'm* one of the Thirty-six? he asked himself. His sins, selfishness, vanity, and dilettantism flashed before his eyes, and he realized that perhaps *he* was the cause of the world's ills. If a righteous man shirked his duty, the consequences could be devastating. Then something bright and golden burst in his mind. He pulled his huge wide-brimmed sombrero over his small head, threw a shawl over his shoulders, and stumbled outside, teeth chattering with excitement.

He stumbled to the edge of Santa Fe, where he hallucinated demons giggling behind palo verde trees and clusters of yucca. He expected an Apache to loom out of the night and chop his head off, but he crashed onward madly, the spines of prickly pear cactus tearing his pants.

"I am one of the Thirty-six," he gurgled, as he rambled toward the glowing in the distance. "Speak to me, Lord of Hosts!" he cried, as his boot was trapped in a prairie dog hole, and he fell onto his face.

He was unable to raise himself, but it appeared the fire was drawing closer, reaching toward him with long, fiery fingers! Diego wanted to run away, but was paralyzed by terror. The burning bush closed around him, setting fire to his mustache, filling his nose with smoke.

He opened his eyes as flames arose from his desk. He realized that he'd knocked over the candle in his religious ecstasy, his house was burning down, his life in danger. "Fire!" he screamed, as he reached for his sombrero, but it was already atop his head. He fled down the stairs, hollering and shouting the alarm. What does this mean? he wondered, as he burst out the front door.

The bucket brigade turned the corner, for the alarm had been given by neighbors. Diego looked backward at his burning office, with all his sacred tomes going up in smoke, not to mention precious religious articles. Am I a foolish old man who set his house on fire, or is this a message from His Holy Name? he wondered. He gazed at his torn pants, shoes caked with muck, thorns, and bits of foliage on his pants and shirt. No, it can't be, he said to himself. They found him on his knees in the middle of the street, hands clasped in prayer, muttering an unintelligible language.

NINE

Nathanial returned to the copper mines, took the hot bath he'd been dreaming about, then shaved, put on a clean uniform, and made his way to the officers' mess.

The menu was the usual beef, biscuits, and beans, washed down with tepid water. Colonel Craig sat at the head of the table, Major Stewart at the other end, with Southerners and Northerners segregated on either side. Nathanial wasn't sure where he belonged on the great issues dividing the nation, so found a space by himself.

Colonel Craig announced: "In case you haven't heard, Lieutenant Barrington ran into Apaches on his way back from the survey. Wisely, he didn't provoke them. Once the Boundary Commission leaves, I hope the Army does something about these damned Apache raiders."

Nathanial recalled the words of Juh, as he said, "The Apaches think we favor the Mexicans over them."

Major Stewart replied, "That's because the Mexicans don't slit our throats when we're not looking. There are no good reasons for Apache marauding."

Nathanial didn't want to argue with higher ranking officers, so silently sliced his beef.

It was silent except for silverware scraping tin

plates, then Lieutenant Jack Whipple said in his Alabama drawl, "Just because Apaches stake people to anthills and pour honey over their faces, they can't help themselves, isn't that correct, Lieutenant Barrington? It's the same argument *some people* use about Nigras. Their brains don't work as well as ours, but they should have the same rights we do. One white man can do the work of five Nigras, and that's ultimately what'll bring about the end of slavery, not the whining of moral cowards like Lieutenant Barrington."

The table fell silent as all eyes turned to Nathanial. Here we go again, he thought wearily. He despised political arguments and considered emotional tirades far beneath the high standards he had set for himself, but seldom reached. "The Spaniards and Mexicans have been committing atrocities against the Apaches for hundreds of years," he explained patiently, "and the Apaches fought back much as you, Lieutenant Whipple, feel the need to fight me. In my opinion, Army officers shouldn't become embroiled in the sectarian strife sweeping our land."

Colonel Craig clapped politely. "Well said, Lieutenant Barrington."

Lieutenant Whipple, a big red-headed freckle-faced farmer's son about Nathaniel's age, had risen through the ranks instead of going to the Point. "Let me ask you a straight-out question, Lieutenant Barrington. Are you opposed to slavery in the new territories?"

"I'm opposed to slavery everywhere," replied Nathanial. "I wish I could go to a land where they had no slavery whatever, but they'd only be arguing about some other burning issue. I find politics the last resort of people who can't converse on any subject that could be of interest to an intelligent mind."

"A subject such as what?" skeptically asked Lieutenant Whipple, whose father owned three slaves.

"Women," replied Nathanial.

The table burst into laughter, for the mere mention of the fair sex improved the tempers of the officers' mess.

"I sure wish I could bring my wife here," said Major Stewart.

The other officers murmured in agreement. "Why is it?" asked Colonel Craig, "that without women, men sink into a state or disorder where they can't even share a peaceful meal together?"

Only two miles away, Jocita stood naked in her wickiup, holding up a White Eyes cotton dress covered with multicolored stripes. She thought it the most beautiful and colorful garment she'd ever seen and marveled at the needlework that had made it.

She slipped it over her head, and the lower hem dropped to her ankles. Then she held out the mirror and looked at herself. Somehow the dress seemed to enhance her appearance, but she couldn't fasten the buttons behind her back. Why did they make it this way? she wondered. But it wasn't necessary to fasten them because her shoulders and breasts held the dress in place.

She raised her leg, but the wide hem didn't bind her. She could work or run in the dress, but it wouldn't last like buckskin. She lowered her head and passed out of the wickiup. It was after the last meal of the day, and families sat around their campfires, while she was alone with her new dress.

She kneeled beside her fire. I am a renowned warrior woman, but what good does it do me? she wondered. And why do I always expect more?

She noticed the little slave boy José passing her fire and offered him a bowl of pinyon nuts. "Take and eat," she said.

"What a beautiful dress," he replied, innocently touching it. "You look like a *Nakai-yes* woman."

Her eyes widened, she leapt to her feet, and an expression of indescribable hatred came over her face. She dashed into her wickiup, tore off the dress, and put on her traditional deerskin blouse and breechclout. Yanking her knife, she cut off a strip of material, then brought it to José. "For a headband," she said. "I'll shall make it for you."

She folded the material into a bandanna and tied it around the boy's head. "You look like a young warrior."

The boy's eyes filled with tears, and all at once he dived onto Jocita, wrapping his little arms around her. She hugged his lithe little body against her and could feel the beating of his heart. "What is wrong?" she asked.

"I ... do not ... know," he said.

She realized that the boy needed a mother, just as she needed a child of her own. *Perhaps I should buy him from old Taza,* she thought. *I will take care of him, and he will give me reason to be happy.* "Would you like to live with me, José?"

"Oh yes, Jocita." He looked into her eyes hopefully. "Could that be done?"

"Come with me."

She took his hand, and together they walked to the wickiup of old Taza. The slave boy Savero was cleaning the metate in a bucket of water, as Taza sat and smoked a pipe near his fire. "Where have you been, you little mouse?" he asked José. "You must fetch water."

"He was with me," said Jocita.

"That does not excuse him," replied Taza. "He has work to do."

"I would like to buy him, Taza. How many horses would you take?"

Taza puffed his pipe. "You do not have enough horses, Jocita. I need these boys to help me now that I am old."

"But you are not old, Taza. You can still work."

"Every day it takes longer to climb into the saddle. Perhaps I eat too much, but I need my boys."

"What about two horses?"

Taza wrinkled his nose. "Why are you giving horses for a useless little urchin? What you need is a wife." Taza laughed at his little joke, but Jocita didn't join in.

"Three horses."

"A hundred horses cannot care for me when I am old. That is why I need slaves."

"You should have married and had children, Taza."

"Not all people have children, as you know. No, I am sorry, Jocita—I need my boys."

She peered into his eyes. "I will fight you for him."

"And if I win?"

"Everything I own."

It was a tempting prize, but Taza measured her rippling muscles and saw power in her eyes. "I could not fight a woman, not even a woman warrior like you, because I could not win either way. Even if I killed you, they'd say Taza has defeated a woman, and I would lose respect."

"What if I were to slap you, and keep slapping you until you fought back. Then what?"

"You are stealing my slave, and I will tell Mangas Coloradas. He will punish you."

"Everyone here is ashamed of your laziness, Taza.

You should rely upon your strong arm, instead of little boys. I am taking this one away, and I will give you three horses. If you do not like it, come and take him back if you dare. And if you harm one hair on his head, I shall feed you to the coyotes. Do you understand me, Taza?"

"How can I say no to the wife of Juh?" Taza smiled graciously as his heart filled with bitter scorn.

Nathanial passed a few days signing reports and requisitions that needed more signatures at other levels of command, until they'd all end at the War Department in Washington D.C., where somebody doubtlessly would toss them into a wastebasket.

When not working on administrative duties, he found time to take his dirty clothing to one of the laundress-prostitutes who'd set up shop among the traders. He made certain his detachment's horses were well cared for and frequently checked the guards.

The only entertainment was the Apache camp, so one afternoon he bought a few bottles of whiskey, put them into his saddlebags, and rode in that direction, hoping to see Mangas Coloradas again. As he drew closer, he noticed warriors sleeping in front of their wickiups, and the encampment had a slovenly appearance that had been absent before. Some of the women appeared drunk, while children ran about like puppies. Put together whiskey and Injuns, and this is what happens, concluded Nathanial.

Mangas Coloradas was nowhere to be seen, but an old woman sat in front of his wickiup. "Are you the wife of Mangas Coloradas?" asked Nathanial.

"One of them," admitted the woman.

"Where is he?"

"I do not know."

"Who is the medicine man in this camp?"

"There are many."

"Who's the best?"

"That is Nana."

She pointed, and Nathanial remembered meeting Nana at John Cremony's tent. The sophisticated New Yorker passed meat boiling in kettles, women rubbing a greasy substance into hides, and men seated in circles, having conversations. "You bring whiskey, bluecoat soldier?" asked one of them.

Nathanial turned a corner and noticed a figure that looked familiar, sitting cross-legged near a fire. Is it she? he wondered. My God.

It looked like the warrior woman he'd observed returning from the raid, bouncing up and down in her saddle. Curiosity overcame common sense yet again, as he steered toward her. She glanced at him sharply, panic came to her face, then she returned to the war lance she was crafting.

He kneeled before her and gazed into swirling magnetic eyes. "We met on the trail awhile back."

"I remember," she said coolly.

He had no idea what to say, and for her, he was a strange golden creature who'd stepped out of the sun. They examined each other's features, and Nathanial realized that every Apache in the vicinity was watching. He coughed nervously. "It is very nice to see you again." Rising to his feet, he reoriented himself, then continued to Nana's wickiup.

Nathanial felt stupefied as he made his way through the Apache encampment. Never had he felt such powerful physical attraction to another woman, *not even his wife* whom he loved dearly and missed desperately. He wanted to turn around and look at the warrior woman one last time, but didn't dare. He recalled her sitting cross-legged on the ground, that powerful yet feminine body, and her dark oriental features. He'd felt the irrational compulsion to take her hair in his hands and touch his lips lightly to hers.

He realized that his heart beat rapidly. I've been in this damned territory so long, I'm going loco, he said to himself as he spotted Nana in front of a wickiup, installing a hardwood tip on a carrizo reed arrow.

Nana appeared sleepy and unintelligent as Nathanial sat cross-legged in front of him. "I'd like to talk with you," he said in Spanish.

"Who sent you to me?"

"Mangas Coloradas's wife said you're the best medicine man here."

"I have the power of geese," replied Nana.

"And what is the power of geese?"

"The power of endurance in war."

Nana looked like anything but a warrior to Nathanial. "How did you come by this power?"

"It was taught me. Do you want the power of geese?"

"I'd like you to explain the Apache religion."

Nana shrugged. "We live according to what the mountains spirits have taught us. And they still watch over us, even now." Nana raised his right hand, and Nathanial glanced at peaks surrounding the valley. "If it were not for the mountain spirits, the People would have died long ago."

He's got rock solid faith, Nathanial realized, but I don't know what I believe anymore. The West Pointer felt unsettled by energies emanating from Nana. "I was taught the Christian religion, but I have committed many sins."

"Purify yourself," replied Nana.

"I can't."

"Then you shall surely die."

Nathanial had difficulty breathing and felt like a horse spooked by something unseen. The hairs raised on the back of his neck. "I've brought you a present," he said, withdrawing a bottle from his saddlebags. "Whiskey."

The Apache's eyes lit up greedily as he reached for the bottle. "Thank you, bluecoat soldier."

Nathanial wanted to ask who the warrior woman was, but this time common sense got the better of him. He arose, bowed awkwardly, and said in a halting tone. "Nice meeting you."

He knew how banal it sounded, but everything appeared turned onto its head in the Apache encampment. Three children stood beside the next wickiup, giggling at him, and a nearby spotted dog barked in disapproval.

Nana disappeared into his wickiup, and soon would be inebriated, Nathanial was certain. I mustn't invest these people with powers they don't have, he cautioned himself. They're killers, thieves, and their extinction is coming sooner than they realize.

Nathanial searched for the warrior woman, but she'd disappeared. He couldn't imagine what it was like to make love with such a creature. He'd wanted to sink his teeth into her throat and wrestle her to the ground. Something violent and brutal was evoked by the mere memory of that muscular but feminine body. He wondered whether she had children, and how many men she'd killed.

He climbed onto his horse and rode back to the copper mines. We'll never be able to reason with these people, he realized. The sheer numbers of America will crush them, and there's not a damned thing anybody can do about it.

* * *

Jocita walked in the chaparral, trying to settle herself down. The bluecoat soldier with sunny hair has placed a spell upon me, she thought. He is an evil sorcerer, otherwise I would not feel so bad.

She shivered, itched, was feverish. He'd appeared like a visitation from the mountain spirits. She recalled the width of his shoulders, the breadth of his chest, his muscled thighs, and the way he filled the seat of his pants. A wave of pure feminine lust made her dizzy.

She considered herself above commonplace considerations, but he was a big, fascinating male being, an she'd wanted to touch him. She broke into a sweat, and it felt as if worms crawled over her body. What is he doing to me? she wondered. I am a chaste woman of the People, and others look to me as the model of behavior. Why am I thinking like a silly maiden?

José peeked into the wickiup, but the warrior woman wasn't there. He wondered where she was as he lay atop the skins. He and his friends had been running up and down hills all day, part of warrior training. When hard-pressed by enemies, warriors left their horses and scrambled on foot into the mountains. This was one reason no one had ever conquered the People.

Jocita's smell was everywhere, like desert flowers in the sun. Her clothing lay neatly folded in a wicker basket near her pillow. Absentmindedly, he rummaged inside, holding garments to his nose. He wished she'd comfort him with hugs, when his fingers fell on one of the *Nakai-yes* dresses that she owned.

Hands trembling, he removed it from the basket. It was light blue, with small yellow designs imprinted onto the fabric. He held it to his nose, and it had the rich smell of another woman, the one from whom it had been stolen. José wondered if his mother had smelled that way, and then he noticed dark spots on the skirt. He brought his eyes closer, scraped his thumbnail against it, and it looked like dried blood.

José gagged, threw the dress into the basket, and ran like a shot out the tent. Eyes of warriors and wives turned as he sped into the wilderness surrounding the campsite. No one went after him, because children were always running about like unpredictable little animals.

José jumped over a paddle cactus and dodged around tall green shrubs. The sun beat down, birds looked at him curiously, and high in the sky, the buzzards circled patiently, waiting for supper. Finally, when far from the encampment, José dropped to his knees behind a raspberry bush, covered his face with his hands, and burst into tears.

The bloodied dress had evoked long-buried memories of his poor *Nakai-yes* mother. José's unprotected young mind flooded with his mother's cries for mercy, the death gurgles of his father, fire sweeping their town. Little José sat heavily on the ground and felt disgusted with his treachery. These people have killed my mother and father, then stole me away. How can I love them?

Nathanial sat in his tent, sipping from a bottle of whiskey. He kept the flap open, so he could see the approach of others. I'm one of those officers who drinks during duty hours, he realized. I've got to pull myself together.

Maria Dolores was far away, and he thought like a rogue once more. Never in his marriage had he lusted for another woman until now. Stirrings from obscure inner organs produced a distortion in his mind. He felt guilty although he'd never even touched the warrior woman, and didn't know her name.

I'm a husband and father, but I desire another woman, he told himself. I'll never see her again, because I will not, under any circumstances, go to that Apache camp anymore. And if I see her riding over here, I'll jump on the nearest horse and head for the hills. I think I'm safe, he thought with a smile, as he raised the bottle.

A shadow crossed the front of his tent. Quickly, the drunkard tucked the rotgut whiskey beneath his pillow. It was Sergeant Duffy. "Got a minute, sir?"

Nathanial sat erectly behind his desk. "What's wrong, Sergeant?"

Sergeant Duffy entered, saluted, and said. "I was jest a-wandering around the Apache camp, and I think I see'd yer old horse in their corral!"

Nathanial recalled Duke II's mysterious disappearance. "Are you sure?"

"I might be wrong, but I don't think so. You'd better have a look at 'im. I can round up the men, in case there's trouble."

"I don't want to go over there right now, Sergeant."

The sergeant appeared thunderstruck. "Yer gonter let 'im keep yer horse?"

The men would never understand, realized Nathanial. "You're right—let's you and I have a look at him. We don't need more men, because that might make everything worse. If it's my horse, I'll talk to Mister Bartlett about getting him back."

"If yer gonter rely on that silly son-of-a-bitch, sir, you better say good-bye to old Duke. From what they tell me, Bartlett wants to give up land that we won in the war against Mexico. He's the biggest goddamned fool I ever seen, outside of James S. Calhoun."

James S. Calhoun had a prominent nose, widow's peak, and wry lips. Superintendent of Indian Affairs for the New Mexico Territory, he sat in his office in Santa Fe, reading a complaint from the Mexican government regarding Apache raiding south of the border. Calhoun, forty-nine years old, suffering poor health, was appointed to his post though connections in the Whig party.

A fine point of law was becoming his Waterloo. According to the Treaty of Guadalupe Hidalgo, the U.S. Army should prevent Apaches from raiding into Mexico, otherwise indemnities had to be paid. The total had reached many millions of dollars, which the U.S. government had no intention of paying. Somehow, perhaps by magic, Calhoun had to remedy the difficulty.

Calhoun was a widower with grown daughters back in Georgia. Another battle-scarred veteran of the Mexican War, he'd risen to the rank of lieutenant colonel, but became a civilian again. Never had he felt so frustrated as in Santa Fe.

The Army couldn't stop the Apaches, and the new military commander of the 9th Department, Colonel William Vose "Bull Moose" Sumner, treated Calhoun like a minor annoyance. Calhoun thought Sumner should be subordinate to him, but Sumner disagreed, and the Army followed *his* orders.

Bull Moose Sumner wanted to subdue Apaches, whereas Calhoun worked for mutually rewarding peace. He'd met many influential Apaches who envisioned their way of life coming to an end, and were ready to become farmers and ranchers.

But other wilder Apaches wouldn't give up old pastimes, and Calhoun received regular reports of raids throughout Sonora, Chihuahua, and Coahuila. They'd even attacked American Army supply caravans in the New Mexico Territory.

Calhoun believed patience and fair treatment could conquer Apaches more effectively than bullets, but it would require sensitivity lacking in Colonel Bull Moose Sumner. The contradictions of Calhoun's assignment, plus the indifference of Washington, were eroding the superintendent's strength. He coughed into his handkerchief as he wrote yet another letter to Washington, D.C., begging for farm implements for Apaches, although none of his previous requests had been honored. *Unless somebody starts listening to me, New Mexico will have a bloodbath even worse than the Mexican War,* he predicted.

The Apache corral was built of sotol slats hammered into the ground and tied with strips of rawhide. Guarded by several warriors, they watched suspiciously the approach of two bluecoat soldiers.

"There he is, sir," said Sergeant Duffy, pointing into the corral.

Nathanial examined the horse, and it surely looked like Duke II. Meanwhile, Duke II was surprised to see his former commanding officer. Neighing, he pawed the ground, then walked toward Nathanial and lowered his head. Nathanial patted between his ears. "I'll be a son-of-a-bitch," he said in amazement.

"Goddamned Apaches stoled yer horse," said Sergeant Duffy. "Didn't I tell you?"

Three of the Apaches guards roved closer and didn't appear happy. "What you doing with that horse?" inquired the stalwart warrior known as Lucero.

Before Nathanial could open his mouth, Sergeant Duffy said, "It belongs to him."

Lucero looked at Nathanial. "You lie."

Again, before Nathanial could say anything, Sergeant Duffy opined, "He's tellin' the truth, 'cause I remember 'im meself."

"Then you lie too."

"Why you son-of-a—"

Nathanial placed his hand on Sergeant Duffy's shoulder. "I'll handle this."

Lucero believed he'd been insulted. "Why do we let White Eyes into our camp?" he asked his cohorts.

Apache warriors drifted toward the corral to investigate the angry noises. Women and children held back, the air thickening with hostility. Nathanial looked into Duke's eyes and wondered how he was being treated by the Apaches.

"Take your hand off that horse," said Lucero.

"Is he yours?" asked Nathanial.

"He is mine," said the voice of a woman.

The warrior woman advanced through the crowd, and Nathanial's knees nearly caved in. Other women wore buckskin skirts, but she had on a breechclout like the warriors, and was deeply tanned, with thin lips, almond eyes.

"Where did you get him?" asked Nathanial, a catch in his voice.

"I bought him in Mexico," she lied.

Odd sensations affected his lower extremities as she came to a halt three feet away. He could feel her body through the distance and clothes that separated them. He patted the horse on the side of the head. "This horse resembles one I used to own, but I guess I'm mistaken."

Sergeant Duffy was shocked. "But that's yer horse, sir!"

"He has similar coloring and certainly is a friendly fellow, but this isn't Duke." Nathanial smiled at the warrior woman. "No offense intended."

"But . . ." expostulated Sergeant Duffy.

Nathanial grabbed his sergeant by the scruff of the neck and escorted him to their horses. "What the hell is wrong with you?" asked Sergeant Duffy as they rode away from the Apache encampment. "That *was* yer horse, y'know."

"You nearly got us killed with your big Irish mouth, Sergeant Duffy."

"Give 'em an inch—they'll take a mile. That Apache woman weren't bad, eh sir? I wouldn't mind nailin' her on the bedspread some night."

"She'd probably break your back, Sergeant, for she looked quite strong."

"Have you ever thought about not drinkin' so much, sir? I think it's makin' yer brain go soft."

Savero chopped wood beside Taza's firepit. The boy was sweaty, dirty, and gaunt, for Taza had been working him hard. Then Savero heard a voice behind him.

"Can we talk?" asked José, eyes red from crying.

Savero lowered his axe. "About what?"

"I remembered my mother, and am ready to run away with you."

Savero made sure no one as listening. "I have been praying for this. You won't change your mind?"

"I would rather be dead than remain with the ones who killed her."

Savero smiled thinly. "Tonight, brother, we will make our run to freedom."

Jocita returned to her wickiup, closed the flap, and sat in light streaming from the smoke hole in the ceiling. What's this? she wondered.

Sorcery or fate had brought her to Sunny Hair again, but how could she fault his behavior, for the horse obviously was his, yet he gave it to her. What should I do?

She was falling in love with a bluecoat soldier whom she didn't even know. Worse, it appeared that he was attracted to her too. She'd always believed one day a great warrior would come to claim her, but didn't realize he'd be a bluecoat soldier. Never had she felt such desire, not even with Juh. Perhaps his light skin and golden hair have captivated me. She considered flirting, then shook her head emphatically. Only dishonor could follow such an act, and Juh would cut off my nose.

According to the holy life-way, a warrior had the right to cut off his unfaithful wife's nose.

At the officer's mess, Nathanial received disparaging glances from the Southern offices when he seated himself on their side of the table. The menu was beans, tortillas, and a spicy beef stew.

"I hope you gentlemen enjoy the meal," declared Colonel Craig. "I've hired a Mexican cook, and hope he doesn't poison us."

"Perhaps," said Lieutenant Whipple, "you should make him taste everything in our presence."

Nathanial replied, "Who'd want to poison you? You're funnier alive."

Lieutenant Whipple believed Nathanial had insulted

him, but wasn't sure how. "Aren't you married to a Mexican, Barrington?"

Nathanial filled his plate with large helpings of everything and proceeded to consume the meal. "That's right."

"They say the Mexicans use spices to hide the taste of rotten meat."

"Seems fine to me," replied Nathanial, chewing away.

"Why'd you marry a Mexican?" asked Lieutenant Whipple. "Aren't Americans good enough for you?"

Nathanial looked toward Colonel Craig for help, but that valiant gentleman preferred to study his officers at play. Nathanial decided to ignore Lieutenant Whipple.

"Does anybody have any idea how much longer we'll be here?" asked Second Lieutenant Howard Dix, the most junior officer present, recent West Point graduate from Maine. "Is the Boundary Commission on schedule?"

Colonel Craig harumphed. "I never saw such a bunch of blundering idiots in my life. All they do is argue about lines on a map, and they're so far over budget, Washington might fire our friend Bartlett at any moment."

Lieutenant Harper said, "I saw you at the Apache camp today, Barrington. Who was that old man you gave a bottle of whiskey to?"

"Their foremost medicine man. His name is Nana."

Colonel Craig cleared his throat. "It's not a good idea to give whiskey to Indians, Barrington."

Lieutenant Whipple chortled. "He has to give it to somebody, sir, because if he drinks any more himself, he'll fall flat on his ass."

"You'd better hope I don't fall flat on you," replied Nathanial.

"I'd drop you in the muck where you belong, Lieutenant Barrington. I can respect a man like Lieutenant Medlowe, who makes no bones about his politics, but you won't take a stand on anything."

"One of these days, somebody's liable to stand on your nose, Lieutenant Whipple."

"Is that a threat, Lieutenant Barrington?"

"If you like."

Lieutenant Whipple turned to Colonel Craig. "Did you hear that, sir?"

"I repeat—I believe in the free exchange of ideas at my mess," replied the commandant.

Nathanial felt his temper coming on like the Hudson River in springtime, but he didn't want to kill anybody in the officers' mess. Instead, he grabbed his hat and was out the door before anyone could provoke him further. The sun had set, the horizon glowed faint orange, and he felt like tossing a bomb into the officers' mess. Sick of his fellow officers, trapped in a pointless career, he couldn't help wondering how his son was doing.

The traders' wagons were lit by coal oil lanterns, which provided a carnival atmosphere. "Help you, sir?" asked a tall, thin trader with a nose like a finger.

"Bottle of your best whiskey."

"It's all the same and comes from the same place— my washtub. Maybe that's why it tastes so bad."

"I'm sure," replied Nathanial as he tossed coins onto the counter, and received the bottle. "You wouldn't happen to know where I could buy a good metal flask, do you?"

"Try Max the German. He's got just about anything a man would want."

Nathanial proceeded to a dimly lit wagon that stood a distance from the others. A sign on the side said in crude letters:

I BUY AND SELL ANYTHING

A table had been set up, and upon it lay guns, Apache deerskin shirts, beads, boots, boxes of ammunition, bags of tobacco, bottles of whiskey, belt buckles; an incredible array of miscellaneous merchandise piled together in no organized manner. Behind the table sat an old man with a long gray beard, wearing an oversize cowboy hat. "Vhat I can do for you, sir?"

"Do you carry a metal whiskey flask by any chance?"

"Got one right here, sir."

The old man reached into the pile and out came a silver flask similar to the one Nathanial had given Mangas Coloradas. Nathanial accepted it, and was surprised to note that it actually *was* the flask he'd given the Apache chief, with the A. T. Stewart label on the bottom. Where'd you get it?"

"Off one of the Injuns. It is very high quality."

Nathanial tossed coins onto the counter, then poured whiskey from the bottle to his old flask. Evidently, Mangas Coloradas had traded it for whiskey or a gun. How strange are the threads of fate, reflected Nathanial, as he held the silver flask in the light of trader's lamps. Welcome home.

Soldiers drifted toward the wagons, and Nathanial wondered where to go. He had his choice of his tent or . . . his tent. A New Yorker accustomed to unlimited night entertainment was stuck at the Santa Rita copper mines.

When in doubt, check the guards. He took another swallow of truly horrible whiskey, then proceeded on his rounds. He walked with his hands behind his back, eyeing bluish-black heavens dotted with stars. In the distance the outlines of mountains looked like great dinosaurs reclining on the trackless wastes of New Mexico. No Broadway concert hall or Fifth Avenue drawing room can compare with this, he told himself. The Southwest frontier is my destiny, and perhaps I was a lizard or a snake in my past life.

He saw himself slithering over the ground like a big diamond-backed rattlesnake, or imagined himself an eagle swooping across the sky. I wonder what they put into this whiskey, he wondered. For all I know, that trader has poisoned me.

"Halt! Who goes there!" The sentry was Private Houlihan, a Philadelphian. "Maybe you should ease off the whiskey, sir."

Nathanial remained perfectly calm. "I hadn't realized it showed, Houlihan. Can it be I'm drunk?"

"I think we can safely say that, sir."

"Tell me, Houlihan. You appear a bright fellow. Why'd you ever join the Army?"

"There was this girl, sir . . ."

He didn't have to say more. Many soldiers had fled women they'd either impregnated or married inadvertently. We're an army of lost souls, reflected Nathanial. "Stay alert, Private Houlihan."

The men are losing respect for me, he concluded, as he continued his rounds. They think I'm just another drunkard officer, and they're absolutely right. He circled back to the wagons, where soldiers and Apaches gathered to trade. The whiskey was going to his head, and he felt old intemperate feelings that usually proceeded trouble of his own making. It was as though he needed something dramatic to alter his present intolerable circumstances.

He felt dizzy, his head swam, and then he noticed

young Lieutenant Dix walking toward him out of the night. "Could I have a word with you, Lieutenant Barrington?"

"What's on your mind?"

"I wanted to tell you, sir, that I admired how you stood up to Lieutenant Whipple's insults at the mess tonight. I agree with you completely—there's far too much politics in the Army, and it's monstrous the way people talk to one another. Sometimes I get sucked into these discussions, and I'm always ashamed afterward. You're a brave man, because you speak your mind."

Nathanial was flabbergasted by this declaration. He'd viewed himself as an unstable and quarrelsome officer, not the kind younger men admired. "Have you ever noticed in the morning, Lieutenant Dix, the odor of death in the air?"

"I don't believe so, sir."

Nathanial pointed to the wilderness. "Do you know what happens in this territory every night? Animals kill each other for food, and even as we speak, there's an owl swooping down on a rabbit, or a snake trying to swallow a baby rat. If you walk out there, and you don't pay attention, you'll become somebody's supper too."

"Here come the Apaches."

Nathanial spotted warriors emerging warily from the darkness. With a jolt, he noticed *she* was among them. Smaller than the others, she moved with the same pride and grandeur. He couldn't take his eyes off her, and then, when he least expected it, she glanced toward him. Their eyes met across the vast distance, like flint on steel.

Nathanial murmured something to Lieutenant Dix, then stumbled toward the wagons, trying to appear

casual. A woman doesn't look at a man like that unless she's telling him something, he reasoned. He felt
like a puppet whose strings were pulled by unseen
forces. The Apaches bartered with traders as Nathanial stood to the side, his silver flask in his right
hand, the stopper hanging loose, as he measured the
warrior woman. Powerful chemicals dumped into his
bloodstream, mixing with alcohol, oxylated tobacco
smoke, and supper. He felt as if something stupendous
were about to happen, and wondered if his months
at the copper mines had destroyed the fine edge of
his mind.

She eased away from the other Apaches, and again,
for a moment, glanced back at him. He saw not a
fearsome warrior woman, but a lady unsure of her
next move. He looked away casually, then took a sip
of whiskey. If he had a shred of common sense, he'd
walk to his tent and forget about removing the blouse
of a certain Apache warrior woman.

Unfortunately, he couldn't stop looking at her. In
the wagons someone fingered a Spanish guitar, and
Nathanial felt giddy. He turned toward her again and
marveled at how exquisitely bizarre she appeared,
with those fierce oriental eyes, high cheekbones, and
jet black hair. Again he desired to dig his fingers into
her flesh, and when finished with that fascinating ad-
venture, he'd like to explore those inscrutable lips with
his tongue, and perhaps he'd learn something new or
old, it didn't matter.

The crescent moon hung like a golden earring from
the Big Dipper. I don't give a damn if I get killed
tonight, he said to himself. The warrior woman walked
aimlessly toward the wilderness, and no one seemed
to pay attention, except Nathanial. The guitarist
strummed a crescendo as Nathanial watched her

breechclout flutter in the breeze. A slick of sweat appeared on his forehead, as a group of soldiers laughed nearby. In the distance, a lobo howled mournfully as a flock of bats flew overhead, chasing insects through the night.

At the edge of the wilderness the warrior woman stopped for a moment and plucked a leaf from a chinchweed. She crushed it in her fingers, as she strolled among the plants, just taking a casual promenade, it appeared, when suddenly she turned and gazed directly at Nathanial.

He felt two rays pierce his brain, and at that moment the flirting came to an end, replaced by something more serious. She tossed the leaf over her shoulder, then strode into the wilderness.

Nathanial didn't respond, because he knew that sagacity was required, a commodity in short supply. No one had noticed her disappearance, while the other Apaches guzzled newly purchased whiskey. Nathanial's heart hammered his backbone, terrified by what he was about to do. He remembered those lips, and his wife was far, far away.

Nonchalantly, as though meandering up Broadway on a hot summer night, he inclined toward the wilderness.

Juh looked like a drunken fool as he passed the bottle to Geronimo. But no matter how much whiskey he consumed, Juh always kept track of Jocita. No suspicious thoughts nagged his mind when she'd walked into the chaparral, for she frequently roamed about alone, but then the bluecoat officer with sunny hair, the same one who'd stopped him on the trail, disappeared at a different place.

Juh wanted to believe they were random events,

for it was inconceivable that his virtuous wife would misbehave, especially with an enemy bluecoat soldier. Everyone knew Jocita was purest of the pure, most devout of the devout, and the one whom warriors wished their daughters would emulate.

Juh didn't dare show concern in front of his warriors, and thought it might be his imagination. Yet earlier he'd seen Jocita staring at the bluecoat war chief with more than passing interest. Hadn't someone said they'd spoken at the camp that afternoon? If I ever catch Jocita unfaithful to me, I'll kill them both, swore the sub-chief of the fearsome Nednais.

Jocita walked deeper into the wilderness, terrified by what she'd done. Despite her better judgment, and against her will, she'd cast not one but *two* significant glances at the bluecoat soldier, and then lured him onto the very land over which she walked. She wanted to flee to her wickiup and hide beneath animal skins, but in another part of her being, she was gratified by her courage.

Usually she felt like a lump of dirt, but the bluecoat soldier made her feel like a woman again. She wanted to be happy, even for a few brief moments, although it violated the most fundamental principles of the holy life-way. The mountain spirits will surely punish me, she said with a rueful little smile.

She wondered if sorcerers had enchanted her, or whether she was a selfish fool. Scratching her arms nervously, she wondered where he was. It appears that I must look for him, she thought. It takes an Apache to find an Apache.

Where is she? wondered Nathanial, crashing through underbrush. Trying to cut her trail, he'd lost his way. Perhaps twenty Apaches will ambush me, skin me alive, and stuff my member down my throat. He reached for his service pistol, but didn't want to appear frightened. What in hell am I doing here? he asked himself. For God sakes, I'm an officer, a married man, a father, a . . .

He saw something move behind a willow straight ahead. It could be a deer, cougar, or an Apache raiding party, or it might be *her*. Nathanial hesitated, but then considered placing his hand upon her naked bosom.

He crossed a small clearing, stepped around the willow, and saw her surrounded by clumps of cactus, yucca, aloe vera, and other tangled foliage, in the soft glow of a clouded moon. Nathanial swallowed a fist that somehow had become lodged in his throat.

She didn't move as he drew closer. One part of her wanted to flee. "What have you done to me?" she asked plaintively in her native tongue.

He didn't understand, as he came to a halt about two feet away. They faced each other in the dim light, and neither knew what to say. He reached for her, but she eluded him. He tried to head her off, but she dodged out of his way. It appeared that she was teasing him, but he heard Apache drums pounding his ears, or maybe his heart, he couldn't be sure.

She ran lightly over the grama grass, and he followed about six feet behind. He lunged toward her, when she abruptly switched direction; he nearly fell onto his face. He heard her merry laughter as she lightly danced away. He redoubled his effort to catch her, the path narrowed, she couldn't dodge effectively, he dived forward, caught her shoulder, and spun her around.

They were inches apart, breathing heavily. There

was nothing more to pretend, no games to play, and they still didn't know each others' names. He pulled her closer, felt her breasts against his tunic, and placed his hand on her firm waist. "You're mine, you savage bitch," he uttered, as he lowered his lips to hers.

She stood still as a statue; his mouth touched hers. All the pent-up suppression of a lifetime swirled out of her, she felt lost, frightened, undefended, and she didn't want to violate the holy life-way. "No!" she cried in the language of the People, as she drew back, swinging her fist.

She caught him on the jaw, and she was no wispy little female. His head spun around, but he'd always been able to take a hard punch fairly in stride. "What's wrong with you?" he asked, grabbing her wrist.

She darted out of his way and caught his mouth on the backswing, splitting his lower lip. "I hate you," she snarled, as she slapped, kicked, punched, and slammed him in a mad frenzy.

First Lieutenant Nathanial Barrington, First Dragoons, was an experienced hand-to-hand fighter, and far stronger than she. In addition, he was unusually fast for a big man. He saw many ways to disable her, but how could he harm such a splendid creature, even if she was beating the shit out of him? He stepped backward, blocking most of her blows, but a few got through to his face, and she was a heavy thumper, considering she was a woman.

In her wild frenzy she saw he wasn't fighting back. Suddenly, she stopped. Blood trickled from his lip, his face was red and puffy, but he was still there, waiting for more. She knew that he'd held himself back for her sake.

"Why you?" she asked sadly.

He didn't understand, and she didn't run when he reached for her once more. "Kill me if you want to," he told her, "but I am going to make you mine."

She couldn't speak English, but no longer could she deny woman's needs. She wrapped her arms around his waist, and touched her lips lightly to his cheek.

Something snapped inside him; his hands roved her back as his tongue skirted the base of her throat. She looked over his shoulder and saw the crescent moon, as he lowered her gently to the ground. She was surprised by how strong he was and figured he truly was worthy of a warrior woman, as she helped him remove her deer skin blouse.

He dug his fingers into her muscled shoulders, and their lips touched for the first time. She was naked from the waist up, he was completely clothed, and they rolled across the grama grass, disturbing the slumber of crickets and grasshoppers. Their tongues lashed each other, and they clawed the other's garments, as if trying to bare their souls.

He realized she was the strongest woman he'd ever known, and there was something almost mannish about her, yet she was completely female, smooth, and soft in a special way. They rose to their knees, where she helped him remove his blue Army shirt, and then went to work on each others' belts. Hers came away fastest, her breechclout went flying through the air, and now she was totally naked except for a left ankle bracelet made from tiny hammered silver conchos.

The sight of the naked warrior woman obliterated what was left of Nathanial's mind. If the entire Apache nation charged him, they wouldn't even slow him down. Hands trembling, he pushed down his officer pants, then yanked off his boots. Now he too was naked, as he drew himself to full height. They gazed at each other, and Nathanial vaguely recalled that he had a wife and child somewhere, but he'd worry about them some other time.

They hesitated, because each feared the treacherous slope down which they were so blithely sliding, but no longer could they control love starvation. They dropped to the bare ground, chewing each other's lips, reveling in each other's touch, while high in a ponderosa pine, a wise old owl gazed thoughtfully upon them humping frantically in the light of the moon.

Savero lay in the wickiup, waiting for his moment to strike. Old Taza was asleep on his back, snoring loudly, but he might be trying to trick Savero.

Savero lay with a five-inch blade that he planned to ram into Taza's throat. He was convinced Taza had killed his parents, and it was time to pay. Savero had learned from bitter experience that he couldn't merely creep up on Taza. He'd have to pounce quickly and kill cleanly, with no screams, otherwise he'd never get away.

Savero rolled onto his stomach, prepared to jump. José was waiting, but somehow Savero couldn't kill Taza. He was frightened, not murderous. Instead, he headed for the exit.

"Where are you going, insect?" asked Taza, raising one eye.

"To the latrine, sir."

"Don't get ideas about running away. And just because you've stolen a knife, it doesn't scare me."

Savero gulped. "Yes, sir." The boy emerged outside, paused, and listened. As expected, he soon heard Taza resume snoring. Savero tiptoed toward the latrine. He saw no one on the trail, but upon arriving

at the smelly place, José wasn't there. Has he changed
his mind? wondered Savero.

"Savero?"

The boy jumped three inches into the air, then realized José had called him. "Where are you?"

José raised his head above a hackberry bush. "You
are late."

"I could not get away from Taza," lied Savero. "Did
you have any difficulties with Jocita?"

"She has not come home."

They heard footsteps on the path, ducked beneath
the bush, and through the leaves saw the great chief
Mangas Coloradas advancing sleepily through the
night. The boys waited until he was finished, then retreated into the chaparral, beginning their long, peril-
ous journey toward freedom.

The wise old owl blinked his saucer eyes at two
creatures, lying beneath him. They weren't moving,
and he wondered if they had died in their great effort.
So fixated was he on the strange spectacle beneath
him, he didn't hear the cougar creeping down the
branch behind him. Something sharp punctured the
old owl's throat, and the scene faded from his eyes.

A few feathers fell to the ground beside the couple
lying in each other's arms, both covered with
scratches, bites, dirt, leaves, and the occasional fleck
of blood. Their chests heaved against each other as
they struggled to breathe.

They wanted to speak, but how could they describe
the ineffable? After a brief rest, they kissed one last
time, then separated reluctantly, unashamed. They
dressed in the darkness. She said something in
Apache, then smiled sadly and turned away.

"Wait . . ." he replied, holding out his hand, but she

was drawing back into the night, and in seconds was out of sight. He heard a faint footfall, that was the end of it. Now he was alone, and Nathanial wondered if the incomprehensible experience had happened at all. He felt exhausted, yet oddly renewed. His back covered with scratches, he touched his finger to his split lip. She punches as hard as my father, he estimated, then shook his head and laughed at himself.

He glanced behind, to make sure her husband wasn't sneaking up on him with hatchet in hand. Then he strapped on his gunbelt, put on his hat, and headed back toward the copper mines. A smile creased his lips, but then a thought came to him, one he'd tried hard to forget during the evening's perversities. I have betrayed Maria Dolores, and our marriage will never be the same.

Jocita prowled far from the main trail because she didn't want to be seen. She felt like a low woman because virtuous wives never give their most precious gifts to strangers, although he had given her most precious gift to her.

She didn't know what to make of it and could never hold her head high again. The People didn't know what she'd done, but the mountain spirits saw everything, and she was convinced illness was headed her way. No longer was she proud of her honor, because she'd flung it away wantonly.

She closed her eyes and recalled how he'd maneuvered her into the strangest positions. He'd been protective, warm, passionate, loving, kind, considerate, but she was a traitor to the most holy precepts of her People.

Yet she knew, deep in her heart, that she'd do it again if the opportunity presented itself. In another part of her mind, she felt perfectly at ease for the first time in many harvests. It was as if sorrow and neglect had been eradicated by the brief time she'd spent in the arms of the bluecoat soldier. Do I love him, and does he love me? she wondered.

A shadow plunged, and before she could draw her pistol, her throat was pinned to the ground. The cruel visage of Juh hovered above her, his fist choking her air.

"I should kill you," he hissed.

"You would do me a favor," she replied.

"You're right—it would be too good for you—little cheat!" He spat in her face. "You pretend to be a proper wife, but no one will ever look at you again."

He held his eight-inch blade before her eyes, then pressed the edge to her nose. She closed her eyes; he was too strong for her, and all she could do was submit to disfigurement. Juh looked down at her and tried to focus his strength for the ordained punishment. He as more hurt than angry, as he visualized how she'd look without a nose. A sob came over him; he dropped the knife and fell beside her, his massive body quaking in sorrow. "This is my fault," he whispered. "I forced you into wickedness when I married again."

"Every warrior deserves children, and I have failed you. I am a bad woman."

He raised his eyes. "Are you in love with him?"

"But my husband—I do not even know his name."

Juh smiled bitterly. "I have betrayed you, and now you have betrayed me. I am the one who should be killed." He held the blade to his throat, but the scene seemed absurd to him as he tried to lop off his own head. He dropped the knife into his sheath. "What are you going to do about him?"

"I will never see him again. Were you watching us, Juh?"

"I was not sick enough for that, but I waited for you to return, and thought I'd kill you, but you foolish little thing—I love you too much. I should be angry, but I feel tired and very old."

"I was in a magic spell, Juh. That is the truth, but I do not know what it means."

"Halt—who goes there!"

"Lieutenant Barrington."

The sentry wasn't part of Nathanial's detachment, and he spoke with a cockney accent. "Pass on, sir."

"Quiet night so far, I hope?"

"Have you been a-wanderin' in the valley sir? Don't you know that's dangerous?"

"Nothing's dangerous when you're ready for trouble, Private—what'd you say your name was?"

"Tommy Gaugh, sir."

"Do you like the Army, Gaugh?"

"It's all right, sir. But when my enlistment is up, I a-gittin' the hell out."

"What will you do?"

"Don't rightly know, sir. I might become a lawyer, or maybe I'll be a farmer."

Or maybe you'll end up back in the Army again, thought Nathanial. "Carry on, Gaugh."

At the edge of the campsite, the twinkling lights of the traders' wagons could be seen. Nathanial tried not to limp as he made his way toward his tent. She'd bitten his lip, neck, and chest, and he felt as if he'd been through a meat grinder. What a woman, he thought wearily. If I were married to her, I'd be dead in an week.

But he was married already, and the cold damp

sheet of guilt fell on him yet again. He wasn't sure what to think, because he'd always believed a man should marry once and be faithful forever. Lights were out in the tents, and one solitary candle burned in the orderly room at the triangular presidio. What if the Apaches sneak up on our guards and murder us in our sleep?

A figure approached in the darkness, and Nathanial's hand dropped to the holster of his service revolver. "Halt!" he yelled. "Who goes there?"

A chuckle came to him through the night. "Is that you, Barrington?" It was brawny Lieutenant Whipple, a bit under the weather. "You look like you've been in a fight," he drawled mockingly.

"I fell down."

"Perhaps you shouldn't drink so much." Whipple was three inches shorter than Nathanial, with a belly overshadowing his belt. "You know—I don't like you much, Barrington. In fact, the word *disgusting* might profitably be used in describing you."

"I thought you were demented when first we met, Lieutenant Whipple, and since then, nothing's happened to change my mind."

"If there's one thing I hate, it's moral cowardice," continued Lieutenant Whipple. "But it doesn't surprise me that you're ashamed of yourself. New Yorkers like you have financed the slave trade practically since the beginning, and kept it going all these years. What I object to is the way you hide behind your famous pretended indifference. Why don't you have the courage of your convictions and admit what you are—a hypocrite?"

Nathanial looked around, but no one was in the vicinity. "You're drunk, Lieutenant Whipple, and I suspect you're one of those deep-brooding Southerners who has spent too much time in the sun. Regarding the courage of my convictions, I consider that a personal insult, but I'll let it ride this time. However, next time you may not be so lucky. Good night, sir."

Lieutenant Whipple snorted derisively. "There he goes, running away yet again. You've married a greaser, and if that's not enough, you're a Nigra lover." The Alabaman leaned drunkenly in the moonlight. "Do you have any idea how much I despise you, Lieutenant Barrington?"

"The feeling is mutual, I assure you."

"There's one way to settle this, and I suppose you know what it is."

Nathanial was exhausted, thanks to an unusually strenuous encounter with a certain Apache warrior woman, but there were certain insults an officer cannot ignore. "Unless my ears are functioning improperly, I do believe you've just challenged me to a duel."

"Your ears are not malfunctioning, Lieutenant."

"I shall send you my second in the morning."

"What's wrong with right now?"

"Do you have any preference as regards weapons?"

"Bare fists, if you don't mind."

Nathanial took one last glance around him, and no one as nearby. "Shall we commence here?"

"Why not? You know, Barrington, you're just too damned piss-elegant for words, like all the other New Yorkers who think they're better than everyone else."

So that's what it is, reflected Nathanial, as he raised his fists. The old antagonism to the biggest and most filthy city in America. He turned to the side, to present a smaller target to his opponent, and was wondering whether to attack or defend, when Whipple shot a stiff left jab toward Nathanial's already-bruised mouth.

Nathanial leaned three inches to the left, the fist whistled past his ear, and then he danced away.

"Are you going to fight or do a Virginia Reel?"
asked Whipple disdainfully.

Suddenly, a large fist appeared in front of Whipple's
eyes. He tried to get out of the way, but it crashed
into his nose, cracking bone and cartilage. When he
raised his arms to protect his face, blows exploded
across his soft belly, taking his breath away. He swung
wildly at his opponent, hoping for a lucky punch, but
instead walked into a solid left hook.

Nathanial knew it was a damaging blow as soon as
it landed, because he'd put all his two hundred and
twenty pounds behind it. Whipple's legs buckled, and
Nathanial watched with curious fascination as the defender of Southern chivalry dropped to the ground.

Nathanial's first instinct was call the doctor, but that
would initiate a court of inquiry and possibly lead to
another setback for Nathanial's already troubled military career. He didn't want to leave Whipple where
an Apache might slit his throat, or a coyote could
chew off his ears, but didn't see any alternative. He
had no great love for people who harangued him over
the great political issues of the day.

Nathanial picked up his hat and continued toward his
tent, hoping no other untoward events lurked in the
darkness. A man can only manage so much chaos in
one day, he told himself. He lit the candle and looked
at his face in the mirror, noticing bruises, bites, and that
hideous split lip. He hung his hat on the peg, pulled off
his boots, and dived onto his cot. Strangest night of my
life, he considered, before falling off to slumber.

Jocita entered her wickiup and noticed the boy
hadn't returned. She assumed he was with friends,

sipped water from a leather bag that once had been the stomach of a deer, then removing her clothing, wrapped herself in animal skins, and wondered if her body would ever recover from the mangling of the bluecoat soldier.

She felt as if she'd fallen off a mountain. There wasn't a square inch of her that didn't ache, but she was satiated in every pore of her being for the first time since the early days of her marriage.

No one had ever provoked her like the bluecoat soldier whose name she didn't know. She closed her eyes and recalled performing certain unmentionable acts upon him. Never had she known such abandon, heights of madness, and depths of depravity. It frightened her to recall that she could be that ... she didn't even know what to call herself.

I must never do this again, she swore. If I see him again, I will look in another direction.

TEN

Nathanial heard haranguing in the distance, as if a preacher had arrived at the copper mines. He rolled out of bed, peered through the opening of his tent, and saw at the edge of the encampment a covered wagon displaying a sign:

PRAYER MEETING

On a platform, surrounded by soldiers and Apaches, a gray-bearded preacher waved his arms excitedly. "Nobody's more smug than the sinner!" he hollered. "And the God-hating atheist is the most shallow man of all. 'Woe to you, generation of vipers,' saith the Lord God. Repent and come to God's own truth, or burn forever in the flames of Hell!"

Thou shalt not commit adultery, remembered Nathanial. How will I ever look Maria Dolores in the eye again?

Old Taza stirred himself to wakefulness. He glanced toward the other side of the wickiup and noted that his slave had already left to prepare the first of the old warrior's many daily meals. A slave boy is better than a wife, he figured, because a slave boy is entitled to nothing.

He stepped outside and was astonished to see no fire in the pit, no corn porridge cooking in the pot, no slave boy in view. That little scum, thought Taza angrily. I'll bet he's playing with his traitor friend, José.

Taza's anger became focused upon Jocita, who had interrupted his tranquil domestic life. I don't care who her husband is, because I am a warrior of the People, and I have rights too.

He stormed across the rancheria, an old egg-shaped warrior with thin legs and hair thinning atop his pate, with a dirty blue bandanna wrapped around his forehead, and a nose like a lump of basalt. He arrived at Jocita's wickiup and called out: "Is my slave boy with you, warrior woman?"

Her voice came to him. "He is not here."

"I do not believe you, Jocita. Have you stolen *both* my boys, for whom I have risked my life on daring raids?"

Jocita pushed aside the tent flap. Her hair was mussed, eyes half-closed, and she looked as if Juh had beaten her. Oh-oh, thought Taza.

"Who are you calling a liar?" she asked pleasantly as she drew her knife.

He held up his hands and grinned, displaying gaps between his teeth. "Not you, warrior woman, but where is my boy?"

"Where is mine?" she replied.

His eyes widened with fury. "Everything was fine before you took José. This is your fault, and I am going to tell Mangas Coloradas what you have done. Only he can give Taza justice."

Captain John Cremony lay in bed, reading a history of England. He'd risen at dawn, for he'd drunk moderately the previous night, unlike most men and officers. Cremony intended to spend a peaceful day performing research. He hoped to become more than a mere translator and scribbler of words, but never had succeeded at anything. What is history but the jottings of people like me? he wondered.

He heard a commotion, grabbed his trusty rifle, and suddenly two small Apache boys ran into his tent. At first he thought they were going to murder him, but instead they dived beneath his cot and jabbered hysterically in Spanish. "We are Mexicans, sir, and the Apaches have captured us! Please save us from them, for the sake of God!"

Cremony aimed his rifle outdoors, but no Apache warriors had pursued the boys. "I won't let them take you, and neither will the United States Army!" he declared staunchly. "How were you captured?"

The boys blurted their tales, then Savero complained of cruel treatment at the hands of the savages. If Savero exaggerated somewhat, in the true spirit of journalism, it was because he wanted to make the most convincing case possible. "If you make us go back," explained Savero, "they will kill us." He ran his finger across his throat to illustrate the point.

"Nobody's going to kill you," said Cremony, "but we'd better have a talk with the colonel." He peered through the opening of his tent, still saw no Apaches in the vicinity, then led the boys outside. They glanced about excitedly, and the older boy appeared more frightened than the younger. "Come with me," said the journalist. "Your Apache days are over."

Taza stood in front of Mangas Coloradas's wickiup as the chief returned from a bath in a mountain stream. "A serious problem has developed," said Taza gravely, as he bowed his head to the great chief. "Thanks to the first wife of Juh, I have lost both my dear boys. They were to be the solace of my old age, but Jocita planted the seeds of rebellion into their minds, and indeed stole one of them from me. You have done nothing to aid a poor old warrior who has always accepted your authority, which is more than we can say for the Nednais."

Mangas Coloradas considered Taza lazy, useless, and unreliable even when Taza had been a young warrior, but Taza always supported him in council. A group of warriors and woman gathered, and Mangas Coloradas didn't want potential supporters to think he might betray their interests.

"It is not difficult to know where they have gone," said Taza with a sneer. "They are in the White Eyes camp. The warrior woman is to blame for this, sir."

Mangas Coloradas looked for a reliable old-line sub-chief, and his eyes fell on brave Delgadito. "Find out where those boys have gone."

The boys trembled as they stood before Colonel Craig. "Evidently the Apaches were quite rough on them, sir," said Cremony, as he completed his testimony.

"Tell them they're safe," replied Colonel Craig, "and the Army will never give them up. If it comes to war, we'll fight for them. I knew those damned Apaches were up to no good, although they've acted friendly. You can't trust them, and there's a lesson in this for all of us. I wonder what else they have in their camp."

Sergeant Barnes looked out the window. "Oh-oh, here they come."

Colonel Craig peered out his window at fifty Indians riding toward Bartlett's wagon. "Barnes—don't blow any bugles, but pass the word that I want every man in front of the presidio, *with weapons*."

John R. Bartlett heard hoofbeats and looked up from the newly drawn map he'd been studying. He'd expected a scholarly day of rest, but a horde of Apaches was headed toward him, led by Mangas Coloradas. Bartlett grabbed his wide-rimmed vaquero hat and jumped to the ground.

The stern-faced Apaches rode closer, while Bartlett smiled at the great chief. "Welcome to my camp, Mangas Coloradas. Have a cup of coffee, and we shall talk together."

"No coffee today," said Mangas Coloradas stiffly. "Two of our boys have disappeared, and we tracked them to this camp. Where are they?"

"The American Army does not steal children, I assure you. Come—search our camp, and we shall settle this matter now."

Nathanial heard footsteps approaching at the run. He reached for his gun, aimed at the tent flap, and Sergeant Duffy appeared, disconcerted by the Colt Navy pointed at him. "At ease, sir," he said.

Nathanial lowered his gun. He'd reawakened with a start and still was in the realm where events could or not be true.

"Big trouble," said Sergeant Duffy, "and the old man wants us all at the presidio. But no shootin' unless he gives the word."

Nathanial had always feared whiskey and mistrust might explode into war at the copper mines, and it appeared the great event had finally arrived. He strapped on his holster, grabbed his rifle, and was on his way out the tent.

Meanwhile, Sergeant Duffy assembled the men. It embarrassed Nathanial to be seen in the uniform he'd worn to bed, but he pulled his bandanna tighter, then noticed the men examining his bruised, disheveled condition. "What're you looking at, Collins?" he asked.

"You, sir," replied Collins with a grin.

"Wipe that smile off your face, or I'll wipe it off for you."

"The hell you will," replied Collins, one of the larger men in Nathanial's detachment.

Nathanial realized he was losing his grip on them. "We'll discuss this at another time." Than Nathanial turned to the others. "You're not to act in a threatening manner, but if there's trouble, it's going to be down and dirty. Sergeant Duffy—march the men to the presidio, and if anybody provokes the Apaches, either by word or deed, he shall spend the rest of his enlistment in the stockade."

Colonel Craig gazed at John R. Bartlett and Mangas Coloradas heading in his direction, followed by a substantial Apache cohort. The colonel's soldiers were in the vicinity, a volatile confrontation on the breakfast menu. He'd already sent the captive boys to the camp of the Mexican Boundary Commission, and they were headed back to Mexico. The American Army does not negotiate captive children, determined Colonel Craig, but how can I calm those Indians?

Apaches would exploit weakness, so he couldn't apologize. But neither could he offer plain talk, since he was outnumbered twelve to one. He angled his mountain man hat low over his eyes, sucked in his stomach, and headed for his meeting with the Apaches.

Bartlett and the Indians came to a halt in front of the presidio, with soldiers hanging about the sidelines, pretending to be wandering aimlessly. Colonel Craig stepped outside, erect, proud, a combat commander to the marrow of his bones.

Bartlett smiled nervously. "The Apaches are rather upset," he said. "Do you know anything about two Mexican boys?"

"Yes, I've returned them to their people."

Bartlett opened his mouth, but had no idea what to say. He was Chief of the Boundary Commission, but the Astor Hotel hadn't prepared him for the tense scene in which he now found himself. Armed Indians and soldiers swaggered about, shooting hostile glances at one another, and it appeared that a melee might break out at any moment!

John Cremony translated Colonel Craig's statement into Spanish for Mangas Coloradas, who appeared astonished by the news. An ominous murmuring began among the warriors, and Colonel Craig realized it was time for the military to take over. He turned toward Cremony and said, "Tell the chief that stealing children is a crime according to United States law."

Cremony translated, as Mangas Coloradas recovered his calm. "But we have won them honorably in war," he tried to explain. "We have come to your camp, we have smoked together, and now you have stolen from us. You must give those boys back."

"Impossible," replied Colonel Craig. "The Army can't violate the laws of the nation."

"You have no right to steal our property!"

"We do not consider children property."

"I have seen the Negritos with my own eyes. You want to deceive Mangas Coloradas, and that is not good."

Colonel Craig didn't know how to explain the difference between Mexican captives and Negro slaves, and wondered if there truly was a difference. "I follow the orders of the Great White Father in Washington, and so must you. You are not permitted to steal Mexican boys."

"But the Mexicans steal our boys and girls. Why is it all right for them, but not us? The Mexicans have invited us to feasts and opened fire with cannon on unarmed people. They have poisoned our wells, sold the scalps of our wives and brothers, and committed terrible murders. You do not return their captives to us, but you want to take ours away!"

"Two mere boys are not worth fighting over," replied Colonel Craig. "We will pay you for them."

"What is money," asked Mangas Coloradas, "to an old warrior who has raised and trained these boys to be his helpers in his old age? Who will cook his meat and gather his firewood when he is feeble? He is too old to find a wife, so he must have slave boys. You White Eyes have slave boys, so why not we?"

Not far away, Nathanial listened thoughtfully to the argument of Mangas Coloradas. It boiled down to arbitrary application of the rules, and who had the most guns. Mangas Coloradas appeared insulted, and his warriors ready to fight. Nathanial maintained his hand near his holster, as John Cremony poured oil on troubled waters. "This is a surprise to all of us," he said with a frozen smile. "Perhaps we should return to our camps and meet again tomorrow."

Mangas Coloradas paused to think through the proposition. What do I care for Taza's slaves? he asked himself. Taza definitely wasn't worth dying for, but the chief couldn't show weakness before treacherous White Eyes. "We want peace with you," declared

Mangas Coloradas. "Tomorrow at noon we talk again."

He turned abruptly and walked back to the war ponies, followed by his warriors. Nathanial couldn't see Jocita among them and wondered what had happened to her. The Apaches mounted up, and electricity seemed to crackle among them, as their horses pranced about nervously. Mangas Coloradas issued an order, and the warriors prodded their mounts. A sound like a bolt of lightning rolled across the campsite as the horses galloped away, carrying warriors brandishing weapons.

The soldiers relaxed now that the Apaches were gone. "Double the guard," ordered Colonel Craig. "I'd recommend that the Boundary Commission doesn't venture out for a few days, because those Apaches are capable of any foul deed, the bloodier the better."

Jocita was awakened by shouting. She grabbed a rifle, poked her head outside, and saw an crowd in front of Mangas Coloradas's wickiup. Something had gone wrong, danger was in the air, and she ran barefoot to discover what had happened.

The most respected warriors and sub-chiefs sat in a circle with Mangas Coloradas, while the other People surrounded them. Taza stood nearby and pointed his finger at Jocita. "There she is—it is her fault! She interfered with my discipline, and that is why the boys have run away."

All eyes turned to her, and she hated Taza for drawing attention to her. Mangas Coloradas appeared greatly troubled, as did the other important sub-chiefs and warriors. Then she noticed Juh move to her side.

"Taza," he said calmly, "another disrespectful remark to my wife, and I shall kill you."

With every step her body ached in some tendon or sinew. "I have been asleep," she said. "What has happened?"

"Savero and José have run to the White Eyes camp," explained Mangas Coloradas. "The White Eyes have given them back to the Mexicans."

Taza announced accusingly: "This is what happens when the holy life-way is violated by foolish women!"

Jocita recalled José's odd behavior the previous day. "The boys missed their relatives," she said. "It is a good reason not to camp near the White Eyes. We should move away from here."

"Does the warrior woman propose to abandon my slaves?" asked Taza.

"We must exact payment," she replied, "and be more cautious in the future."

Taza shook his head angrily. "There is no payment sufficient to satisfy me, because what about the years I've spent training and teaching my dear boys? You are still young, warrior woman, but I am an old warrior."

She looked him in the eyes. "If you are too old to take care of yourself, you should die. That is what will happen to all of us, and we should not rely upon little boys. Besides, if you were not so unkind, they never would have left. You have brought much trouble to the People, old man."

Mangas Coloradas said, "I am guilty of trusting the White Eyes, but can see no point in war at this time. Perhaps we do not understand their views on slave boys, or maybe they are liars—I am not sure."

Juh raised his hand. "There is one possibility that you have not yet mentioned, great Chief. Why not gather your warriors and attack the White Eyes at dawn? They have no business in our homeland, and I do not like them measuring everything with their sinister instruments.''

"Let us give the White Eyes one last chance," replied Mangas Coloradas. "I shall negotiate the best price for the boys, but next time . . .''

A meeting was held that afternoon in the office of Colonel Craig.

"Sir," said Major Stewart, "I propose that we send to Fort Marcy for immediate reinforcements, and all boundary work should cease immediately."

Colonel Craig scowled. "The reinforcements won't get here in time. Any other suggestions?"

Commissioner Bartlett raised his hand. "My staff is far behind schedule. We can't afford to stop now—Congress would never stand for it."

"Let the congressman fight the Apaches," replied Lieutenant Whipple, who wore a bandage on his nose. "Why not attack their camp first? There's nothing like having surprise on your side, and Indians generally don't do well when worried about wives and children."

"Isn't it hypocritical," replied Lieutenant Medlowe, "for an Alabaman to call Indian slavery a crime, but Southern slavery is perfectly fine?"

"There he goes again," retorted Lieutenant Whipple. "The abolitionists inject their foul ideas into any discussion, including our possible massacre at the hands of Apaches."

Bartlett cleared his throat. "Why does the military offer a cavalry charge as solution to all known human problems? Gentlemen, we are witnessing a clash of cultures, where institutions that seem beastly to us are considered normal to others. It is not our mission to teach the Apaches the benefits of civilization, but we must continue our work nonetheless. Therefore we should compensate them adequately for their property. Let them think this is their land, if it pleases them."

Lieutenant Farley cleared his throat. "Perhaps we should trade you to the Apaches, and you can become one of their slaves. Might do you good, sir."

"That'll be enough," cautioned Colonel Craig. "I think it's time Mister Bartlett and I spoke in private."

The officers filed out of the orderly room, leaving the two senior men facing each other across the desk. The door closed, and jangling spurs could be heard, as officers dispersed to their commands.

Colonel Craig leaned forward, folded his hands on his desk, and peered into Bartlett's eyes. "I don't think you appreciate the seriousness of the situation."

"The Apaches want peace, and you must beware of insulting them."

"They're insulted whenever we ask them to obey the law, such as not kidnapping other people's children, or roasting strangers head-down over fires. Once we start making exceptions, that's the end of civilization."

"But they have their own laws—"

Colonel Craig interrupted him. "Their laws are superseded by the laws of the U.S. government. I'm not endangering my men for the sake of your high-minded Indian policy, Mister Bartlett. This is no longer a jaunt along the border, and until further notice, a state of war exists between us and the Apache."

* * *

The Nednais sat in a circle a short distance from the camp, discussing recent events. "Mangas Coloradas is a great chief," admitted Juh, "but sorrow is coming, thanks to his deeds this day."

"We should break our alliance with the Mimbrenos," offered Geronimo. "They no longer have stomach for war. Some talk of becoming farmers—can you imagine? And that Taza is the most loathsome warrior I have ever seen. Such a man would not last a day among the Bedonko."

Warrior after warrior denounced Mangas Coloradas and his efforts at reconciliation, but the warrior woman remained silent, her eyes downcast. How brave he was to follow me, she thought, with his sunny hair.

Her reveries were interrupted by the voice of her husband. "You are strangely silent, Jocita," he mocked. "What do you think should be done?"

"Taza's disgraceful behavior has caused this crisis," she replied. "If he cannot care for himself, he should die like the old wretch he is. Only the holy life-way can save us."

She lowered her eyes like a virtuous woman of the People, but knew she was lying. A payment will be exacted for my transgression someday, she reckoned.

Colonel Craig looked up from his desk. "Have a seat, Barrington. Be with you in a minute."

Nathanial watched the colonel writing upon a sketch of the encampment, evidently planning a more secure defense. The younger officer didn't know why the colonel wanted to speak with him, but had been called by a courier. The presidio was preparing to fight twelve to one odds, and Nathanial wanted to sleep.

Then Lieutenant Whipple entered the office, took one look at Nathanial, and both realized why they were there.

"Have a seat, Whipple."

The Southern gentleman looked comical with the big white bandage on his nose, smudged with something the color of horse manure. The two officers waited for the axe to fall.

Colonel Craig raised an eyebrow. "Have you two imbeciles been fighting, by any chance?"

There was no answer, so Colonel Craig cleared his throat. "Both of you are the worst drunkards among my officers, but surely you're capable of a simple *yes* or *no*. You're the senior officer, Lieutenant Barrington. What do you say about this?"

"No excuse, sir."

"Whipple?"

"No excuse, sir."

"Evidently, you've let your unfriendly mess hall banter spill into other areas. Do you think the men don't know what happened when two officers are covered with bruises, and if I'm not mistaken, your nose is broken—is that correct, Lieutenant Whipple?"

"Yes, sir."

"Let me point out that you are government property, and damaging government property is a court-martial offense. There will be no more fighting in this command, and if I ever smell whiskey on the breath of either of you, I shall drum you out of the Army. We're in an extremely dangerous situation here, and I cannot tolerate fools."

Next morning, two hundred heavily armed Apache warriors arrived at the Santa Rita copper mines, led by Mangas Colorado, Ponce, Delgadito, Cuchillo Negro,

Coletto Amarillo, and Taza. John R. Bartlett greeted
them warmly, but the Apaches appeared in a truculent
mood. Then Colonel Craig made his appearance, attired in a freshly laundered uniform, carefully barbered, boots highly polished.

"Select your top men," he said to Mangas Coloradas, and his words were translated by John Cremony, "then come to my office. We shall settle this
matter once and for all."

Mangas Coloradas didn't want to enter the old
adobe building, but welcomed the opportunity to escape his more vocal critics among the Nednais. "It
shall be as you say," he uttered.

He followed the colonel to a large room with a
table running down the middle. The Apaches sat on
one side, the officers on the other, while Apaches
assembled in a semicircle in front of the presidio,
and heavily armed soldiers lingered nearby, among
them the recently chastised Lieutenant Nathanial
Barrington.

He spotted Jocita among the warriors, but she pretended they'd never rolled naked in the desert less
than forty-eight hours ago. Something told him to
keep his distance, and he wondered if her husband
was sneaking up on him, lance in hand.

Nathanial remained with his men about fifty yards
from the presidio, ready to charge at the first shot.
Another group of soldiers guarded the horses, with a
third bunch in front of the ammunition storehouse.
Apaches outnumbered them in the immediate vicinity,
with the possibility of a thousand more hidden in the
chaparral. Nathanial found himself wondering if the
sun would set on his grave.

*   *   *

Inside the presidio, Mangas Coloradas declared: "We cannot accept your explanation for taking our captives. We thought you were our friends, but you have committed an injustice against us."

"The children asked our protection," replied Colonel Craig. "How could we refuse?"

Mangas Coloradas pointed at Colonel Craig and said, "You came to our homeland and were well-received. Your lives, your property, your animals were safe. You passed through our most sacred places, and we did not obstruct you. Our wives and children visited your houses, an we believed we were brothers, so we brought our captives among you, concealing nothing. We trusted you and thought you understood our ways. How could you turn on us, and poison the good relations that we have worked so hard to build?"

The American Army couldn't grovel before Indians, even when hugely outnumbered. "Four years ago," began Colonel Craig, "my nation was at war with Mexico over this very land. We defeated them, and by the terms of the peace, we must protect them against *you*. In the same way, we offer protection and friendship to you. That is why we—"

He was interrupted by Delgadito, who leapt to his feet and gesticulated furiously. "We do not need your protection, White Eyes! If we had known how treacherous you were, we would never have brought our captives near you! They were made prisoners in lawful warfare and belong to us. If we had known your deceit, we would not have placed our confidence in you!"

Colonel Craig drew his lips into a grim line. "You speak in anger, without reflection, like a boy or a woman. I know that you have suffered much injustice from the Mexicans, as they have suffered from you. It is our duty to fulfill our promises to both camps, regardless of who started the trouble. We mean what we say."

Delgadito appeared ready to attack the colonel. "I am not a boy or a woman!" he shouted. "I am a warrior, I speak with reflection, and I know of the wrongs we have suffered! I had better leave here, or I shall kill you!"

Delgadito stormed out of the room, leaving Colonel Craig in astonished silence. No one knew what to say, then Mangas Coloradas arose. "The owner of these captives is poor," he explained. "He has won them at the risk of his life, and was justly entitled to them. If he does not receive them back, there will be war between us."

The Apaches murmured angrily, and Colonel Craig shivered involuntarily at the forbidden word. Outnumbered, cut off from his base of supplies, he was responsible for the lives of the Boundary Commission members. "The captives have been sent to their people," he replied. "They will never return to you, but we are willing to pay a fair price."

Mangas Coloradas said, "The brave who owns these captives taught them to string the bow and wield the lance. They are like sons, and he has owned one of them six years. His heart cannot be bought."

"The children are gone forever," replied Colonel Craig. "Let my Apache brother name his price."

"What will you give?"

"Come, and I will show you."

Colonel Craig led them to the commissary, where bolts of cloth, axes, candles, and other articles totaling fifty dollars in value were laid upon a counter. It didn't look like much to Mangas Coloradas. "Do you accept this, Taza?" he asked.

Taza's eyes alit with greed, for he could sell the cloth to the Mexicans. Besides, his slaves clearly were gone forever. "Yes."

Gifts were loaded onto a wagon, as Nathanial and Jocita cast surreptitious glances at each other. Negotiations concluded, the Apaches climbed onto their horses and rode back to their camp, and the soldiers heaved a sigh of relief. Colonel Craig said to Bartlett: "We've avoided war for the time being, but how much longer will your work take?"

"Another two months at least."

"Those Apaches won't let bygones be bygones. I recommend that we leave at once."

"Nonsense," replied Bartlett. "I'm sure we're perfectly safe now that the captive issue has been resolved."

Mangas Coloradas was enraged as he rode at the head of the warriors. *They think they have bought us for a few lengths of bright colored cloth, but this matter is not yet settled. I have seen dishonesty in the eyes of Colonel Craig, as if the war father thought he was a great trickster, but in the end he will trick himself.*

"Delgadito!" shouted Mangas Coloradas.

The sub-chief rode forward. "Sir?"

"I want you to carry a message for me. You will ride to Manuelito of the Navaho people and tell him there are many mules and horses at the copper mines, plus weapons, ammunition, clothes, and other valuable goods. Advise him he will receive a fair share if he comes here and helps us wipe out the White Eyes."

That evening Colonel Craig strolled toward the tent

of John Cremony and found the newspaperman at his desk, writing frantically. "Hope I'm not disturbing you," said Craig. "What are you doing?"

"Putting down my impressions of the meeting this afternoon, but everything happened so quickly, can't remember every word."

Colonel Craig chortled softly. "What you don't remember—make up. Isn't that what journalists usually do?" He snatched the pages off the table and held them to the light. "Just as I thought," he uttered. "You've got it all wrong. It wasn't I who spoke with the Apaches, but Mister Bartlett."

"That's not true, sir. It was you, and everybody heard you."

Colonel Craig appeared surprised. "How can that be, since Bartlett is the Boundary Commissioner? And you should soften the language, because we don't want folks back East to think we threatened the poor dear Injuns, do we?"

"But you said the U.S. would go to war over the captives, sir."

"Perhaps you'd better wash your ears, Mister Cremony. I think you'd better rewrite this. You might even mention that you wrote every word verbatim while the discussions were taking place, to give it the flavor of veracity."

"Sir," protested Cremony, "what you're suggesting sounds like manipulation of facts!"

"I have my recollections," replied the colonel, "you have yours, and my officers will sign any affidavit I place before them. We've narrowly averted a massacre, but we're not out of danger yet. Do as I say, and let me remind you that you too are subject to the Articles of War."

* * *

The camp was on full alert, soldiers lay fully clothed in their tents, and guards patroled the wilderness. Meanwhile, Nathanial sat behind his desk, sipping whiskey and smoking the remainder of his tobacco. The Boundary Commission possessed no cannon, and if the Apaches breached the Army's defense, it would be hand-to-hand and man-to-man, the kind of fight in which savages generally excelled.

Nathanial's detachment had been ordered to guard the horses, so he decided to check the corral. Fortifications were dug across the campsite, and even John Cremony had moved his tent closer to the presidio. Nathanial continued toward the corral and reflected on deteriorating Apache–American relations. It didn't escape his notice that the issue was slavery again. At West Point, while studying the Byzantine Empire, he'd discovered that dark-skinned Arabs had enslaved blond Circassians from Russia. *Why is it some people believe they have the right to own others?* he wondered. "Halt—who goes there!" asked Private Collins, with whom Nathanial had argued earlier in the evening.

Nathanial made sure no one was about, then walked closer, stopping two feet in front of the soldier. "You don't like me, do you, Collins?"

Collins made sure they were alone. "Hate your fucking guts, sir."

"What'd I ever do to you?"

"Hell, I can smell the cheap whiskey all the way over here. You might not believe this, but some of us try to be good soldiers. I wouldn't be surprised if you get us killed someday."

No enlisted man had ever spoken to Nathanial in such devastating terms, but each word Collins said was true. "Don't worry about getting killed," replied the West Pointer. "Just worry about killing Apaches, and if you ever take a shot at me, don't miss—otherwise the next shot will be mine."

ELEVEN

The People moved their camp to a hidden gorge deep in the Santa Rita Mountains. One afternoon, guards reported the approach of the Navahos. Elated, Mangas Coloradas rode forth to meet them.

The People and Navahos had been warring long before the conquistadors arrived, and once had been related. Now they were at peace, for Mangas Coloradas gave one of his daughters in marriage to Manuelito, chief of the Navahos, for just such a contingency.

But deep in his heart, the chief of the Mimbrenos considered the Navahos deviants from the holy lifeway. Influenced by the Pueblo People, Navahos had discarded animal skins for brightly colored cloth they weaved themselves, and they emphasized farming along with traditional hunting.

Mangas Coloradas and Manuelito met in a valley near the new Mimbreno camp. After greetings, compliments, and the passage of gifts, the chiefs sat in the shade of a mesquite tree and discussed their joint venture against the White Eyes.

"They have many horses and mules," explained Mangas Coloradas. "Plus enough powder and lead to last many moons. They are far fewer than we, and I propose that we draw close to them at dawn, kill their sentries, and overwhelm them."

Manuelito, thirty-five years old, believed farming offered the best future for his people, but still raided occasionally. He smiled, then asked, "Why?"

"They have stolen captives without warning, and given presents to dissuade us from wiping them out. But we cannot be bought so cheaply. The time has come to resist."

"Hear me, Father-in-law," replied Manuelito. "For every White Eyes you see, a thousand more are coming. You must beware of provoking them, because they have powerful weapons."

Mangas Coloradas raised his eyebrows. "Are you afraid of them, Manuelito?"

"I hate the White Eyes as do you, Father-in-law. They expect too much for too little, and their arrogance is beyond endurance. But perhaps, with a little patience, we can teach them a lesson they will never forget."

Jocita felt nauseated as she prepared her weapons for a new raid. A certain trader had asked for sheep, and Juh was leading selected Nednais to fetch them. Death often came suddenly to the People, and she'd seen perfectly healthy people fall ill and die in a matter of weeks. Jocita thought her sickness was punishment for her wicked deeds.

The only thing to do was consult Nana, so she crawled outside and headed in the direction of his wickiup. I enjoyed one night of pleasure, she considered, but perhaps I must pay with my life.

Manuelito and Mangas Coloradas lay atop a high escarpment, gazing at the White Eyes camp. Manuelito coveted the livestock, for his tribe was learning to breed animals. But he missed the era when he and his warrior friends had roamed freely, with no blue-coat soldiers breathing down their backs.

"First we'll break into their ammunition stores," declared Mangas Coloradas. "They will not see us until we are in their midst. If we strike hard and fast, we shall prevail."

Manuelito counted cattle, mules, and horses. "Warriors will surely die," he replied. "I would not want it to be my son."

"But *all* the White Eyes will die, and we shall be rid of them. How can I permit them to take captives? They do not respect us, Manuelito."

"There are many ways to fight," declared Manuelito, "and why should children be without fathers? The White Eyes can be punished in an even more painful way."

Mangas Coloradas was confused. "Can you speak more clearly, my son-in-law?"

"What if we did not make war on them, but all those beautiful mules, horses, and cattle began to disappear? If they ask us, we know nothing about it, no? Finally, when they have no more horses, the bluecoat soldiers will leave. We shall beg them to stay, but we cannot force them against their will. If they want horses, we sell them at the same high prices they charge us. There are many ways to achieve your goals, my dear Mangas Coloradas, without spilling blood."

Nana the medicine man, sat on animal skins, as Jocita lay on her back beside him. He examined her eyes, but they weren't yellow around the edges. The color of her skin was good, as was her tongue, and her heart beat strongly.

"You do not appear ill," he replied. "Are you sure you are not imagining this?"

"I vomited this morning, and do not feel well enough to go on a raid. Perhaps someone is putting a curse on me, or I have committed a sin and the mountain spirits are punishing me."

Nana chanted old healing melodies as he created a picture of pain with handfuls of colored sand. He was a man of the world, and figured she might be pregnant, although he couldn't imagine how. But he'd learned never to doubt the chicanery of women, even virtuous ones like Jocita. Then, out of the blue, he asked: "Have you been with Juh lately?"

There was silence, then she replied: "What are you saying?"

"You may need a midwife, not a *di-yin* medicine man, Jocita."

At the Silver Palace Saloon a man in a striped shirt plunked a piano shoved against the wall, while two bartenders poured whiskey behind the bar, and one cook flipped steaks at the chop counter. The air was filled with whiskey, frying beef, fresh-baked bread, tobacco smoke, and murmuring of conversation.

Diego Carbajal stood in the darkness, observing carefully. After weeks of meditation upon his stupidities, he'd decided to return to the world of the living. Maria Dolores had furnished a new home and hadn't reproached him for burning down his old one, but he felt like a fool.

He found a broom and proceeded to sweep the floor. It's the least I can do, he thought, as he pushed a growing mound of dirt and cigarette butts down an aisle. He came to a stain that looked suspiciously like blood, but hoped it had been gravy.

I have been lost in abstractions, decided the Talmudic scholar. If I were truly one of the *Lamed Vav,* I wouldn't worry so much about getting killed. A righteous man would go into the world an set an example of godly behavior.

There is nothing wrong with this filthy job, he tried to convince himself, as his nose wrinkled in distaste at a big wet cigar stub coated with dust and dirt. An honest man must perform useful functions, not sit and have fantasies all day long. So what if I saw Ezekiel riding his *merkabah* chariot? It is more important to love one another, as Hillel the great seer has taught us.

"What do you think you are doing?" asked a sharp voice behind him. His daughter eyed him suspiciously, as though he were a madman, and he figured she was right yet again.

"I am no good at numbers," he replied, "and I am too slow to be a bartender. You already have a cook, so I thought I would keep the place clean."

"You are embarrassing me. Have you taken leave of your senses again?"

"How can honest work embarrass you, and you have seen what happens when I spend too much time alone. I can sweep a floor as well as anyone. No job is dirty if it is honest. I want to help my poor overworked daughter. I am not dead yet."

Her eyes softened. "You may do as you please, Father. What is mine belongs to you too. I just want you to be happy."

After she left, Diego resumed sweeping the floor. He made certain not to trip any drunkards with his broom, and tried to be as unobtrusive as possible. After finishing the floor, he emptied the cuspidors into a wooden bucket and flung the contents into the outhouse. I am raising up the holy sparks, he said to himself, as a terrible odor came to his nostrils. How grandiose were my ambitions, but perhaps I am meant to be a humble sweeper of floors, and in this manner I shall uphold the world.

Life returned to normal at the Santa Rita copper mines. One afternoon, during dinner at the officers' mess, the Southern officers were talking about Cuba. "We ought to go in there with about three regiments and kick the Spaniards out," declared Lieutenant Whipple. "The Spaniards have no business establishing a colony so close to our shores, especially since the Cubans want to be rid of them."

"Sure," replied Lieutenant Medlowe, "and then you could turn it into another slave state, correct?"

"Do you think the North should have a permanent advantage in the Senate?" asked Whipple.

"We don't need more slave states, Lieutenant. We have too many as it is." Lieutenant Medlowe waved his hand dramatically. "Can't you see it's wrong to enslave another man?"

"We have taught *civilization* to the Negro," replied Whipple, "and taken him from the state of pure savagery into which he had fallen. Please don't lecture me on slavery, Lieutenant Medlowe, because it was Yankee ship captains who brought the Nigras to America in the first place. You are to blame as much as we, but you're always pointing the finger and wagging the tongue, like the hypocrites that you are!"

"That's it," declared Nathanial as he rose from his chair. "I am tired of this constant bickering, and hereafter I shall take my meals in my tent. Good afternoon, gentlemen." He bowed ceremoniously, then headed for the door, plate in his right hand.

*   *   *

The Boundary Commission horses slept in the valley, guarded by bluecoat soldiers. One was Private Collins, who rode in a circular motion around the herd, while Private Rittenhouse was coming from the opposite direction.

Collins rode with his pistol in his right hand, cocked and loaded, ready to fire. He was alert, tall in his saddle, a serious soldier, not a drunken rogue. West Point reserved a few appointments for enlisted men, and he determined to secure one of them. Spit and polish at all times, Private Collins volunteered for every detail, worked cheerfully, and because of his own high standards, found it difficult to tolerate officers such as Lieutenant Barrington. The word had filtered down that Barrington disgraced himself at the officers' mess, and it was only a matter of time before Colonel Craig drummed him out of the service.

Collins's eyes raked the chaparral, and it appeared the desert was tranquil, with no Apaches waiting to waylay a disgruntled soldier, but appearances were deceptive. Two Apache warriors were concealed only thirty feet away, watching Private Collins pass.

Juh and Geronimo lay on their bellies, armed with bows and arrows. They waited until the guard was gone, then walked casually toward the herd, speaking softly to the horses, because they didn't want to scare them. They slipped bridles over the heads of two outstanding animals, while stroking their manes soothingly; no White Eyes in sight. They walked the horses onto the range and were concealed behind thick foliage by the time Private Rittenhouse appeared, slouched on his horse, dreaming of life back in Munich.

"You wanted to see me, sir?"

"Yes, come in Major Stewart—I'd like to speak with

you." Colonel Craig leaned back in his chair. "I've been a soldier virtually all my life, and my worst difficulties are generally caused by other officers. What do you propose we do about Lieutenant Barrington?"

"Lock him in the stockade, sir. It's just what he needs."

"His father is a colonel in the War Department."

"Can you send him back to Santa Fe?"

"I couldn't find a replacement in time, and I need every experienced officer I can get. Do you think it would be advisable if I sat him down and talked man to man? Or do you think he's incorrigible?"

Major Stewart appeared skeptical. "Barrington is angry about something, doesn't get along with others, and doesn't try. It might be his natural Yankee arrogance, or maybe the whiskey is affecting his mind."

"He comes from an old Army family, and they say his mother is a saint. Well, I guess it won't hurt to try. Tell him I want to speak with him, will you?"

In the camp of Mangas Coloradas, a stolen Boundary Commission mule roasted over a spit. Mule meat was the People's favorite delicacy, and tonight they could gorge their bellies. Juh sliced off a strip of thigh, carried it to his mouth, and chewed contentedly.

"Juh, may I speak with you?" His first wife stood behind him.

"Of course you may speak with me, Jocita. What is wrong?"

She dropped to her knees beside him. "You are going to be very angry, I am afraid. Perhaps we should be alone."

"How can I be angry with my lovely wife? Tell me what is bothering you, and I will help."

She bowed her head and closed her eyes. "I am pregnant, my husband."

Juh's eyes became saucers. "But how can that be?"

"I have been to a midwife. There is no doubt."

The semiforgotten nightmare returned to the Nednai sub-chief. "What will people say?" he asked.

"They will say it is yours, of course."

"But it isn't mine. You and I have not—"

"No one knows, my dear husband," she interrupted. "You are going to be a father again—isn't that wonderful?"

At four o'clock in the morning, Diego Carbajal made his way home from the Silver Palace Saloon. I imagined glorious destinies for myself, he thought with a smile, I wanted to be a great caudillo, and even believed I was one of the sainted *Lamed Vav*, but I am merely a sweeper of floors. Yet even a sweeper of floors can lead the way to righteousness, and not even kings and presidents are guaranteed entrance to Heaven. There is the potential for goodness in everybody, and we must search for the holy sparks.

He faltered, as mild holy ecstasies came over him. Then, as if to answer his question, two dark figures emerged from a nearby alley. They aimed guns at Diego, and evil glints appeared in their eyes. "Put up yer hands," said the one on the left, with a face like a weasel.

Diego raised his arms, wondering if he were hallucinating. The other robber, who resembled a duck, searched his pockets. Diego smiled beatifically as the robber removed twenty dollars and change from his pockets, then stole his watch and chain.

" 'At's all he's got," said the duck.

The weasel aimed his gun between Diego's eyes and

squeezed the trigger. Diego continued to smile as he said, "May the Lord have mercy on your soul."

The weasel faltered, his finger loosened on the trigger, and for reasons not clear to him, felt afraid. "Mister," he said, "I'll let you go this time, but you call the sheriff on us, I'll hunt you down and blow your head off."

"I shall not judge you," replied Diego. "There is a higher law than mine."

"This old greaser's loco," said the weasel. "Let's get the hell out've here."

The thieves fled toward the alley, then Diego lowered his hands, his pockets empty, his heirloom gold watch gone, and he remembered the expression in the weasel's eyes. He was going to kill me, Diego acknowledged, but something stopped him, and it could only be the will of the Almighty. But why would His Holy Name spare my miserable and worthless life?

Can it be that I truly am one of the *Lamed Vav*?

TWELVE

On July 6, 1851, Colonel Craig sat behind his desk, reading the morning report. Five mules and eight horses had vanished during the night, adding to a growing total of mysteriously missing livestock, evidently stolen by Apaches.

The animals needed a large area for grazing, and Apaches were wily adversaries no matter how many guards were posted. It bothered Colonel Craig to know that ignorant Indians were out-foxing him. How long can the Boundary Commission keep on, if Apaches continue stealing livestock? he wondered. Will we have to leave with our tails between our legs, because we don't have horses?

Apaches were waging silent but effective war against him, and he couldn't do a damned thing about it. It'll take twenty thousand soldiers to restore order to this area, but where'll they come from?

Lieutenant Barrington appeared, saluted smartly, and said, "You wanted to see me, sir."

"Have a seat, Barrington." The colonel leaned back in his chair, gazed at Nathanial a few moments, then said, "If I didn't know any better, I'd think you were trying to ruin your reputation. I met your father in Washington years ago, but I simply cannot continue to look the other way regarding your shenanigans.

You've managed to alienate most of the officers, you've been drinking excessively, and it's as if you're losing control. I was wondering if there was anything I can do as your commanding officer?"

Nathanial tried to smile. "I'm not cut out for military life, sir, and I'm resigning when I return to Santa Fe."

Colonel Craig shook his head sadly. "The Army needs seasoned officers, but you're a very troubled man. What's wrong with you, or don't you know?"

"The government lacks the will to deal with Apaches, the Army is full of fools and incompetents, present company excluded of course, and I've had it up to here."

A shot rang out, and both men reached for their service revolvers. Colonel Craig looked out the window, but didn't see a horde of Apaches descending upon the presidio. "Perhaps one of the soldiers has discharged his rifle by mistake," speculated the colonel as he returned to his desk. "It's one thing to resign your commission, but quite another to be drummed out of the Army. That's what I'll have to do if you continue drinking on duty, Lieutenant Barrington. Don't force me to take action both of us would regret."

Suddenly the door was flung open, revealing agitated Sergeant Barnes. "One of the traders has shot an Apache!"

Colonel Craig rushed outside, followed by Nathanial. They ran toward the traders' wagons, where a crowd of soldiers and Apaches had gathered, everyone looking at one another suspiciously. In their midst, lying on the ground, was an Apache with a bullet hole in the middle of his chest, while nearby a Mexican trader's arms were held by two soldiers.

Major Stewart was the ranking officer on the scene. "It appears that the Mexican has shot this Apache whom he claims was trying to steal a bottle of whiskey."

The Apaches appeared ready for war, but Colonel's Craig's men outnumbered them in the immediate vicinity. He raised empty hands to the Apaches. "First, we must be calm."

The sub-chief Coleto Amarillo replied angrily and Cremony translated broken Spanish to newspaper English. "That Mexican has killed our brother, and you must give him to us."

"I am bound by the laws of my country," replied Colonel Craig, "and the murderer shall receive a fair trial."

"A trial for what purpose?" replied Coleto Amarillo. "We have all seen him kill this warrior."

"That is for a judge to decide, but I promise the trial will be fair."

Coleto Amarillo saw himself surrounded by soldiers, so he replied, "I must tell Mangas Coloradas, and he will decide what do."

The Apaches carried their fallen comrade to his horse and tied him head down over the animal's back. "This matter is not yet settled!" shouted Coleto Amarillo as he climbed onto his war pony. The other Apaches followed him away from the copper mines, and Colonel Craig knew he had a crisis far worse than two escaped slave boys. He turned toward the trader who'd shot the Apache. "What's your side?"

"He was trying to steal from me. What should I do—let him walk away with free whiskey?"

"You should have called one of the soldiers."

"By the time the Army did something, the Apache

would have been gone. Do I have a right to defend my property?"

"Lock him in the stockade," said Colonel Craig. "Sergeant Barnes, there will be a meeting of all officers in my headquarters in fifteen minutes. Let's move, gentlemen, because it looks like we're headed for another showdown with the Apaches."

Mangas Coloradas wore the head and hide of a deer as he crept toward two bucks grazing a short distance away. He was upwind of them, working closer through slow painstaking tactics, anticipating roast venison that evening, second favorite delicacy of the People.

The deer were only twenty paces away. Mangas Coloradas aimed his arrow, drew back the string, and suddenly the animals jerked their heads, ears pointing up. Mangas Coloradas let fly, just as the bucks leapt away. The arrow intended for the throat of the biggest, landed in his haunch. The creature bellowed painfully, as he ran erratically into thicker chaparral.

Mangas Coloradas wondered what warned the deer. He cursed his luck, when he heard faint, rumbling hoofbeats. Glancing backward, he saw warriors galloping toward him.

He removed the deer head, then slipped from beneath the buckskin. The warriors drew closer, their horses frothing and hides covered with sweat. Delgadito jumped down and walked swiftly toward Mangas Coloradas. "At the copper mines," he said gravely, "one of the traders has shot Largo. He said Largo was stealing whiskey, but it is a lie—the trader was trying to cheat Largo. The white father will not give us the Mexican trader to punish."

Mangas Coloradas set his lips in a cruel line. "We have tolerated enough insults from the bluecoat soldiers. This time they will accede to our wishes, or we shall fill the copper mines with their blood."

"If I know Apaches," said Colonel Craig, "they'll attack at dawn. We won't hear anything, and they'll be all over us. So keep your eyes open, and make sure your men are on their toes. I want every soldier in position two hours before dawn. If we kill enough of them, I think we can stop them."

There was a knock on the door, then Sergeant Barnes stuck his head inside the office. "Sir—Apaches headed this way, about three hundred of 'em, with Mangas Coloradas himself!"

"Pass the word along," replied Colonel Craig, "and don't fire unless they fire first. Perhaps this matter can be resolved peacefully."

Colonel Craig headed for the door, then his officers followed him out the orderly room. Two columns of Apaches approached from the west, Mangas Coloradas leading. It didn't look like a war party, but Colonel Craig wasn't sure. "Stay ready, men," he said. "Don't fire unless I give the command."

The Apaches wore no warpaint, but all were armed as they rode into camp. Mangas Coloradas appeared unusually grave as he stopped in front of the presidio. He climbed down from his saddle, advanced toward Colonel Craig, and distrusted the friendly smile plastered on the officer's face.

"My dear friend Mangas Coloradas," said Colonel Craig. "Please accept my apologies for what has happened. I deeply regret the death of your warrior."

"You claim to be our friend," replied Mangas Coloradas coldly, "but we demand to see the killer punished. Then we will be satisfied."

"The murderer must be turned over to my government for trial," replied Colonel Craig. "We can put him to work meanwhile, and everything he earns—blankets, corn, or money—we shall give to the family of the victim."

Mangas Coloradas became furious. "Do you think blankets or corn equal the life of a warrior? Would money pay you for the loss of your child? The mother of this warrior requires the death of his killer, and nothing else is just."

Colonel Craig found it difficult to counter the logic of Mangas Coloradas. "You're right—no money can buy the life of a loved one, but who will hunt for that mother now? Is it not better to give her food and bolts of cloth, that she can care for herself?"

"If an Apache had killed an American, he would be dead by now."

Colonel Craig couldn't turn a Mexican over to Apaches so they could cut him into pieces and feed him to the dogs. "The guilty will be punished," he said firmly. "Did not a band of Apaches attack a party of Americans recently on the road to Janos? Did they not kill one of them and wound three others with their arrows? And did they not take all their property? The Apaches did not even bury their victim, but left him lying by the road, food for crows and lobos. Why do we not seek revenge? Because the murder was committed by your bad men, not you. Have you ever punished them? Meanwhile, others of your people steal our livestock, and have you turned the thieves over to us? If you interfere with American justice and continue to steal livestock, we cannot be friends anymore. Thousands of bluecoat soldiers will take possession of your lands, they will kill every Apache warrior, and take your women and children captives."

Mangas Coloradas tried to be brave, but knew Colonel Craig had spoken the truth. "I will hold council, then return with my answer."

The people rode back to their encampment, and a meeting was held in front of Mangas Coloradas's wickiup. The chief listened to varying arguments, while the mother of the victim wailed at the periphery, reminding them of the crime. One faction demanded immediate reprisal, some desired peace at any price, and a few appeared baffled by the shouting and confusion.

Finally Mangas Coloradas rendered his verdict. "It is time to draw the line against the Whites Eyes. First they have stolen our captives, and now they shoot us. We shall take the prisoner by force, and let the bluecoats fight us if they dare."

There was silence, and several warriors felt afraid. If Mangas Coloradas, a voice for peace, wanted war, it surely would come.

Juh rose to his feet and declaimed: "I cheer the decision of the great chief. There must be war, and if you say there will be dead warriors, well—there are dead warriors now. In the old time, some cautioned against fighting the Mexicans, but we have pushed them out of our homeland. So shall we do with the White Eyes."

Scatterings of warriors applauded the outspoken Nednai sub-chief, and among his admirers was Lucero of the Mimbrenos. "The White Eyes are huddled like sheep," he said. "It is time to show whose laws have prominence in this land."

Lucero's statement was greeted warmly, and the war party gained adherents. Then Ponce arose and said, "They behave as if they own the land, but they have not paid for it, and neither have they won it in lawful war. They will take your wife, children, land, and horses, but still not be satisfied. Sometimes I think they want our very souls."

Manuelito, chief of the Navahos, watched them work themselves to fever pitch. He was an outsider, his motives questionable, but he saw catastrophe looming for the Apaches. Finally, he raised his hand. "My friends—may I speak?"

They looked at the slim, loose-limbed chief as he arose in their midst. "My people have had many dealings with the White Eyes," he began, "and the more we killed them, the more they came." The young chief raised his finger in the air. "But if their livestock continues to disappear, they will leave on their own. This unholy crime shall never be forgiven, but the White Eyes can pay in other ways."

Two days passed, soldiers remained on alert, and the threat of Apache attack was imminent, Nathanial had stopped drinking. He suffered headaches and occasionally shook uncontrollably, but supervised his men closely, and spent much time with his spyglass glued to his eye, which didn't help his headache. He was forced to ease the pain with laudanum, which produced its own drawbacks, such as hallucinations.

One morning, sitting in front of his tent and scanning terrain through his spyglass, he heard someone shout: "Apaches!" Sergeant Duffy pointed to the foothills of the mountains, where two columns of Indians advanced, Mangas Coloradas in front. It appeared the Apaches wanted to talk, but Nathanial held his hand near his pistol.

Colonel Craig, surrounded by his staff, aides, and guards spilled out of the presidio. The Apaches were heavily armed, and a few young bucks looked ready to lance somebody. Poppy juice invaded Nathanial's brain, and he felt like laughing at the absurdity of the confrontation. There's plenty of land for everybody, he reasoned. What are we fighting about?

Colonel Craig stepped forward to meet Mangas Coloradas. "My brother, I am happy to see you. What have you decided?"

"We have decided peace," said Mangas Coloradas. "If you give me your word that justice will be done."

Colonel Craig raised his right hand in the air. "You have my word."

"I don't believe you, thought Mangas Coloradas, but he smiled and shook the colonel's hand.

"This is great moment!" declared Colonel Craig. "We have proven that peace can be won if sensible heads prevail!"

Your livestock will not prevail, reflected Mangas Coloradas wryly. "We promise to be friends, but a mother is wailing in her wickiup tonight, with no one to bring her meat."

"Take two head of cattle, and I shall give her all the Mexican's money, goods, and other belongings. We Americans want to be fair, but we insist that justice be done."

"Yes—your justice, not ours."

"If the murderer is punished, what does it matter?" asked Colonel Craig. "Come, sit and smoke with me."

Mangas Coloradas waved his hand from side to side. "No more smokes," he said. "Now is for mourning."

Mules dragged the trader's wagon toward the Apaches, cattle were brought, and the formal exchange took place. Then Mangas Coloradas climbed onto his war pony and rode proudly out of the camp, followed by his warriors, the wagons of goods, and

two steers. This matter is not yet ended, thought
Chief Mangas Coloradas. I shall defeat you the Navaho way.

Peace came to the Santa Rita copper mines, on the
surface. The Apaches stopped visiting the Army camp,
and the Boundary Commission continued its work.
Livestock was reported missing nearly every day, and
John R. Bartlett was forced to pay high prices for
replacements. Sometimes he suspected he was buying
the same animals over and over again.

Meanwhile, the Department of the Interior complained about his expenses, and Bartlett passed much
time arguing with Army surveyors who accused him
of ceding too much territory to Mexico. Often he regretted leaving his erudite little store in the Astor
Hotel.

One morning he was handed a report concerning
ten mules disappeared during the night. It was the
final straw. He stormed across the encampment,
barged into Colonel Craig's office, and yelled: "The
Commission can no longer perform its duties because
you are unable to protect my livestock! I don't have
enough mules to pull my wagons—don't you
understand?"

Colonel Craig made a mock serious face. "You
don't think the dear Apaches have *stolen* them, do
you?"

"What are you going to do?"

"I don't have enough men to guard every mule and
steer, and we don't know where the Apaches moved
their camp. It would be nice if you used your influence
in Washington to get us reinforcements."

"I have *no* influence in Washington, and in fact
may lose my job any day. Colonel Craig, this expedi-

tion is rapidly becoming a costly and embarrassing debacle."

"We'll commence a search," replied Colonel Craig, "but I imagine your mules are in another territory by now. As far as I'm concerned, this Commission was a harebrained idea to begin with, and I have no idea why the Apaches haven't massacred us long ago. Be on your guard, Mister Bartlett, and maybe you'd better move inside the presidio."

Nathanial sat in his tent, working through the mound of papers in front of him. As detachment commander, he had to file reports and requisitions, plus maintain careful records. He was writing a report on a broken wagon when suddenly he caught a clear image of himself bent over his desk, tongue sticking out the corner of his mouth.

At my age, Napoleon had conquered Italy, Egypt, and Turkey, while I command forty men in this godforsaken New Mexico Territory, he evaluated. I dreamed of becoming a famous general, but instead remain in constant difficulty with commanding officers, and the men dislike me because I'm a drunkard.

Occasionally the craving came on him so viciously, he wanted to run to the traders. I'm leaving the Army, so what does it matter? he asked himself. He looked in the mirror, and his face had taken on a sickly green hue. Sometimes he experienced double vision, and occasionally terrible fatigue came over him.

Sergeant Duffy came to a stop in front of the tent. "The old man wants to see you, sir. It's important."

Nathanial pulled on his hat and ran across the clearing. His heart chugged, he thought he'd faint, but finally entered Colonel Craig's office, pleased to note

he was the first officer to arrive, except for Major
Stewart, the executive officer.

Then other officers crowded into the room, and
Lieutenant Whipple shot a disdainful expression at
Nathanial. When all were present, Colonel Craig
began his presentation. "We lost ten more mules last
night, and the time has come to show the Apaches
they can't continue to steal from us with impunity.
Half our escort will defend the camp, while the other
half will commence a hunt for missing Army
livestock."

Colonel Craig pointed to the map and described
where the search parties would go. Nathanial discovered he was headed for the mostly uncharted mountains west of the copper mines. "Any questions?"
asked Colonel Craig.

Nathanial wanted to keep his mouth shut, but the
plan seemed ludicrous at best. "Sir, it'll be awful easy
for Apaches to cut off those detachments. I don't
think it wise to antagonize Indians in an area where
we're outnumbered by such a large margin."

Colonel Craig stared at him. "*You* don't think it's
wise, Lieutenant Barrington? Would you rather let the
Apaches steal our livestock, while we twiddle our
thumbs? The detachment commanders may leave
when their men are ready, but I expect all of you
gone by noon tomorrow. I'm not sending you to be
slaughtered, as Lieutenant Barrington has so cleverly
suggested, but we must be firm with these damned
Apaches, otherwise they'll steal our eyeballs right out
of our heads."

Nathanial found Sergeant Duffy at the corral, super-
vising shoeing of a horse. "We're going on a scout,"
said the detachment commander in a loud voice, so

all could hear. "I want to travel light, so no wagons or tents. We'll live off the land, like the Apaches."

"No tents, sir?" asked Sergeant Duffy. "What if it rains?"

"You're not afraid of a little water, are you, Sergeant Duffy?"

Nathanial packed saddlebags, then thought of writing to his wife, but time wasn't sufficient for the deeper sentiments he wished to convey. Instead, he sat at his desk and worked on official correspondence, trying to get as much out of the way as possible. The odds were he wouldn't find Apaches, but detachments had been attacked before.

Next morning, after breakfast, Nathanial threw saddlebags over his shoulder, then put on his wide-brimmed silverbelly hat. The men had formed in two ranks before his tent, and Private Rittenhouse held Nathanial's new horse, an army nag renamed Duke III. Nathanial lay his saddlebags over Duke III's haunches, then climbed into the saddle. "Move 'em out," he said to Sergeant Duffy.

Nathanial rode to the head of the column, where he joined his scout, Donald Pennington. "Take the point!" ordered Nathanial.

The former Texas Ranger spurred his horse, who proceeded to trot onto the open range. Nathanial's horse followed at a steady walk, with Sergeant Duffy and the rest of the detachment behind, the guidon flag fluttering in the breeze. *Wouldn't it be a hoot if I were killed while waiting to resign my commission?* wondered Nathanial.

A skinned, gutted, and beheaded mule roasted over hot coals, its delicious fragrance filling the air. Delgadito watched his two wives turn the spit, his stomach yawning in hunger. He and Coletto Armarillo had stolen ten mules from the Boundary Commission, and they were giving the clan a feast.

Delgadito had moved his warriors and their families to a crook in the Mimbres River, site of much game, and here intended to spend the rest of the summer. The other mules were on their way to the Commancheros, to be traded for ammunition, whiskey, cloth, trinkets, and blankets.

Why travel to Mexico when there's merchandise at the Santa Rita copper mines? figured Delgadito. He saw no great difference between the White Eyes and the Mexicans, and it irked him that the White Eyes believed their so-called laws superseded those of the People.

The White Eyes had better stay away from me, he decided, because I am not as gentle as Mangas Coloradas. The only way to keep this land sacred is to drive back intruders wherever they are found.

Three days later, Nathanial lay on his belly and examined through his spyglass a trading post consisting of three interlinked log cabins, no Indians in the vicinity, a few horses and mules tied to the rail. "Let's buy some flour," he said to Sergeant Duffy, "and maybe they've got vegetables, but tell the men to keep their eyes open."

Nathanial and his detachment rode down the incline toward the trading post. Pennington had reported smoke that morning, and Nathanial assumed the Apaches had burned something down, but evidently the trading post was useful in dealing stolen goods.

Whatever happens—I'm not buying whiskey, Nathanial ordered himself. Only a complete derelict would get drunk in the middle of the Apache home-

WAR EAGLES

23

about now. Four mules and four horses loafed at the
rail before the ramshackle, rough-hewn trading post.
Nathanial climbed down from the saddle and in-
spected them, but spotted no army brands. While returning to his horse, the front door opened and a stout
miner with a black spade beard minus a mustache appeared. "Somethin' wrong, soldier?" he asked in a
cocky, insinuating tone.

Nathanial smiled and said, "Just looking for stolen
mules, but these have never been in the Army."

"I paid fer 'em in real American money. You
know—you've got a lot of nerve, lookin' over my
property that way."

Nathanial maintained his false grin. "Just doing my
job, sir. Meant no offense. Sergeant Duffy—direct the
men to dismount, and then I'd like you to accompany
me inside. When we're finished, the men can buy
whatever they need."

Nathanial tied his horse to the rail as blackbeard
returned to the trading post. Sergeant Duffy slapped
alkali out of his vaquero hat. "I'm ready, sir."

"Watch my back, and I'll watch yours."

Nathanial entered a low-ceilinged, murky room with
four unpainted tables and chairs. On shelves were
bolts of cloth, bottles of whiskey, cans of beans, bags
of flour, sugar, and coffee beans. Four men stood in
front of the counter as two worked behind it. "Can I
help you sir?" asked one of the latter, fortyish, with
a salt-and-pepper mustache.

"Ten pounds of coffee," said Nathanial, "Five
pounds of sugar, and twenty pounds of flour, if you
don't mind."

"Yes, sir."

The storekeeper made a move, when the customer

with the black beard banged his fist on the counter. "What the hell's goin' on hyar?" he demanded. "We were afore that officer!"

The storekeeper smiled. "We don't like to delay the Army, because where would we be without them?"

"The damned Army makes more trouble than it's worth, seems to me."

Nathanial tried to grin. 'We're in no hurry, sir. Take care of this customer, since he was first."

"It's going to be a while," said the shopkeeper. "These miners are a-gonna be out thar fer quite a spell."

"We're in no hurry," replied Nathanial as he dropped to a seat at a nearby table.

Sergeant Duffy sat opposite him, looked around warily, and said in a low voice, "I'd hate to git caught inside this place, sir."

"While we're waiting, you don't think we should order whiskey, do you?"

"No, sir."

Meanwhile, at the counter, blackbeard mumbled loudly. "Soldiers ride this territory as if it's theirs, and everybody's got to git out of their way. They're all scared of Apaches, but that don't mean they don't live high off the hog. They wear their fancy pants, and think they're better'n everybody else."

Sergeant Duffy couldn't let that one pass. "Where in the hell would miners be without the Army?" he asked in his rolling brogue. "Yer damned bones'd be a-bleachin' in the sun, but at least we wouldn't have to listen to yer flappin' lips no more!"

No one moved inside the trading post as a gust of wind blew across shake shingles. Then blackbeard laughed too loud, hitched his thumbs in his greasy suspenders, and said, "Did you hear that, boys? Ain't that how it is—a bunch of ignorant immigrants are runnin' around tellin' native born Americans how to live? And the funny part is we're a-payin' their salaries!"

"And a bargain yer gittin'," replied Duffy. "Every civilian with a few cents in his pocket thinks he owns the Army. If it weren't fer the Army, you probably would've been skinned alive long ago, and I think it'd be the best thing that ever happened to you."

It became silent again in the trading post, and an frown came over blackbeard's face. "I don't give a damn what uniform yer wearin', friend. Nobody talks to Jasper Wheatly that way."

He walked toward the table as Nathanial rose with Sergeant Duffy. "Now hold on," cautioned Nathanial, trying to be conciliatory. "We don't want trouble."

"Siddown, fancypants," replied Wheatly. "I'll take care of you later."

Sergeant Duffy and Jasper Wheatly were on a collision course, and Nathanial felt it incumbent upon him, as the government's duly appointed official in the trading post, to get in the middle and separate the combatants. "No fighting," he said. "It's against the law."

The miner slapped Nathanial's arm out of the way. "Who the fuck're you talkin' to?"

"Sir," interjected Sergeant Duffy, "it's my fight, if you don't mind."

"Stay out of this," ordered Nathanial. "It's an Army matter now."

Wheatly appeared incredulous as he stared down his nose at Nathanial. "That son-of-a-bitch Irishman insulted me, and if I have to whup yer ass to reach him, that's okay by me."

"You'd better settle down," said Nathanial firmly, "or I shall arrest you."

The miner couldn't believe his ears. "You shall arrest me?" he replied, mimicking Nathanial's West Point intonation. "You think you're man enough?"

"I told you before—I'm not looking for trouble. We're here on government business."

"People like you don't work, so you jine the Army."

"I've wasted enough government time with you." Nathanial turned toward the counter. "We'll take our order first."

Wheatly grabbed his shoulder, spinning him around. "Yer gonna wait yer turn like everybody else!"

"Take your hand off me," said Nathanial icily.

"Make me," replied the miner.

Nathanial brought one up from the floor, and it was zooming toward Wheatly's head before the latter could get out of the way. It connected with a solid *thunk,* and Wheatly went sprawling backward. No one had the presence of mind to stop him as he backpedaled across the floor, crashed through the window, and landed in a trough of water outside.

The soldiers in the yard had been smoking and relaxing as the body hurtled into their midst. They reached for their pistols, and a moment later the door opened. Nathanial dragged the miner out of the trough, because he didn't want a drowned civilian on his hands.

"What're you gonna do with 'im?" asked Sergeant Duffy.

"Leave him here, I suppose."

"I think you done broke his jaw."

"I'll break his head if he ever talks to me like that again." Nathanial took the miner's guns and knives, carried them into the trading post, and dropped them onto the counter. "Give them back after we're out of here."

"Yes, sir," said the clerk. "I'll have your order fixed in a few minutes, sir."

Nathanial turned to the other three miners. "How're we doing today, boys?"

"Jest fine," said one, removing his hat. "We ain't lookin' fer trubble are we, Jethro?"

"Hell no."

José, the former captive boy, was brought to Fronteras, where the *alcalde* adopted him. Everyone told José how fortunate he was to live with such a notable man.

But Jose didn't like Fronteras, and school bored him to the point of headaches. No longer could he hunt with friends, or run wild as young deer over the desert. José thought Fronteras stank, and the other boys made fun of him while Elena, daughter of the *alcalde,* teased him. Often José found himself missing the People.

I don't like *Nakai-yes* food, thought José one evening as he sat to dinner with his new family. The portly *alcalde* was positioned at one end of the table, his obese wife at the other, with Elena opposite José. A maid brought a platter covered with roasted pig, but the People had taught that pigs were unclean, since they ate snakes.

José craved mule meat, but Mexicans didn't appreciate that great delicacy. The former child of the People looked out the window at mountains in the distance, and his eyes filled with tears. I loved the People, he realized. But I don't like Mexicans.

"Are you all right, José?" asked the *alcalde.*

"I'm fine, sir."

"Poor boy," said the *alcalde's* wife, genuine compassion in her voice. "Life with Apaches must've been horrible." She squeezed his hand warmly. "You're safe now. We'll never let the savages harm you again."

Her cheeks were puffy, her fingers like sausages, and she had drenched herself with vile perfume. José couldn't help remembering Jocita's strong body hugging him. Jocita didn't stuff her mouth with candy all day long and sprinkle herself with stinky substances.

"Can't you say anything, José?" asked the *alcalde* gently.

"I was just thinking about something," the boy replied.

"You've had terrible experiences, but they are over," counseled the *alcalde*. "And it is never too early to prepare for your future. Perhaps someday you'll own a store, and you might even become *alcalde* yourself. Forget the past, because a bright new future lies ahead. You can do anything you want if you put your mind to it."

Two suns later, a herd of cattle stolen by Nednais grazed at the edge of Delgadito's camp. Juh, leader of the raid, sat with Delgadito at the latter's wickiup, smoked, and laughed at the foolishness of the White Eyes.

"The White Eyes are confused," said Juh delightedly. "No matter how many guards they post, their livestock continues to fly away. They hold meetings and walk around with worried faces. They know it is us, but cannot prove it. Soon we shall have every animal they own."

"There is a camp of diggers not far from here,"

replied Delgadito, "and they have a big herd of cattle. Perhaps, after you dispose of what you have, you and your warriors can join me in capturing them."

Juh spat at the ground. "The only thing worse than White Eyes soldiers are White Eyes diggers. We shall be pleased to help our Mimbreno brothers."

Delgadito's sharp eyes picked out a rider galloping toward the encampment. "Bluecoat soldiers!" hollered the rider, pointing behind him. "About forty headed in this direction! They are following the cattle tracks and should arrive at midafternoon!"

Juh snorted. "Shouldn't we bloody their noses?"

"If we do, the diggers will hear of it and maybe remove their cattle. No, move your property away, then come back later."

"What if they attack you?"

"If they see no cattle, why should they attack me? I am a good law-abiding Indian brother, no?"

The Nednais herded their cattle away from the encampment, while Delgadito sat in front of his wickiup and waited for the White Eyes to arrive. Meanwhile, the People went about their usual business so as not to appear suspicious to the bluecoat soldiers. Then the soldiers appeared on the horizon, and it wasn't long before they were riding into the camp. Delgadito arose in front of his wickiup. "Let us have sport with them," he said.

Warriors, maidens, and children made way as the bluecoat soldiers rode toward Delgadito's wickiup, led by a tall officer with a sunny beard. The bluecoat war chief raised his arm, and the soldiers came to a halt behind him. Sunny Beard climbed down from his horse, walked toward Delgadito, and said in Spanish: "Are you in charge here?"

"I am," replied Delgadito, raising his chin, looking Sunny Beard in the eyes. "What do you want?"

"I am Lieutenant Nathanial Barrington, and we've tracked cattle into this camp. Where are they?"

Delgadito blinked in mock confusion. "I have seen no cattle. We are not ranchers."

"The tracks lead to this village, according to my scout," replied Nathanial.

"Perhaps he does not know a horse from a cow."

"If we determine you had anything to do with them, we'll be back."

"We are always happy to see the White Eyes," replied Delgadito with an eerie frozen smile.

"Sergeant Duffy—move the men through the village, and Pennington—see if you can pick up the cattle trail."

The bluecoat soldiers moved forward in a clatter of hooves and jangling equipment. They tried to sit proudly in their saddles, although weary, sun-beaten, their uniforms raggedy. Even the old women shot contemptuous glances.

The tense moment passed as the bluecoat soldiers roved onto the open land. The prominent warrior Lucero happened to be in camp that day, and he sidled next to Delgadito. "It would be easy to ambush them in the broken canyon country. You and I together, Delgadito—what do you say?"

"It is tempting, but I must respect the judgment of Mangas Coloradas," replied Delgadito. "We must not provoke the bluecoat soldiers . . . yet."

It was three o'clock in the morning, and all was still in Fronteras. José climbed silently out of bed, looked out the window, and opened the door to his closet. On the floor in back were his moccasin boots, with his breechclout stuck into one of them, and his red headband in the other.

He took off his nightshirt, put on his breechclout and moccasin boots, tied the bandana around his head, and looked at himself in the mirror. A child of the People gazed back at him. In the bottom drawer lay his old Apache knife, which he jammed into his belt.

He opened the door and looked into the hall. The *alcalde* and his wife snored, and little Elena was fast asleep. José crept silently to the back door, paused, and wondered whether he'd survive bears, rattlesnakes, wild dogs, killer cats, and poisonous lizards. If apprehended by enemies, he could be made a slave or killed on the spot.

José slipped out the door and headed for the edge of town. In an alley a sleeping drunkard stirred as the boy leapt over him, but when the drunkard opened his eyes, José was gone. He paused in the shadows of the stable, waiting silently for the sentry to pass. The sentry looked straight at him, but saw nothing except murky darkness. The sentry turned the corner, and the boy got down on his belly. He crawled slowly and silently toward the open land, hoping no one looked out the window at that moment, otherwise he might receive buckshot in the back.

José blended with night hues as he reached the first clump of cactus. He took one last look at the evil town, then began his long dangerous trek back to the Mimbreno homeland.

"Looks like they split the cattle three ways," said Pennington. "Take a look fer yerself, sir."

Nathanial perched on his hands and knees and tried to make sense of random impressions on the ground.

Sergeant Duffy asked impatiently. "What're you gonter do, sir?"

"What do you recommend, Sergeant?"

"I think we orter attack that village back there. You can see the cattle went right through."

"In the absence of hard evidence, I don't see how we can attack peaceful Indians," replied Lieutenant Barrington. "No, we're going to follow one of these trails and see where it leads. I have a feeling they meet again farther down the line. Move the men out in a column of twos, please."

"Sir—don't you think the men could use a rest?"

"They can rest when we return to the copper mines, but we'll never catch the Apaches unless we move as fast as they. You've received your orders, Sergeant."

Seven suns later, Delgadito and his warriors were leaving to harvest the miners' cattle they'd been observing for the past moon. Women, children, and aged warriors cheered their passage onto the naked desert. Juh took his position beside Delgadito, with young Geronimo, Lucero, and Jocita back among the other warriors. They were thirty in all, and even old Taza was there, for it appeared an easy raid.

Taza wanted to obtain cattle, but if he found an opportunity, hoped to murder the warrior woman in a manner where blame would reside with the White Eyes. You have cheated me, but Taza will not be denied vengeance, he told himself.

Old Taza felt tired although the raid had only begun. But many outstanding warriors would be his eyes and ears, and naturally he'd demand his fair share when the time came to divide stolen cattle. He also was in the market for one good slave, a girl this time, and maybe, when she grew older, Taza might marry her. I am not too old to have fun, thought old Taza as he looked at the back of the warrior woman. And neither am I too old to kill my enemies.

The jackrabbit's ears were pointed in the air, alert for dangerous sounds. When satisfied he was alone, he looked at pinyon nuts scattered on the ground. He'd never seen them strewn quite that way before, but his appetite got the better of him.

He inched closer, sniffing the ground systematically. No strange smells, configurations, or shadows hinted danger. He glanced up, but no hawk swooped toward him, claws outstretched. Neither were owls perched in trees, watching his every move. The pinyon nuts gave off faint tantalizing fragrance as he hopped closer. He could fill his belly quickly, a rare happenstance for a jackrabbit.

He came to the nuts, sniffed, lowered his head, and sank his teeth into the biggest nut. It's oils and juices exploded in his mouth, and he was munching happily when suddenly something pulled his leg! He screamed and struggled to break away, but then a knife cut his throat; he went limp on the ground.

José examined him with the eyes of a rabbit connoisseur, then sucked nutritious blood out of the rabbit's arteries. He lay the rabbit on the ground and skinned him with deft strokes of his knife. When the rabbit was pink, José sliced off a piece of thigh, placed it in his mouth, and chewed. He couldn't risk a fire, not even with wood that didn't smoke. He lay strips of meat on a rock, to dry them in the sun, and then dug a hole with a branch, for sips of water through a reed.

After his meal, he dropped the strips of semidry

meat into his pouch, and resumed his trek toward the Santa Rita Mountains.

"I hate to say it, sir, but . . ."

"They've divided again?" asked Nathanial.

"Looks that way."

Nathanial took off his hat and wiped his forehead with the back of his arm. It was early afternoon, hottest time of the day, and he was surrounded by mountains pulsating red, orange, and yellow, while the heady fragrance of greasewood filled the air. Lizards no wider than pencils scurried along the foliage; the desert seemed alive with them. "Well follow the trail to the right, Sergeant."

Sergeant Duffy's mustaches twitched with barely suppressed rage. "Why not the trail to the left, sir? I mean—what the hell does it matter what trail you take? We're just a-wastin' time no matter how you cut it, and I think you don't have a goddamned brain in yer head! The only way to teach 'em a lesson is burn down their camp!"

The mining camp employed modern techniques, with a sluice gate instead of men panning individually for gold. One crew shoveled dirt into the fast-moving water, while another searched for gold nuggets in the basket at the end. They hadn't found much ore, but with the optimism common to their breed, expected to be rich within a year.

They labored assiduously, and their herd grazed peacefully on the nearby meadow. Majestic blue mountains thrust toward the sky, the scene pastoral and bucolic, when an Apache head appeared from behind a rock outcropping in a nearby ravine.

No miner noticed the odd movement, and neither

did the cattle, but a mule began to bleat pathetically. The head belonged to Delgadito, whose sharp Apache eyes studied every facet of the camp. Only two miners guarded the herd, he noted.

THIRTEEN

It was dawn in the miner's camp. Even the dog was asleep, not to mention two scraggly cats. A half mile down the valley, the herd slept, protected by two guards.

One was Ronnie Dowd, the weasel-faced deserter and murderer. He'd changed his name to Mike Turner, and no one asked where he'd come from. The weasel understood well the ways of the Apache and never relaxed vigilance. As a soldier, he'd seen the results of Apache raids.

The cattle bestirred themselves, as the first glimmer of dawn appeared on the horizon. Dowd and his chum Gus Ethridge planned to massacre the other miners after they accumulated a reasonable quantity of gold, but unfortunately that seemed a long time in the future.

Dowd heard a sudden *twang*, and jerked to the side as an arrow pierced his left pectoral muscle where it connected with his shoulder. At first he didn't know what hit him, then saw an Apache crouching behind a prickly pear cactus, aiming another arrow. A wave of pain shot through Dowd as he fell to the ground. "Injuns!" he gasped and fired his rifle wildly. "Halp!"

The miners came roaring out of their cabin, carrying new breech-loading rifles. They saw distant Apaches trying to stampede the herd, so flopped onto their bellies and opened fire. But the Apaches were too far away, and the miners watched with dismay as their herd was rustled away virtually beneath their very noses.

Sipping breakfast coffee, Nathanial was startled by shots in the distance. "Sergeant Duffy—tell the men to mount up!"

Sergeant Duffy didn't argue, because he knew war when he heard it. "Let's prepare to move out, men."

"Aw shit," said Private Toohey, "whoever it is, let 'em kill each other if they wanna. What does it have to do with us."

"I've given you an order, Private Toohey."

"But I ain't finished me bacon yet."

Toohey jabbed his fork into a strip of bacon, when suddenly the plate exploded in his face. He wiped bacon grease off his eyelashes and saw Lieutenant Barrington lowering his boot.

"You were ordered to mount up, Private Toohey."

"Right away, sir," replied Toohey, a strip of bacon stuck to his shirt, as he slunk toward his horse.

An orderly saddled Duke III as Nathanial studied his maps. Thanks to the U.S. Topographical Corps, he had no idea where he was.

Sergeant Duffy rode closer. "The men are ready, sir."

Nathanial climbed onto his horse, then addressed the men. "I suspect we're hearing Apaches, and if you're looking for a fight, this might be it. Remember your training, follow orders to the letter, and whatever you do, don't shoot the dragoon next to you—especially not your commanding officer." Nathanial pointed his yellow-gloved finger straight ahead and hollered: "Follow me!"

The People's warriors managed to prevent the herd from stampeding, and now concentrated on confiscating the miners' fine new rifles. The warriors advanced on foot, firing arrows or antiquated rifles, as they closed with the miners.

The warrior woman dodged from boulder to tree, shooting her rifle steadily. She'd volunteered for this last raid, to imprint her unborn son with a taste of the warrior life. It appeared half the miners were dead or wounded, with the rest retreating toward their log cabin. The warriors sang war songs as they rushed the remaining miners, when suddenly Delgadito hollered: "Stop!" The warriors halted, and a terrible thunder came to them. "Bluecoat soldiers!"

Warriors ran for their mounts as the sound of charging dragoons came closer. Delgadito's eyes flashed excitedly as he leapt onto his war pony's back. "Get the herd moving, my warriors!"

"But," protested Juh, "the cattle will slow us down."

"The White Eyes are far off, and they will not follow us into the woodlands that lay ahead. Hurry—you Nednais—do as I say!"

Hollering and shooting pistols, the People succeeded in terrorizing the herd. Within moments it was rampaging south, with warriors galloping at its rear and sides, urging the frightened animals onward. The warrior woman glanced back over her shoulder and saw the mining camp disappear behind the last rise. Ahead lay woods excellent for ambush, and there they'd demolish the bluecoat soldiers. Let them come, thought the warrior woman, as she raced alongside the herd. We will pick them off one by one, and their weapons shall be ours.

Nathanial and his dragoons galloped toward the log cabin, where miners tried to doctor fallen brethren. A cloud of dust billowed forward as Nathanial climbed down from the saddle.

The miners rose to meet him, and it looked like a bloody fight had occurred. "Apaches done stoled our herd," said one of miners.

"How many Apaches?"

" 'Bout thirty, and if you ride hard, you might catch 'em."

Nathanial returned to his horse, climbed into the saddle, and pointed in the direction the Apaches had gone. "Forward—hoooooo!"

Raising himself like a jockey boy, Nathanial raced across the valley, followed by his hard-charging dragoons. He felt wonderfully exhilarated and had to admit once again there was nothing quite like an all-out full-tilt hell-bent-for-leather cavalry charge. Wind whistled past his wide-brimmed cowboy hat as he motioned the men forward with his gloved hand. "Don't let them get away!"

Delgadito sent the herd forward with ten warriors, then organized the remainder for an ambush. They tethered their horses in a sheltered area, then stuck branches into their hair and covered their bodies with dirt.

Delgadito and several of his best shots climbed to the sandstone bluffs overlooking the cattle trail. From the distance he heard the approach of bluecoat soldiers. They invade our land, cheat us at every opportunity, and expect us to surrender? Delgadito asked himself. Not today, my white-eyed friends.

Taza narrowed his eyes at the warrior woman perched at the mouth of a cave overlooking the ambush area, while he lay beneath two inches of dirt on the ground below. In order to shoot her, he'd have to angle his rifle upward, which others might see. Taza gnashed his teeth in frustration.

He'd expected thirty warriors against ten miners, but it was turning into a fight against a sizable number of bluecoat soldiers. Perhaps, if we kill enough of them in the first volley, we can prevail, thought Taza. Otherwise . . .

Nathanial brought his detachment to a halt at the edge of the forest, then took a sip from his canteen. He'd been on the frontier long enough to know an ambush when he saw one.

"Well?" asked Sergeant Duffy impatiently, his little red nose twitching at the aroma of pine needles wafting toward him.

Why should I risk my life, and my men's, for miners' cattle? Nathanial asked himself. Is the Army supposed to provide protection for any greedy fool who digs where he doesn't belong?

West Point prepared Nathanial to fight the Napoleonic Wars, but instead he found himself pursuing Apaches in a region where right and wrong depended on whether you wore a breechclout or trousers. Then a gust of wind caught the American flag fluttering on the guidon pole, producing a *snap* sound. As long as I'm wearing this uniform, I've got to go by the book, he told himself.

"If yer a-waitin' fer Christmas," said Sergeant Duffy, "It's more'n six months away."

Again Nathanial ignored him. "Mister Pennington?"

"Sir?"

"I think there's an ambush waiting for us in there."

"So do I."

"Sergeant Duffy, I want two skirmish lines right here."

"But sir," said Sergeant Duffy. "If there's an ambush, why are we ridin' into it."

"We're going to keep our eyes open, Sergeant, and not let ourselves be taken by surprise. Our job is recover that herd, remember?"

Sergeant Duffy spat at the ground. "Two skirmish lines right here!"

The men and horses performed the maneuver they'd practiced countless times on the parade ground, and soon were dressed right, covered down, and ready for war.

Nathanial drew his Colt, faced the men, and said: "We're advancing on my command," he told them. "There are probably Apaches waiting for us, so at the sound of the first shot, dismount and return fire. Now draw your pistols and make sure they're loaded."

The men checked weaponry as Nathanial motioned his scout closer. "I won't ask you to take the point, Mister Pennington, because I don't want to make you a decoy. You'll ride alongside me, but we want to see them before they see us."

"The Apaches are very good at hiding themselves, sir. I don't think this is a good idea."

Nathanial wondered if he'd be dead in the hours to come, then turned toward his men one last time. "Cock your hammers," he ordered, "but whatever you do, don't shoot your bunkie by mistake. It's time to earn your pay, gentlemen. Forward hooooo!''

On his mossy ledge Delgadito watched the approach of the bluecoat soldiers. He'd expected them to come in a column of twos, but they'd spread out and appeared alert, guns at the ready, which meant they expected ambush. Delgadito didn't like the look of it, but too late to run away.

He carried an old musketoon and kept the bore clean with a special rod. He crawled forward on his elbows and knees, rested his chin on the edge of the rock shelf, and waited patiently. *Just a little closer, and I shall destroy you White Eyes bastards.*

Not far away, the warrior woman, covered with dirt and twigs, spotted the sunny-haired officer though an opening in the trees. *It's him!* she realized. Many Apache rifles would be aimed at the officer, for a warrior tries to kill his enemy's leader first.

She recalled rolling naked on the desert with Sunny Hair and couldn't bear to see him killed. A deep imperative caused her to pick up a rock as big as her hand. She drew back her arm and tossed it through the air.

The forest was cool and sweet-smelling as the detachment advanced. The dragoons aimed their pistols straight up in the air as they scanned tree trunks, boulders, crevices, and clumps of bushes. Birds sang above them, flitting from branch to branch. It was an idyllic forest landscape, no Apaches in sight.

"I heard something," said Pennington. "I think we'd better dismount and proceed on foot."

Nathanial decided to take his scout's advice for

once, because Pennington had fought Apaches, Comanches, and Mexicans during his years as a Texas Ranger. The West Pointer turned in the saddle to issue his dismount order, as something incredible slammed into his head.

He nearly blacked out as the woods exploded with gunfire. He heard Sergeant Duffy order the men to take cover, and then somebody yelled: "Lieutenant Barrington is down!"

"No, I'm not," Nathanial muttered, but then realized his face lay on pine needles. "What's going on?" he asked himself as someone screamed, and it sounded like his own voice. He felt himself being carried away, laid behind a huge boulder.

"How is he?" asked Pennington.

"Bleedin' like a son-of-a-bitch," replied Sergeant Duffy. The doughty old warrior watched the dragoons deploying as he'd taught them in many drills, and every fourth man led horses to the rear. "Keep firing!" shouted Sergeant Duffy. "We've got them where we want them!"

"We have?" gurgled Nathanial as blood trickled down the side of his head.

The soldiers had been warned moments before the trap snapped closed, and Delgadito was furious. But at least he'd killed the bluecoat officer.

He sang a victory song as he examined the smoke-filled forest before him. Steady Apache fire raked the bluecoat soldiers, and he was proud of his warriors. "Keep shooting!" he bellowed. "Kill them all!"

Delgadito didn't know that one Apache rifle wasn't firing. It lay cold in the hands of the shocked warrior woman, for she'd seen the father of her unborn child fall. A bullet ricocheted off a rock wall near her head, forcing her to retreat more deeply into the cave. There she sat cross-legged, eyes closed, praying for the fighting to end.

The warrior woman assumed a soldier tried to kill her, but Taza had fired the round that sent her backward. I did it! he thought exultantly. Revenge rolled like honey over his tongue, but lost its flavor quickly in heavy fire coming his way.

The soldiers were fighting back, but as a precaution, Taza had dug his position behind the others, for ease of exit. This is not the raid I bargained for, he told himself. The time has come to depart this foolishness. Taza looked in all directions to make sure no one was observing him, and then crept backward, his chin scraping the ground.

Nathanial opened his eyes, and a bullet *zanged* off the boulder beside him. He touched his fingers to the bandage around his head, then remembered that Apaches had ambushed his detachment. He had the worst headache of his life. He rolled to his knees, pulled his pistol, and felt curiously queasy, as if he were looking down on himself from above.

Sergeant Duffy crouched behind the corner of the boulder. "You'd better lie down, sir. You've taken a shot to the head."

"I'm perfectly fine," replied Nathanial, although he was having double vision. "What happened?"

"We're holding them off, sir. Collins is dead, O'Neil is wounded, and as for you, they say if a head wound doesn't kill you outright, it can't be serious."

"Quite right," replied Nathanial, although he heard bells tolling above the gunfire. He peered from the boulder and saw orange flashes through the smoke.

The battle appeared evenly matched, but he wondered if other Apaches were poised to strike him in the flank. For all he knew, he could be surrounded by the whole Apache nation.

Nathanial thought he saw something move in a clearing toward his left. His vision distorted, he raised his pistol and fired a wild shot. His gun kicked into the air, smoke bellowed around him, and he thought the motion stopped. His head felt as if a slab had been hacked off with a hatchet as he thumbed fresh cartridges into the chambers of his revolver. He still had that floaty feeling as he raised his pistol, aimed in the general direction of the Apaches, and squeezed the trigger.

The bullet bounced off a rock, which provided a long deadly edge, and then whizzed into the retreating Taza, slicing his spine. All feeling departed the old warrior's legs, and next thing he knew, he was on his way to the spirit world. Never again would he require the services of slave boys.

It gave Delgadito great pleasure to shoot bluecoat soldiers, instead of pretending to be friends. He remembered how they'd stolen the two captives at the copper mines, and then shot Largo. The bluecoat soldiers behaved as though they were superior beings, and it was glorious to see them cringe beneath his fire. Delgadito shouted insults and taunts at the White Eyes, and then, to show his utter contempt, he performed an Apache's most insulting act.

Delgadito turned around, exposed his hindquarters to the bluecoat soldiers, and slapped his buttocks, while shrieking vile insults above the din of gunfire.

*   *   *

Nathanial wondered if he was hallucinating as he peered through his spyglass at the Apache warrior exhibiting his posterior. "Mister Pennington, do you see that Apache dancing on the ridge up there?"

"Yes, sir, and I was just drawing a bead on him."

Pennington possessed one of the new Wesson rifles, said to be accurate at four hundred yards. It had been fitted with especially calibrated sights, and the former Texas Ranger lined them on his target. The Apache was leaping about excitedly, slapping his fanny as Pennington squeezed the trigger.

Delgadito believed himself beyond the range of enemy rifles and felt wonderful releasing pent-up loathing, when a mule kicked him in the rear end. The force drove him forward; he crashed his chin into a rock wall and was pierced by fiery pain. Holding his warrior mind steady, he assessed the damage. His left leg was paralyzed.

The bluecoat rifles had greater range that he'd believed. "To the horses!" he shouted.

Juh and Geronimo grabbed each of Delgadito's arms, then helped him down the side of the mountain, amid tufts of grama grass exploding from bluecoat gunfire. Finally, they reached their makeshift corral, where warriors fired back atop nervously prancing war ponies. Delgadito was tied to his saddle, given the reins, and the haunch of his horse slapped hard. The animal lurched forward, carrying the nearly unconscious Delgadito from the battle; behind him warriors fled frantically. No victory songs were sung as bullets zipped about like angry bees.

Nathanial sat against the boulder, sipping from his canteen. His head felt as if portions were missing in action, but Sergeant Duffy reassured him it was "just a graze." Nathanial touched the blood-caked bandage on his head. If I don't get out of the Army soon, he told himself, I shall be killed.

Sergeant Duffy returned, campaign hat perched on the back of his head. "Two dead, sir. Six wounded. No horses lost. How do you feel?"

"I've got a mild headache, but that's about all," lied Nathanial. "Tell the men to mount up. We're going after those Apaches."

Sergeant Duffy looked at him in disbelief. "What're you gonna do with the dead, sir?"

"We'll take them with us."

"They'll start to stink in a while."

"When they do, we'll bury them."

"What about the wounded?"

"They'll have to keep up."

"Sir, if you don't mind me sayin' so, I think that bullet affected yer mind. How many ambushes do you want today? It's time to return to the copper mines."

Nathanial growled and pulled himself to his full height. Towering over his first sergeant, placing his hands on his hips, he said, "Duffy, I'm getting damned tired of arguing with you. From this moment on, you're going to obey my orders without question, or I shall place you under arrest. Do I make myself clear?"

"I think you'd better sit down, sir."

"There's nothing wrong with me," replied Nathanial as fireflies danced before his eyes. How odd, he thought. I never saw fireflies at this time of the day. Then his mind went blank, his knees turned inward, and he went crashing to the ground.

The People's warriors made camp that night in an abandoned pueblo nestled against a mountain. They ate dried meat in the darkness as guards watched their backtrail. The raid had been disastrous, and Delgadito lay stomach down on his blanket, gasping for air, his left buttock covered with cactus sap and wrapped in deerskin. Two warriors had been killed, three wounded, the cattle lost, and maybe they'd replace Delgadito with a new war chief.

The pain made him delirious, and it felt as if a giant were gouging his left buttock with a knife. But his pride was hurt worst of all, and he hated the White Eyes with renewed vigor, even as he feared their medicine. Delgadito couldn't help marveling at their weapons, but the White Eyes stole the People's land.

I will obtain one of those rifles for myself, thought Delgadito. Death has not claimed me, and other battles will come. Next time I shall do better.

The warrior woman lay on the far side of the cave, wrapped in her blanket. Her belly felt uncomfortable, and she realized that her warrior days were over, or at least until after the child was born. She wondered about the child's father, for it appeared that he'd been killed. Her life had taken new directions since she'd lured the strange golden warrior into the chaparral.

She could feel the child growing within. She never knew such anguish as when she'd seen Sunny Hair lead his soldiers into the forest. He is probably dead, she reflected, but surely the mountain spirits have brought us together for a purpose. It is my duty to bring this special child into the world.

Overshadowed by cottonwood trees, a stream trickled softly into the night. Nothing moved, not even the breeze, with stars emblazoned above. Then a semi-naked boy appeared beneath the bow of a tree, his eyes darting furtively as he inched toward the water. Streams were the most dangerous places, but José had to drink, for night was safer than day. He'd sat hidden for a substantial period and observed nothing threatening, but couldn't be sure; he half expected a cougar to drop upon him at any moment.

At water's edge he dipped his hand like a cup, drank silently, but didn't notice two eyes watching him from upstream shadows. José filled his water bag warily, then covered his tracks with quick sweeps of a branch, his every movement carefully observed.

Nathanial couldn't sleep, due to the pain in his head. Every time he turned, he thought his skull cracked. He kept reliving the crucial moment when he'd turned around to speak with his men. If he'd remained on course, the bullet would've drilled the middle of his forehead, and wild dogs would dig him out of his shallow grave that night.

He'd feared his brain was injured, his thinking never the same, and imagined himself a ragged old man sitting in the corner of a lunatic asylum, drooling onto his beard. There's no doubt I'll be killed if I keep at this soldier business, he said to himself. If I'd had any sense, I never would've gone to West Point in the first place. Raising his hand, he touched the bandage caked with blood atop his head. Then an odd thought came to mind. Wouldn't it be funny if the warrior woman shot me?

FOURTEEN

Maria Dolores Carbajal Barrington came to a street of lavish homes, but that didn't prevent her from wearing a Colt Dragoon in a holster concealed by her serape. Her nose ever to the business winds, she'd heard about a certain gentleman who wanted to sell a mansion, and she needed larger quarters for her family.

She felt invigorated by the open air, far from domestic responsibilities. She'd hired maids, but still tried to spend an hour or so every day with her increasingly rebellious son, who tended to break whatever was given to him. She feared he'd be the kind of child the others wouldn't like at school, but if she didn't keep an eye on her investments, they'd all go down the drain. Perhaps everything will be easier with a larger house, she hoped.

Written directions led to a rambling two-story adobe structure that looked like a fortress in a neighborhood of similar residences, each surrounded by more property than her present neighborhood. Waiting by the front door was a dignified fortyish gentleman attired in a blue business suit. He tipped his spotless white sombrero as she approached. "You must be Mrs. Barrington."

She wore a light cotton purple dress gathered at her

waist and buttoned high at the throat. "And you must be Señor Galindez."

He sported a salt-and-pepper mustache, long side whiskers, and had a nicely shaped head. "It's a solid house, only three years old, but you really can't appreciate it from the outside."

"I've admired it many times," she replied. "Why are you selling?"

His smile disintegrated. "My wife died recently, and I can't live here without her." The bright sun became dark gloom as he unlocked the door.

"Do you have children?" she asked.

"Two boys. I'm taking them back to Mexico as soon as I get rid of the house."

He showed her a large sunken living room with a natural stone fireplace and beautiful striped Navaho blankets hanging from the walls like tapestries. The furniture was crafted of dark wood, the kitchen magnificent, with palatial bedrooms, and Maria Dolores fell in love with the structure.

"We were happy here," Señor Galindez mused sadly as he led her through the dining room, where twenty guests easily could be accommodated.

She noticed he was somewhat elegant as she caught his profile in the library, his features strained by tragedy. She wanted to embrace him compassionately, in brotherhood and sisterhood, but then recognized more than altruism.

She caught herself, for every woman learns at an early age never to admit certain thoughts to others. Instead, she smiled and said, "What's your price?"

He mentioned a reasonable sum and agreed to let the house be checked by her carpenter. If all went well, Maria Dolores and Señor Galindez would sign legal papers in three days.

She felt thrilled as she walked back to her office. Even the great hacienda in which she'd been raised wasn't as lovely as the house she'd just seen. Señor Galindez and his wife spared no expense to create their beautiful and comfortable dwelling, then the family lost its mother. *If something ever happened to me, what would become of Zachary?*

Then she realized that her husband might as well be dead, for all the good he was doing her. *I should divorce Nathanial, marry Señor Galindez, and merge families. It wouldn't surprise me in the least if my spouse was in bed with a filthy, diseased prostitute right now, but Señor Galindez is a refined and cultivated gentleman. I don't love him, and in fact barely know him, but after a few years, who could say?*

Sleeping deeply in late morning, José felt something clamp around his throat. He opened his eyes, and a warrior of the People was holding him down. "I have been following you for days," said the warrior. "You're a smart little fellow, but not smarter than Chatoosh. Get up." Chatoosh turned Jose' loose, and the boy raised himself to a sitting position.

Chatoosh was short, muscular, with one eye half closed, and a scar on his chin. "You have a lot to learn," he said.

José had thought himself safe, but neglected to cover his tracks at certain times. "I have escaped the *Nakai-yes* and am on my way to the clan of Mangas Coloradas. My mother was the warrior woman, Jocita."

"You lie, for Jocita is a barren woman." Chatoosh grabbed José by the neck. "Be careful what you say, for I am not afraid to kill little boys."

José was terrified. "What clan are you with?"

"My own clan."

José knew of outlaws from the People living alone in caves, preying on travelers. "What are you going to do with me?"

"I think you'll be my slave. Or, if I became hungry, I might roast you over a fire. Don't even think of escaping, for I have sharp eyes, I never sleep completely, and am the finest tracker you ever saw. You are mine like a dog or horse, except dogs are funny, and horses have useful functions. I might even kill you one of these days for the fun of it."

Nathanial returned to the copper mines on a rainy August day, riding at the head of his detachment. Drops of water fell from his nose, and the gash on his head was a mass of dried blood, hair, twigs, and something that looked like a petrified insect. Nathanial called his detachment to a halt in front of the presidio, told Sergeant Duffy to dismiss the men, and entered the orderly room. "The colonel in?"

Sergeant Barnes sat behind his desk. "He's inspecting the horses. What happened to your head?"

"A scrape with Apaches, nothing serious. How's the boundary work progressing?"

"Couple more weeks and they'll be done, according to Mister Bartlett. But there's one problem. We're losing livestock faster'n we can replace them."

"I'll keep my detachment's animals separate if you don't mind. If the colonel wants to see me, I'll be with Dr. Webb. Anything else happen that I should know about?"

"Have you heard that gold has been discovered in the Pinos Altos mountains?"

"I've seen miners, but nobody's said anything about a gold strike."

"Hundreds of 'em are pourin' into the area, and it's only a matter of time before the Apaches kill 'em all."

The great chief Mangas Coloradas chuckled in the darkness of the wickiup. "Of all places to get shot, did it have to be in the buttocks, Delgadito?"

Delgadito lay on his stomach, groaning in the darkness. "How embarrassing to be shot there," he whispered. "Do you remember the bluecoat chief with the sunny hair—you had spoken to him once? I think we shot him when the fighting began."

"He was an excellent warrior," replied Mangas Coloradas, "but even excellent warriors die, and sometimes they are shot in the buttocks." Mangas Coloradas patted Delgadito's shoulders confidently. "Soon you will be well, my warrior brother, and we shall do much fighting."

Dowd wasn't especially chagrined that his co-deserter, Ethridge, had been killed in the Apache raid. They'd been friends of sorts, but a dead man can't blab information about certain crimes committed in the past. Dowd felt brand new as he sat around the campfire with the other surviving miners.

He munched beans and bacon, wary of the others as they were of him. None really knew much about the other, and Dowd couldn't be sure he wasn't the only thief and murderer in camp. The deserter lived in fear he'd run into someone with no morals, compunctions, or doubts, like himeself.

He puffed a cigarette silently as the others talked about their favorite subject: what they'd do after they hit the mother lode. Dowd guessed they'd blow it all within a short period, and so would he. But he could always steal more, for at least he had a regular profession.

"How about you, Turner?" asked one of them.

Dowd realized they were talking to him, using the false name he'd chosen. "I don't want to work no more," he blurted, "and I guess I'd hire me some dancing poopsies to take care of things, if you know what I mean." He grinned. "But first we have to find gold, and sometimes I gits discouraged."

"Hang on, feller," said white-bearded Old Bill, their unofficial leader. "Gold's been found in these mountains, and whar thar's some, thar's usually more. Don't forget the Comstock lode started with a few small nuggets. Hell, if we're not careful, we're liable to find gold rocks big as yer fists just lying on the ground, waitin' to git picked up."

Chatoosh lived in a cave far from trails and hunting grounds of the People. He never stayed in one place long, because he believed the People were hunting him for the murder of his brother. Other warriors became sub-chiefs and respected warriors, while no one had ever cared much for Chatoosh. The People made fun of him, but when his own brother joined in, he had to draw the line.

Now he was a renegade, but life wasn't bad, especially with a playmate. He gazed across the cave at the boy gnawing a bone. At least I won't have to gather wood anymore, dig mescal, or tan skins, thought Chatoosh. But first I must break his rebellious spirit.

Chatoosh was tempting José with a pistol lying on the floor. The boy kept glancing at the weapon, measuring whether he could grab it and fire a quick shot.

Go ahead, thought Chatoosh. I'll break your arm,

and you'll learn the best lesson of your life. But the boy didn't move, because he wasn't as dumb as he looked. He's biding his time, thought Chatoosh, but so am I. He'll never be a good slave until I give him a sound beating.

Colonel Craig frowned as he looked out his office window at the returning Boundary Commission wagons. "By God, I hope this is the end," he muttered as he put on his hat.

He ambled toward the commission and noticed many workers on foot, as horses continued to disappear. The bookseller from the East sat beside the driver of his wagon, and it came to a stop in front of the presidio.

"Good morning, Colonel," said Bartlett with a tip of his hat. "I'm pleased to say we've finished our work at this area, and I'd like to proceed to Fort Yuma day after tomorrow."

Colonel Craig saluted. "Just what I hoped you'd say, sir."

Colonel Craig's spirits soared as he returned to his office. He sat behind his desk and thought about the long, simmering summer with Mangas Coloradas, Ponce, Delgadito, and the other Apaches. At last the ordeal was over.

In laudanum stupor, Nathanial lay motionless on his cot. Random images drifted across his mind, and sometimes he saw himself marching across the plain at West Point, or a child growing up on Washington Square. At least once a night he refought Palo Alto, but his favorite hallucinations were those involving Maria Dolores. I'll never leave you again, he swore.

He heard the rustle of the tent flap, opened his eyes,

and Sergeant Duffy stood before him. "Are you well enough to hear some good news, sir? The Boundary Commission is done, and we're headed back to Santa Fe day after tomorrow."

Nathanial wanted to perform a dance, but the laudanum held him to the cot. I'll be with Maria Dolores in a few more weeks, he said to himself and closed his eyes. My prayers are answered, and my army days are just about over.

Chatoosh sat in a corner of the cave, smoking his pipe and watching the boy working an antelope hide. Sweat poured down José's forehead, and Chatoosh was pleased to note that José was properly afraid of him, thanks to a few kicks and slaps administered along the way.

He's a good worker, Chatoosh had to admit. Working hides was woman's work, but Chatoosh had done it as a boy. His father enjoyed humiliating him, and Chatoosh was secretly thankful when the old man had died.

"Do you remember your father?" asked Chatoosh.

The boy appeared surprised. "Yes, I do."

"What happened to him."

"He was killed."

"By the People?"

"Yes."

Chatoosh scratched his head. "The People killed your *Nakai-yes* father, but now you're running back? I do not understand."

"I have been raised by the People," replied José, "and I missed the holy life-way."

"What about your parents?"

"I do not think about them anymore."

"You are a traitor to your people, no?"

"But who are my people?" replied José. "My parents, or the ones who have trained me to be a warrior?"

Loyalty, thought Chatoosh, puffing his pipe, as the boy massaged blubbery substances into the antelope skin. *He has a family among the People, but why do I feel pity?*

"Take a rest," muttered Chatoosh. "And don't worry about wood for the fire. I'll get it."

The boy blinked in surprise as the renegade moved into the chaparral.

It was the last supper at the Santa Rita copper mines, and tables had been set outside the presidio for one last feast. Chunks of steer roasted over open fires, and a special ration of whiskey was issued to the dragoons.

Amid the revelry John Cremony sat in his tent, hastily writing his journal. He'd fallen behind in his entries and wanted to finish everything before his departure. Due to his whiskey ration, or perhaps sloppy thinking, he confused Lieutenant Whipple with Lieutenant Barrington in his account of the fight west of the copper mines. To spice the account further, he wrote himself into the scene, a first-hand account having more immediacy than mere restatement of official reports. Cremony never let facts interfere with a good story, and no one would know the difference except a handful of mostly illiterate soldiers.

Cremony's dream was to publish a book and make lots of money. *There's a deeper truth I'm trying to convey here*, he mused. *The truth of my bank account.* Laughing softly, he took another sip of whiskey.

In the lawyer's office Maria Dolores signed official

documents and then watched Señor Galindez affix his name to them. The widower wore a dark suit and black cravat as he perused the papers one last time. "Everything appears in order," he said as he signed the papers. Then he shook Maria Dolores's hand. "I trust you shall enjoy your new home."

They departed the lawyer's office and faced each other on the sidewalk. Wagons clattered in the middle of the street, vaqueros and soldiers rode past, and someone fired a gun nearby.

"I'll be leaving in the morning," said Señor Galindez. "It has been lovely meeting you, Mrs. Barrington."

She gazed at his melancholy brown eyes, and he'd told her he studied to become a Jesuit priest before getting married. "It is a shame you are leaving so soon," she replied, "because we were just starting to know each other."

His businesslike features softened in the shade of his wide, spotless sombrero. "I have thought the same thing, but my plans are made, and besides . . . you are a married woman."

She laughed sardonically. "I have not seen my husband for so long, sometimes I forget what he looks like. Yet somehow I can't help thinking . . ." She let her voice trail off meaningfully.

"I have thought the same thing." He removed his sombrero and bowed low. "You are a beautiful woman, Mrs. Barrington, and many times reminded me I am still a man. But above all, we must be true to ourselves, and to God. I hope you enjoy your new home, and may the Virgin bless you. Good day."

He kissed her hand, then strode away, leaving her standing with her leather case full of documents. She decided she'd married the wrong man, but then remembered the admonition of Christ. If you sin in your heart, it is the same as sinning in actuality.

Maria Dolores crossed herself as she headed toward her new home. Señor Galindez is free to marry, she pondered, but I must remain single. This is a cruel thing that Nathanial has done to me, or I have done to myself.

How much longer before another man like Señor Galindez comes along? she wondered. What if I become weak, and a man like that is flirtatious. She could imagine giving herself to Señor Galindez if they were alone with a bottle of wine.

The line between sin and virtue was far flimsier than she'd imagined. Perhaps, if I paid a certain sum to the bishop, I could have my marriage annulled. That worthless husband of mine has brought me to this sorry pass, and this is what happens to women who marry soldiers.

No official ceremonies marked the departure of the U.S. Boundary Commission from the Santa Rita copper mines. It was September 15, 1851, and the sun shone brilliantly on the caravan as Colonel Craig took his position at its head. No photographer captured his orange dragoon bandanna fluttering in the wind as he raised himself in the saddle and peered at his scouts advancing toward Fort Yuma. The crusty old colonel took one last look at the presidio and thought: Am I glad to be getting the hell out of here. He lifted his gauntleted arm and moved it due west. "Forward hoooo!"

Not in victory did the Boundary Commission depart the Santa Rita copper mines, and many dragoons were walking due to stolen horses. But their labor was complete, and they had to continue drawing their line all the way to Californio.

Nathanial and his detachment were back at the presidio, making final adjustments prior to their own departure. He smoked a cigarette as he gazed at the section of chapparal where he'd encountered the warrior woman. Sometimes he wondered if it had been another of his drunken dreams, but you don't get scratches and bites from a dream. *She broke more rules than I when she met me,* he surmised. *What a strange Apache she must be.*

Sergeant Duffy marched toward him and saluted. "The detachment is ready, sir."

Nathanial turned around and saw his men formed in two ranks before him. A private stood with his horse, so Nathanial promptly climbed into the saddle. He gave Duke III the spurs, and the russet stallion trotted to the head of the formation. "Scout forward!" shouted Nathanial.

Pennington trotted ahead as Nathanial arrived at his position in front of the column. The men gazed back at the presidio, as if aware something significant was coming to an end. *We've become a footnote to history,* figured Nathanial. *No one except the most esoteric historians will ever give a second thought to the U.S. Boundary Commission of 1851, although it was the most interesting summer of my life.*

"Ready to move out, sir," said Sergeant Duffy.

Nathanial raised his fist in the air and shouted: "Detachment—forward hooooo!"

Duke III clomped forward, carrying Nathanial back to Fort Marcy. Behind him clattered his detachment of armed dragoons, and not even the entire Apache nation could prevent them from reaching the fleshpots of Santa Fe, especially with three months' pay waiting.

Nathanial fully expected half of them in the stockade within one week after their return, and wasn't sure he wouldn't end there himself.

How can I look Maria Dolores in the eye after what I've done? he wondered.

Mangas Coloradas and his Navaho son-in-law, Manuelito, lay on a ledge and watched bluecoat soldiers riding away from the Santa Rita copper mines. "Will you admit my strategy was correct?" asked Manuelito.

"You have taught me a valuable lesson, my dear son-in-law," replied Mangas Coloradas. "We have lost no warriors, and even Largo would be here if he had stayed away from their camp. There can never be peace between the White Eyes and the People, but at least we have won today."

Manuelito nodded, but he could see the Apache life-way slipping into the breeze. The youthful Navaho chief wanted to tout the joys of farming and weaving, but would earn his father-in-law's contempt.

Other members of the clan also observed the departure of the White Eyes, and among them was the warrior woman. Her sharp eyes discerned golden hair beneath the hat of the officer at the head of the smaller detachment.

He is alive! she realized happily. She closed her eyes and gave thanks to the mountain spirits. Whenever I look at my child, I will see his face, while he is free to ... what? She knew nothing about him, although she'd seen the White Eyes wedding ring on his finger. He is going to his wife, but I'll bet he never tells her about me, as I shall never say anything about him. The warrior woman smiled wistfully as she watched the sunny-haired officer merge with the horizon and disappear.

*   *   *

It was an afternoon barbecue in Neshoba County, Mississippi. Clouds of pungent smoke rose into the air, children played among heavily laden tables, and their parents feasted upon succulent roast pig, yams, potatoes, and biscuits, among other delicacies.

A stage had been constructed at the edge of the clearing, and the featured speaker was introduced by Alderman Adam Twitchell, a bald-headed, clean-shaven politician wearing a cream-colored suit. Red, white, and blue banners adorned the stage, and the sign above the podium declared:

HERO OF BUENA VISTA

TRUE TO THE SOUTH

"And now, ladies and gentlemen," declaimed Alderman Twitchell, "it is my privilege to present the man you've come to see, the man who stands as a bulwark against the enemies of the South, our own *Senator Jefferson Davis* of Brierfield!"

Farmers and wives rose to their feet and pounded hands enthusiastically, as a tall, slim, austere-looking gentleman walked onto the stage, then firmly shook hands with the alderman. Although dressed in dark tailored civilian clothing, Jefferson Davis somehow carried the air of the battlefield about him.

The hero's dignified bearing won the crowd to his favor instantaneously, because most Washington politicians took off their fancy suits when they arrived in Neshoba County and dressed like farmers or woodsmen. But Senator Jefferson Davis refused to pander for votes, and instead relied upon reason, the oratorical arts, plus compilations of facts to back his arguments.

He readied his notes at the podium, unruffled by thunderous applause. A member of the planter class,

Jefferson Davis never doubted his authority. He stood erectly, although his left eye was blinded by a cloudy film, and his neuralgia headache throbbed in the hot sun. He had not come to Neshoba Country because he loved electioneering, but he was standing up for a way of life he considered threatened by powerful forces.

He began speaking in a low voice, like a college professor offering a seminar to his favored students. "You have heard it said that I am a disunionist," he told them, his eyes slowing sweeping the audience as he stood at attention behind the podium. "But if I have a superstition which governs my mind and holds it captive, it is a superstitious reverence for this great Union of ours. I agree with our beloved former president Zachary Taylor that we must enact laws favorable to *all* regions of our nation, and not just certain powerful groups, otherwise we shall have replaced the tyranny of King George with the tyranny of manufacturers from certain parts of this nation which I shall not name, to spoil this fine barbecue afternoon."

Members of the audience chuckled, because Jeff Davis was funnin' with them. Sure he was a big national hero, West Point officer, and U.S. senator, but he was plain folks beneath his fine suit. They hadn't forgotten his remark about President Taylor, as he reminded them that he'd been a former intimate at the White House.

Jefferson Davis sipped water, then resumed in a more urgent voice. "I come to you today from my duties in the U.S. Senate, to ask your support. I am running for governor of Mississippi because you and I deserve better than Henry Foote. Now there's a man who changes his mind according to how the political wind is blowing. Today he says he's a unionist, if you can trust him, but Henry Foote will say *anything* to get into the governor's mansion!"

Jefferson Davis raised his right fist in the air. "But everyone knows what Jefferson Davis stands for, and has always stood for. I'm aware there are some among you who wish I'd sit down and let them finish this good food in peace, but I say to you that our beloved Mississippi is in the gravest danger. The Compromise Bill of last year is a farce, and only a matter of time before it falls apart. The Compromise has settled nothing!"

The last word came like a shot from a Mississippi Rifle, and for the first time Jefferson Davis pounded the podium. The air crackled with electricity as one of the most famous orators in America hit his stride. Final bronzed rays of the afternoon sun came over the combat commander's face as firelight flickered across his blind left eye.

"Ladies and gentleman," he continued, "let's make no mistake about the most important issue before Mississippi today. The Northern industrial power seeks to dominate the South, and that's what this election is really about. Who do you want to lead Mississippi through the hurricane that lies ahead, the man who drifts with the wind, or Jefferson Davis, your senator!"

The crowd became raucous with applause, hats flew into the air, and mothers held up babies so they could see the great man. Jefferson Davis leaned toward them, his spare frame energized with conviction, and everyone could see this wasn't a bad actor trying to fake human emotions.

"Ladies and gentlemen," roared Jefferson Davis, "the whip with which they chastise us is called *slavery*, which *they* have introduced to this land, and indeed *forced* upon us. Let us make no bones about it, my friends: Slavery is a Northern institution, not a Southern one. But it doesn't end there—then they forced us to sell cotton to them for prices lower than we could receive in London, and when we protested, they leveled the most disreputable insults at our character and institutions."

Jefferson Davis raised both hands to the heavens. "It is enough for me that our way of life has been established by decree of Almighty God, that it is sanctioned in the Bible, in both Testaments from Genesis to Revelations. But nothing will satisfy them who daily assault us, and nothing will terminate their persecution of us.

"No, Jefferson Davis is no disunionist, but I can envisage a day when this section may need to separate itself from the other. And if the other section does not let us depart in peace and seeks to force its will on us, Jefferson Davis will fight! And I will fight to the end, my friends, for the principles which we all hold dear. If that's the kind of governor you want for Neshoba County, I'd appreciate your vote on November 2nd. Good day to you, and thank you for inviting me here."

The people were taken by surprise, for political speeches generally lasted hours. But Jefferson Davis was stepping backward from the podium. Aged grandmas in their prettiest dresses applauded noisily, and small boys tried to whistle like their fathers, who'd tell for the rest of their lives about the day they'd heard Jefferson Davis speak the truth in Neshoba County.

A woman stepped onto the stage, and everyone recognized the jewel of Natchez, Varina Howell Davis, second wife of the great man. She embraced her husband, the crowd roared approval, and then the candidate and wife stood side by side, flowers raining upon them, as huzzahs reverberated across the audience, like cannon fire at Buena Vista.

Jefferson Davis squeezed his wife's hand, for he was ready to collapse, so frightful was his headache. But instead, he raised his free hand and waved to his friends in the audience, not omitting local political leaders, especially their children. The applause told him he'd spoken to their most heartfelt concerns, and the hero of Buena Vista was held in high esteem in Neshoba County. But business had improved since the Compromise had been signed, the North–South strife had muted somewhat, and a small measure of peace was loose in the land. Jefferson Davis knew he was out of step with his times, yet persisted in believing he saw farther ahead than most.

Jefferson Davis basked in the applause, but his one good eye filled with burning cities and blackened fields carpeted with dead soldiers. War was coming, and he saw himself in the vanguard of Southern resistance, holding the banner of Mississippi in one hand and his sword in another, as he accepted the crowd's thunderous accolades.

It was supper on the open range, and Nathanial sat a short distance from the men, his tin plate covered with a broiled reddish slab of mule deer. Pennington had shot it earlier in the day, enough to feed the whole detachment. They hoped to be in Santa Fe within fifteen days, providing the Apaches didn't interfere.

The men glanced surreptitiously at Nathanial as he dined. He had no idea he'd become an object of curiosity to them. They were surprised he was alive, after he'd led them into the ambush, a clear target with gold shoulder straps. By that single act of courage,

he'd won the grudging respect of his uniformed outlaws, outcasts, and failures from all over the world.
Dragoons were paid to pursue Apaches, not let them
run off with one hundred head of American cattle.

A whispered legend about the strange officer had
been building ever since he'd punched the miner
through the window of the trading post. The men had
served under martinets, easy-going officers, drunkards,
and fools, but they'd never met anybody quite like
Lieutenant Barrington. The latest word was he was
resigning his commission!

"Oh, I wouldn't worry about that," said Sergeant
Duffy as he gathered around the campfire with the
other men. "He may be foolin' hisself, but he ain't
foolin' me. There's nothing a man like Lieutenant Barrington can do on the outside 'cept git into trouble, if
he doesn't git himself killed first. I seen 'em come, I
seen 'em go, and that one'll be back afore long, mark
my words."

In a ramshackle Illinois roadhouse, Judge David
Davis of the 8th Circuit Court opened his eyes in the
middle of the night. A candle glowed nearby as lawyer
Abe Lincoln read a book.

They were two to the bed, while on the other side
of the room, lawyers Ames and Bramwell slept together on a straw mattress. Accommodations weren't
the kind the legal eagles preferred, but at least they
had roofs over their heads.

"Don't you ever sleep, Abe?"

The large, lumpy weather-worn face turned toward
the judge. "Hope I'm not keeping you up, sir."

"How are you going to defend that murderer tomorrow if you don't get some sleep?"

"You're right," agreed Honest Abe. "I just want to finish the page I'm on, and then I'll join you."

Judge Davis was exhausted from a day trying cases, followed by several hours on the road. He closed his eyes as Abe Lincoln returned to Plutarch's *The Lives of the Noble Grecians and Romans.*

Abe Lincoln was a voracious reader, and his interests ranged from the science of Euclid to the philosophy of Ralph Waldo Emerson, but on that night he was curious to know how the great men and women of antiquity had governed themselves.

He happened upon an unusually interesting passage when Judge Davis had called out to him. It described the final moments of Julius Caesar on the floor of the Roman Senate.

But those who came prepared for the business enclosed Caesar on all sides, with their naked daggers in their hands. Which way soever he turned he met with blows, and saw their swords levelled at his face and eyes, and was encompassed, like a wild beast in the toils, on every side. For it had been agreed they should each of them make a thrust at him, and flesh themselves with his blood.

Abe Lincoln closed his eyes, sickened by the violence and horror of great Caesar's fall. Yet it was no mere story, and it had transformed history. Men stuck their blades into their brother out of jealousy, hatred, ambition, and all the usual abominable reasons, sometimes even disguised as the highest patriotism, reflected Abe Lincoln.

He lay the book on the floor, blew out the candle, and smelled burnt tallow in the darkness. He could feel Judge Davis sleeping next to him and wished he had a bed of his own.

The former backwoods rail splitter remembered the words of Shakespeare describing the death of Julius Caesar. "Oh what a fall there was, for when he fell— you fell, I fell, and Rome fell." Abraham Lincoln shuddered in the darkness, for the account of Caesar's assassination had moved him deeply. He'd seen dead soldiers as a captain in the Black Hawk War and never forgot their angry wounds.

Abe Lincoln feared the misuse of government power, and that's why he'd voted against the Mexican War, defying the popular will of Illinois. He'd received many pounds of angry letters, but at least no one tried to stab him. Some folks are made for politics, and others become country lawyers, he decided, as he sought to make himself comfortable on his side of the bed. It's a wise man who doesn't get them mixed up.

FIFTEEN

Nathanial's detachment spotted Santa Fe in distant haze. Bearded, covered with dust, they usually made camp at dusk, but maintained their march, anxious to reach wives, sweethearts, or houses of ill fame. They hadn't bathed since the copper mines, and their animals anticipated rubdowns followed by a peaceful night in the stable.

Nathanial sat erectly in his saddle, hat slanted low over his eyes, determined to lie to his pretty wife, because he never, never, *never* under any circumstances would relate certain tales concerning the Santa Rita copper mines.

The first thing a woman checks is physical evidence, but mercifully the bites and scratches had healed. Nathanial had "known" certain women before meeting Maria Dolores, and in fact had been considered something of a swine during his bachelor years. But sooner or later every swine goes too far, and he knew how ferocious women could become, the cruel remarks they made, and the sharp objects they had a tendency to throw, the dear little darlings.

He'd lied to women on countless occasions and knew all the tricks of the boudoir arts, but never had he lied to his beloved wife, mother of his son, partner of his life, flesh of his flesh.... Santa Fe loomed out of the gathering shadows, one of the southwestern frontier's biggest and wildest towns, adobe buildings jumbled together and ablaze with light, with whorehouses to suit every budget. The sound of a guitar wafted across the chaparral as the detachment's animals pulled together for the final haul.

Excitement grew as the soldiers drew closer to the "Sodom and Gomorrah" of the New Mexico Territory. Nathanial knew they were planning monumental debaucheries, and even he was in the mood for a good solid binge, but instead had to report to Maria Dolores.

He wished he weren't a cheating husband, but that stain never washed away. And he knew he'd do it again, because he could not resist the warrior woman. She was the female counterpoint of himself, a stone-cold killer when necessary, and a new experience whose ramifications he still was trying to decipher.

The Army horses clomped down Palace Avenue, headed toward Fort Marcy. Night denizens watched from sidewalks and alleys; it was always good to see the Army. The dragoons passed the *Parroquia*, the parish church, then rode through the gates of the fort. Nathanial headed for the command post headquarters, while his men veered toward the stables.

It was after taps, most lights out on the post, and faint sounds of revelry could be heard in Santa Fe. Nathanial knew that Maria Dolores was probably in bed, wearing one of her simple high-necked cotton gowns, for Maria Dolores was a proper lady, a rare and magnificent creature built to his scale, unlike usual small women, while her bosom was pure rhapsody in form. The more Nathanial thought about his wife, the more he desired her, and regarding certain events that occurred in the chaparral, they never really happened, did they?

Nathanial halted Duke III at the command post, climbed down from the saddle, and threw the reins over the rail. What purpose would it serve to tell Maria Dolores the truth? he asked himself as he climbed the stairs to the command post. It would only make her angry, and she might even kill me. Sooner or later there comes a time when a man must lie to his wife for the sake of domestic tranquillity.

He opened the door to the orderly room and saw the Charge of Quarters sitting behind the desk, a sergeant Nathanial vaguely remembered. "My detachment has returned from the Santa Rita copper mines," said the weary officer. "I'll report formally in the morning, but please make a note for your records."

The sergeant wrote on a square of paper, and Nathanial was about to return to his healthy-bodied wife when a door opened behind the desk, and a fearsome-looking, white-bearded colonel appeared. It was Colonel Edwin Vose "Bull Moose" Sumner himself, newly appointed commander of the New Mexico Territory, like a biblical prophet in army uniform, working late.

"Welcome back to Santa Fe, Lieutenant Barrington," he said in a clipped professional voice. "I've been receiving reports on you. Could you come to my office?"

Nathanial followed the colonel down the corridor. Bull Moose Sumner was another hero of the Mexican War, descendant of one of the oldest families in Boston, and a long-time Indian fighter. The commander's office contained boxes of documents piled to the ceiling. "I don't suppose you know we're moving," said

Colonel Sumner, as he sat behind his desk. "I'm establishing a new camp east of here, Fort Union."

Nathanial was taken by surprise. "Why?"

Bull Moose Sumner wasn't accustomed to receiving questions from his subordinates. "Santa Fe is a sink of vice and extravagance, or in other words, a bad influence on the men. The only reason I'm here is to complete some duties, and you're one of them." He opened a drawer in his desk and withdrew a sheaf of papers. "It appears that you've beat the hell out of a civilian—is that right?"

Nathanial remembered the miner in the trading post. "He threw the first punch, sir. Was I suppose to stand and take it?"

"Yes, because he's written to numerous politicians, who in turn have written to the War Department, who have asked me to submit a full report. Naturally, I have a tendency to side with the officer in these circumstances, but subsequently I've received word from Colonel Craig that you've been drunk on duty and have engaged in belligerent acts toward your fellow officers. Do you have any explanation for this unmilitary behavior?"

"I'm tired of making explanations, sir. Tomorrow morning you shall have my resignation on your desk, and I hope you'll pass it along without delay."

Colonel Sumner expected a plea for understanding followed by a heartfelt confession and the promise to reform, not the end of a military career. "Impulsive acts have been the hallmark of your service," he observed, "but you're an excellent officer in many respects, good with the men. Don't you like the Army, Barrington?"

"I mean no disrespect, sir, but I'd like to get out as soon as possible."

Bull Moose Sumner narrowed his eyes at the ugly shrinking scab atop Nathanial's dome. "You've been wounded, and according to your records, you haven't had a furlough for over two years. Perhaps you should take a few weeks off, to think things over. Then, when you're ready, we can discuss your future further."

"I've given this matter plenty of thought already," replied Nathanial. "I'm not the man I was when I joined the Army, and I think it's time for a change."

Bull Moose Sumner nodded solemnly, and he looked like Moses sitting on Mount Sinai. "I too am not the same as when I joined, and I know the short-comings of the Army perhaps better than you, but don't think civilian life is so wonderful. A man has to *do* something with his life, and you don't strike me as a layabout, are you?"

"I'd make a first-class layabout, sir. The world seems absurd and pointless to me."

"It *is*, but I hope you're not thinking of destroying yourself." Bull Moose Sumner leaned forward and said confidentially: "You haven't gone mad, have you?"

"I wonder if we could continue this conversation at another time, sir."

Colonel Sumner wasn't accustomed to being cut off by junior officers, which made him admire Nathanial more. "You're dismissed, Lieutenant. Please convey my compliments to your lovely wife."

Nathanial was bearded, filthy, but eager to see Maria Dolores. He walked swiftly across the parade ground, saluted the guards at the main gate, crossed the square before the Palace of Governors, and plunged into the streets of Santa Fe.

The more he thought about his wife, the more anxious he was to place his hands upon her voluptuous configuration. Yet it wouldn't be the same, because of the warrior woman. His skull ached dully, but he was sure it would heal faster once he got into bed with his beloved wife.

Wait a minute, thought Nathanial. How do I know what *she's* been doing while I was away. After all, she's an exceedingly attractive woman by any standard, and wedding rings are mere challenges to male predators such as I was prior to marriage. She's a flesh-and-blood woman, and I'm sure she's had certain temptations. Perhaps she'd been unfaithful too and is guilty as I.

Nathanial stopped in the middle of the sidewalk, unable to continue. Something told him he was headed toward an extremely trying scene with his wife. I need a drink, he thought, but if she smells whiskey on me, there'll be hell to pay.

The house was dark, and he imagined her sleeping peacefully, unaware that her husband was descending upon her. He stepped onto the porch, and his eyes spotted the sign: FOR SALE. He knocked stupidly on the door, though he knew no one was within. Where's my wife? he wondered. His first instinct was she'd run off with another man.

Maybe an old letter of hers is on its way to the copper mines, and we crossed on the trail. Here I am back in Santa Fe, and my wife has flown the coop. He drifted toward the saloon district, guitar music floated on the breeze, and he heard the roar of men's voices.

He arrived at the Silver Palace Saloon, where a crowd stood outside, passing bottles, joking, gesticulating, getting rowdy. Nathanial opened the door, stepped into the shadows, and maintained his hand near the holster of his service revolver.

The audience was subdued, as every pair of eyes ogled three scantily clad young women dancing upon the small stage, while a man sat at a piano jammed against the wall and plunked the keys. The dancers weren't renowned ballerinas, just local talent with pretty faces and nice figures. His eyes fell on his strange father-in-law observing the girls from the end of the bar. The old boy looked ready to wrestle all three of them, and it would probably kill him.

"Hey—watch where the fuck yer goin'!"

Somebody pushed Nathanial as he made his way through the crowd. Finally, he came to Diego Carbajal, who noticed his approach at the last moment. An expression of fear came over the old man's eyes, as if the Spanish Inquisition had finally caught up with him, but then he recognized his son-in-law.

"Where's Maria Dolores?" asked Nathanial.

"She's moved to a beautiful new home." The old man repeated the address. "Have you just arrived?"

"Yes, and I was just leaving. We'll have a drink sometime."

Nathanial never felt at ease with his father-in-law, as if a mere West Pointer weren't good enough for Diego Carbajal's daughter. The officer hastened for the door, delighted to know his wife hadn't run off with a rival. He ran like a hound dog through the night streets of Santa Fe, headed for his opulent new home.

Maria Dolores was awakened by a knock on the door. Instinctively, she reached for her Colt hanging in its holster from the bedpost. "Who's there?"

Her maid burst into the room. "Your husband is home, Señora Barrington."

Maria Dolores was thunderstruck. His boots approached down the hall. He'd followed the maid to his wife's boudoir and now stood in her doorway, hat in hand, an uncertain smile on his face. "Just arrived," he said uneasily. "Good to see you."

The maid lit a lamp, and Maria Dolores could smell her husband across the room. His uniform was filthy and tattered, he wore a beard that looked like it had mopped a few miles of desert, and there was something wrong with his head. "Is it really you?" she asked.

"I'm not sure," he replied.

She stepped toward him, touched his hair, saw the scab. "What happened?"

"Somebody shot me, but Sergeant Duffy said if a head wound doesn't kill you straight out, it's nothing to worry about. How's Zachary?"

She stared at the familiar stranger. "Zachary is fine, but we have missed you, Nathanial."

"I've missed the both of you, too."

She turned to the maid. "Fix a bath for my husband and set out his robe."

The maid bowed as she retreated from the room, leaving husband and wife alone.

"Where does Zachary sleep?" asked Nathanial.

"I'll take you to him." She held the lamp and led him down the corridor, like an Arabian priestess in a mosque.

"This is some house you have," he said. "Have you become rich in my absence?"

"I have not been happy, Nathanial. When you are gone, the family is broken apart."

"I told Colonel Sumner I'm resigning my commission. I thought of you constantly while I was away."

She opened the door and illuminated little Zachary in his crib, cuddling his teddy bear, fast asleep. His face seemed more finely formed, and he bore a striking resemblance to Nathanial's mother, but with a certain Mexican influence. "His health has been good?" inquired the concerned father.

"He has been very bad since you have been gone."

They returned to her bedroom, stood awkwardly with each other, then, suddenly she stepped toward him dramatically and looked into his eyes. "Have you been with another woman?"

"Of course not," he replied, unable to look at her directly.

"I think you are lying."

"I am not lying."

"I can tell when you are lying, Nathanial."

He gathered together every ounce of his strength and managed to look at her. "I'm not lying."

"Who was she—some prostitute you met in a cantina, or did you seduce a girl from a nice family?"

"My dear, I was with about two hundred other men in one of the most remote parts of New Mexico. I think your imagination is running away with you, perhaps because you're guilty about something *you've* done."

"Me?" she asked in a little voice.

"Have *you* been with anybody else?" he asked.

"There is *nothing* a man will not say. Who was she?"

He wondered how she'd divined the truth, or whether she was just bluffing. Her eyes burned into him, and he felt like a sneaky traitor. Dropping onto a chair, he covered his face with his hands. "It's true," he admitted.

She wanted to crash the lamp into his skull, but it might set fire to her new hacienda. "What was her name?"

"I don't know. She was an Apache woman. Something happened ..."

"I can't imagine what," replied Maria Dolores, a murderous tone in her voice. With an angry screech she reared back her arm. He could block her blow easily, but instead closed his eyes and let her land one good one on him.

Maria Dolores was bigger than most men and had a wallop like a boxer. He saw stars, his headache worsened immediately, but he grabbed her wrist before she could whack him again. "That's enough," he said firmly.

Their bodies touched, her breasts jutted into him, and he felt the strength go out of her. "I hate you," she replied. "You have betrayed me."

"What about you?" He took her chin in his fingers and forced her to look into his eyes. "What have you been up to in my absence, my dear?"

Tears filled her eyes. "There was a man ..." she began.

Livid, Nathanial reached for his revolver. "Who was he?"

"It was nothing, but I felt something for him. Perhaps ... I don't know."

"You didn't ..."

"No."

"I don't believe you."

Fire flashed from her eyes. "How *dare* you doubt me."

They looked into each other's eyes, then burst into

laughter, their marriage becoming bedroom farce. Confused, frightened, giggling nervously, they didn't know what to do.

"It just happened once," he explained. "I don't even know her name, and probably will never see her again. She belongs to one of the wildest southern tribes, and if I hadn't been lonely, it would never have happened. Anyway, I've decided to resign my commission. I need my family, otherwise I get into trouble."

"It was the same with me—I was lonely—he was a good man, and I sinned in my heart, which wasn't as bad as what *you* did, but it was bad enough. You must never leave me alone again."

"Never," he swore to the impossible task.

He reached for her, touched his tongue to her throat, and felt her hefty body against him. Nearly as tall as he, she was another female mirror image of himself, and sometimes he wondered if he were really in love with Lieutenant Nathanial Barrington.

He felt her hands on his waist, and she was, quite simply, the most erotic creature he'd ever known. He had the urge to tear the gown off, but Maria Dolores wouldn't approve of destroying good clothing. He could feel her warm fragrant naked body beneath the cotton gown.

He laid her gently on the bedspread, then removed his clothes. She watched her big blond beast returning after depositing his seed with another woman. But I am not perfect myself, she admonished herself. For better or worse, this is my man.

He lowered himself onto her, and his headache vanished. An old married couple well-skilled in each other's physiognomy, they soon were performing the horizontal fandango as faint sounds of guitars drifted through the half-open window. Nathanial touched his tongue to her caramel ear. *I don't care what Bull Moose Sumner says,* he thought. *I'll never leave this woman again.*

Chatoosh peered through poplar branches at little José diligently rubbing down the horses. It appeared the boy was talking to the animals, and Chatoosh couldn't help noticing they were at ease with him, although they behaved finicky and sidesteppish whenever he, Chatoosh, was around.

Chatoosh felt jealous of the boy, but killing him wouldn't absolve the pain, and might even make it worse. *I have been evil,* thought Chatoosh, *and that is why the horses hate me. This boy carries a special gift that I would love to steal, but it is his alone. It would be wrong to harm such a child.*

Chatoosh pushed his way through the chaparral, as the boy reached for his bow and arrow. "It is only me," said the warrior. "I have been thinking about you."

The boy appeared fearful as he resumed brushing Chatoosh's horse. "What do you want me to do, Chatoosh?"

"I have decided to bring you home."

José dropped the brush in astonishment.

"You slow me down," explained Chatoosh. "You should be with your mother. At dawn we leave for the Mimbreno encampment."

José stared at him, trying to understand. "Why . . .?"

"Perhaps the mountain spirits have influenced my decision," replied Chatoosh. "You are a good boy, but I have been cruel to you." Chatoosh's voice caught in his throat. "I am sorry."

"You could not help yourself," replied Chatoosh.

"Prepare yourself for the journey, and do not think I want to be friends with you. Stay away from me, or I might kill you yet."

The great chief Mangas Coloradas rode into Gold Canyon, accompanied by his grandson, Little Antelope, on his new horse. They stopped at a stream, climbed to the ground, watered the horses, and then drank.

"I like this place, Grandfather," said Little Antelope. "It is so beautiful."

"No more beautiful than other canyons," replied Mangas Coloradas as he kneeled at the water's edge.

"But the rocks are so bright." Little Antelope picked up a nugget big as a sparrow's egg. "They are like fire."

"Do not be fooled by shiny things, because that is what the White Eyes do. They would kill each other if they found this place."

They peered across the valley at a huge gold vein like a diagonal stripe across the face of a mountain. Mangas Coloradas picked up a heavy gold rock large as Little Antelope's fist. It would buy many horses, jewels, and bottles of whiskey, but where was the honor in selling pieces of the ground?

The White Eyes dug up sacred mountains, and many warriors and sub-chiefs wanted to fight, but Mangas Coloradas had learned a lesson from Manuelito. There is a peaceful resolution of every problem, he told himself, as he beheld the smoldering depths of the nugget. Would it be better if I brought the diggers to one place, so they will leave the rest of the homeland alone?

*   *   *

The maid Juanita held Zachary's head with one hand while washing his face with the other. "Be still," she said crossly. "Don't you want to look nice for your father?"

Zachary had been told the great man had returned, the house was in an uproar, and he'd even heard his mother singing in other rooms. The boy tried to cooperate as Juanita dressed him in a clean pair of light blue pants and a red shirt, then tied his little shoes. She brushed his hair, looked at him critically, and her expression seemed to say: He'll do.

She carried him across the corridor, down the stairs, and to the dining room, where the boy saw his father and mother sitting at the table. His father looked enormous as he arose from his chair. Then he rushed toward his son and took him in his arms, smothering him with kisses. "I've missed you so much," said the war hero. "I hope you've been a good boy."

"No," said his mother, "he has been crying all the time, but he is not crying now."

"I'm not leaving my family ever again. Maybe you can give me a job at one of your businesses, my dear."

"You should rest awhile and let your head heal."

Zachary touched his hand to his father's scab. "What?"

"A bullet went through there, Zachary."

Mother appeared cross. "Don't talk to him about those things."

"My son's not afraid of anything, right Zachary?"

Zachary kissed his father's cheek. "Right," he tried to say.

"What are you going to do today?" asked his mother.

"I thought I'd spend the day with you."

"But I must work, Nathanial. Do you think my businesses run themselves?"

"Then I'll take care of Zachary. We can go for a walk together."

"I hope you do not show him cantinas or other places where bad people go."

"If there's any trouble, I'm sure Zachary and I can take care of ourselves."

"You will be careful with him, Nathanial? I don't want you drinking in his presence."

Maria Dolores left for her office, and soon thereafter Nathanial escorted Zachary into Santa Fe. The boy rode his father's shoulders as the fragrance of desert foliage wafted by. They passed through the gate at Fort Marcy, soldiers drilled on the parade ground, and the American flag whipped the sky.

They came to a house, Nathanial knocked on the door, no one answered, so Nathanial and his son looked through the window. It appeared deserted. Next thing Zachary knew, he was on his way across the parade ground. Men saluted his exalted father, and then Zachary Taylor Barrington was carried into a dark cramped room with clothes, bottles, and cans piled on shelves, accompanied by exotic but not unpleasant smells. "Good afternoon, Lieutenant Barrington. Who you got there with you?"

"My son, Zachary."

"He looks like he's ready to take command of this Army post."

"He'd probably do a better job than Bull Moose Sumner."

The sutler cleared his throat, then glanced toward the corner, where Colonel Bull Moose Sumner was examining a pair of pants. Nathanial realized he'd just undermined his career yet again, and young Zachary

felt fear through his father's arm. But Bull Moose
Sumner smiled at the boy. "I'm sure the lad *could* do
a better job than I. If he wants the command, he can
damn well have it."

Nathanial cleared his throat. "I was looking for
Lieutenant Hargreaves, sir. Has he been sent to Fort
Union?"

"Yes. The Jicarillas have been raiding again, and I
think we'll see action before long. I trust you're feeling
better now that you've had a night's rest."

"I feel more strongly than ever that I want to resign
my commission. This isn't the place to discuss it, but
I just thought I should let you know."

"If you want to resign your commission, I certainly
won't stand in your way. You appear headed for a
court-martial anyway, and perhaps it's the best thing.
I'll hate to lose you, Barrington, but nobody's
irreplaceable."

Colonel Sumner paid for his pants, patted little Zachary atop his head, then departed the sutler's store.
Nathanial felt embarrassed in front of his son, but
his son thought the hero had given a good account
of himself.

It appeared that Lieutenant Beauregard Hargreaves
of Charleston, South Carolina, was at Fort Union.
Beau and Nathanial had been roommates at West
Point, served together on General Taylor's staff in the
Mexican War, and had fought Apaches together out
of Fort Marcy. During their West Point days, Na-
thanial had visited Beau's home in Charleston, while
Beau had spent vacations on Washington Square.
Beau was about the only man Nathanial could speak
with openly, but Beau was at Fort Union.

Nathanial wondered what else to do with Zachary.
He couldn't take the boy on a ride through the coun-

try, because the country was full of Apaches. He was tempted to have a glass of whiskey, but Maria Dolores would slap his face. "Let's go for a walk," he said to Zachary.

Zachary felt himself flying through the air, landing on his father's shoulders. Horses pranced in the streets of Santa Fe, pretty ladies waltzed over planked sidewalks, and the striped barber's pole always fascinated Zachary. The boy thought they were going to church, but his father stood across the street from the cathedral, making no move to the door.

Nathanial had been raised an Episcopalian, became Roman Catholic to marry Maria Dolores, and wondered whether to become a free-thinker. He was tired of sermons, and too many ministers behaved as if they'd graduated from drama academies. Santa Fe was mostly saloons and cantinas, so he returned to his new home, handed Zachary over to Juanita, and found his books in a room on the second floor, with a desk and chair.

He looked at the books his mother had sent him, but had no desire to improve his mind. He resided in the bosom of his family, but somehow didn't feel at home. Wandering through the mansion, he liked the Spanish-Moorish architecture, the quality of furniture, and was reminded of his mother's home on Washington Square.

He came to an open door that led to the cellar. At the bottom of the stairs were odd pieces of furniture, a stack of lumber, and sealed crates. Nathanial flopped onto a chair and spread out his legs. The cellar was cool, musty, smelling of old fabrics. Now at last he was alone with his thoughts, or so he imagined. Creaks came to him from upper floors of the mansion. What should I do? he asked.

He closed his eyes and let his mind wander. Images of Palo Alto flooded his consciousness, mixed with skirmishes he'd fought against Apaches. Who am I and what do I want from the world? he asked himself as something moved on the far side of the cellar, behind a stack of boxes.

In an instant Nathanial was on his feet. "Who's there?" he asked, drawing his revolver.

"D-don't shoot," said a male voice.

"Stand up, and hold your hands high."

Nathanial saw a curly black head rise above the crates. It belonged to a frightened Negro in his late teens, wearing a dirty shirt and work pants, holding a book. "I didn't mean no trouble, sir. I was just readin', that's all."

"What is it?" asked Nathanial.

"The Bible, sir. Please don't tell my massa, because he don't like me readin'."

"Who's your massa?"

"Mister Braithwaite, sir. He said he'd kill me if he caught me readin' again, so when I ain't busy, I comes over here. I live right next door."

Nathanial stared at the Negro, inspiration for strife at political meetings, saloons, and officers' messes across the nation. "What do you do for Mister Braithwaite?"

"I work in his kitchen, sir. But my momma taught me to read."

"What's your name?"

"James, sir."

"I'm Nathanial." He held out his hand. "You may come here to read anytime you like."

The Negro looked wary, for he'd never shaken with a white man before. Finally, he reached forward, their hands embraced briefly. "Thank you, sir."

Nathanial always felt uncomfortable around slaves, so he headed for the stairs. If I had the courage of my convictions, he thought, I'd buy that poor darkie and turn him loose.

SIXTEEN

"This is the worst idea you have ever had, Mangas Coloradas."

Delgadito wore a bandage around his rear end, as he spoke with his distinguished chief. They crouched behind pine trees and gazed at miners below, sluicing gold alongside a stream sacred to the People, a place of visions.

"Is it better," asked Mangas Coloradas, "to let the White Eyes dig our sacred lands, or simply give them all the yellow metal they need, and then they will leave us alone."

"It would be better to gather them in one place where we could kill them," replied Delgadito, "but if you walk into that camp alone, there is no telling what the White Eyes will do to you."

"When I tell them about Gold Canyon, they will fall at my feet and worship me. For gold is the most important thing to them."

"Mangas Coloradas, I urge you to rethink your plan."

"I have given it sufficient thought—my mind is made up. Do not worry about me, for I have spoken with General Stephen Kearny and Commissioner John Bartlett. I know how to negotiate with the White Eyes. Wait for me here."

The mighty chief arose, and with great stateliness, mounted his war pony. Delgadito shook his head sadly, for he fully expected Mangas Coloradas to be murdered in the minutes to come.

One of the diggers noticed an Apache riding down the mountain. "Looka thar!"

They pounced onto their rifles and glanced about nervously, expecting Apache encirclement. But a voice came to them from above. "I am alone, and I come in peace!" called Mangas Coloradas.

The miners put their heads together, and one was deserter Dowd, the weasel. "I think we should shoot the son-of-a-bitch," he suggested.

"But he's unarmed," replied Dougherty, a tall bony miner from Boston; he'd attended Harvard for one and a half years. "Let's hear what he has to say."

"Might cost yer neck," said Dowd. "Any man who'd trusts an Apache is signin' his own death warrant."

"We've got guns, and he hasn't. Nothing to worry about," said Dougherty.

"Big son-of-a-bitch, ain't he?" asked Ryan, an escapee from the potato famine in Ireland. "I wonder if'n he's really alone?"

"Looks it," said Morgan, former Pennsylvania blacksmith, scanning the mountains, but his eyes passed over Delgadito shaking his head in dismay in the pine forest above. Oh mighty Life-giver, please spare Mangas Coloradas, prayed the sub-chief.

Mangas Coloradas felt like laughing, for the White Eyes were practically sniveling, yet were armed. "I have come to help you," the chief said, with a little bow to set them at their ease. Then he climbed down from the saddle. "I have watched you waste effort, for there are no yellow rocks here. If you want them—come with me. I will show you where yellow rocks are lying on the ground. You do not even have to dig."

It was silent as they reflected upon the Apache's extraordinary offer. "Think he's tellin' the truth?" asked Manning, a former Ohio farmer.

"Hell no," replied Dowd, aiming his rifle at Mangas Coloradas. "He just wants to lead us into a bushwhack. I think he's a thievin', lyin' Injun."

Mangas Coloradas found himself surrounded by rifles and pistols. Now, too late, he realized the correctness of Delgadito's position. All he could do is raise his chin like the great chief he was, suck in his belly, and say, "If you do not trust me, I may as well leave."

"Not so quick, you redskin bastard," replied Dowd as he exchanged his rifle for a bullwhip.

The great chief refused to run from diggers, so all he could do was stiffen his frame as the lash snaked around his bare chest. Biting his teeth in rage and pain, he raised himself even higher as the next pass wrapped around his face, nearly blinding him. He spun around, in time to see a length of lumber zooming toward his skull. It cracked him, his eyes filled with black ink, and he dropped to the ground.

One bunch of miners wrestled him down, while others bound him with rawhide, as Delgadito watched helplessly. They tied the chief to a tree, then the lash sang again.

A red scar appeared on the chief's back, but no sound escaped his lips. The strip of black leather whistled through the air, and each blow tore Mangas Coloradas's flesh. Blood dribbled down his back, but the great chief hung onto consciousness. I shall show these White Eyes how to die, he told himself, straining to maintain his regal calm throughout the torture.

The miners took turns whipping him as they passed the jug around. Some spat in his face, and others threw rocks at him. Finally, his eyes went white, his head dropped, and tension departed his legs.

"Is he dead?" asked Dowd, smoking a cigar.

Manning took the Apache's pulse. "No, he's still alive."

"Not fer long." Dowd drew his pistol.

"Hold on," said Dougherty. "What the hell you want to kill him for?"

"Because a good Injun is a dead Injun."

"I think we should send him back to his people, and let them see what we do to Injuns who bother us. Time they learned we don't tolerate Apaches."

They threw a bucket of water at Mangas Coloradas, and he came to his senses as they were untying him. He felt so weak, he could barely stand, and then one of them kicked him in the buttocks; he went flying onto his face.

The miners thought it the funniest sight they'd ever seen, the chief struggling to his feet. Covered with blood, nearly paralyzed with pain, he walked in measured steps to his horse, for he still was chief of the People.

The miners giggled, snorted, and threw stones, but he didn't try to dodge them, to show his disdain for White Eyes. With great effort he climbed into his saddle. Sitting erectly, he rode toward the thickest chaparral and felt certain they'd shoot him in the back. He nearly fell off the saddle a few times, but soon was alone in the wilderness. So great was his pain, he couldn't turn around to see whether the miners' camp was out of sight.

Delgadito popped his head from behind a sumac bush. "So," he said, but added no reproaches, for he didn't prefer to further humiliate the chief. Mangas Coloradas permitted himself to droop in the saddle as he and his warrior brother rode alongside each other, hearing miners' laughter recede into the distance behind them.

The sign said:

I BUY AND SELL CATTLE
T. Braithwaite

Nathanial opened the door and entered a room with three clerks writing furiously at desks. "I'd like to see Mr. Braithwaite."

"He's busy, sir. Should be free soon."

Nathanial sat on a chair, picked up an old copy of the Charleston *Mercury*, then laid it back down. A group of businessmen were ushered outside by someone who looked like a Mississippi gambler. After much handshaking and back-slapping the gambler returned and noticed Nathanial. "You want to see me?"

"If you don't mind."

"Always got time for the Army. I'm Tom Braithwaite."

Nathanial followed him into a large office overlooking the stockyards. Braithwaite was corpulent, with a blond mustache and three wattles for a chin. He sat behind his desk and said, "Are you buying or selling?"

"Buying," replied Nathanial.

"I've got plenty of stock, and I'll beat anybody's price. What do you need?"

"Actually, I wanted to buy your slave, James."

Braithwaite appeared surprised. "I thought you were after cattle for the Army. Who told you I'm a slave seller?"

"I'm your next-door neighbor, and I'm willing to give you a fair price for him."

Braithwaite frowned. "I wouldn't take your money, Lieutenant Barrington, especially since we're neighbors. James is the most worthless slave I own, and you practically have to kill him to get him to do anything. His favorite trick is acting dumb, but he's really too smart for his own good. I think the best thing for James is a bullet between the eyes."

"I'd like to buy him anyway."

Braithwaite narrowed an eye. "You aren't a nigger-lover, are you?"

"I think I can get work out of him, and I'd be happy to take him off your hands."

The cattle broker shrugged. "You've been warned and don't come crying to me when he turns out to be useless."

Braithwaite named his price, cash exchanged hands, and Nathanial left with a bill of sale for one male Negro, aged eighteen, good health.

The bloodied Mimbreno chief rode across the encampment, and the People gazed at him in awe. His back was covered with dried blood, his face lacerated and bruised, his august pride absent.

A terrible outrage had been committed against the People—that was clear. His wives and brothers helped him down from his horse, he limped toward his wickiup, and Nana arrived with blessings and incantations. The chief was helped inside and laid upon soft antelope skins. Nana kneeled over him, listened to his heart, then examined his wounds. "What happened?"

Mangas Coloradas opened his mouth with great effort. "I have defended the White Eyes in councils, and overruled those who desired open conflict. But we have tolerated the vermin long enough. From this day forward, I recommend war."

*   *   *

Maria Dolores began work early every day, while Nathanial lay like an oriental potentate in bed until noon. Servants cared for his clothing, prepared baths, and brought any delicacy he desired. It reminded him of growing up on Washington Square, with a woman still in charge.

After the first meal of his day, he usually spent a few hours with his son, then drifted toward downtown Santa Fe, where he visited saloons and cantinas, drinking and talking with bullwhackers, hunters, itinerant preachers, dog-eared gamblers, gold-hungry miners, and all the other forms of life attracted to the bright lights of Santa Fe. In addition, he often played poker with strangers, losing small and sometimes large sums, but got into no fights, and never went home reeling.

On weekends a group of neighbors would band together and ride to a nearby spot for a picnic. On Saturday evenings there was no lack of social affairs, since Maria Dolores was becoming a leading business figure in Santa Fe.

Nathanial couldn't explore the countryside, thanks to Apache hostility, but Santa Fe offered many diversions for a man of jaded tastes, including traveling theatrical companies and musical orchestras. He soon was on a first-name basis with the mayor and other local dignitaries, for everybody liked Lieutenant Barrington.

Sometimes he felt uneasy about his future, and his disquietude increased as the end of his leave approached. Finally, early one morning, Nathanial dressed in a new tailored uniform, kissed his wife and son good-bye, and headed toward Fort Marcy.

He was rested, healed, barbered, and carried his letter of resignation in his back pocket. He reported to the command post headquarters and asked if Colonel Sumner were there.

"He's gone to Fort Union," said Sergeant Bradley, the new sergeant-major. "Your orders are to report there without delay."

"Sorry, but I'm resigning my commission." Nathanial handed the declaration to the sergeant. "My family is in Santa Fe, and this is where I'm staying."

The sergeant appeared confused. "Maybe you'd better talk to Captain Milligan. He's in charge now. Would you have a seat?"

Nathanial realized that Colonel Sumner had tricked him, and his resignation had been delayed needlessly. I don't give a damn what they do to me, thought Nathanial. I'm not going to Fort Union.

"He'll see you now, sir."

Nathanial strolled into the office of a former upper-classman at West Point. They shook hands, although they'd never been close friends. But they were West Point brothers, despite everything.

"You didn't really refuse to obey orders, did you, Lieutenant Barrington?" asked Milligan.

"I just handed in my resignation, and I'm not leaving my family again."

"Take them with you. Fort Union permits wives, unlike Fort Webster."

Fort Webster was a new post under construction at the Santa Rita copper mines, named after Secretary of State Daniel Webster. "I could never ask my wife to leave Santa Fe. She has business interests here."

"That's not the Army's fault. Your orders are to report to Colonel Sumner at Fort Union."

"I'm suffering blurred vision, constant headaches, and dizzy spells. I need more sick leave."

"Until your resignation goes through, I suppose?"

"Correct."

The miners ate bacon, biscuits, and beans for breakfast, washing it down with large quantities of thick black coffee. They denied themselves nothing although the pickins had been mighty slim thus far. Despite sophisticated mining techniques, they weren't accumulating enough gold to pay expenses, and naturally everyone blamed everyone else for their misfortune. A vast reservoir of bad feelings flowed among them, with the coffee.

"I knowed this valley was bad luck," exclaimed Dowd, although he'd voiced no objections when first they'd settled in the area. "I think we should find us another stake."

Old Bill raised his arm in protest. " 'At's the way it always is. Just when a camp gits close to paydirt, the miners move on. Then the next bunch comes, and they're the ones who end with the boodle. I seen it happen time and time again, boys. That's why that Injun wanted us to move, because he knowed we was a-gittin' closer. We can't give up now."

Manning snorted derisively. "That Injun was full of horseshit, and we sure showed him a thing or two. You'll notice we ain't see'd no more Injuns since we kicked the livin' shit out of 'im. You got to stand up to the bastards."

"I don't like workin' fer nawthin'," replied Dowd, "and I don't think there's a damned thing in this valley 'cept bad times."

"I think we should stay," replied Daugherty, the Harvard man. "We've already found gold, and where there's some, there's usually more."

"There ain't no rules in this business, boys," said Old Bill, "but I got a hunch about this place. Who knows, just a few feet more and maybe we'll find nuggets big as yer heads. I heard it all a million times, and it can happen to us—you'll see."

Dowd spat at the ground. "This old coot has heard everything and done everybody, but if he's so smart, how come he ain't rich? I think he's a jinx—you ask me." Dowd drew his pistol and aimed at Old Bill. "Shaddup, or I'll blow yer haid off."

A red splotch appeared on the front of Old Bill's shirt, and Dowd wondered if he'd shot him, but no gun fired. Then Dowd realized that the hardwood point of an arrow extended through the blood. The old miner pitched onto his face, the shaft poking out his back. Dowd was stupefied as arrows whistled through the air, piercing heads, throats, and torsos of his partners.

It happened so fast, Dowd wondered if he were dreaming. A silence came over the campsite, and he realized he was the only one still standing. The other miners were dead or groaning in pain. Dowd spun around, his gun trembling, but only chaparral was there. He became frightened as something moved behind a barrel cactus. Dowd turned and received a war club in the face. It sent him flailing backward.

When he opened his eyes, he was surrounded by Apaches. They held his arms and brought him to his feet. Standing before him was a certain Indian with fading whiplash scars across his weathered face.

"Remember me?" asked Mangas Coloradas.

"No," lied Dowd.

Mangas Coloradas barked an order, and Dowd was carried kicking and screaming toward a wagon wheel. They turned him upside down and tied him securely to the spokes.

Dowd knew what was coming, and all he could do

was shriek at the top of his lungs. But he could only kick his feet, for everything else was secured tightly to the wheel, his pleas in vain.

Several times during his Army days, then-Private Dowd had seen what would befall him. Upside down, disoriented, he watched as they lay dry twigs and branches beneath his very head. His life passed before his eyes, he saw himself as the lowdown varmint that he was, and for the first time since a child, feared the wrath of God.

If there was Heaven and Hell, he knew damned well which direction he was headed. He became terrified, wept and whined pathetically, and saw them bring fire to the branches and twigs. Smoke filled his nostrils, heat rose to the bottom of his head, and he went berserk, blubbering, drooling, and bellowing like a buffalo. Blisters formed on his black, singed pate, and an awful new smell rose to his nostrils.

Mangas Coloradas watched dispassionately as the miner's head was engulfed in flames.

Maria Dolores sat in her office, estimating the cost of a hotel she intended to build, but her mind kept wandering back to her son, husband, and marriage.

Nathanial had become a variety of saloon rat she knew only too well, from ownership of the Silver Palace Saloon. He gambled, drank, and swapped lies with the best of them, but at least he engaged in these pastimes away from home.

Maria Dolores loved her husband dearly and couldn't imagine being married to anyone else. The marriage would suffer additional strain after Nathanial became a civilian, because he expected to work in her business, but unfortunately didn't know anything about buying and selling, and indeed seemed to have an aversion for it.

Business was like chess, except Maria Dolores couldn't afford to lose too many games. Nathanial was well-mannered and highly educated, so naturally all the other wastrels and drunkards loved him. He could probably become mayor of Santa Fe if he put his mind to it, she calculated. I'm sure he's a brave soldier, but sometimes I feel like his mother.

He became stubborn whenever she made suggestions, as if her opinions didn't matter. He was a big angry animal, and she constantly had to placate him. The early months of their marriage had been idyllic, but now they were growing in different directions.

Despite his faults, he was an excellent husband in some respects, she had to admit. Maria Dolores often heard other women bemoaning their husbands' failing romantic powers, but Nathanial was a courteous and gallant gentleman, still good-looking despite the wear and tear of the Apache Wars, and when it came to certain interludes best not discussed in public, he was wonderful.

Perhaps I should be thankful, thought Maria Dolores. It doesn't matter whether he earns money, because I have enough for all of us. If he wants to be a wastrel—what do I care? As long as he remembers where his bed is, this marriage will survive.

Colonel Bull Moose Sumner sat in his new office at Fort Union and read another formal request for a military escort from Superintendent of Indian Affairs James S. Calhoun in Santa Fe. Evidently Calhoun wanted to arrange a peace conference with Mangas Coloradas, chief of the Mimbrenos, to stop attacks against miners in the Pinos Altos Mountains.

Bull Moose Sumner was from the school that said Indians respected one thing: naked force. He considered Calhoun a typical well-intentioned idiot who tended to get others killed. *I'm not risking my men for the sake of civilian nonsense,* decided Bull Moose Sumner. *Calhoun can go to hell for all I care.*

Bull Moose Sumner wrote a brief rejection letter within the guidelines of official correspondence. He placed the letter in his outgoing box, then picked the next document atop his incoming box and removed it from the envelope.

It was the resignation from Lieutenant Barrington, and Colonel Sumner frowned yet again. The Jicarillas and Utes were on the warpath in the east, Mimbrenos raided the south, and the Chiricahuas marauded into Mexico at will. Bull Moose Sumner had a full-scale three-pronged Apache War on his hands, but New Mexico was far from Washington, and the American people, in their supreme wisdom, didn't want a large standing army.

Bull Moose Sumner's forces were spread so thin he couldn't afford special detachments for silly Indian commissioners. The battle-hardened commander had no illusions about Lieutenant Barrington and knew him to be an insubordinate, quarrelsome, hard-drinking officer, the black sheep of a respectable New York family, but evidently also an effective leader, and they weren't easy to find.

There were two kinds of officers in Bull Moose Sumner's estimation. One group learned how to function in war, and the other didn't. Background, education, and courage had nothing to do with results, but Lieutenant Barrington had become a solid frontier officer.

Many times Bull Moose Sumner had thought of

handing in his own resignation. But he'd been fighting for America so long, he couldn't give up now. If he wants to resign, I can't stop him, sighed the old warrior, as he wrote a letter that consisted of one sentence: I regretfully accept the resignation of Lieutenant Nathanial Barrington.

The door to his office opened, and Sergeant Ferguson, his sergeant-major stood there. "Sir—an important message from Captain Milligan at Fort Marcy."

Bull Moose Sumner unfolded the correspondence and read about more massacres of miners in the Pinos Altos Mountains. He wondered if the Mimbrenos, Jicarillas, and Chiricahuas were acting in concert to hurl the Americans from the land they claimed.

"All leaves are canceled," he told Sergeant Ferguson, "and soldiers imprisoned for minor crimes will be released as of today. Captain Milligan will send every soldier he can spare to Fort Webster, from which a campaign will be mounted to counteract Apache depredations in the Pinos Altos Mountains. Please have those orders on my desk within the hour."

Warriors, maidens, wives, and unmarried *bi-zahn* women danced around a bonfire, as drums pounded and lutes were plucked. It was a sacred Property Dance, celebrating the influx of new wealth into the tribe.

The booty was guns, ammunition, clothes, blankets, and tools that they could sell back to the White Eyes, a mountain of largesse near the bonfire. Copious quantities of sacred *tizwin* were consumed as the People leapt about and shook their hips with glee. Miners were being driven from the Pinos Altos Mountains, and soon the homeland would return to normal.

The great chief Mangas Coloradas danced happily with his youngest wife, when a sentry galloped into the celebration. The drumming came to a halt, and the atmosphere became ominous as the sentry reported to the great chief.

"The captive boy named José is coming—the one who was stolen by the White Eyes at the copper mines!"

Everyone was stunned by the news, especially the warrior woman sitting with her big belly among the circle of women singers. She arose as José approached cautiously, followed by a warrior whom she vaguely recognized. Mangas Coloradas wondered if sorcerers were playing tricks upon him as the boy bowed before him.

"Do you remember me?" asked the boy.

"You are José, who has run away from the People."

The boy struggled to maintain himself erect. "I have made a mistake, and I want to return to my mother."

He looked around and saw her heavy with child, walking toward him. She dropped to one knee, and he wrapped his arms around her. "I have missed you so much, Jocita."

Tears filled her eyes as she hugged him against her. "My son has returned," she said. "I am thankful."

"I do not know what I was thinking when I left, but I remembered my *Nakai-yes* mother, and I . . ."

"Hush," said Jocita. "There is no need to speak of such things now, for they have been washed away by yesterday's rain."

Everyone noticed the strange nervous warrior standing to the side, carrying an old rusty rifle. "And who are you?" thundered the great chief Mangas Coloradas.

Before the warrior could speak, José said: "This is

Chatoosh, and he saved my life when I wandering alone in the wilderness. Without him, I could never have arrived here."

"I know that warrior!" said a voice in the assembly. "He has killed his brother!"

A woman made a weird ululating sound with her tongue as a shiver passed up Chatoosh's spine. This is what comes of good deeds, he thought darkly. "Yes, I killed my brother," he admitted, "and I killed him out of jealousy, but I have given you back this boy, and it is only fair that you let me leave in peace."

José shook himself loose from Jocita's arms and walked respectfully toward Mangas Coloradas. "He could have killed or enslaved me, but instead brought me back to my people."

"Chatoosh," said Mangas Coloradas, "there is no more evil deed than killing your brother, but this time you have saved a life. We are your People, because you have shown compassion to a helpless boy. Now you may remain among us if you wish."

Chatoosh bowed low. "I have dwelled alone for many harvests, and perhaps there is another lost boy out there, needing to be saved."

Chatoosh looked one last time at José, then turned abruptly and ran into the darkness. He was gone as suddenly as he arrived, leaving José with Mangas Coloradas, the warrior woman, and her husband Juh.

There was silence for several seconds, then Mangas Coloradas said: "Let the celebration proceed!"

Drums reverberated across steep mountain defiles as callused fingers plucked gutstrings. Juh of the Nednais took one of José's hands, while his mother, the warrior woman Jocita, held the other. They led him to the celebration, where José danced with warriors, maidens, *bi-zahn* women, his old friends, and even camp dogs. His blood pulsated in time to the music, and the boy felt the energy of the mountain spirits flow through him. My journey is over, he thought happily. Now I am back with the People.

Nathanial liked to nap in his backyard during the afternoon, pondering thoughts he considered profound. Often he'd prop up the pillow and gaze for hours at the Sangre de Cristo Mountains silhouetted against an endless azure sky.

Tension drained from his muscles, for it was his first real vacation in years. What's the point of pushing myself to exhaustion? he asked himself. They can give New Mexico back to the Indians for all I care. What is this warped sense of duty that keeps propelling me onward?

As a young boy, he'd decided upon a profession where his life would be in constant danger. What kind of fool would devote his life to the Army? he asked himself. He spotted a tiny dot high up in the sky and thought it the result of excessive drinking, but then realized a big old eagle was up there, searching for prey. What a perspective that bird must have, speculated Nathanial. He sees hundreds of miles, from Apache camps to Army posts, stagecoaches to trading posts, empty mines and filled graves. Why can't I take the long view like the eagle?

He heard a back door open and assumed his wife or one of the servants was coming to inquire if he wanted food, or perhaps a tall glass of lemonade. This is the life, Nathanial thought contentedly.

But he didn't hear his wife's skirt; it was jangling spurs and a steady measured military tread approaching. He opened his eyes and was dismayed to see a tall stringbean sergeant headed for him. Nathanial had never seen him before. The sergeant came to a halt beside the supine Lieutenant Barrington, threw a salute, and said, "Captain Milligan wants to speak with you without delay, sir."

"I've handed in my letter of resignation, Sergeant. Sorry, but I'm on leave."

"Colonel Sumner has canceled all leaves, and Captain Milligan says your resignation hasn't taken effect yet."

"Tell him to court-martial me if that's the way he feels. I was shot in the head recently, and do believe I've lost my mind."

"Captain Milligan said he'd have you arrested and thrown into the stockade if you didn't come back with me. The Mimbreno Apaches have gone on the warpath, and we need to reinforce Fort Webster."

Nathanial wished he could join the eagle high in the sky, but duty was calling. "I'll be right with you."

"Lieutenant Barrington reporting, sir."

"Have a seat, Lieutenant."

Nathanial dropped to a chair, fearing he'd pop the buttons on his uniform. He'd gained several pounds during his too-brief sick leave, but all he'd done was eat, sleep, and drink a variety of alcoholic beverages.

"I'm afraid I have bad news. All leaves have been canceled."

Nathanial shrugged. "Surely Colonel Sumner doesn't mean *me*, because I'm recovering from a wound to my head. Often I have dizzy spells, and sometimes I become disoriented. I don't think I'm fit for duty, and perhaps you should have the doctor look at me."

"The doctor has gone to Fort Union, and we're even releasing prisoners from the stockade. We need everyone we can get, because the detachment at Fort Webster is in danger of being overrun. We're expecting a company from Fort Union to help out, and you'll join them. You've been to Fort Webster, and I'm afraid you're going back."

"I don't suppose it concerns you that I've already tendered my letter of resignation."

"Not in the least."

Nathanial parted his hair and showed his scar. "I'm not quite right in my mind, sir."

"You never were—not even at West Point. Lieutenant Barrington, you have approximately a day and a half to settle your affairs. I expect you prepared to leave for Fort Webster at dawn on the day after tomorrow."

Nathanial trudged back to his hacienda, certain he'd be killed in the upcoming campaign. *I threw myself in West Point prison at the age of eighteen, and nobody, not my mother, father, or uncles tried to stop me. What the hell have I done to myself?*

He arrived at his hacienda, where Pedro, one of the servants, opened the door. "Are you all right, sir?"

"Where's my wife?"

"She has gone to the bank, sir."

"She's always at the bank, or a lawyer's office, or some other goddamned place," muttered Nathanial.

Nathanial wondered how his beloved wife would take the news, but he knew that his son would throw a tantrum in which no one could control him. *We can all have a good cry, and then I'll ride off to war like a knight of the Round Table, except the Apaches will skin me alive.*

"Where's my son?"

"In his room, sir.'

Nathanial climbed the stairs, realizing he'd been neglecting Zachary as of late. He opened the door and saw the fruit of his loins sitting on the floor, playing with blocks, while a maid knitted on a corner chair.

"I'm taking him with me," said Nathanial, and he lifted his son off the floor.

Zachary found himself hurtling through the air, and then he landed on his father's shoulders. His spirits improved immediately, because he always had fun with his father. Down the stairs, out the door, he rode happily into the bright-colored streets of the city, his father holding his legs for support. If only it could be this way always, thought little Zachary.

Halfway to the bank, Nathanial wondered whether he should interrupt his wife in the middle of important business negotiations. Perhaps we should talk in the privacy of our home, he determined. And since I have all day tomorrow to prepare for the trip, maybe I should step into this saloon and have a conversation with my son.

Nathanial lifted Zachary from his shoulder, and carried him in his arms through the door of the low adobe saloon. Everyone seemed to know Lieutenant Barrington as he introduced his son to the bartender, waitresses, and prostitutes. "Put a glass of whiskey on that table over there," said Nathanial.

He carried Zachary to the table, sat the boy upon the bench against the wall, and lowered himself beside him. Zachary was fascinated by the smells of whiskey and tobacco that he always associated with his father. He heard his father talking to him, but it was difficult to make out words in the constant din.

"Listen, Zachary," said his father, raising a glass of whiskey with one hand, and a cigarette with the other, "I haven't been a very good father, but when you're older, I'll teach you how to ride horses—we'll even go on hunts together. I'll introduce you to my Apache friends if they're not still on the warpath." Nathanial placed his hand on his son's shoulder. "My boy, a substantial portion of this town will be yours someday, at the rate your mother is going, but remember you're a man, and sometimes men are forced to endure hardship, danger, and even ... well, maybe you're too young for this stuff right now, but just remember you're the son of a soldier, the grandson of a soldier, the great-grandson of a soldier, and the great-great grandson of a soldier. Someday, if you're good, I'll teach you how to play poker."

Nathanial sipped his glass of whiskey, wondering whether to play a few hands before going home, as his son stared at him in reverence. In the little boy's eyes, his father appeared the most splendid and rugged individual in the world, head and shoulders above other men, strong, steady, with a friendly voice and playful manner. "Da-da," said Zachary, reaching for the great man.

A shadow fell over the table as the boy drew back his hand. His father was looking at a heavyset, well-dressed fellow carrying a glass of whiskey, advancing toward the table. "Barrington, I've been looking for you."

"Good day, Mister Braithwaite," replied Nathanial affably. "Have a seat."

"I don't sit with the likes of you!"

Zachary sensed trouble, because his father wasn't smiling as he rose slowly and deliberately from the table. "What's on your mind?"

"I saw James the other day, and you should have heard the way that Nigra talked to me. He said he was as good as me. You know—it's bastards like you who are ruining this country." Braithwaite pointed his finger at Nathanial's nose, and the saloon grew very still. "You teach Nigras to hate their rightful masters and incite them to riot. If the day comes when slaves rise up and kill white women and children—there'll be rivers of blood in the streets because of soft-hearted fools like you!"

The angry Southerner's words reverberated off the walls of the saloon, then Nathanial replied: "My son and I came for a drink, and that's all we want it to be."

Braithwaite threw back his head and hollered: "First he hides behind his wife's skirt, and now he's hiding behind his son's diapers."

It was the wrong remark to make to a man who'd just been dragooned back into the dragoons. Nathanial lifted Zachary off the table and placed him in the arms of a kindly-looking nearby prostitute.

Zachary coughed at perfume arising from her body, so different from his mother. Meanwhile, Nathanial turned toward the cattle broker. "I have a right to dispose of my property as I wish. If you don't like it, you know your recourse."

Braithwaite reached for his pistol, and so did Nathanial a split second later. But a split second can be a long time in a dueling situation, and Braithwaite's gun barrel cleared his holster as Nathanial was just grabbing his own iron. Braithwaite fired too high; the bullet zipped through the crown of Nathanial's wide-brimmed hat, which flew off his head. Then Nathanial pulled his trigger—*click*—a misfire. Braithwaite's arm trembled as he thumbed back his hammer for the next shot, but Nathanial threw his pistol at Braithwaite's face, then dived after it.

Zachary watched with mounting interest as his father crashed into the hostile man. Fists whizzed through the air, his father nearly got knocked off his feet by a solid blow, but then responded with a flurry of short chopping punches that sent his opponent reeling backward. Braithwaite bounced off the bar, came back at Nathanial, and both men stood toe to toe, trying to beat each other into oblivion, when suddenly Braithwaite's head snapped backward, then he tripped over a cuspidor and landed on his back. A crowd surrounded Lieutenant Barrington, slapping him on the shoulder.

"Great punch, Nathanial!" shouted one gentleman. "Let me buy you a drink."

"Don't mind if I do," replied Nathanial.

Nathanial carried his son to the bar, sat him atop it, and drank the first of several free whiskies. Meanwhile, women with powerful perfume were fussing with Zachary, kissing him, and telling him how pretty he was. A piano player struck up a tune, and several men at the end of the bar started singing. Zachary decided it was more fun than playing with blocks in his room.

The next thing he knew, he was on his father's shoulders, and they were headed out the door. "Time to go home," said the old boy, whose eye had turned purple, with a red mark on his cheek. "Let me do the talking, because Mother is going to get awfully mad. The great paradox about her is she got her start in the saloon business, but hates saloons. She might even raise her voice and throw certain articles about, so get ready for the worst, my boy."

They arrived at the hacienda; Nathanial opened the door cautiously and peeked inside. "Is my wife home?" he asked one of the servants.

"She is in her office."

A door slammed upstairs, and he heard his wife's voice. "Who's there?"

"Me," replied Nathanial, trying to sound confident despite opposing terrors.

Holding her skirts, she rushed down the stairs. At the bottom, when she could see them better, her normally placid countenance transformed into something resembling a mountain cat. "Where have you been?" she demanded. "You have been drinking, fighting, and you have taken Zachary with you?" She picked the boy up, hugged him tightly, kissed his plump cheek. "Have you taken leave of your senses, Nathanial? I cannot believe you would do such a thing."

From Nathanial's point of view, there was nothing wrong with exposing his son to the world in which men lived. He wanted to explain this to his beloved wife, but she was ordering a maid to give Zachary a bath. Zachary wailed and reached futilely for his father as the maid carried him to his room.

Nathanial and Maria Dolores faced each other in their sumptuous parlor. "I'm afraid I bear bad news," said the husband. "The Apaches are up to their old tricks, and I've been ordered back to the copper mines."

"Good." She saw hurt on his face, but kept on rolling. "You are an irresponsible fool."

The words stung more than a hard punch to the jaw, but his West Point pride didn't betray him. "If I'm such a trial, madam—good day."

Nathanial reeled toward the door, and Spanish pride prevented her from stopping him. She watched him march unsteadily out of her life, the door closed behind him, and she dropped to a sofa, to gather her thoughts.

My husband lacks common sense, she reflected, and he exposed my son to danger. Was it simply animal lust that brought us together? I can never leave him alone with the baby again. Maria Dolores knew her husband was going to war, but somehow it didn't bother her.

Nathanial stopped at the first saloon on his way to Fort Marcy. He ordered a glass of whiskey and tarried for a time, mumbling to himself at the bar as the man in the apron refilled his glass a few times, and waitress-prostitutes offered the delights of their persons. His next stop was a cantina full of tough Mexican vaqueros, and he found a vacant table in a corner, consuming two glasses of mescal in rapid succession, while continuing his angry conversation with his wife, although she wasn't there.

It wasn't long before he was wandering the streets of Santa Fe, a cigarette dangling out the corner of his mouth. He searched for Fort Marcy, but Santa Fe appeared a foreign city. He found no familiar guideposts, while imps and fiends lurked in alleys, anxious to waylay a lost wandering Army officer, or so it appeared to his alcohol-soaked eyeballs.

He felt disoriented, as though his mind had a broken wheel. He was going to war, his domestic life a shambles, and he didn't know whether to feel guilty about taking Zachary to the saloons. How else will he learn what it is to be a man? asked Nathanial, although a part of him lectured that he was a worthless drunk and was leading his son down the primrose path practically before the lad could walk.

What is a man? wondered Nathanial. And what the hell do I care what people think of me? Zachary spends too much time with women, and they'll make a pantywaist out of him. If a man's afraid to fight for his rights, he won't have any before long.

Across the street sprawled the Silver Palace Saloon,

one of his wife's many investments. Normally, he stayed away from the establishment, so as not to embarrass her, but now, in a gesture of defiance, stormed toward the door.

It was the cleanest saloon he'd seen that night, with the girls a cut above the other places. My wife is trying to dominate me, thought Nathanial, as he bellied up to the bar. If she thinks she's too good for me, she can kiss my ass.

The bartender poured a glass of whiskey. "On the house, Lieutenant."

"What for?" snarled Nathanial.

"It wouldn't be right to charge the boss lady's husband."

"She can go to hell, and so can you." Nathanial threw coins on the bar, then stumbled toward a table against the back wall. He sat heavily, slurped the top off his whiskey, and felt in a murderous mood. Goddamn women are always trying to domesticate us, but men need to cut loose once in a while, and that goes for Zachary too, although he's only seven months old.

A familiar figure walked down the aisle, his father-in-law. Oh-oh, thought Nathanial. This has got to be the strangest bird in Santa Fe.

Diego sat at the table. "Nathanial, you're drunk," he said disapprovingly.

"Mister Carbajal—evidently you haven't received the news. Your daughter has thrown me out, and I'm going on a scout tomorrow. Something tells me I won't be back."

Diego placed his hand on his son-in-law's mountainous shoulder. "You're a drunken lout, and you don't appreciate your family."

"I took your grandson to a saloon and showed him what it's like to be a man." Nathanial punctuated his statement of questionable fact by pounding his fist on the table.

"Tell me, Nathanial—who do you think will impress God most on Judgment Day, the righteous man or the drunkard?"

"What Judgment Day? There's nothing here but whiskey, bullets, and Apaches."

Nathanial pushed himself up from the table and saw himself surrounded by drunken louts just like himself. They guzzled, gambled, and made roaring pronouncements that made no sense at all. Nathanial craved fresh air, passing a man in a bearskin cap dealing a hand of seven-card-stud. Then suddenly a big, broadshouldered bullwhacker arose from his chair, got his spur caught on one of the legs, and lurched into Nathanial, who merely pushed him out of his way as he continued toward the open sky.

"Hey—who the hell d'ya think you are?" demanded the bullwhacker.

Nathanial didn't realize he was being addressed, so busy was he bemoaning his fractured marriage, and he was going back to the Santa Rita copper mines, where he almost certainly would be decapitated by a poor misunderstood Apache.

Frustrated, baffled, and bruised, Nathanial reached for the door, just as a hand landed on his shoulder. "I asked you a question, mister, and I want an answer."

The bullwhacker was bigger in the shoulders than Nathanial, but the old war madness kicked in, carrying the thrill of mortal combat bequeathed down the centuries from Nathanial's Celtic warrior forebears. "What's on your so-called mind, friend?"

"You just ran me down, and I ain't heard no apology."

The bullwhacker's powerful arms bulged and filled

the sleeves of his shirt, but he also had a big gut. Meanness glimmered in his eyes, for he'd just come to town after several days on the *Journada del Muertos*.

"I apologize," said Nathanial, ever the West Point gentleman. "I guess I've been drinking too much."

The bullwhacker's face softened. "I feel so goddamned loco, I'm ready to kill somebody."

"Let's have another drink—on me."

Two big men plowed toward the bar, and everyone got out of their way. Two glasses of whiskey were placed before them, and they toasted each other profusely, then tossed the contents down. It hit them simultaneously, both blacked out momentarily, then returned to Santa Fe.

"I've got to be going," said Nathanial. "Got a lot to do tomorrow."

"But you just arrived!" protested the bullwhacker. "Maybe you'd better have another drink. Bartender—where the hell are you?" The bullwhacker yanked out his Colt, aimed at the ceiling, and pulled the trigger.

The cartridge exploded, propeling the ball upward. Splinters fell to the bar, and everyone become extremely silent in the Silver Palace Saloon.

"Friend," said Nathanial, "I think you'd better put that away."

"What the hell for?" The bullwhacker turned toward Nathanial and aimed at him. "Don't tell me what to do with my gun!"

"I'm afraid you might shoot somebody by mistake."

"If I shoot somebody, it sure as hell won't be a mistake, and if you ..."

Nathanial saw the bullwhacker's attention flicker, so he lunged forward, his hand knocked the gun downward, then it fired, blowing wood chips out of the floor. Nathanial brought his elbow around, slamming the bullwhacker's nose, bending it out of line. At that point everybody in the vicinity dived onto the bull-whacker and wrestled the gun out of his hand.

The bullwhacker struggled to stay on his feet, but the combined weight of three vaqueros, two miners, and one bank clerk forced him to the floor. Nathanial didn't need an interview with the local sheriff, so he shoved his way to the door, then walked swiftly toward Fort Marcy.

Disheveled and demoralized, he was saluted by dragoons guarding the gate. He headed for the Bachelor Officers' Quarters, aware he was stumbling like a buffoon, but struggling manfully to retain his West Point posture. The guards would pass the word that he'd come home drunk, and another misconduct notation would be made in his folder, but he was long past caring about his military career.

Many rooms were vacant at the Bachelor Officers' Quarters, since most dragoons had been transferred to Fort Union. He found his old musty-smelling lodging, threw open the window, unrolled the mattress, took off his hat and boots, and collapsed.

In a red silk robe, Maria Dolores wandered her spacious home. She bumped into furniture and kicked things over, so dazed was she by the sudden collapse of her marriage. Servants watched from shadows, whispering and worrying.

I still love Nathanial, Maria Dolores admitted, but why? How can I remain married to a worthless drunkard unable to care for his son? From room to room she walked aimlessly, frightened and angry at herself. I should have waited till he was sober, but he hasn't been sober for weeks. She realized that Nathanial needed encouragement, not disapproval. Maybe I can talk with him early in the day, when he's still lucid.

She devised new and exciting plans for reforming her errant husband, although she knew that drunkards seldom reformed and generally drank themselves to death if they weren't killed first in an altercation.

She took a bath, changed clothes, and was sitting to breakfast when her worried father arrived. "I saw your husband last night, and he was in quite a state," said Diego as he sat at the kitchen table. "Then he got into a fight with a man who came within three inches of killing him."

Maria Dolores behaved as if this scandalous information was of no consequence, but secretly it infuriated her. So he didn't go to the fort when he left, but instead resumed his drunken wanderings. "Sometimes I think my husband is *un pocito loco*," she confided to her father.

"I knew this would happen before you married him," her father stated matter-of-factly as he reached for the sticky buns. "I don't deny that Nathanial can be quite charming at times, if you like the befuddled kind, but don't you think it's time to find a responsible husband?"

Maria Dolores rushed to the nearest mirror, where she examined new imaginary wrinkles beneath her eyes and at the corners of her mouth. I'm becoming an old married woman because of that crazy *gringo* I have married, she thought. Perhaps my father is right, and any effort to reform Nathanial will be in vain. "But I'm still in love with him, I think," she complained.

Diego didn't prefer to continue denigrating his son-in-law, and actually, in a strange way admired the big, hard-hitting officer. And didn't God give every man a purpose, even drunkards like Nathanial Barrington? Then a stupendous thought came to the secret practitioner of a forbidden ancient religion. What if my son-in-law is one of the *Lamed Vav*, the sainted Thirty-six?

"I thought this was where you'd be."

Nathanial's old West Point classmate, Lieutenant Beauregard Hargreaves, stood at the foot of his bed, a wry expression on his ruddy features. "I heard you were being sent to Fort Webster," continued Beau, "so I volunteered to go along for the ride. I thought we could have some fun together."

Despite headache, stomachache, and foul taste in his mouth, Nathanial was happy to see his best friend. They'd even courted the same woman, Beau's current wife, the former Caroline Harding, daughter of the recently retired major of dragoons. Beau and Nathanial had been not only roommates but partners in pranks since their plebe year at the Point.

Nathanial felt embarrassed by his torn uniform, black eye, pulped lips, and contusion on his forehead, where somebody had punched him during the course of the previous evening. "I need a drink," he said.

"I don't believe I've ever seen you like this before," said Beau. "Good God—you look like hell, Nathanial. You'd better pull yourself together."

"I've resigned my commission," explained Nathanial, "but they won't let me out of the Army. In addition, my beloved wife has thrown me out. I have the premonition that I'm going to die within the next two or three weeks."

"I wouldn't let Captain Milligan see you like that, Nathanial. You look like someone shot at you, missed, then hit you the second time around."

* * *

Nathanial checked his horses and men, in that order, to assure preparations were underway for the move back to the copper mines. Then came time to retrieve clean uniforms and equipment from his former home. On his way from the stable to the front gate, he turned a corner and nearly ran down Captain Milligan.

"Lieutenant Barrington—do you have any idea what you look like?"

"Sir—I fell down a flight of stairs last night and damned near killed myself."

"Was that before or after the fracas at the Silver Palace Saloon? Lieutenant Barrington—the men in your detachment are relying upon your leadership, and I shall put you in shackles and chains if one hair on their heads is harmed because of your stupidity."

No longer master of the mansion, Nathanial sneaked in via the kitchen door, where no one would announce him to his wife. Like a thief he darted up the stairs, but nothing escaped the eyes of his wife's servants.

He entered his bedroom, pulled the bedspread off the mattress, spread it on the floor, and threw two uniforms onto it. Then he added his straight razor, underwear, an extra pair of boots, a few shirts, and his saddlebags. There was a knock on the door, and his heart nearly stopped. "Who is it?"

The door opened on James, his former slave, now an employee of his wife. "I heard you're goin' to war, sir."

"Last night I nearly went to war over you," replied Nathanial. "You should watch how you talk to people like Mister Braithwaite."

"He's mad because he can't boss me anymore."

"Could you fix me a bath before I leave?"

"I'll have to ask your wife, sir."

Next, Nathanial visited his son in the nursery. The boy played with toy wooden soldiers, a gift from Nathanial's father, and Nathanial got down on the floor with his progeny, kissed his cheek, and said, "I'm going away, and we may not see each other for a while. I expect you to take good care of your mother."

Nathanial embraced his little boy as Maria Dolores opened the door. She saw father and son kissing, and her eyes became salty.

"I've come to say good-bye," said Nathanial. "I'm not looking for trouble, and I haven't had a drink all day. Of course, it's still morning, but . . ."

He had no idea what to plead, so made his bitter smile and headed for their former bedroom. She followed him, tears streaming down her cheeks; she couldn't help loving and hating him.

They came to the room where they'd performed intimate acts in the recent past. Maria Dolores wore an all-black dress with a high white collar. "I do not think we should part this way," she said.

"You're the one who threw me out."

"You must stop drinking if you care about your family."

"There's nothing to do except go to saloons. You should have given me part of the business to manage."

"Managing a business is no simple matter, and you don't know anything about it anyway. Besides, you're always drunk."

He looked her in the eye. "I can't get along without you."

"You will have to change."

"Why can't you get used to being an Army wife?"

"I thought you were resigning your commission!"

"It hasn't been accepted yet, and I'm on my way back to the Santa Rita Mountains. If other Army wives adjust to their husband's careers, why can't you?"

It grew silent in the bedroom where they'd shared intimacies on numerous occasions. Each knew they might never see each other again, and they'd always felt a certain attraction. The bed was a few feet away, and she offered no resistance as he maneuvered her toward it. She tasted blood upon his lips, then they reached for each other's buttons, clasps, and hooks. "I will give you something to live for," she whispered into his ear, and the mattress groaned in protest.

SEVENTEEN

A cloudless sky beckoned as the column of dragoons snaked across the endless plain. They rode in two files, with the stars and stripes in front, a guidon flag to the side, flank guards, and scouts leading the way south over the *Journad del Muertos*.

Many soldiers wore tan canvas pants, not blue wool Army issue trousers, and a few sported buckskin jackets with fringes, like mountain men and Indians. Each had exchanged his high-crowned dragoon cap for a light-colored broad-brimmed vaquero hat molded into a shape and style to suit the raffishness of the wearer.

Three horse lengths before the guidon rode two first lieutenants, also topped with wide-brimmed vaquero hats, but with regulation military tunics and gold shoulder straps. They sat erectly in their saddles, wore gauntlets, and demonstrated a certain West Point panache as they advanced deeper into the Apache homeland.

Beau's black mustache covered his upper lip, while long, curly side whiskers framed his face dramatically. He raised his hand to shield his eyes from the sun as he peered ahead.

Nathanial dozed in the saddle, orange bandanna covering his nose and mouth, thinking about his wife and their passionate farewell. He was determined to rescue his marriage, or so he thought that day. Her kind and loving heart, the majesty of her walk, her innate goodness, and numerous other traits all had combined to ensnare him yet again, and sometimes he felt like a prisoner of romance.

"Do you know where we are?" asked Beau.

Nathanial roused himself. "I haven't the slightest idea. Did you ever realize—back at West Point—we'd end up like this?"

"Never." Beau looked at him curiously. "Nathanial, have you ever stopped to think what you'd do if the Northern and Southern states went to war against each other?"

"I hope it'll never happen," replied Nathanial. "But I'm sure the politicians will continue blundering along, and the Compromise seems to've worked for the time being."

"Maybe so, but the South's leading thinkers are calling openly for secession."

Nathanial turned toward his old friend. "What will *you* do, Beau, if the South secedes?"

Beau shrugged. "I'll fight for South Carolina, sir."

"I'd hate to face you across a battlefield."

A strange expression came over Beau's face. "Could you kill me, Nathanial?"

"I doubt it. Could you kill me?"

"Never."

Nathanial held out his hand. "Let's always be friends, no matter what the politicians say."

Beau clasped his hand. "Friends to the end, but I hope the end doesn't come."

Nathanial raised his spyglass and saw the scout signaling toward the sky, where a flock of buzzards circled. "Perhaps an antelope keeled over and died," guessed Nathanial.

"It may be more than an antelope," replied Beau. "We'd better alert the men."

Maria Dolores kneeled in a pew, fingering rosary beads. Please protect Nathanial for the sake of his son, Virgin Mary.

She felt guilty about fighting with Nathanial, but found his lackadaisical approach infuriating. Sometimes she wanted to grab his shirt and shake sense into him. She'd never forgive him for his love affair with the Indian, because she suspected it was not as casual as he'd claimed. Her husband was essentially mindless when it came to certain matters, like most men, yet he was unfailingly polite and essentially decent, although he'd fallen away from Holy Mother Church in recent months.

I'll give him a job and make him think he's important, although I'll have to check all that he does. Despite everything, he's a wonderful man in many ways, and that has to stand for something, *madre mia*. And he's usually very good with the baby. We'll be fine once his resignation become official. I wonder where he is right now?

The dragoons wore their bandannas over their noses to muffle the noxious odor. According to the tracks, a wagon train of miners had been riding the *Journada del Muertos*, probably headed for the Pinos Altos Mountains. Buzzards dived squawking out of the sky, landing behind the next rise. Each soldier sought to strengthen himself for the horror that lay ahead.

Nathanial rocked back and forth in the saddle as he approached the crest of the hill. He'd seen massacres, mutilations, and rapes, but the smell penetrated his bandanna as the *conducta* came into view.

The wagons had been burned to the ground, with semi-eaten, decomposing cadavers. Nathanial's practiced eyes could surmise where the Apaches had hidden, waiting patiently for the miners. He imagined gold diggers playing mandolins and singing songs as they rolled along, an adventurous bunch of vagabonds waltzing blithely into a hail of well-aimed arrows.

Nathanial engraved the terrain into his mind for his official report. The smell became more pronounced, but he thought the men should see what they were fighting. As their officer, he'd have to set the example.

He rode stolidly into the carnage, then stopped his horse and climbed down from the saddle. "Sergeant Duffy—appoint a detail to count the dead!"

Beau dismounted and joined Nathanial, who was removing his notebook from his saddlebags. "You don't intend to spend the afternoon here, I hope."

"Just long enough to make my report."

Nathanial wrote his approximate location, noting prominent terrain features, while Beau gazed calmly at heaps of bodies. "I never dreamed," he said, "that such savagery could exist."

Nathanial took azimuths of mountains, then consulted his map. Sergeant Duffy marched toward him and said, "Eighteen dead, sir. Including three women and one baby."

Nathanial felt as if someone had punched him in the stomach, but betrayed no emotion. After completing his notes, he drifted closer to the wreckage. Tattered dresses of women could be seen, and Nathanial guessed they'd died alongside the man, probably firing rifles. The Apaches aren't the only ones with warrior women, he mused.

Then he noticed a small bloody object approximately the size of a loaf of bread, lying near one of the women. He wanted to pretend it was nothing unusual, although he knew exactly what the object was.

If children were too little, Apache warriors merely killed them. A wave of revulsion and rage came over Nathanial as he lowered himself to one knee near the corpse of the child. He calmed himself by praying for the little one's soul.

It seemed the most brutal act imaginable, far beyond the bounds of ordinary warfare, attaining the truely diabolical. Nathanial had heard tales of babies massacred by Apaches, but it was another matter to actually see it.

No longer could he remain aloof from the scene. Yes, this is what we're fighting, Nathanial told himself, balling his right fist. The infant had been around Zachary's age, but the Apaches didn't want him in their so-called sacred homeland. Nathanial imagined his son's head smashing against a wall and wanted to scream for Apache blood.

They think they've got the right to do anything, including killing babies, he told himself. Yes, Apaches are beautiful pastoral nomads and root-gatherers, but they're also brutal murderers. Their religion is fascinating, and they have produced outstanding individuals, such as Mangas Coloradas, but when you come right down to it, we're talking massacres. Nathanial felt deeply shaken by the carnage before him. How can I stand by the blood of children?

Jefferson Davis returned to Brierfield in November to await the results of the election. In days to come, as votes were tallied across the length and breadth of Mississippi, the gubernatorial candidate roamed his plantation and tried to figure ways to make it more productive.

Brierfield consisted of eight hundred acres, mostly in cotton, and sixty-one slaves. The overseer was a Negro, and Jefferson Davis had built a schoolhouse and church for his darkies, and supported those too old to work. The aristocratic hero of Buena Vista liked to think of his plantation as a big family, and he truly liked his slaves, often playing with their children. He preferred to believe most slaveowners were as benevolent as he and shrugged off abolition criticism of cruelty to slaves, considering it merely anti-Southern rhetoric.

One day, while inspecting horses in the barn, he thought to himself, this isn't a bad life at all. The cloudy film had vanished from his left eye, and the neuralgia had diminished considerably. He began to feel like a Mississippi planter again, instead of burdened by the afflictions of the world. He was contemplating buying more land when a familiar figure appeared in the doorway at the far end of the barn.

He rushed toward his wife, fearing something terrible had happened. She carried an unfolded document. "A messenger just brought the election results," she said, eyes filling with tears.

I lost, thought Jefferson Davis, his heart sinking through the dirt floor. He read the numbers and felt rejected by the very people for whom he'd fought all his life. With no one to see him besides his loyal wife, he balled the document and tossed it onto the pile of manure in the nearest stall.

"You were defeated only by about one thousand votes," soothed Varina as she touched her lips to his cheek.

"The people of Mississippi have spoken," he replied, trying to sound cheerful. "And maybe it's a good thing, because I was just thinking that I'd like to remain here for the rest of my life, with you, Varina."

"The people don't appreciate you," she said bitterly.

"You and I are retiring from public life as of today, my dear. If the people want that scoundrel Henry Foote for governor, to hell with them. It's time to tend our own garden for a change."

EIGHTEEN

Coughing blood into a reddened handkerchief, Superintendent of Indian Affairs James S. Calhoun sat in his office at Fort Marcy, writing another letter to Commissioner of Indian Affairs George W. Manypenny in Washington, D.C.

Calhoun's health had been deteriorating steadily, but he remained at his post, trying to pacify Indians. Somehow he'd caught a strange slow-acting disease, his body unable to throw it off, and he wondered if Apache medicine men had put a black magic hex upon him.

The continual gnawing debilitation made him furious, for nothing could be done about it. Winter was coming, and he wasn't sure he'd survive. He wanted to make a treaty with the Apaches, but that goal seemed more elusive than ever. Clutching the pen in his hand, he bent over the document and scratched:

Dear Commissioner Manypenny:

Apache depredations have been continuing unabated, despite the alleged military genius of Colonel Sumner. I have asked the colonel for a military escort, so I could meet with Chief Mangas Coloradas, but the colonel refused, demonstrating once again his usual pigheaded resistance to new initiatives. Colonel Sumner evidently believes he's been appointed King of New Mexico, and tends to rely on brute force in difficulties with Apaches, although brute force has never worked with them before.

I remain convinced that the majority of Apaches would lay down their arms if they were offered an alternative way of life. It would require approximately a half-million dollars, but I believe warriors would settle on farms if provided seeds, implements, and assistance. They are an intelligent and industrious people, and many of their leaders realize their present way of life is coming to an end. We have the opportunity to make a new beginning in New Mexico, if the government acts now.

The paper went blank, Calhoun's head dropped like a rock, but he awoke a split second later, thus saving his nose from being smashed. Often he lost consciousness and knew one day he'd never awaken again. I wonder how long I have left? he asked himself. Perhaps it's time I inquired into the purchase of a good solid coffin.

The ink had smeared on the letter, which meant he'd have to write it again. Perhaps I should tone down the language, he decided. If Colonel Sumner ever sees what I think of him, he'll only become more obstructive. I'm looking for a diplomatic resolution with the Apaches, but old Bull Moose Sumner wants to win more medals. How many men will die for his vanity?

American immigration to the Pinos Altos Mountains came to an end, and the Mimbreno Apaches found it easy to elude random patrols of lost, wandering bluecoat soldiers. Meanwhile, in the northland, Chief Chacon and his Jicarilla Apaches continued on the warpath, and Bull Moose Sumner decided to make an example of them. He ordered all available units to Fort Union for his forthcoming campaign against the rebellious Chief Chacon.

At Fort Webster Lieutenants Barrington and Hargreaves were ordered north with their detachments, to participate in the upcoming campaign. They arrived at Fort Marcy after eighteen uneventful days on the *Journada del Muertos*, and although directed to proceed to Fort Union without delay, they decided to let men and horses rest and refit for a few days.

Nathanial and Beau shook hands in front of the command post headquarters. "If she throws you out," said Beau, "the Bachelor Officers' Quarters at Fort Union isn't so bad."

Beau headed for the sutler's store, while Nathanial aimed toward the fateful meeting with his wife. He'd been anticipating it since the massacre on the *Journada del Muertos*, wondering how she'd accept his latest career decision.

He hadn't drunk anything except alkali-flavored water since leaving Santa Fe, and the active outdoors life always agreed with him. He felt strong, healthy, and irrepressible as he turned onto the street where she lived.

It was dusk, and candles burned in windows of the mansion. He hadn't notified Maria Dolores he was coming and hoped she wasn't in bed with a smooth-talking vaquero. He wore his usual dusty uniform, hadn't shaved since leaving Fort Webster, but alertness gleamed in his eye.

He knocked on the door, and a servant promptly opened up. "Is my wife home?" asked Nathanial.

The servant appeared astonished. "Please come in, sir. I'll tell her you're here."

Nathanial stepped into the parlor and stood next to a Mojave tapestry in red, gold, and black. There was a commotion on the second floor, then Maria Dolores descended the stairs, carrying Zachary in her arms.

"You're home," she said as she crossed the parlor floor. "I was beginning to think I would never see you again."

"You're not that lucky," replied Nathanial as he lightly kissed his wife.

Zachary reached for the silver lieutenant's bar on the hero's left shoulder strap. Nathanial took his son in his arms. "I hope you've been looking out for your mother."

Maria Dolores smiled at both of them; the boy was the mirror image of the father, but with Mexican highlights. "Was your resignation approved?" she asked.

His face drained of blood, and she knew something terrible was going to happen.

"I've decided to stay in the Army," he said.

There was silence for a few moments, then she replied: "I cannot believe my ears."

"I saw a baby not much younger than Zachary, killed by Apaches. No one in New Mexico will be safe if it weren't for the Army. I cannot walk away from my duty."

Her beautiful crystal dreams shattered before her eyes. "But you said you were going to become an engineer! You have done enough fighting! Let someone else have the honor for a change!"

Zachary was fascinated by his father's shoulder strap and tried to tug it loose.

"I've been transferred to Fort Union," said Nathanial, "and you and Zachary are coming with me."

She felt as if he'd hit her over the head with an Apache war club. "Fort Union? But my business is here in Santa Fe!"

"What's more important—your business or your family?"

"Why do I have to give up my business? Why can't you give up the Army?"

"You can go into business anywhere. What the hell do we need all this money for anyway? Zachary requires his mother, not more real estate. You say you love me, but is it just lies?"

"I still think you have been in the Army long enough, and it is time to find a new profession."

"You don't have to make up your mind right now," Nathanial said soothingly, "but why don't we talk it over more leisurely in the bedroom upstairs?"

President Millard Fillmore sat in the Oval Office of the White House, his desk covered by stacks of documents. He was distracted by a meeting he'd had that morning with the prominent Albany Whig leader Thurlow Weed.

Weed had told him it would be unlikely the party would nominate Millard Fillmore for president in the convention that summer. It appeared that the "conscience" Whigs were dissatisfied with Fillmore's support for the Fugitive Slave Law, while the "cotton" Whigs never forgave him for signing the Compromise of 1850. Fillmore couldn't get elected without substantial support within at least one section, and neither wanted him, Weed had explained patiently, and Weed was one of the most skilled political strategists in the nation.

Millard Fillmore wore a dark charcoal lawyer's suit with white shirt and maroon cravat. Some said he was the most handsome man ever to win the White House, with his full head of gray hair, solid round jaw, and air of rectitude. Unfortunately, government had ground to a virtual halt, due to dissension between North and South.

He couldn't imagine who'd be chosen president that year, and he didn't see how anyone could govern the fractious United States of America. Would the Whigs put forth abolitionist Senator Daniel Seward of New York, and alienate the Southern wing of the party, or General Winfield Scott, and make a bid for patriotic Americans in both sections?

The leading contenders among Democrats were Senator Lewis Cass of Michigan, who'd lost to Zachary Taylor in 1848; Senator James Buchanan of Pennsylvania, an amiable fence-straddler acceptable to both Southerners and Northerners, and Senator Stephen Douglas of Illinois, considered by many the most ambitious man in America.

President Fillmore reached for the nearest stack of documents, for even the president had to keep the paper moving. On top sat a request from Commissioner of Indian Affairs George Manypenny, attached to a letter from James S. Calhoun, Superintendent of Indian affairs in the New Mexico Territory. President Fillmore's practiced eyes sliced through the verbiage, just another plea for public money.

The former Buffalo lawyer had never seen an Apache in his life and possessed only vague notions about the New Mexico Territory. Some claimed it was barren desert, and others said abundant minerals and nourishment for cattle could be found in the far-off land. Can't Americans ever agree on anything? wondered Millard Fillmore.

The request had been scaled down to fifty thousand dollars, much less than war against the Apaches, but President Fillmore was besieged by requests for appropriations from every department, as if the federal government had taken on a life of its own, constantly enlarging, shouldering new responsibilities, requiring additional funds.

President Fillmore wasn't the most decisive man to sit in the White House, but didn't care to give up politics yet. If I run for office in the future, I don't want opponents to hit me over the head with expenditures I made in the White House. Why not let my successor worry about Apaches?

Millard Fillmore shrugged as he placed the letters from Manypenny and Calhoun to the side, his casual gesture affecting thousands of Americans in the New Mexico Territory. But Santa Fe was far from Washington, and seemingly insignificant compared to more pressing issues such as tariffs, internal improvements, Cuba, and continuing acrimonious debate over the Gordian Knot of American politics: slavery.

NINETEEN

Maria Dolores sat in the Army carriage, part of a caravan lined in front of the presidio at Fort Marcy. Zachary rested beside her, gazing avidly out the window at formations of soldiers riding by.

What have I done? wondered Maria Dolores. Sometimes she thought she'd gone loco for yielding to her husband's wishes, but she didn't think the family could withstand another long separation. Love is more important than money, she tried to tell herself.

She'd left her businesses in care of her father, who somehow had become fairly adept at management. A transformation had come over the old scholar during past months, as if he'd miraculously become rational.

Maria Dolores expected crude quarters at Fort Union, but at least she'd have Nathanial and Zachary. Nathanial is my man, she told herself, and I married him for better or worse, till death do us part. But if he ever tells me he's been with another woman, I shall kill him.

Sometimes Maria Dolores wondered about the strange Apache woman who had lured her husband into the chaparral. She was a good judge of men, Maria Dolores admitted ruefully. Nathanial had stopped drinking and returned home from Fort Marcy after work every day. He seemed to function better when he had duties and responsibilities. It was like the halcyon first year of their marriage, but now they were moving into the middle of hostile Jicarilla territory.

"Da-da," said Zachary, pointing his pudgy little finger out the window.

He'd spotted his father riding toward the carriage, wide-brimmed hat slanted low over his eyes, wearing a splendid blue uniform with polished brass buttons and glittering military insignia, the orange bandanna around his throat, and carrying a gun at his waist, with an Apache knife sticking out his boot. In the bright morning sun Zachary's father appeared a mythic figure, king of life and death, bouncing up and down in his saddle. Zachary would remember that particular gleaming vision of his father for the rest of his life.

Lieutenant Barrington leaned forward and touched his hand to his son's cheek. "If you see any Apaches, punch 'em right in the nose." Then he turned to his wife, who was smoldering on the opposite seat.

"I wish you wouldn't speak to him that way."

He always deferred to her, now that she'd agreed to accompany him to Fort Union. He could tolerate any hardship, as long she was near. "I know this is an ordeal for you, Maria Dolores, but I'll try very hard to be a good husband. If we love each other, we can endure anything. Perhaps we took our marriage too much for granted before."

She reached for his hand. "I know it will not be easy, but I will never let you get away from me again."

He removed his hat, leaned into the carriage, and his lips touched hers. "I love you with all my heart, Maria Dolores."

Duke III made an impatient move, and Nathanial's head struck the door of the carriage. Then he heard someone call: "You're wanted at the head of the formation, Lieutenant Barrington!"

Nathanial straightened in the saddle, put on his hat, and tossed his wife a regulation salute. "You'll always be my commanding officer, dear," he declared. Then he wheeled his horse and trotted toward the guidon flags as he took one last glance around Fort Marcy. His eyes fell on a sallow face looking out a window, Indian Superintendent James S. Calhoun, unhappy about being stripped of military protection. Nathanial took his place at the head of the column, alongside his friend Beau. Both West Point officers were in high spirits, it was a beautiful day, and a pleasant journey lay ahead, they hoped.

"Would you like to do the honors?" asked Beau.

"I believe it's your turn," replied Nathanial gallantly.

Beau raised his arm into the air. "Detachment—forward hoooo!"

Guidon flags shot into the air, orders were passed through the ranks, and the dragoons began their journey toward the Jicarilla homeland. The band played the traditional old Army tune, "The Girl I Left Behind," and Nathanial couldn't help remembering the smooth-muscled warrior woman writhing beneath him amid dirt and twigs at the Santa Rita copper mines.

I wonder what became of her, reflected Nathanial as he rode through the gate, tossing a sharp West Point salute to the guards. She'll always be part of me, and I'll bet she'll never forget me either. But maybe I dreamed the whole interlude one night when I was blind drunk at the copper mines. Is the warrior woman only a representation of my wicked, wicked desire?

*   *   *

Lawyer Abe Lincoln argued a case before the Illinois Supreme Court that winter, and at the end of the day, after the give and take of legal maneuvering, repaired to a tavern in the area, to relax before going home to his often difficult wife.

He was joined by lawyers, judges, clerks, and other members of court. Their dining companions were traveling salesmen, farmers, gamblers, and shopkeepers. They sat at long tables, with an open fireplace supplying heat, and no one was a better storyteller than Honest Abe Lincoln.

Sometimes the discussion turned to politics, and then Abe would lean back and listen to contending arguments, a pensive expression on his face. Occasionally he'd offer his opinion on this or that burning issue, and sometimes he appeared unbearably sad as he gazed into flaming tongues of fire.

Occasionally he speculated on returning to politics, not as a candidate, but a Whig campaign organizer, worker, and spokesman. The Whigs traditionally stood for internal improvements, such as roads and canals constructed with tax dollars, thus developing the resources of the nation. He didn't think he could change the world, but a mind here or there might be influenced.

Whenever the topic of slavery was raised, Abe Lincoln weighed conflicting viewpoints carefully. He believed increasingly that slavery could never be abolished without Southern insurrection, but it should be prevented from spreading to new territories. Then, he hoped it would die of natural causes in its final Southern bastions.

One evening, after Honest Abe expressed this view in a smoky crowded Springfield tavern, a semiinebriated lawyer from Savannah visiting friends in the vicinity leaned across the table and said, "Mister Lincoln—you know very well that slaves in the South are often treated better than factory workers in the North. Why don't you worry about the mess in your own backyard, instead of pointing at ours?"

It was one of the oldest proslavery arguments, and the rail splitter born in a log cabin had heard it many times. Honest Abe lay down his knife and fork, turned to his inquisitor, and replied, "What you say is true—there are doubtlessly slaves who receive better treatment than some Northern laborers. But there is no permanent class of hired laborer in America, and twenty-five years ago *I* was a hired laborer. In this great nation of ours, the laborer of yesterday can labor on his own account today, and tomorrow will hire others to labor for him. Although some gentlemen claim slavery is a boon to the Negroes, I've never heard of anyone who wanted to become a slave and take advantage of its supposed benefits. My good sir, labor is the common burden of all people, and the effort of some to shift their share onto the shoulders of others, is the great durable curse of our times."

In the season known as Many Leaves, Chief Mangas Coloradas and his retinue journeyed south to the Sierra Madre Mountains, home of the Nednai People, to participate in an important Cradle Ceremony. Jocita, wife of sub-chief Juh, had given birth to a boy, and leading warriors and chiefs from all across the homeland gathered to pay homage.

On the morning of the ceremony, Nana, the *di-yin* medicine man, was already at the warrior woman's wickiup, where she and Juh sat cross-legged on the ground. Jocita held the infant in her arms, and nearby lay the cradle board crafted by Nana during the previous night of oak, ash, and walnut, with sotol stalks for crosspieces, and special holy amulets affixed to safeguard the baby from evil spirits. The latter consisted of turquoise beads, lightning-riven wood, and tiny bags of pollen.

Nana kneeled before the baby and applied four dots of sacred pollen to his cheeks. Then he threw pollen to the four directions, to sanctify the encampment. Next, he took the naked babe from Jocita, held him high over his head, and turned in a circle, presenting him to the four holy directions. Nana sang songs and uttered prayers, then placed the child into his new cradle board, and handed him back to Jocita.

She positioned the cradle board so the child could see the feast and dance that followed, and the little fellow appeared highly alert to the rejoicing. Jocita tied the right paw of a badger to the front of the cradle, to guard her son from fright, plus bird claws and pieces of wildcat skin. Then she took the child's tiny hand in hers, and the warmth of her warrior spirit flowed into him.

Juh sat on the other side of the cradle, his chest puffed with pride, although he knew in another corner of his mind that the baby was part bluecoat soldier. But he preferred not to dwell on that doleful fact, for it did not further his cause.

The people ate roast mule, drank *tizwin*, smoked tobacco, and danced long into the night, celebrating the birth of a new warrior among the People. At the height of the festivities, swept away by maternal devotion, the warrior woman held her baby in the air. "One day he shall be a great chief of the People!" she declared.

No parents disputed with the warrior woman, for it was a common enough salutation at Cradle Ceremonies. But Jocita deeply believed her son would attain the position of Mangas Coloradas in the future, and she silently swore to do everything possible to bring about that end. She hugged the infant warmly and kissed his forehead. "And thus a great man is sent into the world," she whispered.

The child smiled toothlessly, like a tiny shriveled old man, as if he understood every word she'd spoken.

A column of dragoons headed east across the grassy swales of Kansas, and a massive herd of buffalo watched silently from the distance. The dragoons were on escort duty, and their charge was the ailing James S. Calhoun, former Superintendent of Indian Affairs for the New Mexico Territory.

He'd departed Santa Fe several weeks ago, accompanied by his newly made coffin lashed to the top of the stagecoach. The journey had been grueling, he'd suffered a precipitous decline in health, and yesterday, wracked with pain and illness, he'd lapsed into a coma, but came out of it that evening.

Now he felt himself sinking again and wondered if death were imminent. He gazed dully at grazing buffalo as far as he could see, and knew their days were numbered also. This is the land of death, he thought, and soon it shall claim me.

He reflected upon the futility of his life, for he'd never really amounted to anything. Arriving in New Mexico with the highest aspirations, then he'd run into Bull Moose Sumner, and still hadn't received a response from Commissioner Manypenny about settling Apaches on farms. It will cost more in blood than the price of farm implements, thought Calhoun, but nobody in Washington cares about Apaches.

Dizziness came over him, and he thought he saw

Apache warriors and maidens riding alongside his stagecoach, waving mournfully at him, smiling sadly. "Good-bye, my friends," mumbled Calhoun as he raised his hand and made the sign of peace. "We shall meet again in the happy hunting ground."

The death rattle rose in his throat, his head fell forward, and he sagged to the floor. I knew I'd have use for that coffin someday, was his last thought, then the final breath of life escaped his nostrils, another casualty of the Apache Wars.

Apache warriors continued raiding into Mexico, with the U.S. Army unable to halt their reign of terror. General Winfield Scott, commander of the Army, asked for ten million dollars a year for ten to twenty years to defend Mexico against Apaches, and Congress practically laughed in his face. Approximately eight thousand troops, representing more than two-thirds of the regular Army, were stationed with Lieutenant Nathanial Barrington, Lieutenant Beauregard Hargreaves, and Colonel Bull Moose Sumner on the southwestern frontier, to subdue the fearsome Apache.

Meanwhile, Mexican citizens pointed to Article Eleven of the Treaty of Guadalupe Hidalgo and demanded reparations amounting to millions of dollars for damages incurred by Apache marauding. The total grew each year, while many congressmen and senators agreed that the Mexicans were legally entitled to indemnities.

A diplomatic crisis ensued due to Apache depredations into Mexico. In smoke-filled rooms, distinguished statesmen from both nations sought an honorable way out of the dilemma. It was political suicide for American politicians to raise taxes to pay off Mexico, while

Mexican officials couldn't hope to remain in office if they didn't hold America in compliance with the Treaty of Guadalupe Hidalgo, for which so many patriots had died.

James Gaddsen, the American minister to Mexico, hit upon a possible solution. The Mexican treasury was nearly bankrupt, but it possessed land it couldn't defend in northern Mexico, where Apaches committed their worst crimes. Cash and land became the grease and oil that eased the path for a new agreement between America and Mexico.

The agreement became known as the Gaddsen Purchase, signed in 1854 by President Franklin Pierce, the former Democratic New Hampshire senator who'd won the White House against Whig nominee General Winfield Scott in 1852.

The Gaddsen Purchase stipulated that Article Eleven of the treaty of Gaudalupe Hidalgo be rescinded, and a new international boundary was established farther south, giving the United States 29,644 square miles of new Apache homeland. Finally, the U.S. would make a one-time cash payment of ten million dollars to the starved and desperate Mexican treasury.

With deft strokes of quill pens, the line drawn by John R. Bartlett's U.S. Boundary Commission of 1851, with its many achievements, deeds, and sacrifices, was wiped out for all time.

Often, as Lieutenant Nathanial Barrington led his company of dragoons through the new paid-for territory, he recalled that oddly hallowed summer of 1851, with Captain John Cremony, Colonel Lewis Craig, and that fine old Astor Hotel scholar, James R. Bartlett. What a strange time it had been, Nathanial often reflected, as two distinct cultures met briefly at the Santa Rita copper mines.

Lieutenant Nathanial Barrington had become a fairly sober, capable, and experienced officer, with a reasonably satisfying family life, and another baby due that fall. But at odd moments of solitude, after hours in the saddle and his mind drifting lazily, he took secret pleasure in remembering a certain lithe and dangerous Apache warrior woman.

With a wistful smile and melancholy tear, he recalled wrestling in the dirt with her at the Santa Rita copper mines. For as long as he lived, he'd never forget her high cheekbones and almond eyes, how she'd slapped his face, then kissed the blood away. Did you ever exist, or were you just a phantom? he sometimes wondered during long scouts across sunbaked valleys.

Perhaps one day we'll meet again, my warrior queen.